BOOK ONE
of

The Adventures of Benjamin Manry

BENJAMIN MANRY

AND THE

Curse of Blood Bones

Owen Palmiotti

Benjamin Manry and the Curse of Blood Bones

Published by Wheatmark®
610 East Delano Street, Suite 104
Tucson, Arizona 85705 U.S.A.
www.wheatmark.com

International Standard Book Number: 978-1-60494-106-7
Library of Congress Control Number: 2008924583

"Adventures are great…
because they are fun,
exciting, and make for
an interesting story.
That is, if you survive to tell it."

=BM-

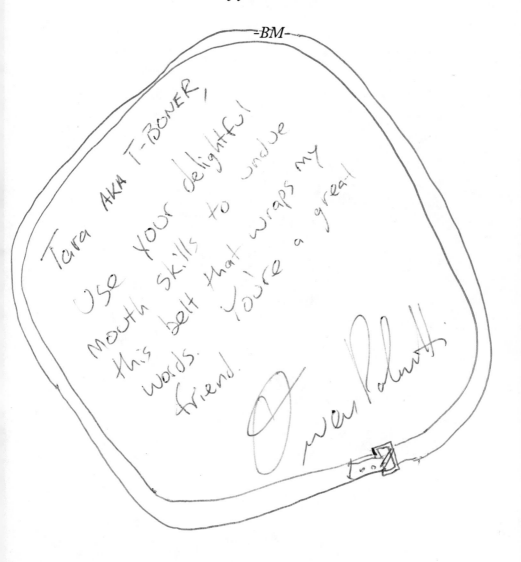

Tara AKA T-BONER,

Use your delightful
mouth skills to undue
this belt that wraps my
words. You're a great
friend.

For my mother, Lorraine Palmiotti, may your memories bring happiness to all that knew you. The dedication is perhaps the hardest feat to write, even worse then the actual manuscript. This novel took many years of thought and countless hours of my time to actually create what I wished. This is for all those people who want to write, but don't. Use my words as that motivation to strive for your goals. Attain everything you wish to hold close. This is for all my high school friends who listened to me endlessly while walking through the halls of Monroe-Woodbury. This is for all my buddies who passed me on campus at SUNY Maritime, drink to the Dome! This is for all my shipmates who I've sailed around the world with, coffee in hand and eyes glancing out at the foaming seas. This is for my amazing family and best friends, who all helped me through some rough times. But lastly, this dedication goes out to me, because after all, I've never had a prouder moment in my young life than when I wrote THE END. Enjoy!

1

January 14th, 1763
Boston, Massachusetts

The flames danced in each cut of the scarlet stone. As he pushed a coin over the tabletop, the bartender placed a bottle of red wine within reach. Bringing a hand over the neck, he retrieved the bottle between sea-weathered fingers. He let off a deep sigh under the protection of a large draped cloak. Between swigs he took in the atmosphere, enjoying the loud music and boisterous laughter. He removed the ring off his pinky and placed it in the palm of his hand, rotating it slowly. The memories of its origins filled his eyes with emotion, but he fought off the urge to reminisce with a quick shake of his head. Minutes turned to hours as he sat there atop the barstool listening intently.

A local approached the bar through a crowd of drunks, pushing his way until he was face to face with the bartender. "William, get me the normal. I can't take this taxation anymore. All I've saved from my last year's wages are nearly gone, between debt and these new linen tariffs. My wife can't even purchase the materials to clothe our family!"

"Aye, Jonathan, it's just not right."

"Every three months I hear that sound, it utterly disgusts me!" the angered man pounded the table, spilling the freshly poured mead.

"Those armed carriages are beginning to sound familiar. They come from all corners of the colonies, from Albany and Philadelphia to Charleston and even Williamsburg!"

Jonathan let off another angry assault on the wooden countertop. "The King's taken all my, er, all our money," he paused to catch his breath. "As I came up the walk, I saw the vessels taking on stores."

The bartender nodded, wiping wet hands on a cloth tied around his waist. "Aye, I wonder how much gold's in the holds."

"Ha! Don't get me dreaming. Pour me another mead my friend," the conversation carried to the mysterious sailor still seated in the corner.

Hearing all that he had needed, Hernando Audaz stood from the stool. Through the crowd of drunken sailors and locals, he made his way for the door, hiding his face beneath the gray cloak. He looked over his shoulder as the tavern faded into the distance. Several vendors approached him with the day's catches, but he ignored the crates of codfish and continued on through the snow-covered streets to his sloop, *La Monzón*.

2

JANUARY 27TH, 1763
PORT OF ST. AUGUSTINE

A group of sailors leaned over the railing, lowering a hawser to the longshoremen waiting below. As the men hauled on the lines, the schooner slowly kissed the rope fenders on the pier. Ordinary seamen lowered the gangplank into place and Arthur F. Nelson, captain of the Frendrich, paced down with a quick gait towards the harbormaster's office. Once inside, Nelson was greeted warmly.

"Hello, my dear friend! It has been quite some time, eh?"

"Yes, yes it has. I hope all is with you. Do I have any messages?" Nelson asked.

"Ah, yes indeed. Here you go," the harbormaster slid the folded paper across the counter.

Nelson eyed the initials set in the wax, certain that he had seen the marks at some earlier time as he began to unfold the letter:

January 18th, 1763

Captain Arthur F. Nelson,

With the utmost urgency, your presence is required at the Castillo de San Marcos. When you arrive, tell the guards at the ravelin that you are there on urgent busi-

ness. Once through, enter the sally port. Count five paces from whence you enter. There will be a wall on your left. Feel for a grooved track and a handgrip. Inside is where you must meet my representative.

Colonel Victor Smith
Boston, MA.

✖✖✖

Nelson remembered the man's name and his friendship with the Dominion Governor of Boston, James Elliot. He trekked up the incline that surrounded the perimeter of the fortification. Two guards came out of the ravelin and approached the figure at the base of the castle.

"Name and business?" inquired the taller soldier.

"Captain Arthur F. Nelson, here for orders."

With a nod, the soldiers opened the portcullis as the large wooden door creaked with every inch. The soldiers touched the brim of their red hats in salute and let the man pass.

"Five, four, three, two, one," he counted aloud.

He reached for a lone candle that rested in an old, decrepit holder. Once his eyes adjusted to the poor lighting, he noticed the groove at the base of the wall and then finally its handgrip. He planted his feet and pushed hard with his shoulder. Slowly, the door budged enough to allow him to pass through.

A curl of blue smoke rose from a dark silhouette. "Welcome."

Nelson glanced at the back of a chair. Exposed was only the feather from atop the man's felt hat. He stood and turned, facing his guest.

"Reporting as requested," Nelson stood proudly.

"Yes, yes I see that, Arthur. Take a seat," said the man pointing to a chair.

As he became comfortable the man in front of him remained standing, blowing smoke rings into the musty air. "You may be thinking why you are here. Well, in a moment, you will undertake quite a mission. Do you think you can handle this?"

Nelson nodded, "Of course, sir."

"I do not wish to speak of the details of these matters. Although you and I are the only ones present, you can never be too careful. Instead, take this."

The letter was pushed across the smooth surface of the grand oak table.

A smile grew on his face as he scanned through the message. "I accept these terms."

He sighed with relief, "Good, we knew you were the right man for the job," he reached a hand across the table, his fingers skirting the edge of the note. "Let us burn the evidence of our plans."

The candle flickered beside him, spitting flame several inches as the message caught fire. He held an edge and rotated his wrist, allowing for the flame to spread. He dropped the message and watched it fall lazily to the stone floor at their feet.

Pulling out a drawer from the desk, he brought out a bottle and two wine glasses. "I hope you are a gentleman and accept this lovely wine. It is aged thirteen years."

"Of course, who can refuse such an offer?"

He poured into each glass, "Here, drink up my friend."

They touched the rims in a toast to success and sipped until the remnants of the wine were fast flowing through the body. After another round was downed the man looked across the table, "Go off with you then. The mission must be carried out with a swift wind. When completed, report to the governor of Boston."

3

PRESENT DAY
ST. AUGUSTINE, FLORIDA

enjamin Manry glanced up from his doodling and eyed the clock at the front of the room, staring just slightly above his teacher's auburn hair and thick, square glasses. His piercing blue eyes were transfixed on the timepiece as the second hand made its slow journey around the center. He clicked his pen to a song that played over and over in his head. He continued shading in the lines of the ship. His drawing began to take a life of its own.

As the clock struck two, Ben inched his body closer to the edge of the seat. He ran a hand through his short, dark brown hair and sighed with impatience. Five minutes until his weekend would start, five excruciating minutes of Peruvian canals and South American irrigation techniques. He was flirting with time; as each second struck, his smile would grow ever larger.

He snapped back into focus when he heard a clap of the textbook close shut. Mrs. Jacobs concluded the class with the typical ending, "Read the next two chapters, and study for a quiz based on the reading."

It was the same routine every day: Go to class, get assigned work, go home, and do the homework. Ben was different though. Unlike other kids who would waste a day in front of the television, he and his two best friends would explore the wooded area around their property, go canoeing, and seek adventures.

As he fiddled with the combination to his locker his older brother, a senior, slapped him on the back.

"How was class?"

He looked into his brother's hard, brown stare. "Same stuff different day. Where's Sal?"

"At his locker, let's go bug him."

After closing the flap to his pack, he stood vertically, stretching out the kinks from a long day of sitting. Four inches separated their nearly identical appearance. The pair sauntered around the bend in the hallway, passing several friends. A few waves and several hellos later, they were at Sal's locker.

"Hey guys, what we doing today?"

Harris stared at his classmate, "Well, we aren't doing anything if you keep wasting your time in your locker."

Sal ran a hand through his black, silky hair repeatedly until he was content with how it fell. He finished looking in the mirror with a smile of content.

Harris chuckled, "Dude, you're such a girl. Calm down, we're just going to the truck."

Closing the locker they set off, navigating through groups of hacky-sacking skaters, around girls gossiping about their college boyfriends, and nerds who always had their laptops open as they discussed the latest traded stocks and bonds. Finally, they emerged through the double swinging doors, exiting the school that they had grown to dislike after the years of the daily repetition.

Molly Wiggins waited at the bottom of the staircase. She was a cute blonde who had been head over heels with Sal since they met at the Freshman Halloween Dance. A smile grew as she waved to the group, her stare focused on Sal. "Hey guys."

Sal stumbled in a struggle to find the right words, as his complexion turned red, his gaze turned towards his feet, "Uh, um hi Mo…"

She opened her mouth, but before anything came out, Ben

stepped in for his friend. "Sal says hi. Sorry, we're running late, but we'll talk to you later. We really should all hang out sometime, maybe you could bring a few of your friends and we can go out to the movies?"

She chomped on the bait, "Sounds great, talk to you guys later."

As their feet hit the blacktop of the parking lot, Sal whispered for only Ben's ears.

"Thanks man."

Their walk turned into a sprint as they continued their journey. The truck was located at the far end of the parking lot, requiring the group to run through columns of numerous vehicles, dodging cars as everyone tried to leave the school grounds at the same time.

The lights of a large SUV backing up caused Ben to halt in his tracks. He stared at the backs of his fleeing friends, watching the gap between them grew. He was losing seconds in the pursuit. Harris fumbled with the handle, opening the door and jumping in. Sal was next, running around the bed of the truck, diving into the passenger's seat. The key met the ignition box, and with a turn, the engine roared to life. He backed out of the slot without looking back, and then floored the gas pedal.

Ben's hand slapped the rear bumper as the blue pickup truck propelled forward. Ben kept pace, just an arm's length behind. This was not the first time his friends pulled the prank on him, and probably would not be the last, but within several seconds, Ben managed to leap into the open bed as Harris maneuvered around the lot.

He tapped against the window and a second later it slid open, "Good pursuit, very excellent form with your sprint and a near-perfect landing. I'd give you nine and a half out of ten, half a point off for not having gotten my seat."

"Oh shut up, Sal. I got delayed. Did you see that guy; he just backed up into my path."

"You're always full of excuses."

✖✖✖

They pulled off the town road onto the gravel path that wound through the Manry estate, twenty-five acres of beautiful land, with a stream running through the center. The truck passed over a small wooden bridge, by the dock that housed two canoes and a dinghy, and finally reached the paved driveway of the majestic, yet homey two-story palace.

As the stood before the house, which had been passed down from father to son since it was built in 1778, they were greeted by Margie Manry. "Boys, before you go out and have fun, I need the wine cellar cleaned up. Your father is going to start building the addition in a few weeks. He wants it all cleared up down there. I think he said we'll start knocking down the wall on the long weekend coming up."

"Yes, mother," the brothers said together, Sal following on their heels.

4

"Men, I learned of some excellent news. We share berthing in the same harbor as three vessels. They're transporting a quarter year's worth of colonial taxes to London. There are two sloops of war, acting as the convoy for a thirty-two-gun frigate. The facts are simple; we cannot win in manpower or firepower."

After a slight pause, his cousin and first mate raised a hand, "Hernando, what if we engage them internally?"

"Álvaro, I was thinking the same. I know that they will be heavily armed and crewed. We must solely focus on the frigate; it'll be a third of the people that we have to fight. We'll be undermanned, but I'm not terribly concerned. We'll need to sneak onto their ship…"

The crew nodded throughout the discussion. "Men what do you think? Shall we loot and plunder the English?"

5

A hand reached forward, opening a rickety door to the cellar. Harris, as usual, led the group down the staircase as he made his way through the darkness. He reached upwards for the cord that hung from the ceiling, but Sal blindly stumbled into his back.

"Hey, watch it buddy."

"Sorry, I can't see anything. Why don't you have a switch upstairs, it'd make this a whole lot easier.

Harris pulled on the cord, illuminating the sole bulb to the twenty foot square cellar. "Well, if I had built the cellar I would've placed the switch more conveniently!"

Ben gazed around at the cellar, part of the original eighteenth century house. "Guys, stop arguing, we'll never get the job done."

"Well, I guess we should look through the stacks of newspapers," Harris began the commands. "Sal, maybe we can use something for those projects coming up. If not, I guess we can just throw them out," he paused. "Ben, would you mind going upstairs to get a few black garbage bags and a roll of twine for the boxes?"

Sal and Harris moved towards the stacks of papers that covered a majority of the floor as Ben made his way for the staircase. They began sorting through the papers, discarding irrelevant items, and placing anything of use in one pile. Ben reentered the cellar with a box of rolled up bags and pulled out two. He tossed the plastic wads to each waiting hand, and then placed the box and the twine on a small desk next to the closest wall.

"Ben, I found an article about Peru. You think you could use that for Jacobs?"

"Uh, yeah I guess. It wouldn't hurt."

This continued for a half hour. There were four bags at their feet, three bags were full of discards, and one contained their treasures, the items they thought yielded promise.

Harris scratched his head. "Um, let's fold up the empty boxes. We can tie them up with the twine. After that I guess we can look through the others."

As Ben peered into one of the cardboard boxes, his hands fell on some familiar items. "No way, I thought mom threw these out!"

Harris joined his brother, looking at their childhood toys. "Yeah, these are definitely going in the treasure bag."

Ben smiled, "Without a doubt."

Sal went to a neighboring box and reached in, pulling out an old photo album. He placed the top one on his lap and began to flip through the pages. He let out a laugh that made Ben and Harris jump.

"You guys looked so cute when you were kids."

Harris wrestled the book from his friend's hands. "Shut up, let me see tha…"

He began laughing before he could finish the sentence. They were kneeling beside the Christmas tree, wearing two light blue wool-knitted sweaters. The label read Harris- 8, Ben-7.

"Wow, just over ten years. We sure did grow."

Harris returned the look. "Yeah, man. You're still a shrimp though."

Ben ignored the comment and the group continued to look through the remaining boxes, placing the albums in the treasure sack to look through them later. It was an hour into their chores when they moved the large oak cabinet, revealing a wine rack carved into the stone cellar. It held rows of old bottles, six high, by ten wide.

Sal smiled, "You guys want to crack one open and enjoy some wine?"

Harris pulled out bottle after bottle and placed it in a line.

Through the accumulated dust, the three could see a purplish hue. It was not until the last bottle that left the rack until he noticed something different.

"Guys, this bottle's empty."

The three began to scrape off the thick dust with hurried fingers, looking for a date on the bottle, a label, or something that could yield information.

Harris reached out to his brother. "Hey, let me see the empty bottle."

Ben placed it into his brother's hands.

As Harris began to scrape off more dust, his fingers moved with intensity, "Hey, move out of the light! I see something inside. Looks like something rolled up. Maybe paper or some kind of parchment, it's hard to tell."

Harris gripped the cork that plugged the bottle. It fell out with a gentle tug. He then tipped the bottle over and tapped the bottom, causing the contents to fall into his lap. His eyes strained, noticing a few engravings.

"Let's go upstairs later and look at the bottle, it looks like a date or initial or something, I can't see it that well."

Ben glanced down, "You're right. It looks like a note, a message in a bottle."

Ben strained, but could not hold back the laughter as Sal bobbed his head, dancing while he sung the song in the English accent.

"Ha…ha…ha…you are quite the comedian eh?"

Sal smiled towards Harris, "Oh, you know it."

They stared closely, recognizing the rough sketch of an island in the center. "Can anyone make out the writing?"

Harris eyed his brother before gazing at the map; studying one jagged edge, as if it had been ripped out of a bound journal.

Blinded by an adventure for the weekend, they failed to turn the discovery over.

iguel studied his friend before him and let off a chuckle, "Hernando, you look good. If I didn't know you, I'd say you could pass for a British officer."

He sensed his friend's sarcasm, "Well, that is the plan after all, heh?"

The two enjoyed a nice laugh as they led their men down the wharf. Minutes later they arrived in front of the *HMS Courtesy*. As the Officer on Deck hailed down to them, Hernando Audaz switched to his best English accent as his Spanish skin took refuge under the blanket of night and sheets of falling snow.

"Good evening. It is I, Lieutenant Clifford Johnson of your neighboring *HMS Georgia Rose*. As per our captain, we're to switch out my twenty-five best gunners between the *Courtesy* and the *Rose*. Rumor has it that *Blood Bones* is preying these waters and *he* wants to be careful. Is that all right with you or shall I be required to discuss orders with your captain?"

The young man appeared nervous at the mention of Blood Bones, the most feared pirate on the Atlantic coast and Caribbean. "Aye, I'll pick the men. If we do confront this bastard you speak of, we'll be well prepared. I appreciate the warning; I'll tell our captain. Just wait here, I'll return momentarily," he mouthed in what seemed one breath.

He watched the man turn, heading at a quick gait for the companionway ladder that led below. Miguel whispered, "Hernan, do you think all will fall into place?"

He rubbed his goatee and then ran a hand through his hair until the movement shifted the hat atop his head, "Of course. The plan was well thought out."

The Officer on Deck returned to his post with twenty-five marines. He cupped his hands around his mouth, hoping his voice would carry over the howling wind.

"Sir, I've informed my captain of the plans. I'm sending my men to the *Georgia Rose*. Again, I thank you for the warning and would be delighted to have you aboard."

Hernando Audaz watched as the line of men walked by, heading less than a quarter mile down the wharf. Judging the distance, he calculated the alarm would be raised in under five minutes. Time was not in their favor.

As he filed up the gangway he lowered his head, touching the brim of his hat to the Officer in a manner to cover his face, yet to present the salute. The young man returned the gesture as the men came aboard. Hernando led his men to the bow of the vessel to meet one last time before they put the plan into action.

7

Harris adjusted the coiled-spring lamp. "Okay, so any ideas?"

Three faces looked down at the map, studying what lay on the desk. The ink had turned to a brownish dye with the years. Their excited eyes failed to notice the smears of blood upon the material.

"Harris, turn on the scanner. I got something. We'll scan it and then maybe do an image search, see if it gets any hits. That may give us something to work with."

His brother nodded with a smile, looking directly at Sal, "At least someone's thinking."

Sal laughed, "Ha...ha...ha...I see that you have countered in our comic battle. A battle of charm and wit, of..."

Ben shook his head, "Do you ever not talk?"

The laughter slowly faded to just their combined breathing. They sat enjoying the silence of the room, only hearing the computer beep throughout the start up process. After the scanner and computer were up and running, Ben handed his brother the page to make the scan. As he placed it face down, he realized there was a message on the backside.

It was written in Spanish, and sort of scrambled around. Arrows pointed at random angles and curves, going from an X to the next X, followed by a number. Below this tangle of lines there seemed to be a chart, with the numbers one through eight, with yet another number written out and the word "pasos" beside it.

"Sal, that means paces, right?"

He looked it over quickly, "Yeah, what I'm thinking is that each leg of the journey, from X to X, is a number. One is the first leg and it is twenty paces until the next leg of the trek. The second leg of the journey is another twenty. It looks to be about forty-five degrees from where we would be walking last. So on and so forth."

He inched to the edge of the seat, "You think this is authentic?"

Sal appeared over Harris's shoulder. "It looks old. Let's try and find a date, or something."

Ben looked back at the computer and then to the scanner. "How about we scan it first, and then we can check it out as the search works its magic?"

The others nodded in agreement. They placed it on the glass and then closed the lid. After pressing a green button on the power panel, the machine roared to life. Moments later, the image appeared on the computer screen. Ben gripped the mouse, moving the small hand icon over the 'Edit: Copy' option.

He then went online and typed in the search box, waiting for the server to update the web page. Seconds later, he maneuvered his mouse around the page, clicking 'Yes' to some options, and 'No' to others. After he was content, he hit 'Copy/Paste' inserting the scanned item into a query box. He limited the search to 'islands/bodies of land/maps.'

Harris removed the map from the scanner and placed it on the desk. Ben's eyes looked at the area below the chart, seeing two lines of text: 'Una caja sin bisagras, sin la llave, o sin la tapa, mas tesoro dorado dentro de es Escondido,' followed by a date, 1763.

"Hey, do you think this is a riddle or a clue or something?"

Sal looked at it for a moment, translating the words in his head as he dissected each line word by word.

"A box without hinges, key, or lid, yet a golden treasure, inside is hid"

They paused and let the phrase sink in. "Golden treasure? You think this is a treasure map?"

He smiled towards his brother. Harris replied, "Maybe, I wonder if we got any hits yet."

The website showed half downloaded images as the blue scale at the bottom of the screen was halfway full.

Sal ran a hand through his hair. "A box without hinges, key or lid, yet golden treasure, inside is hid. Yeah, it's a riddle all right."

Harris interrupted, "Let's have a look at the bottle first, I have a feeling all of this is somehow related."

Ben reached over towards the bottle, his fingers gripping it just enough to move it closer to the light. He flipped it over so that the three of them could study the markings he saw earlier in the cellar.

"It looks like, DWV. There's a date also, 1742."

Harris put a hand on his brother's shoulder. "Good work. Open another search window and type those in."

As Ben was clicking the mouse, Sal slapped his thigh, causing both boys to turn their heads towards him.

"Wait a second. 'A box without hinges, key or lid, yet golden treasure, inside is hid.' I know what that means…"

Harris interrupted anxiously, "What?"

Sal continued, "An egg. Think about it. A box could mean a container or something right? Do eggs have hinges, keys, or lids? The golden treasure is the yolk. It's got to be an egg."

Harris sighed, "What does an egg have to do with a treasure map. Twenty paces around the egg, fifteen paces yet again. No, it can't be an egg. I'm positive about it."

Sal replied, "Then what do you think it is, Mr. Wise-en-heimer?"

"Listen, I'd bet my life on it," he sounded angry.

Ben zoned out the arguing as he opened the original search window, listing eight sites. He skimmed through each option, and smiled once his eyes looked at the third one. "Guys, guys, shut up. Look, I think I found what we're looking for."

They stared at the map on the computer monitor, just a little bit out of scale in comparison to the original. Its shape was not the typical circular one, but rather, an oblate spheroid, having a bulging center.

"Wait a second. 'A box without hinges, key or lid, yet golden treasure, inside is hid.' You said the answer to the riddle was an egg, right Sal?"

He looked at Ben and responded, "Yeah, an egg. So, you think this island is egg-shaped?"

"I have to agree, it does look egg-shaped," Harris said reluctantly.

"Okay, so we know a few things: this riddle, relates to this island. There's also a date that was below the riddle, 1763. On the bottle, there is also a date, along with initials."

"Let's take it one step at a time, bro. Click on the link for this egg-shaped island. We got to find out where it is."

Ben looked at his brother as he clicked the mouse. A second later, the name, "Roosevelt Island, St. Augustine, Florida" appeared. His jaw dropped and his eyes popped out of his head.

Harris shook his head. "No way, there's absolutely no way. Do you guys realize we can explore it tomorrow?"

"Hey, let's do some research first. I've heard some stories about it. I don't know anyone who's even been to it before," Ben replied.

"Okay, okay. Let's read what popped up."

Their eyes scanned through an excerpt of the local newspaper dated in the early 1980's:

...Roosevelt Island is rumored to harbor a curse, a curse that makes St. Augustine home to more than its title, the oldest European city in America. Supposedly between the years of 1763 and 1764, the gruesome pirate, Captain Blood Bones, had snuck through the defenses of the battery guarding the harbor. Some of his men were seen drinking in the local taverns along the main streets of the city. It is rumored that along with his men, he also had a mage or a wizard in company. This man had placed a curse on the

*island to defend it from being looted. To this day, no one
has discovered any sign of the treasure…*

Ben heard another series of beeps, his search for 'DWV, wine, 1742' finished with ten hits. He clicked the mouse and then turned to the others.

"Hey guys, take a look at the second search, something about Durbanville Wine Valley."

They turned to Ben. Harris replied, "It's hard for Sal and I to see over your shoulder to read what it says. Can you read it aloud?"

Ben began, "Durbanville's heritage and links to the early Cape of Good Hope date back over three centuries. Then, wild animals roamed the Renosterveld and the indigenous people traded with the early pioneers at the Cape. Originally, with Biesjes Craal, Elsjes Co-rael and Bommelshoek, the Pampoenkraal border outpost supplied the Dutch East India Company with fresh produce as well as meat. In the early 1700s vineyards were established in the area."

He paused to take in the information.

Sal nudged Ben with an elbow. "So, we have sixty bottles of early 18th century wine, down in your cellar?"

"I guess so," Harris said dryly.

Ben replied, "But…what's that got to do with our 'egg-island' and Captain Blood Bones. From what I see, it just tells us that our relatives drank expensive Merlot."

Harris cut in with a chuckle, "At least they had good taste!"

Sal smiled, "One point for Harris. I'm still winning though, in the ever-continuing comic battle of charm and wit."

Ben let out a deep sigh. "Guys, this is huge. Can't we save the humor for later?"

The group chuckled for a bit, and then continued on their quest for answers.

"Hmm, I got another idea," Ben called out.

Harris replied, "What's up?"

"Well, it's just 1763 and Captain Blood Bones haven't really been linked together yet. I think they are two important pieces of the mystery. Remember the article about the island. It mentions between the years of 1763 and 1764, that's as much as a year later than the date on the map."

"Man, you're right."

He looked at Harris, "So yeah, I think the next step is for us to do a third search, linking 1763 and Captain Blood Bones."

Sal nodded in agreement.

Ben attacked the keyboard with nimble fingers. The blue scale at the bottom of the web page began to fill the entire box, seconds later the page was loaded: 'Boston, January 16, 1763: Pirate Attack on Three British Ships in Boston Harbor.'

After clicking on the link, Ben smiled, knowing he had found something. The silence was interrupted abruptly as their mother yelled through the floorboards, rattling the boy's feet. "Boys, come down for dinner!"

The three simultaneously replied, "In a second!"

They shook their heads to ward off the thought of food, though the intoxicating smell lingered in the air.

"Okay, back to the search," Sal tried to break the silence.

Ben scanned through the first few paragraphs of the Boston News-Letter and began summing up the article:

"In the early hours of the sixteenth day of January, three British vessels were anchored in the harbor, awaiting several documents required for their journey to London. Three months of colonial taxes sat in the holds of the *HMS Courtesy*. One of the convoy ships, the *HMS Georgia Rose*, burnt to the hull as it collided with a pirate vessel that was ablaze. The remaining convoy ship picked up all survivors, pirate and British. About half of Blood Bones' crew were captured or killed in the conflict, but amazingly he managed to escape, sailing away aboard the *HMS Courtesy*. It passed the battery and escaped to sea. As for the rest of the captured crew, they were then sent to the dungeons of the Castillo de los Tres Reyes del Morro in Havana, Cuba to spend eternity in the bowels of darkness."

Sal looked confused, "Wait, so how did he get onto the *Courtesy*?"

Ben scanned the words closer. "It says that no one is exactly sure as to how he accomplished this feat, but rumor is he and his men snuck on and then took over the ship."

Harris interjected. "This guy seems brilliant. His commandeered ship didn't even get fired upon and he escaped with three months worth of the American colonies' taxes. Do you have any idea how much that would be worth today, nonetheless back then?"

Ben replied, "Yeah, it's a lot."

Sal laughed, causing the others to join in.

"Hey, how bout we get some food. All this talk of money and treasure is making me hungry."

Ben slapped his brother on the back, "Yeah, let's talk about this after we eat."

8

Miguel followed Hernando closely as the two walked towards the officer standing guard at the gangway, "I have some requests of you."

The young man saluted, "Sir, of course. What can I do?"

"How many men are on deck right now?" Hernando asked.

"Sir, we've ten marines and fifteen seamen. At the end of the watch another dozen or so will come on deck and we'll lift anchor and sail out of the harbor in convoy with the *Georgia Rose* and the *Savannah*."

"Good. Well, I'm thinking ahead. Just in case, we can mount several swivel guns on deck. Order your marines to retrieve ten guns from below. I think if we mount four on both sides, evenly spaced and two fore and aft, that would be enough for the defense against *this* bloody pirate."

"Aye sir, but wouldn't it make more sense to send the ordinary seamen?"

"We might need them on deck to ready for sea," he replied convincingly.

"Aye sir, I'll do that right now."

✖✖✖

As the twenty-five marines from the *Courtesy* reached the gangway of the *Georgia Rose*, a voice carried down from the gangway, "Hark, who goes there?"

A man replied, "Just reporting, sir. We've orders to join with your crew. Can we be led to your Commanding Officer so we can go over the plans that were assigned to us?"

He called back down in a questionable tone, "Remain there while I retrieve the captain."

The men on the wharf stood still, chatting amongst themselves until the two figures called down to them, "Permission granted."

Once all were aboard, the man at the front of the assembled line sounded off, "Sir, Lieutenant Alec Greenbough of the *Courtesy,* reporting as ordered."

The captain was simply puzzled. "Reporting for what?"

"Sir, Lieutenant Clifford Johnson, of the *Georgia Rose,* came with about twenty or so men to our vessel just before. He had a message that Blood Bones is preying the waters nearby the harbor and that you gave *him* permission to switch out marines between ships. He said they were the finest gunners from the *Rose.*"

"Something's not right. You said Lieutenant Clifford Johnson?"

"Sir, unless I heard him wrong, but I swear he said that name."

The captain closed his eyes, knowing something serious was to occur. "This is not good. We need to warn the *Courtesy* that the men you speak of are imposters. I don't have anyone by the name of Clifford Johnson on board, nor did I grant those orders."

❊❊❊

Within half a minute the deck was clear. Miguel moved to the railing beside the Officer on Deck, glancing off into the wintry harbor. Hernando signaled his man with a nod of the head and Miguel unsheathed the knife on his hip.

"Do as I say or you will die," he whispered as he pressed the blade into the man's neck.

The Officer nodded slowly, enough to let his attacker know his decision, but not enough for the blade to inflict any damage. He noticed the darker complexion of the man who had introduced himself as Lieutenant Clifford Johnson.

"Lock your men below deck, batten the hatches. Get your ordinaries to cut the lines and lift anchor. Raise sails and steer out of the harbor."

His complexion reddened. "And may I ask who you are?"

He placed a hand on the brim of his hat, removing it with a sweeping motion across the front of his body. "My friends call me Hernando, to my crew I am captain, but you know me as Blood Bones."

"And what if I refuse?" replied the British officer.

"You'll meet Davy Jones himself, for he was the first to have refused an order of mine. Miguel, we are wasting time."

With a flick of the wrist, the young man fell to the deck.

A sailor swabbing the deck nearby ran over to interrogate. "Sir, may I ask what happened?"

"Just an imposter, we're lucky I saw him come aboard. I'll go below decks to inform the captain of what happened. I think it's best that we ready the sails now; trouble looks to be brewing on the pier. I want the ship ready for sea immediately."

"Yes sir."

He quickly passed the message, watching the ordinary seamen run the decks with haste.

"Sir, if we place a couple of swords between the handles, the hatches won't open."

"Good work, Miguel. The hatches cannot be opened from below; they'll have no way of escape. Now, hurry!"

"Yes, captain."

With the telescope pressed to his eyes, he scanned the decks of the *HMS Savannah*, pleased to see that there was no commotion on board the other ship. His gaze shifted towards the *Rose*. As he blinked away several snowflakes from his eyelashes, he noticed the ship emerge with life.

※※※

The captain of the *Georgia Rose* led a squad of marines down the gangway, forming his men into columns of three. They marched quickly, moving with urgency.

"It's an awfully good night, tonight," said a man emerging from the shadows.

The longshoreman led a group of ten out into the middle of the lane, obstructing the path.

The captain called out, "Get out of the way or we'll have you arrested."

With a hand in his pocket, the longshoreman gripped the pouch of gold coins that a mysterious cloaked sailor had given him earlier. "But these are our docks; you must pay the toll if you wood like to pass."

"Listen, we do not have time for this, move or we will be forced to take drastic measures."

The longshoremen fell back several feet, allowing the marines to advance further. The man replied, "Aye, that'll cost you too. We let you have a yard," he chuckled in his half-drunk state.

"Charge them!"

The marines lowered their rifles, using them as clubs in their forward charge. One man was clubbed to the ground as the rest fled backwards, allowing the marines to regain their ranks and continue down towards the *Courtesy*.

✖✖✖

"All lines are cut and the anchor has just been raised," a sailor screamed to Hernando Audaz over the noise as the chain slid down the spill pipe to be stored on the deck below.

His eyes focused through the telescopic glass, first on the *Georgia Rose*. Men littered the weather decks, preparing the vessel for sea. He then adjusted his view towards the wharf, noticing his hired longshoremen succeed in delaying the pursuing marines. After wiping a layer of snowflakes off the lens, he continued to scan the bare decks of the *Savannah*.

Audaz snapped to attention when he heard a volley of gunfire come from the pier. The vessel was less than half a pistol's shot away when he heard the thuds of the lead bullets hitting the decks and bulwarks of the *Courtesy*.

"Get down! Find cover!"

His men kissed the deck as another volley filled the air, the sound carried in the cool wintry night. The sails let out and began filling with a strong offshore wind, propelling the vessel from the British gunfire.

As the ship left the berthing area and passed by several anchored ships, Audaz looked astern to find sailors climbing the rigging of the *Rose*. She had just raised anchor and took in all lines. By the time the canvas would be filled with wind, the *Courtesy* would have at least a quarter mile on its pursuers.

✹✹✹

La Monzón cruised slowly back and forth by the entrance to the harbor, flying the British flag. They waited anxiously with primed cannons, ready to fire the chain shot into the enemy's rigging. With a reduced crew, maneuverability was slow. Only a few were on deck; the remaining men were below decks manning the gun carriages.

It was a long and anxious wait for Álvaro Audaz as he continually scanned the waters around him. He could see the battery that protected the harbor; it looked asleep. His eyes moved from the fort to the entrance of the harbor, trying to pick out the first set of white sails. He let off a large smile upon seeing the flying canvas.

✹✹✹

"Sir, they have a decent lead on us. I figure that by the time we exit the harbor and are in good winds, we'll be able to overtake them," Greenbough said to the captain of the *Georgia Rose*.

"Yes, Alec. I cannot believe this, someone will be blamed. They just bloody walked onboard."

"Sir, do you think they got any more tricks up their sleeve?"

"Let's hope not, I bet Blood Bones is probably heading south-wards to his lair. I've heard rumors that it's near Port Royal. I don't know if you've heard this tale, but supposedly a small group of his men changed their bad habits and snuck away from the island. So guess what he did?"

"Uh," he paused. "He chased him?"

The captain of the *Rose* replied, "Of course, but the four escaped and revealed his hideout. Also mentioned was another lair some-where off the coast of Florida, but isn't really specific. Anyways, this guy's tricky, but I think he used up all his magic."

"Let's hope so. This wind needs to pick up, it died down again. Look, they're almost out of the harbor," he pointed. "The *Savannah's* lagging behind. Hopefully it doesn't come down to a straight up fight against the *Rose*. They have too many guns, eight more than us."

"This is true, but they only had twenty-five men with them. How will they sail the frigate and man the guns at that same time?"

"Well, if they all got onboard the ship, convincing everyone they're British Naval Officers; I couldn't tell you what they are ca-pable of doing. It's like they are always one step ahead of us, no matter what."

9

$\mathcal{I}$ n the dinning room, the three teenagers helped Mrs. Manry place the food on the table. As they were distributing the silverware between each setting, the man of the house, John Manry entered through the doorway carrying his black briefcase and a duffel bag.

"Hey, guys, good evening Sal. How's everyone doing?"

The couple kissed in greeting, and then John emptied the duffel bag's contents into the washing machine.

"How'd you do today?"

John turned to his wife. "Oh, it was a great game of racquetball. I was down eighteen to fifteen and then had a huge comeback," he paused and looked at Sal, "Your father played well though. When you see him next tell him that I can't wait for the next game."

Jorge Draben and John Manry were best friends, just like their children were. The two worked at the same firm together, John as a sales representative and Jorge as an accountant. The duo consulted with various clients and together they had made their business quite successful in the St. Augustine area.

"I'll tell him in a few days; Ben and Harris asked me to sleep over tonight."

John Manry's tall frame moved towards the dinning room table to take a seat. "Oh, all right. It's a pleasure as always. So, how was school today?"

His blue eyes looked around the table, spotting his older son first.

Harris replied, "Eh, class, class, and more class. Senior year is going well though. I just applied to UCF, UF, and Sanford Brown yesterday, I'll find out in a few months if I get in."

His eyes then moved to the younger son.

"Um, took a few quizzes. Learned about the irrigation in Peru, drew a few nifty sailboats on my notebook," he summed the day's events.

The father shook his head, ignoring the last statement. His gaze then looked to Salvador.

"Well, sir. Been busy, I got an early decision into Webster; I also applied to the same as Harris."

"Oh, following in your father's footsteps are we?"

Sal smiled, "Yeah, I guess you could say that. Most likely I'll go to Webster."

As the males talked at the table, Mrs. Manry finished the preparations and then the group began to eat.

"So, what's adventure this weekend?"

Harris gave a quick glance to Sal and Ben before turning to his father. "Oh, just going fishing overnight for a day or so. I think we'll take the plastic canoe out and explore around the stream and lake."

"Ah, sounds fun. When I was a kid, I used to explore around that area too."

The group continued eating, talking about the plans for the cellar extension, along with college acceptances and several other topics. Everyone threw their trash out and then they washed the dishes together. After everything was put back into the cabinets, Ben, Harris, and Sal ran upstairs to the computer room.

"Okay, so where did we leave off?"

Sal looked at Harris, "Just talking about this pirate dude burying treasure onto an island that looks like an egg."

Ben cracked a smile. "What do you plan on studying in college anyways? You could definitely be a comedian."

"You think?"

"No, I was just trying to catch up to you guys; I'm a little behind in the comic battle of wit and charm."

Harris fell out of his chair rolling in laughter. Ben couldn't help but laugh too, leaving Sal the only one breathing normally.

"Ha...ha...ha, very funny."

"I thought it was."

Harris regained his composure and then checked the clock that sat on the desk.

"Hey guys, it's just after seven, let's start packing for tomorrow so we can relax."

"Sounds good," replied Sal.

"Sal, can you go into the fridge and get like...nine bottles of water and a few boxes of granola bars from the kitchen closet? Ben, go into the closet and get out the camping equipment: tent, matches, and backpacks. Can you think of anything else we need?"

Sal shook his head. Ben answered, "Yeah, pocket knifes, hatchet, flashlight or a lantern. I guess we should pack a fishing rod so dad won't get suspicious."

"Yeah, good call bro."

✖.✖.✖

ℳr. Manry banged on the door the following morning to wake the boys up for breakfast, causing Ben to jump to his feet. He shook Harris and Sal, and then slipped on a fresh t-shirt from his drawer. The three hurried down the stairs towards the kitchen, with the smell of bacon, eggs, and toast getting stronger with each step.

When they took a seat at the table joining Mr. and Mrs. Manry, they each poured a glass of orange juice.

He stared down at a cheese omelet, three strips of bubbling bacon, and a piece of toast with butter melting on it.

"So, when are you guys heading out?"

He looked at his father, "Eh, after we eat, we'll throw everything into our packs and get some gear from the shed," said Harris.

"What're you trying to catch?"

He let off a smile, "Eh, whatever comes our way."

His father laughed a bit and then replied, "Yeah, that's usually how it goes for me."

❌❌❌

*I*t was just after nine in the morning when they arrived at the small, wooden dock. Once Sal sat down inside the midsection of the canoe, Ben passed the gear to his waiting hands, while Harris moved to the metal cleat at the edge of the dock.

"Get in, I'll push off and then hop in," Ben said as he started unwinding the line off the cleat.

Harris stepped in and took a seat in front of Sal. Ben held the line in his hand, and then pushed the canoe to angle it away from the pier. As he did this, he stepped in, taking place in the remaining seat. He leaned down and pulled the third oar from between Sal's legs.

"So, which way?" asked Sal.

Both Harris and Ben pointed at the same time, "Off to the right."

It was as if they were destined to say that phrase, leading the canoe down the little stream that connected to the lake and also the Atlantic Ocean by the Matanzas River. The three of them were facing astern, pulling hard on the oars, propelling the canoe forward.

Ben called out a quick cadence, "One, two, pull, one, two, pull…"

Sal called out over Ben's shoulder, "Why are we going so fast?"

"So we can explore the island sooner. I can't wait!"

After the exchange, the only thing heard was the dipping of the blade into the water, and the gurgle of propulsion. This was not the normal kind of silence, the kind that everyone experiences every once in awhile, but rather, a silence that was eerie. They all had the feeling they were being watched. Their eyes darted around, scanning the bushes and foliage that lined their path. The hair on Sal's neck stood straight as the canoe maneuvered around several rock outcroppings in the middle of the stream. The width opened for a few hundred feet, and then shrunk to just the width of the canoe. Harris looked over his shoulder and saw that the waterway began to curve.

"Ben, we want to go a little to the left, hold water for a bit."

He dunked the oar below the water and held it there for a few seconds, feeling the canoe swing a few degrees to the left.

"Yup that's good, you can start rowing again."

Sal turned his head towards Harris, "How much further?"

As Harris turned his head to see what was to come, the canoe slammed hard into a fallen tree that blocked the waterway. With a load crash, the boat came to a sudden halt.

"What the hell was that?" Ben yelled out.

Harris twisted his torso so that he could see the limb protruding from the murky water below.

"Shit, there's a fallen tree. You guys want to try and chop it?"

Ben turned his body to investigate. "Hell no, it'll take too long. Let's try and get to the side, I'll jump out onto those rocks, and then I'll move it."

They maneuvered the plastic shell enough so that Ben could step out onto the rocks. "Toss me the bow line. I'll tie off the canoe."

His brother passed him a coil of cotton rope; Ben stepped back and then wrapped the bitter end around the trunk of a sapling, tying it off quickly with two half hitches. He scanned the area for the source of the problem. He took a few steps and then made a left into the woods. The tree was cracked in half, split in a recent thunderstorm.

He stooped down, bending at the knees and hips. His hands wrapped around the tree, gripping tightly with the effort. With a powerful squat, he lifted the tree out of the water several inches.

"Keep going, you almost got it!" yelled Harris.

He strained his muscles, the waterlogged wood not budge any further. "Dude, it's not going any more. It's stuck."

Harris peered into the water, seeing if there was anything in sight. "It's too murky, I can't see through it!"

Ben jerked the tree back and forth, hoping to dislodge what was below.

"Want me to jump in and free it?"

Ben shook his head. "Nah, then you'll get wet. Why don't we just lift the canoe out of the water and carry it."

Sal smiled. "Ha…that's why he's with us. He's got the brains of the bunch."

Harris 'accidentally' kneed him in the back. "Sorry. I must've slipped."

Ben chuckled. "All right, get out of the boat. You two fat asses will make it impossible to carry out!"

"Oh shut up bro. I was just trying to get some more adventure in before we go to the island."

"Well if you want, I'll carry out the canoe. You can feel free to hack away underwater at a snagged branch. That's totally up to you."

Sal got out of the boat. "I'm with Ben. I could use a laugh watching you wrestle with a branch."

Harris turned red. "Fine, you're lucky I want to see this island just as much as you guys do. If I didn't, I'd be wrestling that freaking branch in a second!"

Ben smiled, "You'd probably lose."

Sal let out a good laugh before placing a hand over his mouth. Through loosely positioned fingers, he let out, "Score two points for Ben."

Harris stepped out beside Sal and the three moved beside where they were seated earlier, Ben in the stern, Sal amidships, and Harris at the bow.

After untying the line from the sapling, they each grabbed the rubber handgrips with one hand, and then placed a hand below the bottom to cradle it.

"One, two, three, lift," called out Harris.

They lifted the canoe to chest level and then took several steps backwards, aware of the rocky terrain that lined the stream. They sidestepped in unison until they were well clear of the tree obstruction and then moved forward until they were at the water's edge.

Harris led the group, "Ready to lower. One, two, three go!"

The boat was then placed into the water and they each took their respective seats. They continued paddling down the winding stream, ducking their heads below sagging vines and branches from the overgrown woods on either side the stream. After several strokes, they emerged out of a twisted stream into a large lake, within sight of the egg-shaped island and the two boulders that marked the landing spot.

10

Alvaro went below decks to check the angle of the guns once more before the first volley would be launched. As he stared through the porthole, a second column of canvas came into view.

"Gentleman, man the guns. Our target is in sight. We need to get off an effective broadside that'll cripple their ship. We don't have much time. The fort could come to life at any second!"

Inside each barrel sat a length of chain and bar shot on top of powder. The fuses were primed and ready. Each gun leader obeyed the orders. They went down the line repeating, "Ready to fire."

❉❉❉

Lieutenant Alec Greenbough eyed the *Courtesy* rounding a spit of land, on its approach to the battery. He changed his view from the starboard side and looked left. The moment his eyes adjusted to the snowy darkness, he saw five bright flashes of light.

"Hit the deck!"

The bars and chain flew through the sheets of falling snow, spinning towards the rigging above. The spray of projectiles nearly took off his head; slicing spars, tackles, and rigging just several feet away. A sail dislodged fell to the deck, trapping several men underneath. The central mast split in two, sending splinters flying in a massive explosion of wood.

He tripped in his escape to avoid the splinters that showered him like a heavy rain. There was a slight pain in his calf as he tugged on his breeches, revealing several long gashes.

"Hard over, I want to give them a broadside before they can re-load their guns!"

The message was relayed to the gunners below to ready for battle. The helmsman fought the strain as he forced the rudder to the large angle.

As the *Rose* revealed its broadside to the attacking vessel, the lieutenant saw the flashes of the muzzles again, and the sound of the explosion.

"Get down!"

✖✖✖✖

Álvaro looked on as the first volley damaged the sails and rigging, smiling with the fact that the vessel lost at least a knot or two in speed. The vessels ran parallel courses, just two hundred yards away. When the debris settled, a full complement of the English broad-side floated through the air towards Álvaro and his men. The can-non balls arced downward, crashing into the deck and through sails. Shreds of canvas slowly descended to the men below as an explosion of splinters showered the sailors.

The gun crews below began loading for a second volley, adjust-ing the angle as the vessels closed in range. Another series of chain shot flew through the air, shredding sails and spars. The English ship altered to port, closing in for a boarding.

"Helmsman, hard to port; make sure we clear their bow so we can let off a broadside at minimum range. I don't want them to be able to board us just yet…"

He then raced towards the companionway ladder. As he paced down the wooden stairs, he felt the ship take the great angle

"Men, once clear of her bow, shower her with grape shot."

The sailors replaced the bar and chain shot with canvas bags full of metal shards and small rods. As he emerged on deck, another vol-ley from the *Georgia Rose* landed at his feet.

The vessels were now closing in towards each other, with *La Monzón* cutting the bow of the English ship. He felt the shake of the deck as the rudder continued its struggle. The instant the ship was broadside to their enemy the gun crews lit the fuse to the cannons, sending projectiles of metal that mowed down the English marines.

Almost clear of the *Rose*, the English let off a volley from their after cannons that crashed into the side of the *La Monzón*. One ball entered through the gun port; the cannon exploding, killing the gun crew on the carriage. A fire erupted as the surrounding barrels of gunpowder were showered with sparks and hot metal.

✖✖✖

*H*ernando Audaz peeked through his spyglass, noticing the initial shots sent towards the English. He studied the curves of the ship that had brought him his fame and glory. All was going according to plan; the *Courtesy* had passed by the battery without any detection and the trap was set for the two English vessels. He maneuvered the ship two points to port, heading for the open Atlantic Ocean. Their rendezvous was the easternmost part of Belle Isle Inlet, out of detection from the harbor's battery and English ships.

Then he noticed the returning gunfire from the HMS *Georgia Rose*.

Miguel stood beside his captain, "Sir, what do you make of this?"

"Just a hindrance, our men are experienced. The English will sustain rigging damage that will take it out of the battle. Once my cousin steers the ship out of the engagement, we will meet up and sail southwards for Port Royal where we'll ransom the captured crew for more gold."

Miguel smiled at the prospect of such a large profit, "Between that and the tax money, we'll retire and buy a villa and have any woman we desire!"

He let out a laugh, "Does that not happen already?"

The two snickered as their bodies rested against the stern railing.

✖.✖.✖

Alvaro heard something rumble below his feet. Without thinking, he ran for the companionway, emerging into a sailor's worst nightmare; a fire. Men were swatting the flames with their shirts, attempting to delay the fire's spread. The trails of the black gunpowder continued to catch, setting off lines of little explosions.

"Men, we must extinguish the flames before it reaches the magazine!"

✖.✖.✖

Still standing at the stern of the *Courtesy*, the two figures snapped into focus when they heard the explosion and witnessed flames shoot out from *La Monzón's* gun ports. Hernando Audaz looked on, seeing the English vessel alter course and begin its pursuit of his cousin's crippled command.

Even with the damaged rigging, the *Rose* managed to close the distance between the two ships. His eyes focused through the spyglass, seeing grappling hooks thrown, bringing the ships together like lovers. Marines swarmed out onto the deck of the English vessel hooting and roaring with life.

Between the gunfire and the clinking swords, he watched his men back away from the fight, looking as if they were giving up. This was not like them at all. He began to think they were up to something.

✖.✖.✖

Lieutenant Greenbough and the captain of the HMS *Georgia Rose* led the marines as they jumped the gap between ships. They met a resistance of ten, who seemed to be guarding the central companionway.

"Find out what they are hiding!"

A dozen marines obeyed the command, charging at full gait with their blades high, ready for battle.

Greenbough's hand felt for the handle of his pistol. Taking sight of the first man he gazed at, he squeezed the trigger. They continued their charge forward, only to find a row of pirates drop to their knees. Only one man remained standing with a lit fuse beside the barrel of a swivel gun.

"Get out of the way!"

The man pressed in the fuse; balls, nails, and shards of metal projected outwards, fanning out across the deck. Numerous marines fell to the deck, clutching their throats, faces, and stomachs.

Twenty men were slain with one shot from the powerful mini-cannon. After the dust settled, the marines pushed forward cornering their enemies against the rail.

"Surrender or die!" Greenbough called out.

A pirate with a blade pressed to his chest replied with a laugh, "I'm afraid it's already too late."

✖✖✖

As the flames entirely consumed the second deck of the schooner, the powder magazine began to spit fire; sending boards and men flying upwards. A hole that ran the entire breadth of the ship splintered off, exposing the flames of the deck below to friend and foe. Many lost their balance as they slid to their fiery deaths.

The fire spread yet further, engulfing the main deck of *La Monzón*. A violent explosion hurled more splinters into the air, injuring men aboard the English vessel and further wrecking havoc to the trapped sailors. Several marines began chopping at the boarding lines to free their vessel from the inferno. To no avail, the vessels clung together like a stubborn farewell.

Within a minute, the fire spread to the *Georgia Rose*, setting it too ablaze. Men jumped off the burning vessels into the surrounding waters, only to have men land on their heads in the hurried escape. The sacrifice saved the remaining crew of *La Monzón*. The fifteen men rowed away in the skiff, their laughter carrying over the water.

✖✖✖

Álvaro called the cadence, "Heave, one, two, three, heave, one, two, three, heave…"

They had disappeared into a cloud of snow and were a little more than thirty yards away from the flames when they spotted the *HMS Savannah* bearing down towards them. The ship was the last to prepare for sea, about twenty minutes behind the convoy. Álvaro watched as a man focused on them through a bronze scope. A few moments later, the ship altered its course to intercept the skiff.

"Men, prepare for a collision!"

The distance between the sloop and the skiff closed greatly, sail power winning the race versus oars. Soon the bowsprit protruded above a man at the tiller.

"Sir, what should we do?" the man screamed to Álvaro.

Before an answer could depart his lips, the skiff dissolved under the impact; rising with the swell one last time before she sunk to the depths of the harbor.

✖✖✖

He looked on as the explosions of burning gunpowder filled the harbor. He could do nothing about it; there was no chance of turning the *HMS Courtesy* around to rescue his fallen comrades. He was already out of the battery's range, almost rounding another spit of land that lead out to the ocean, but the scene flashed through his mind once more.

"If only the marines locked below would fire upon their own vessel, then a rescue mission would be possible, but then I would put to risk all what we have accomplished so far. We could lose this treasure that I stand upon, a frigate laden with three months worth of colonial taxes," he whispered to the wind.

And for a moment, Captain Blood Bones had a fixation with greed, forgetting any possible chance of rescue for his cousin and his shipmates.

11

Harris jumped out of the canoe, splashing into the cool water, turning up the mud that lined the bottom of the lake. This body of water separated them from civilization, cutting them off from any human contact, both an eerie and thrilling concept for the eager young men.

Harris tugged at the bow of the canoe, dragging it onto the embankment that surrounded the island. He stared up at the tall pines and peered into the wild underbrush. Once inside the shadow of this ominous forest, no one would be able to see them.

Harris and Sal excitedly scrambled out of the canoe and opened the map fervently.

"Ok, so I'm thinking this is the starting point. It's the only noticeable break in the bushes all along the edge of this place," Sal noted.

"Yeah, I think so too, it's got to be. Let's go!" Harris exclaimed. He and Sal shouldered their backpacks, itching with anticipation.

"Hey! Hold your horses. Let me make sure this canoe's not going anywhere. Should we cover it up, so no one sees it from shore?" Ben inquired.

"Nah, who cares? It shouldn't take that long anyways. Come on!" replied Sal.

Ben gave one last heave and the canoe became securely beached. He grabbed his own pack from the canoe, and walked towards the other two that awaited him at the entrance of the woods. He sighed;

scanning the blackness that loomed before them, looking for any signs of the island's rumored supernatural activity.

"Ok, so we've figured out that these numbers here on the map are paces," Ben looked down at the map.

"Why's the path so ziggy-zaggy?" Sal asked to no one in particular.

"It's probably just to confuse us, like they do in the movies. We just have to make sure we follow it exactly," he replied.

Harris grabbed the map from his younger brother and took off, beginning the adventure.

"Fine," Ben huffed with frustration.

The younger Manry scrounged for the water bottle that rested in the side pocket of his pack, and took a big swig while glaring at Harris.

"Let's see. Well, we'll start the counting right here where the brush begins, where the map says to," Harris said.

He moved a branch out of his way as he took the first step into endless darkness. They were startled at how the bright sunlight was completely blocked out due to the foliage that towered over their heads.

Sal and then Ben fell in line behind their leader.

"Wait. Hold up," Ben said, squinting to see anything that surrounded him, decided to retrieve the flashlight from his backpack.

"Good idea," Harris said.

Both he and Sal paused to take their flashlights out. After clicking them on, they set out with determination to find the treasure.

"One...two...three..." Harris counted aloud the first set of twenty paces delineated on the map. Ben scanned the treetops that enveloped them with his flashlight. A chill ran down his spine. Peculiarly, all was quiet except for the crunch of the twigs and leaves beneath their trudging feet.

"Oof!"

"Ahhh!" Sal yelped as Ben barreled into him from behind after having tripped over a tree root.

"Geez! You scared the crap out of me!" He heard Harris snicker beneath his breath.

"Sorry man. You can't see anything in here," Ben explained.

"Twenty! Hmm, now where to go from here?" Harris questioned.

They stopped for a quick break, surveying the spot. The leader scanned the map with his flashlight.

"Hey! Look at this!" Ben reached down, moving the branch of a fern to reveal what he had spotted. He picked up a small stone on the ground that was quite unique. It was bright white in color beneath a crusted layer of accumulation. He wiped the dirt off and gasped.

"Whoa!" He had turned the rock over to expose the letter 'M' that had been crudely carved into it. "I wonder what it stands for," he said excitedly.

"We got to be on the right track. Maybe they're markers, or checkpoints," Sal theorized.

Ben pocketed the stone. "We'll check out the next spot when we get there for another one."

"The map shows that we have to shift our course about forty-five degrees to the right. Well, looks like we're going to have to blaze a new path through these trees if we're going to follow the directions exactly."

Harris adjusted the direction of their path, grabbed hold of a large branch, and pushed it out of his way, making an entry for the group. The branches seemed to grapple with the young men, using great force to push them this way and that as they plowed through the unexplored territory. Ben's water bottle was wrenched from his backpack, falling carelessly next to a tree stump.

Sure enough, after some scrounging in the dirt of the next point on the map, there, embedded in the dirt, was a black stone with the letter 'z' engraved into it. The adventurers were thrilled, and eager to continue on. They plowed through the dense forest, following the map and counting aloud the number of paces that were outlined. The next set of paces was the longest stretch; forty paces.

"Thirteen…fourteen…fifteen…Ack!!"

Harris sprawled backwards, bumping into the chest of his brother. Harris rubbed his face with his hand as he crouched low to the ground.

"What the hell was that?! Did you guys see anything?! I just got hit in the face by something!" Harris exclaimed.

"No way, there's nothing out here!" Sal nearly shrieked. This attempt at reassuring the other guys proved useless.

Ben whipped his flashlight in every direction, attempting to shine light on whatever attacked his brother and to also ward off any creature that might be after them, but nothing could be seen.

"Maybe a branch just ricocheted back or something," Sal offered a possible solution.

"That's just it. It felt like a branch hit me, but with a lot of force. And I wasn't even touching it!" Harris explained, frustrated with the situation.

"Let's just keep going," Ben said.

But as they would soon come to discover, the trees on this stretch of the path seemed to have a life of their own.

"God damn it!" yelled Ben as a branch swung down from above, hitting him atop his head. "What's going on?"

"No way, they're alive!" Sal yelled over the rustle of the moving branches that surrounded them. "They're haunted or cursed or something!"

"We got to keep going! We need to find that treasure! Twenty-two…twenty-three…twenty-four" Harris continued.

The tree limbs persisted to hit the young men, but they became mere annoyances, never striking with the tremendous amount of force that the first attack entailed.

"Forty!" Harris shouted, and, with that, the branches immediately stopped, and once again, the forest became quiet.

Ben moved his hands through the dirt and found the next rock; they were now one step closer to their goal. The next three sets of paces went smoothly, with no interferences, but when they reached the last stretch of fifty paces, more trouble arose.

"Thirty-eight...thirty-nine...forty..."

"Ah!"

Harris and Ben whirled around to find that Sal was not with them. They raced back along their path, Ben making sure to count backwards in his head so that they would be able to resume their journey.

"Help!" Sal said with a look of fear and worry in his eyes, his chest slowly sinking further into the quicksand.

Ben quickly unfastened his belt and threw an end to Sal, who wrapped it around his palm. Harris joined in, both using all their strength to free their friend from the mysterious goo. Sal scrambled to his feet and gathered the brothers in his arms to give them a big hug.

"That's always been one of my biggest nightmares. Thank God you guys heard me!" Sal said and he let out a sigh of relief.

"Isn't it weird? We both had walked along the same path before you, Sal. Why didn't we sink into that stuff?" Ben questioned.

"This place is definitely haunted or something," Harris concluded.

Sal brushed most of the quicksand from his clothes, watching as the clumps flew to the ground and then they continued to push on. After what they had just experienced, it seemed as if nothing would stop them from finding that treasure.

"Fifty!" Just ahead, the opening of a menacing-looking cave lay before them. The boys froze in place, jaws dropping as they scanned the ten-foot high mouth of rock in the hillside. It was almost as if the rock face smiled at them, welcoming them for what was to come.

"This is it," Harris said. "The treasure's in there."

He ran forward, without giving an ounce of thought.

"Hey, we can't leave Harris to find this treasure all by himself," Sal said with a laugh.

"I know that, I just would've liked to have gone in at the same time."

12

A messenger rapped on the door of James Elliot, Dominion Governor of Boston. The stately gentleman clad in his finest linen robe rose and made his way to the door as his legs struggled to support his weight. Before turning the knob, he donned the hairpiece that hung on a wooden peg beside the entryway.

"Yes, yes, come in."

The familiar young face looked up to the large man.

"Sir, I was requested to bring this urgent message to you."

His well-manicured hands reached for the sealed delivery.

"Take a seat."

Placing his gilded monocle over his left eye, he began to slide a silver letter opener under the wax seal. His heart raced as his eyes took in the mirrored initials that stared him in the face. With a heavy sigh, he began reading:

Governor Elliot,

> *I regret to inform you that one hundred and fifty of your men are below deck chained by the feet, ready to face my wrath if you do not fulfill my requests. They are as follows:*
>
> *Firstly, I demand that you meet me personally at the rocks of Cohasset, midnight, tomorrow night, escorted solely by the messenger that has been sent to you as well as a horse drawn carriage laden with items that will be*

mentioned. *To put your uneasiness to rest, it will only be me meeting with you. If you have any officers follow-ing you, in an attempt to ensure your safety, I can assure you—you will not be safe or alive for long.*

Secondly, it is requested that you provide us with enough provisions to make a journey of two weeks. This entails casks of fresh water, rum, loafs of bread, and salted meat. Also, we require lumber, nails, and munitions. Limit yourself to two carriages.

Lastly, I wish to exchange your men for my men who survived, in addition for ten thousand gold pieces. If you want to see your men alive and well, heed my warnings and do as I say.

Blood Bones

His face contorted with anger.

The messenger inquired, "Uncle is everything ok?"

He shook his head, "Who does this man think he is?" His fist slammed the table with boiling rage. "We will end his mockery!"

☠☠☠

Two days passed, the imprisoned marines remained locked up in the bowels of the ship, without food and water. All of the lanterns below were removed to allow for a pitch-black atmosphere, breaking the prisoners will to live. The ship lay at anchor off the Graves, an island less than four and a half miles east of the battery protecting Boston harbor. Audaz paced the deck, waiting for day to turn to night. In his mind, he began to formulate what he believed the British Dominion Governor would do in response to the ransom note.

As midnight approached, he and a group of six hand-picked men rowed from the anchored vessel to the meeting spot on the rocks of Cohasset. Between the flooding tide and the power of their oars, they soon touched bottom. He jumped out and his gray robe dipped into the cool water. Once the skiff was dragged out and secured, Audaz tied the hands of his men together with rope.

"Men, remember that you wouldn't have eaten anything in the last several days. You'd be filthy dwelling in the same disease-ridden space below decks. Act the role; we shall deceive them once again!"

✖✖✖

*J*ames Elliot and his nephew led the two horse drawn carriages down the familiar streets of Boston. Inside each carriage sat a half dozen huddled British soldiers, armed with pistol, sword, and musket. Once clear of the main streets, he navigated the caravan through side alleys and finally onto a dirt trail.

They followed the curved path for quite some time, while the Dominion Governor looked anxiously out the window at a strip of beach and the rocks of Cohasset. The carriages paused at the tree line before closing the distance to the awaiting men. In just a few minutes, they were twenty paces from the fire. He glanced around, viewing the scene. Captain Blood Bones was standing alone, his robe fluttering in the wind. Six men, bound in rope, sat side by side before the wind-whipped flames.

The two leaders walked towards each other with their heads low, as if both were hiding something from the other.

"I have the supplies you requested," said the burly man, "Your men are safe and will be returned tomorrow morning once the exchange is made."

Audaz snickered at the comment. "I have six of yours by the fire for a down payment. I shall send them to join you right now. Likewise, on the morrow I will allow your remaining men to rejoin with you."

He turned his neck slightly, still keeping the Dominion Governor in view. "Get out of my sight, you scum!"

The group of six stood as one, shaking sand off their breeches with tied hands as they walked over to stand behind the governor.

Elliot's eyes stared at the men as they passed him by.

"The light skin of an honest Englishmen; perhaps he did not trick us this time. Now he'll be in for a surprise," he mumbled.

✺✺✺

*J*ohn Elliot lay with musket focused on his target, but did not dare pull off the shot until his uncle gave him the signal. The teenager watched the pirate hand over the captured sailors, but was not able to hear the passed words due to the howling wind. He blinked a few times to rid his eyes of the dust that lived in the filthy blanket above him.

"Come on, uncle. Just move a bit to the right," he whispered, waiting anxiously for the gesture.

✺✺✺

*T*he moon shone through the dancing clouds as the snowstorm had ceased the night prior and the shifting winds brought in the scent of the sea. He could easily view the entire beach without straining his eyes. While discussing the plans of further releasing the other's prisoners, his eyes scanned the area wearily; his focus then shifted to the carriages itself. He wondered if he was wrong in his presumptions about the rather cumbersome man standing before him.

"Governor, I believed I asked you to be accompanied by your messenger? I have yet to see him."

"Well, Blood Bones, can I call you Blood Bones? He had to run an errand and could not make it. I am sorry, it is just I tonight."

Audaz smiled, stunned at the man's wit. "I see. Yes, call me Blood Bones," he added in a whisper, "Allow me to prove my reputation." He continued, "Well, I lived up to the first part of my deal. I want my supplies now. Tomorrow, I would like to then conclude the remainder of our agreement."

"Yes, yes of course. Let me show you the wares."

He watched as his uncle managed to about-face, giving a slight nod as the man reached for the handle to the side door of the carriage.

With a cough, he signaled his men to free themselves of the weak bonds. Elliot had his back turned towards the pirate captain, who charged and let off a yell that broke the silence that lingered.

The moonlight reflected off the metallic barrel, just enough for Audaz to notice.

A loud muzzle flash erupted from atop the carriage, sending a musket ball hurling at Blood Bones. The ball missed his chest, ripping cleanly through his left shoulder. Having little effect on the man's forward progress, he barreled into Elliot, just as the man's grip on the handle opened the carriage door. The hidden soldiers spilled out of the small space, joining the fight as the pirates began to split up; several men running to blockade the door of the second wagon while the rest raised their swords.

Elliot slashed at the air beside Audaz. The blade missed his face by an inch as it clinked into the rocks at their feet. Audaz mastered swordplay in his early years, receiving lessons from his father, and honing them in his short stint in the Spanish navy. The two leaders touched blades multiple times as the surrounding area began to fill with redcoats engaged in hand-to-hand combat. The deceptive pirates had a piece of rope tied around their right elbow to distinguish friend or foe.

He was surprised how the obese man managed the blade. He studied his rival's quick and strong slices, looking for weakness.

"He only fights from one side, leaving his left side vulnerable. He parries well, although at times he is slightly delayed. His attack is stronger than his defense," he thought to himself.

With a quick feint, he tricked Elliot into blocking high, revealing a small window of opportunity for his blade to slice at the man's stomach. Drawing blood, he continued on the attack, slashing high and then low, left and then right. His blade was parried away, but he continued on, cornering the Dominion Governor against the carriage. Blood Bones changed his fighting style once again and now slashed in quick arcs. As his own personal engagement progressed, his men had overcome the remaining British soldiers. They watched, cheering on their captain as he parried the skilled governor.

Sweat glistened on both men's brows with the strenuous efforts from both parties. Blood Bones now tried a different approach; instead of arcing the attacks; he now lunged with quick jabs. The first of which caught the man by surprise, slicing him low under his ribs. The blow knocked Elliot back, crashing hard into the carriage, revealing a clear path towards his neck. His blade instinctively met his opponent's weakness, slicing deep into the man's throat. The man fell to his knees, a sheen of fresh blood flowing fast down his chest.

✪✪✪

Having no clear shots, he laid down his musket beside his hip. All he could do was watch his uncle face his slayer's blade. The thought disturbed him; he had never seen a man kill another, regardless of it being in battle or in cold blood. In his brief service of two years to the Crown, the most deadly thing he had seen were paper cuts from the many piles of letters strewn throughout the offices in the battery.

He now watched as Audaz commanded his troops to throw the bodies into the empty carriage, locking the doors once all the British were inside. Shifting the blanket, he made sure he was shrouded from their view.

"I can't believe they forgot about me. Thank God," he sighed.

"What now, captain?"

He turned to his men. "Burn it all. There's nothing of value here. This, this will show the British," shaking a fist into the air.

He watched as two men grabbed a handful of boughs from a nearby bush, heading towards the bonfire. Setting the green shrubbery ablaze, they returned to the carriages.

"Get it done with. Someone knows of the meeting also. When they come to investigate, they'll realize that we mean business."

The two pairs of horses whinnied in fear as the pirates spread the fire, tossing burning limbs onto each carriage.

"Set the horses free. They're innocent; they have done nothing wrong here except n delivering these men to meet their fates."

Once done, they watched as the flames kicked up. Suddenly there was a stirring motion on top of the first carriage.

A young lad jumped down, landing hard on the ground. The boy curled in pain as he held his sides. He coughed for several minutes until he could manage to breathe regularly. Once he regained his composure, he looked around at pointed blades.

"Ah, and you must be the messenger…"

The teenager looked at the man who had slain his uncle. His body shuddered with another series of coughs.

"You are killing innocent men!" he managed through gritted teeth.

Audaz replied, "By associating themselves with these scoundrels, they can no longer claim innocence!"

"Then go along and kill me! I am loyal to the Crown, which means I am guilty as well," his chest stuck out with pride.

Audaz snickered at his bravery. "You are brave, boy. Now run off with you. I shall send your uncle's replacement a message within the week, but until then, leave."

The boy unsheathed his sword, ready to fight any who dared cross blades.

"Do you have to learn the hard way? Obviously it runs in your family, now get out of here," he waved his hand in disgust.

After a long stalemate of gleaming eyes, his sword found comfort in the scabbard. He looked deep into the man's eyes and said, "This is not over. You will be slain."

With that, the young messenger hurried off into the dark of night, not looking back once for fear of being chased.

✹✹✹

*J*ohn Elliot returned with haste to the safety of his home. When he rapped on the door, he was sweaty and breathing heavily. His mother opened the door and instantly knew something was unusual.

"What's wrong dear?"

Between pants, he managed, "Uncle took me…We went with twelve men to make a prisoner exchange…The pirates deceived us killing everyone except me…They told me to take a message to his replacement."

The words slowly sunk in, her complexion left her features. She had lost one of her closest childhood friends and her brother-in-law.

She closed her eyes, saying a prayer that lingered on her lips. "Oh my Lord," she opened her eyes, "Your father is sleeping; I'll go wake him. You can go wash up, you're a mess!" she said, attempting to lighten the mood.

He ran to the changing room and dunked his wrists under the cool water, he swirled them around and then bent down, splashing water onto his face. He could feel the sweat and ash slide off his wet cheeks and into the bowl.

When the family reunited beside the fireplace, his mother had passed him a blanket to warm up. His father was tying on his leather boots as he trembled with fear.

"I'm going to the Governor's headquarters. John, you can stay here with your mother."

He shook his head, "No, I'll come."

Mrs. Elliot watched as her husband and son stood up and walked to the door.

"It's all right, there's nothing to worry about. Go to bed, we'll be back by sun up."

They hurried around the house to their backyard. Fenced in were a watering hole, a barn-like overhead full of hay, and three beautiful white horses.

"If you'll get the horses ready, I have to get something quick."

Several minutes later, Mrs. Elliot watched the two figures pass by the front porch at a full gallop; John craned his head as he passed, and saw a shadow beside the flicker of a candle in the window.

They rode on through the town, heading towards the Dominion Governor's large estate. Beside the mansion was a barrack of men that guarded the city. Once they transited from the cobble-stone main streets onto the brick inlaid walkway, they hopped off the white stallions, and tied the horses to a wooden post.

They approached a group of laughing figures, silhouetted in cigar smoke. He paced up the stairs to the landing. "Nicholas Elliot, the Governor's brother. I need to come in right away."

The man sensed the urgency in his voice and waved them inside.

After being led to a group of officers finishing the night's last paperwork, Nicholas looked for Victor Smith, his brother's favorite subordinate.

"Victor, I've some rather unpleasant news. The Governor and a small force of troops went to meet Captain Blood Bones to discuss the prisoner exchange. My son was there, and he was lucky enough to have survived. Those bloody pirates killed every last one of our men, burning the dead and alive, showing no remorse. Something has to be done!" he said with an angry tone, smashing a closed fist into an open palm.

The officers closed their eyes and each said a silent prayer for their lost comrades. Victor's brown eyes turned red with anger, "How shall address this problem?"

His gaze was not focused on any one person, the question directed to all those present. John craned his head back and forth, to look at the faces of each man in attendance. He then saw paintings and drawings hung up on the walls. A bookshelf in the corner of the room sat quietly, looking as a book had not been opened in years.

Finally a man replied, "We should hunt him down. I believe all the captured pirates from the wreck were sent down to Havana."

Victor added on, "Yes, I was informed this morning. They were brought to Castillo de los Tres Reyes del Morro. I suppose we could send someone to look for him, but where would he go? Bloody hell, this pirate already deceived us twice!"

Nicholas chipped in, "Yes, it's the least we could do for my brother. Do we know of anyone capable of finding this murderer, Captain Blood Bones?"

The men pondered for a long while, thumping their hands against their sides. "I had a man do a few errands here and there, but I don't think he is capable for this sort of mission," a voice called out.

Victor ran a hand through his long salt and peppered hair. "I know of a man, his name is Nelson. I worked with him several times, and he has an impressive record. What's today's date?"

"Sir, three hours into the midnight watch, January 18th," said a voice listening in.

Victor continued, "If I'm not mistaken, he will be arriving in St. Augustine within the week. We can send out a dispatch rider immediately. Do we have any messengers available?"

A man replied, "No, sir. My messenger was dispatched four days ago; he should arrive within a fortnight."

Victor shook his head, "No, that will not help."

Another officer replied, "I believe I might have one also, but he won't be in for another three days."

An air of disappointment filled the room, all seemed to be lost. "Is there anything we can do then?" asked the favorite of the late Dominion Governor.

At the age of fifteen, John Elliot showed the qualities of leadership needed for such a brave and daring mission. "Sir, I will dispatch the message to St. Augustine."

All eyes turned to the corner of the room.

His father replied instantaneously, "No, you will not. This is very serious."

"Yes, but father, ask any one of these men. I've carried messages for each and every one of them."

Nicholas Elliot sighed, "This is different though. This is not just an ordinary message."

"Father, if you had been standing in my shoes and saw what had happened through my eyes, it would be a different story," he paused, sticking out his chest with pride. "I am as capable of any of the others; I'm a skilled rider, and could get there quicker than anyone else."

Victor let off a slight smile. "I will agree only if your father allows you."

"No, it is settled, my son will not ride."

"Father, you don't understand, I have to do this. This is what uncle would want. Plus, I know these trails well."

Finally after all pondered their choices, Victor spoke again. "All in approval of our own, John Elliot, to dispatch the message say aye. All opposed say nay."

The responses were unanimous; he beamed a large smile. The scenes of what progressed earlier that night flashed before his eyes, and then he remembered what he had said.

Victor dismissed everyone except the father and son. The man took out a sheet of parchment and placed it before him. Opening the ink jar, he dipped the quill in, and began writing. The sounds of the pen etching into the paper made John jump in anticipation. Finally, he took out a block of wax and held it over a candle that lit his workspace. Melting the wax, he let several drips pour onto the fold of the letter. Before it could harden, he placed Boston's seal on it, labeling it as official business. He then began writing another letter.

He nodded for John to come near, "Whatever you do, do not let this slip into enemy hands. You must get this to St. Augustine with haste, the survival of one hundred and fifty of our marines, retrieving the lost taxes, and avenging your uncle's death depend on this," he paused. "The first message is to be brought to the harbormaster at the port; this will end up going to Captain Arthur F. Nelson. The second must be brought to my representative at the Castillo de San Marcos. Now, go off with you and rest up. You have quite a long journey ahead of you."

The young lad stood at attention, saluting his uncle's favorite.

"Aye sir, I'll dispatch the message."

"Dismissed, good luck and God speed."

As his son turned and began to walk through the doorway, Nicholas Elliot placed a hand on his shoulder, saying, "Son, I'm proud of you."

✖✖✖

*A*s the sun rose several hours later, John awoke to his mother and father standing beside his bed. His mother placed a hand on the headrest. "I've made you a nice, big breakfast. Come down to the kitchen once you've cleaned up."

"Yes, mother."

He watched as his parents left the room, and then pulled on his breeches. Instead of wearing his redcoat, he pulled a wool sweater over his long sleeve cotton undershirt. He stared out the window, noticing frost on the ground. He then moved quickly to his closet and pulled out his father's old wool pea coat, carrying it loosely in the crook of his elbows.

After washing his hands and face, he hurried down the staircase and strolled into the kitchen. The smell of fresh poached eggs and ham filled his nostrils. Living on a farm yielded many advantages given the hard work to maintain it; his household was always full of fresh meats, milk, and vegetables.

The three ate in silence, his younger brothers and sisters still in their beds sleeping contently. Once finished, he stood up from the table and placed his dishes in the washtub.

"Honey, don't worry about them, I'll give them a good scrubbing later. Go pack your things and I'll get some food together for your journey."

"Thanks, mother."

After placing a scarf around her neck, Mrs. Elliot joined the two by the stable, carrying a large sack. She gave it to her husband who then placed it in the leather saddlebag on the horse's right hip. On the opposite side, John had packed a cooking pot, flint and steel, and other wares that he'd need on the thousand mile trek.

"Give everyone my regards. I should be back in a few weeks."

His mother held back the tears. She was familiar with these sorts of occasions, though still found it hard. "Goodbye, give your mother a kiss."

After he kissed his mother, his father stepped in, extending a welcoming hand.

"Here son, you're doing a fine duty. You'll have to help me more around the farm when you get back; you're almost a man now."

He reached for his father's hand, gripping it tightly. He looked deep into the man's eyes that hovered above his.

"Thank you for letting me do this, it's something I had to do."

"I now understand. Go off with you lad and return safely."

He only looked back once as the horse galloped off the property. He yanked on the horse's reigns and headed for the main road. In his mind, he had mapped out the route he would have to take.

On the first day, he rode until the moon took over the sun. He stopped by a creek, watering his horse. As the beautiful animal slurped the water, he filled his canteen and began arranging camp. He broke off twigs from a nearby tree and then returned with a handful of kindling to start the fire. After the fire was made, he took out his cooking pots and made a cup of tea. Drinking it down in a gulp, he felt the warmth flow through him again. It would be a long night in a string of many.

13

The *HMS Courtesy* began its southward passage down the eastern coast of the colonies. The vessel stayed out of sight of land during the day, but at night would skirt the coasts. Passing through the Bahamas, the vessel changed course for the eastern end of Cuba. The next leg took them on a southwesterly course, heading for their hideout near Port Royal, Jamaica.

It was here where they joined their fellow brothers of the sea; pirates who would band together and seek refuge and shelter in the well-protected area known as Hunt Bay. For the last several years, he and many others would meet here on a regular basis, to trade their plunder and escape from on-looking eyes.

They lived by a secret code and the hideout's location was known by few, if this location ever fell into their enemies' hands, it would be the end for the men who dwelled upon these hidden beaches. It was a perfect location; the hills that engulfed the bay were large enough to shield the tall masts of the numerous vessels that could be found there at any given time.

As Captain Blood Bones and his crew maneuvered the sails, the *HMS Courtesy* passed astern of several moored ships. A horde of men ran out to investigate the vessel that had dropped anchor, just a cable length away from the smooth beach lining the bay. A red pendant flew just inches below the black pirate flag, as was customary to prove their identities.

Later that night, Blood Bones met with the seven other ship's captains who were present.

"My brothers, listen closely. I have just captured an English ship, and inside are one hundred and fifty British marines. I believe we should put them to work; larger huts for the captains, along with other structures, perhaps an improved pier?"

Several nodding heads caused him to continue speaking. "The blasted pier we have now I built using the masts of a captured Dutch merchant. It's time for something, more, upscale. Also, we can work them in the sugar fields."

"That would be most profitable," said one.

"Indeed," another voice echoed across the room.

The group began fantasizing of an ever-increasing amount of gold that would fill their already laden purses. Their laughter rang throughout the encampment, reverberating against the chains that latched each pair of marines together. They were forced out from below decks into a vast array of dinghies that ferried the soldiers to the beach and then split into groups designated by Captain Blood Bones, the leader of the hideout.

14

The two young men squinted in an attempt to see anything in the darkness that shrouded their surroundings. They stood in a small atrium that had been naturally formed within the hill. Gradually their eyes adjusted and before them materialized a narrow passageway, just wide enough to walk side by side. They saw a flicker ahead. Sal, eager to catch up with his friend, plunged into the darkness of the tunnel. Ben sighed and followed like a shadow.

As they made their way, they came to realize a noticeable slope downward. The rocky walls that encircled them were covered with ghostly cobwebs that danced with the wind of a small draft that wound its way through the tunnel.

"Come on, wait up!" Ben's voice echoed along the walls.

"You hurry up!" Harris replied some twenty feet ahead, making clear to them that there was nothing that was going to slow him down.

They continued on for another fifteen minutes. The descent would take them beneath the massive body of water on which they were just canoeing.

"Whoa!" Harris said ecstatically, his voice carrying to his friends. The stragglers sped up their pace, eager to discover the source of excitement.

They emerged from the tunnel to find Harris's mouth wide open, his flashlight's beam shining down into what appeared to be a deep ditch. But, with closer inspection, it was far from a simple hole in the ground. The three stood at the edge, scanning the depths of a foreboding underground river with their flashlights. A rushing current lay twenty-five feet below where they were standing.

Harris, somewhat tired from the lengthy descent, grabbed hold of a rope cable, crudely fastened to a natural rock formation that crossed the rushing water. A second rope lay at their feet and had been nailed into the ground with a large spike. This was the only way in which to traverse the thirty-foot wide river. What was most peculiar about the mysterious river was that there were ten-foot wooden poles jutting up from the dark churning water, each sharpened to a point. With one slip, a trespasser could easily be impaled. As Sal scanned the immense depths of what lay before them, something golden shimmered and caught his eye.

"Hey, what's that?" he asked aloud.

Ben moved his beam towards the area.

"No way, it can't be. It's a skeleton!"

Harris rushed to their side, his own source of light combining with theirs. "And the light's reflecting off of his front golden teeth! Look, four other skeletons!" Sal said elatedly, almost overcome with glee knowing that surely treasure must lie ahead.

"You sound a little too excited. Show some respect," Ben said reproachfully.

As he spoke, Sal shook the cable that passed near his head, almost confident that this was a bad idea.

"I wonder who they were," Ben speculated, studying the obstacle that loomed before them.

"Well, obviously they had no balance." Sal chuckled at his own joke. The brothers just glared at him.

Ben, very confident with his own sense of balance, placed his feet on the rope that was nailed into the ground and clutched the rope that ran just above his head, and set off to reach the other side of the rocky canal. The rope quivered with his weight as he made his way. Slowly but assertively, he placed one hand in front of the other and shuffled his feet along the length of rope. Harris and Sal watched from solid ground as their companion dipped lower and lower as he approached mid-way. He was precariously close to the pointy tips of the makeshift spears.

"That wasn't so bad! Come on you guys!" Ben shouted to his brother and friend from across the rapids.

"Not it!" snuck in Sal as his finger touched his nose.

"Fine, you don't have to be so immature about it. I'll go," Harris said with a hint of frustration in his voice.

Although Harris was the same build as his younger brother, he was taller. The height and slight weight difference was on his mind as he grabbed the hand rope. He began to shimmy across, unable to not look down at the horrific scene below. He continued on, there was no turning back now. Only grazing the top of a spike with his foot, Harris made it beside his brother.

Sal grasped the overhead rope and took the first step. Mid-way, the skeleton with the golden teeth caught his eye. For some reason this pile of bones captivated him. He must have been another pirate in search of Blood Bones' treasure. Then the young man caught sight of what was wrapped around the fleshless neck of the skeleton, the tattered crest of Spanish occupied Puerto Rico, used as a bandana.

He began envisioning his ancestors as swashbucklers attacking and seizing other ships. Wrapped in his thoughts, Sal paid little attention to the very important task at hand and slipped, his leg banging into the side of one of the sharpened posts.

"Sal!" Ben shouted; the worry in his voice echoed off of the cavernous walls.

"I'm good," Sal was lucky to have had a sturdy grip on the rope.

He regained control and continued to shuffle along. With a tremendous sigh of relief, Sal stepped onto solid ground, happy to leave the rope bridge behind.

Harris led the way down the tunnel, noticing the terrain slope further into the pits of the earth. After having gone perhaps one hundred yards, they emerged into a cavern that was smaller than the previous. In fact, it was as small as a typical household room. The ceiling was no more than eight feet high and the room itself was twelve by sixteen feet.

The space was barren, except for a very intriguing mosaic depicting skull and crossbones in the middle of the floor, with several images missing. The stones were set within a circular background of black stones.

"Do you think the treasure's buried under the skull and crossbones?" asked Harris.

"Well, we really didn't bring digging tools," Ben stated the obvious. "So it wouldn't do us much good if it were."

"Hey, look at this you guys," Sal had observed that there was a small inscription carved above the entryway of the room. "Esto corre de frente a la parte posteriora del barco, y en el otro lado de la parte posteriora al frente," Sal called out for all to hear.

"What's it say?" Harris asked.

"It's a riddle. 'This runs fore to aft on one side of a ship, and aft to fore on the other.' You guys know more about boats than I do. What's it mean?"

"Well, let's make a list. Maybe it's sails?"

Ben looked at his brother, "What about rigging or planks?"

Sal shook his head at both, translating in his head. "Na, those both don't work, none of those fit what the riddle describes."

Harris stroked his chin in deliberation.

"I got it! It's the name of a ship!" Ben smiled.

"Yeah, that might be it! Way to pull that one out of your ass," his brother replied sarcastically. "Let me see the stones."

"I know, it's a gift," he replied with a smirk, handing the colored stones over.

"So, what's the name of a ship have to do with anything?" wondered Sal.

"Well, these guys are pirates. Maybe we just found a clue, not the treasure. The gold's probably at the bottom of an ocean, long gone with the sunken boat it was hidden on," Harris said pessimistically.

"I don't know," Ben shoved his hands in his pockets, feeling for the remaining stones.

The adventurers stood there, thinking hard about the possible correlation the riddle had with their journey. Ten minutes went by as they stood in silence.

Harris hurled a stone onto the ground in frustration. "Damn it! We've come so far!" he said, thoroughly agitated.

"Hey, check that out!" Sal said as he pointed at the discarded stones that now lay just outside the black edge of the mosaic. Jaws dropped as it became apparent that these stones belonged to it.

Ben scrambled to take all of the stones out of his pockets. "I wonder which one goes where?"

There were eight empty spots, aligned with one another horizontally. Sal knelt down and gathered the stones, making sure the letters all faced up: *o-e-n-l-m-z-ò-n*

"Maybe we need to make a word out of them," Ben said, looking over his friend's shoulder.

"But what word?" he looked up.

"You think it has to do with Captain Blood Bones? I mean, it is *his* treasure," Harris asked.

"Whoa, whoa, whoa. I got an idea. What'd that article we read online say? What was his ship's name?" Sal asked, his excitement growing.

"Something with an 'M'," Harris paused.

"El...El...Monzòn!" Ben recalled, jumping to his feet and doing a little dance in celebration.

Sal rearranged the stones, spelling the name of the fabled ship. He flipped them over, and slid them into the empty slots in sequential order, to make complete the ominous image.

At first nothing happened, but then, as if by some mysterious force, the wall before them began to vibrate, in small spurts at first and then more violently.

"What's going on?" Harris shouted over the rumble of the wall. "Is it an earthquake? Oh man, if I die in this place..."

They ran to the entryway, clinging to each other for dear life. The room was trembling and quaking to and fro, as the opposite wall began to shift to the left, revealing yet another passageway that had lay undisturbed and hidden. They sighed with relief when the shaking stopped.

"How creepy was that? I mean, how'd it move like that?" Harris said in disbelief.

"Blood Bones must have cursed this place somehow," Ben offered. He too was in as much shock as the others, still not believing what he had just witnessed.

The size of this next passageway did not leave much room for their height, and they had to stoop as they trudged down deeper beneath the lake above. It was the shortest of the three passages, and after only having traveled about fifty yards, Harris was the first to poke his head into the next chamber.

Ben pointed his flashlight upwards. The beam disappeared into the endless black of darkness. Weighing their options, the only way to travel now was up the wall furthest from the entrance. The three young men were standing in a vertical shaft.

"Are we supposed to climb this thing, with no equipment? I mean, come on! We don't even know how high it goes?"

The beam of light lit up his first handhold, but Harris's skepticism did not deter Ben's motivation. He was already five feet off the ground as Sal gave light to the path above. Harris shrugged his shoulders, sighed, and joined Sal in assisting his brother. Small rocks and soot spiraled down the vertical tunnel every so often, getting into the eyes of Sal and Harris.

"Watch it up there!" Harris called to the almost indistinguishable silhouette that was his brother.

"Okay, okay. Hey! I made it! It wasn't too bad, about twenty-five feet high. Come on you guys!" Ben shouted down.

Sal grabbed the first rock handhold in reach and turned to Harris with a big grin on his face. Having worked at the local gym manning the imitation rock wall there, his ascent went without faults.

"Let's go slow poke!" Sal yelled down.

He gingerly clutched the first rock, making sure his grip was secure, and then jammed his sneaker into a foothold. Harris picked his way slowly but surely up the wall. When he reached the top, and just as he reached for his brother's outstretched hand, the rock his right foot was supported by crumbled beneath him. His body shot down, but luckily, Ben and Sal were quick enough to grab hold of him.

"Thanks guys," Harris said as he sat sprawled out on the shelf of rock.

They sat with propped elbows, catching their breath. Ben craned his neck and shined the flashlight around, only to see the rough shape of a wooden desk. On closer inspection, there was a piece of paper tacked to the wooden surface with a knife.

Sal's voice echoed off the walls, "Congratulations on making it this far, but do not let greed be the end of you."

They pressed on, advancing through the vast cavern. Each interpreted the message differently.

"Treasure," thought Ben.

"Another obstacle," Sal mumbled.

Harris let off a skeptical, "We're screwed."

As they walked down the corridor, they came to a spacious lobby area. On either side there were side tunnels, six in total. The group stopped to explore each passageway. To their surprise, each ended up in a cavernous room with treasures scraping the high ceilings.

"Holy cow!" Ben screamed.

They went from one cavern to the next, mentally noting the total treasure increasing exponentially with the discovery of more and more jewels, silk rugs, pottery, gold and silver bars, and stacks of chests laden with American colonial taxes.

Each member of the party continued to beam with anticipation as they reached the last and final cavern. A skeleton sat guarding this lone chest. Tattered rags dangled from the bones of what remained of the man. A ring inlaid with a scarlet stone reflected the beams from their flashlights.

"This must be Captain Blood Bones," Ben muttered through a smile.

He felt the heat the room emanated and took off his windbreaker, laying it in the corner of the cavern.

It opened with ease as Harris lifted the unlocked lid. The chest held four objects: a staff and three beautifully crafted gold medallions, each strung with faded leather. Three hands reached in, donning the golden treasure around their necks.

"Isn't it weird there's exactly three?" Ben nudged Sal, he stared at the pattern that encircled a crudely scratched X. It was unlike anything he had ever seen before; the medallion had a stunning, yet eerie appeal. He was drawn to it. He was destined to wear it.

"Um, who cares? We found the treasure!" Sal gave a victorious pound to the air.

"I guess, I still think it's weird though. Doesn't it seem like they were here for us?" Ben replied, slowly succumbing to the mood of success and victory.

"Ben, you think too much, way too much," Harris laughed, "Who wants the honors of holding it?" his eyes looking down at the remaining item.

He raised the three foot long staff out from its safekeeping. Their eyes studied the handgrip, moving slowly up the shaft and finally resting at a garnet headstone. His fingers slid across an indentation, sliding a trigger-like release forward. The gears inside clicked and their excitement heightened.

"Try pulling it?" Ben offered, looking at the mechanics of the item.

He tugged, but to no avail.

"Twist it" Sal inched closer, feeling left out.

"Yeah, you're right," he said after twisting one turn. "There is definitely something hidden inside," as he finished, a rolled letter fell into his lap. "It's written in Spanish."

Sal moved alongside his friend, his eyes scanned through the message:

"Me llamo Capitán Huesos de Sangre, el pirata despiadado que ha invadido muchos pueblos, saqueado, y ha matado a muchas personas. Felicitaciones, respeto su viaje arduo a encontrar mi tesoro. Mis tesoros son ahora suyo. A pesar de que estoy muerto, continúo proteger mi tesoro. Desgraciadamente usted no entenderá el significado de estas palabras, para lo se maldice. Usted no se dará cuenta de esto hasta que usted descifre este mensaje. Vaya con Dios en este viaje que tomará usted a 1763."

"So what's it say," Ben inquired eagerly.

"My name is Captain Blood Bones, the merciless pirate that has invaded many towns, plundered, and has killed many people. Congratulations, I respect your grueling trip to find my treasure. My treasures are now yours. Despite that I am dead; I continue to protect my treasure. Unfortunately you will not understand the meaning of these words, for it is cursed. You will not realize this until you decipher this message. Go with God in this trip that you will take you to 1763."

They looked at the larger font that appeared throughout the message. He turned to Ben and Sal, "What does 'le ahora maldicen a 1763' mean?"

He answered Harris instantly, "You are now cursed to 1763."

As the phrase left his mouth, a yellow beam of light flashed out from the staff. It pointed straight up, touching the center of the cavern. Four objects in the room grew bright orange: the three medallions and the scarlet stone of a ring. These orange beams angled up to meet at the yellow peak, forming a light show around the pyramid. The light began to crisscross, filling in the gaps between the four legs. From the apex to the ground, the entire pyramid was full of clashing yellow and orange light.

The room swirled around the staff and the group: a gust of wind howled originating at the top of the radiant cone, spiraling down like a corkscrew. The windbreaker in the corner of the room flew by in circles with increasing speed. There was a loud imploding sound, as the cone of light and energy collapsed. Then the wind stopped, the jacket fell down abruptly: it looked carelessly tossed into the middle of the room. Everything located within the cone of light vanished into the reversal of time.

15

OFF THE FLORIDA COAST
FEBRUARY 1ST, 1763

The *Frendrich* was sailing southwards, staying within sight of the Florida coast. The voyage down had been pleasant, there was always a strong wind filling the sails. The watch relieved itself as the hourglass renewed. It was four in the morning when the captain came on deck to look around and check the general safety of the ship. He was a prudent mariner, always making sure his vessel and crew were safe, never overlooking the slightest detail. After a long inspection, he was content and went back to sleep.

Two hours later the skies did not brighten. The eastern horizon was painted in a deep, blood red color.

"Go wake the captain. Something's unusual."

The cabin boy nodded to the mate.

Moments later, Captain Nelson emerged from a shadow and confronted Charles, "Aye?"

"Sir, what time was sunrise the last few days?"

Nelson closed his eyes, reliving the past week. "A little after the first hour of the 0400 watch, I'd say around 0530."

"Yes, I've flipped the hourglass twice since coming on and look at the sky."

The pair glanced upwards and the captain replied, "You're right, something's wrong, a storm's heading this way."

"Oh, and captain, she's still following us."

"*Fatasma Negra?*"

"Aye."

"Good, that is good news."

Before the captain could return to his quarters, a flash of orange and yellow light slashed through the red sky. There was an ear piercing sound of the wind's velocity increasing, causing the ship to rock back and forth to dangerous angles. Sails ripped and timbers cracked. The top of the after mast fractured. Just as suddenly as the sky lit up it reverted back to normal and the red faded to a dull, overcast gray.

✺✺✺

An otherwise peaceful morning erupted into utter chaos as swirls of eerie patterns of light filled the sky. A vortex was created as space and time bended, releasing infinite energy, creating deafening sounds resembling thunderclaps. Time, in its essential state, was being reversed. A cluster of objects fell from the heavens into the warm Caribbean water. There was a splash and then a series of heads popping up. They held onto an old chest, their faces just inches above the ocean waves.

It had been closing in on three hours. They were in the middle of the shipping lanes, floating with a strong current just off the coast of Florida. About a mile away, there seemed to be a trading vessel flying English colors with no sails run out.

"Do you guys see something far to the left?" asked Ben.

"Yeah, what do you think it is?" asked Sal curiously.

"From what I can see, it looks like our rescue is here," Ben said with a sudden burst of energy.

"Do you think we can catch up to them?" asked Harris as he shivered to the long exposure.

"Well, the ship looks like it has its anchor down. We may have a decent chance if the current leaves us alone," Ben said as he weighed their chances, not even mentioning what could happen if they missed the ship.

✺✺✺

The surrounding waters were far too deep to anchor, but as the ship cruised, they checked the available water under the keel by dropping a weighted line. Once finding a suitable anchorage, a melodic sound calmed the sailor's nerves as the chain spilled out the hawse pipe, splashing into the blue water below. Crewmembers worked together to get the *Frendrich* in shipshape condition for the remaining voyage. The master carpenter studied the crack at the top of the after mast.

He yelled to his apprentice, "Joseph, hand me my wooden mallet and a sheet of metal."

The young boy ran off to his master's cabin to fetch the repair kit, returning shortly with a canvas bag filled with items. The carpenter removed the needed tools and began to work. He placed the sheet of metal on the nearest rail and began banging the edge with the mallet, bending it to match the circumference of the mast. Once done, he brought the brace over to the mast and placed it over the splintered section. He pulled out a dozen nails from his pouch and began to nail the brace into the wooden mast.

Joseph was called again and a few moments later came on deck holding a long, thick piece of line. The carpenter began to tie off the repaired section for additional strength, starting with a slipknot. Every couple of inches, he placed a tight half hitch until the job was finished. Captain Arthur F. Nelson came over to study the mast and was satisfied with the repair until they would make a port call.

❈❈❈

They eventually made it alongside the waterline of the *Frendrich*; the chest crashed alongside the ship, bumping with each wave.

"Shh, don't make any loud noise, or they'll hear us," whispered Ben.

Ben looked up at the task that faced them, a long ascent up the long shots of chain. He released his hold on the chest and grabbed the rust colored anchor chain. Hand over hand; he quietly made progress.

He was tired and waterlogged, but his determination drove him on. The tip of his head peered over the gunwale. He grabbed hold and pulled himself to the edge, maintaining his position as he looked around. When his feet found the comfort of the deck, he looked down with thumbs up. Sal grabbed the anchor chain and exhaled deeply. He began scaling the long chain; hand over hand until he was out of breath, sitting next to Ben.

Sal then peered over the gunwale, motioning Harris to climb. Harris cursed and then grabbed the chain. A minute later Ben was pulling his brother onto the bow of the *Frendrich*.

A mysterious figure appeared from the shadows behind the forward mast, "And may I ask whom you are?" said the man smoking a pipe; a whisk of blue smoke seeped through his open mouth.

The wind kicked up now, sending a mystifying shiver down the trouble-laden teens.

"Don't think you'll fool me, answer the question," pressed the man again.

"We fell from the sky and we were floating on a chest and needed to get out of the water," Harris answered on the whim.

"Yeah right lads," he said. "Stowaways you are!"

"Sir, we're not stowaways, we're from the future," Sal said without thinking of how absurd his response would sound.

There was a moment of pause. "Could you take us back to Florida, sir?" asked Harris.

"Bloody no, we've business to tend to," he said.

"And where's that?" Ben replied.

"England, after a small detour," he thought of Blood Bones hanging from a noose.

"We're going to England?" asked Harris.

He changed the topic quickly, "By the way, my name is Arthur F. Nelson, captain of this magnificent beauty, the *Frendrich*. What're your names, lads?"

"Well, I'm Ben Manry, my brother Harris, and our friend Sal Draben."

He glanced towards Nelson and guessed his age to be around

thirty. Atop his head sat a black leather hat that covered a mane of flowing black hair. Ben noticed a small and neatly trimmed goatee on the man's square chin.

"Charles, put these boys in some quarters and give them some warm broth," a mischievous smile brewing on his face.

Charles Marconi came out on deck, walking briskly towards the group standing around the foremast. He was the First Officer, standing five ten with grayish brown hair tied back in a ponytail, "Aye sir, what room shall they be put in?" asked Marconi.

"The cell," the captain said slowly, emphasizing the term.

Marconi stood in front of the captain and gave a weird wince. The captain nodded; a group of men emerged from the shadows and led them below decks. Nate Brodkin, the Second Officer, watched as the strange newcomers took slow and labored steps, obviously tired from the ordeal that they had just gone through.

Pacing down several companionways, they shoved the dazed boys into a small cell. One-inch thick bars, set four inches apart made up the storage cell for prisoners. The captain closed the heavy door and twisted the key counter-clockwise. Ben's eyes readjusted to the change in lighting, watching the three men turn and head up towards the companionway.

"Help, what's going on? Why are we locked up?"

He watched as the captain's head turned slightly. With hesitation, his neck lingered in this position. Expecting an answer, Ben's eyes began to close. Even if Captain Nelson replied, he wouldn't have heard.

✖✖✖

*N*ate broke the silence at the table, "They could be telling the truth. Remember early this morning when that orange and yellow streak flew through the sky. Maybe that's it. Ah, let's finish eating and we'll find out what really happened."

"Eh, the months truly string to years, we've been venturing these oceans for too long. I've seen some bizarre things in my days," Nelson sighed. "Hopefully this is our last assignment."

"Aye, the sea spray's getting to our heads," the men laughed together.

❉❉❉

*H*e remained lying on the deck, sprawled out attempting to sleep. A series of footsteps stirred him awake. With a glance, a small aged man entered, carrying a tray with three plates of rolls with a cup of tea each. Jensen McCafferey made his way towards the cell, placing the tray on a desk below an open porthole. He let out a deep sigh as fresh air and rays of sunlight spilled into the space. Opening the cell's door, the man placed the tray down on the wooden deck. The Third Officer locked the door and turned on a heel, leaving the room.

Ben watched as the man turned away and walked up the crooked steps that led back up to main deck. Before he could shuffle over to the platter of food, he collapsed once again, beginning another brief stint with his face buried into the wooden deck.

❉❉❉

*"W*ake up guys I think I hear something," he stirred from his sleep several hours later. He got to his feet slowly and shook Sal and Harris.

"Where do you think we are?" Harris yawned, studying the metal bars that constrained them.

"I don't know. I was out of it pretty much the entire time, but I think I saw something. We walked down two sets of companionways, so I assume we're on the third deck."

"How's that help us?" Harris asked.

"You asked me where I thought we are. Give me a break," he stared at his brother with an evil eye.

Ben closed his eyes in thought; pondering the beginnings of an escape plan.

16

The gray mist hid the *Fantasma Negra*, shrouding her from English eyes. For the past week, El Perro Loco had been just out of sight, waiting for the perfect opportunity to make a move. With the thickening fog, the pirates littered the decks, eager to cast the grappling hooks in boarding. The distance closed, but the vessels were still out of range.

"Helmsman, two points to starboard," Mad Dog gave the command.

The rudder caught and the ship turned slowly. Feeling the vessel take the angle, he smiled as he heard the gun ports open below. Orchestrating a perfect symphony of shots and recoils, El Perro Loco let off a broadside. The shells sliced through the thick mist, spiraling towards the rigging of the *Frendrich*. The volley was effective, catching the English sleeping, or at least, that is what the pirates had believed.

✖✖✖

Nelson stood at the rail with his officers. "Men, all's well. They have taken the bait. They will come with the mist."

They waited, knowing that they would have to take several broadsides for the plan to succeed. He cringed as the gun ports erupted, sending the chain and rods hurling through the air. The shredding of the sails above sent a shiver down his spine. He hated this feeling, taking damage to a ship to lure his targets in. But this is what he had to do, and it worked every time.

"Run out the guns! Hard over to starboard!" he eyed the progress of the pursuing ship, making a quick calculation in his head of the speed and distance needed for the maneuver.

✖✖✖

"Match her turn," he said to the helmsman.

The gap slowly closed as El Perro Loco let out every inch of sail to his advantage. The small lougre relied on its maneuverability and speed, rather than its armament. Several stern chasers were shot off from the English vessel, tearing through sails and spars overhead. The distance between bowsprit and stern continued to diminish. After a half hour his vessel had come within pistol shot of the schooner.

"Hard to port, ready cannons for a broadside!"

The rudder caught, causing the ship to heel over to a steep angle. Once the vessel steadied, his men had their eyes pressed to the barrel of the guns, awaiting his command.

"Fire!"

✖✖✖

The vessels danced upon the sea, tacking from starboard to port, and back again. The skilled seaman evaded fire while exchanging broadsides, though an occasional stray would hit home. The distance continued to close as munitions changed from chain shot to grape shot. The decks were covered with splinters and smoke as Nelson stood tall beside the helmsman. He looked up; a tangle of spars and ripped sailcloth swayed with the wind from the splintered mast that hung dangerously overheard.

"We cannot afford to continue this," he paused, knowing the time had come. "Take in sail, let the fight begin!"

❌❌❌

The first grappling hook was thrown and the two ships came swiftly together like lovers. A group of pirates swung over the open water from the crow's nest. El Perro Loco stood fearless, placing a plank between the gaps of the two ships and led ten of his men towards the awaiting sailors.

He sent twelve men to fend off the attack. Several more waves of pirates jumped the four-foot gap between the two ships to get in on the action. The battle had started with a feint cry from a sailor as El Perro Loco took the man's life with a flick of his wrist.

Blue smoke and the smell of fresh gunpowder filled the air as handguns were fired back and forth. Within the first few moments of the battle, the pirates had evened the fight, coming on stronger now with greed and bloodlust in their eyes. At least two Englishmen were slain for every pirate.

Nelson reached into his munitions pouch, feeling for the depleted gunpowder and shot. With a quick sidestep, he maneuvered around a group of entangled swords and turned on a heel, heading for the companionway to go to his cabin. He then remembered he had three young and fit men below decks.

❌❌❌

"I think he's coming, I hear footsteps behind the door!" Ben shifted his gaze from the entranceway. "Get in positions!"

Ben's plan was put into effect, but it was not Jensen McCafferey to come down with the afternoon meal: it was the captain, running at a full gait down the companionway. He screamed over the noise of the battle above as he pulled out the set of keys from his breast pocket, "I'll make a deal with you lads. If you fight with us and we win, we'll drop you off at our earliest convenience. Is that fair enough?"

"I thought we heard cannon fire. What's going on?" Ben took the lead.

"We've engaged El Perro Loco, now are you with us or not?"

"Who's El Perro Loco?" Harris interrupted.

"Listen lads, I've no time to answer your feeble questions. Do you want to stay in the brig, or fight with me and gain your freedom?"

"Yes sir," said Ben without thinking, coming to the conclusion that the sooner they got out of their dilemma, the better.

"What are we going to fight with?" asked Sal looking at his empty hands.

"Follow me to my cabin, and then we'll return on deck," he wrestled the lock off with hurried fingers.

✺✺✺

The group emerged as one from the shadows of the companionway hatch. Nelson forged the path with a raised sword and pointed pistol. In his absence, another half dozen men had fallen. Ben reached down for a sword: it was light and deadly, the blade already stained red. They stood there for a second, together for what they thought could be the last time.

Five pirates noticed the commotion to their left and charged forward. Already outnumbered they began to quiver with fear. Ahead, leading the oncoming pirates was El Perro Loco. Each had a sword held high in their hand; the leader had his finger on the trigger of a rustic antique, eager to take the life of one more Englishman with the small handgun.

Their swords waved in the air, inviting rival blades to unite as one. Speckles of light gleamed off the Toledo steel as the sun snuck its rays through the gray sky above. The two groups merged, struggling for advantage. Nelson backed away as he took a slice of his opponent's neck. As the blades danced again, he noticed the tip was stained red.

An ear-deafening eruption momentarily silenced the metallic kisses that echoed across the deck. El Perro Loco fell to the ground, headless. Nate Brodkin stood behind a swivel gun, smiling as the blue smoke spread in the easterly breeze. He then ran over to join

Ben, who had pushed forward into the enemy's embrace. Between the two, they coordinated their fighting like an experienced duo.

Nelson picked up El Perro Loco's fallen sword and with two blades in hand, swung them around unmercifully: one in wide arcs and the other in short jabs. Harris and Sal joined up with Ben, who now faced the last two remaining pirates. They grouped together and stood in a triangle formation, hearing Nelson and his Second Officer cheering them on.

"Tell them something in Spanish," said Ben with an evil grin.

"Good day scoundrels. We are all mages with powers and will turn you both into worms," Sal started, and dramatically threw down his sword as if in anger. "And then we will use your puny bodies as bait while we fish for the largest and most ferocious creatures in these seas."

Confused and looking at the strange teenagers, the two men shook their heads and leapt off the ship into the blue water below.

✖✖✖

"Good job, lad. What did you think of the battle?" Nelson asked with a smile.

"For my first, I'd say it went well," said Ben, with his head held high. "I'm surprised I fought that well. I've always dreamt of being in a sword fight."

"It looks like we won, I don't see anything else," Brodkin interrupted.

"Err, yes it does. Gentlemen, I must apologize for what happened earlier. I hope you accept. Without your help, we might have lost this magnificent ship. I thank you. Let's look for survivors and then we will rest," said Nelson.

"That sounds good," Harris said content that they were no longer in a dimly lit cell, or floating on a chest at the mercy of the sea.

The men dispersed to search the decks of the two vessels. They counted only nine men left after the large skirmish. Nelson went down into El Perro Loco's personal quarters and rummaged through his desk. He brought out the cargo manifest and as he fingered through it a smile grew on his face. He continued looking through the desk and brought out two more books, one was a journal and the other was the logbook. Gripping these documents in his hand, he let out victorious laugh. He would finally get to understand the man that had preyed upon so many merchant sailors, bringing their lost souls redemption at last.

✖✖✖

Captain Nelson sat at his desk in his quarters aboard the *Frendrich* and lit an ivory inlaid pipe. Inhaling the fumes, the tobacco began to relax his body. His hand reached down by his leg, pulling on the desk drawer. Reaching in, he took out a lock box and laid the safe on his knees. He popped open the lid with a turn of a key and then reached for the document.

His fingers massaged his goatee for a brief moment before reaching for the feather pen. Dipping it in a jar of ink, he scanned through the list in front of him. Once he found El Perro Loco's name, he held the quill tightly in his hands as he marked a solid line, crossing it out. His gaze moved one line down; the next name on the list brought a smile to his face.

"Sir, there's a spit of land sighted. I'm sure it houses the harbor of Freeport, Bahamas. With the wind in our favor, I believe we could make it by the end of my watch."

He looked up to see the face of Nate Brodkin. "Yes, that is where we'll berth for the time being. We'll sell off our plunder and refit. Make a towline connecting the *Fantasma Negra* to our stern, it'll be slow, but we cannot split our crew. We're already undermanned as is."

"Yes, sir."

17

Today

"**I** want to know where Sal is. John, how long have they been gone?"

The four parents eyed each other as they sat around the dinning table.

"Jorge, Linda. The three were going on an overnight fishing trip to the island in the center of the lake. They left yesterday morning."

Linda Draben was a quick-tempered and overly protective mother, "For the love of God, so you are saying three teenagers have been missing for over a day. We have to go to the island and bring them back. Oh, my son will be grounded when I get my hands on him."

Jorge touched her arm, "Hun, don't worry, they're big boys. They'll be fine, I'm sure they'll return tonight, I mean, it would only have been a day and a half right?"

His male counterpart nodded, but both wives stared angrily. John reluctantly picked up the phone and dialed the police. "Hello Bill, I was wondering if you and Tom could come by my house when you can…We have a slight dilemma that we could use some help with… Uh, yes, thanks. See you in ten."

✖✖✖

The doorbell rang loudly and broke the minutes of silent waiting. The two officers walked into the room and greeted their friends. "Hey ya'll."

"Bill, Tom. The reason we asked you to come is because our sons are missing."

"When were they last seen?"

"They left yesterday morning on an overnight fishing trip, and they should have been back by now. We were wondering if you could accompany us to the island and look for them."

"Of course, we'll find them. There's nothing to worry about. I'm sure they're on one of their adventures like normal."

The group of six squeezed into the police car and drove down the long twisting driveway leaving the Manry estate. The silent drive ended up in a dirt parking lot. Once out of the car the group ran towards the pier. Bill stepped down into the motorboat and primed the engine. It started on the third pull and the rest boarded evenly. The roar of four-stroke engine propelled them across the watery expanse.

"Guys, I see their canoe! It's tied up to a tree in the inlet," Mr. Draben stood at the bow, pointing to the beach.

The chug-chug of the engine died out once the boat had touched bottom, Tom stepping into the knee-deep water to pull the boat in. Once all stepped onto solid ground, they looked for footprints.

"That's where they entered, look at the opening in the foliage," Bill said, studying the ground.

The two cops led the search party down the trail, their flashlights slicing through the darkness. They could see broken limbs and branches here and there, leading straight. After continuing on the path, they noticed there was a cluster of footsteps. It then angled off and the group continued on. They went forward on this angled path, and without realizing it, nearly stepped on a discarded half-full water bottle that was hidden by a bough of leaves beside a stump.

"Yup, they've been here alright," as Bill reached down to look at the evidence.

Continuing their search, Bill pointed to yet another recent path. They followed it for a few paces and then stopped, once more angling off on a different tangent. The parents were determined to find their sons. After each phase in the search, there was a new clue as to where the boys had paused and stopped. Luckily, it was a fresh trail and they made good time.

"Should we go in?" Mrs. Draben stared open-mouthed at the cave entrance.

The group pressed on, plunging into the darkness as the beams of light barely lit their way.

"It's amazing how three young men did this. I wonder what they were looking for?"

Mr. Manry turned to his wife and replied, "It appears like a hunt, like a treasure hunt. I know the kids are big into pirates and treasures, knowing them, they probably found something."

The policemen turned to the concerned father, "John, you don't think they really went looking for that old rumor about Captain Blood Bones, do you? I read it could've been anywhere along these here parts."

"I really don't know. They're quite capable of anything, when they put their minds together."

The cave was dark and musky as they followed the path and continued on as it angled down. The width of the passage grew until they paused when they heard a gurgling sound several feet ahead. They peered out in the opening, seeing a rope bridge joining two landmasses with a fast flowing river of rapids below. The scene took their breath away, causing them to just stare at the long poles that had impaled the long dead skeletons.

"Let's cross the bridge, it shouldn't be that difficult because we know that the kids finished it," Bill said, attempting to get their attention off the spikes below.

The men of the group filed over the rope bridge first, waiting at the other end for the women. Once all were on solid land on the other side of the pit, they regained concentration and looked at what lay before them, another side trail. They walked on this until they reached an opening, with what seemed to be a mosaic at their feet. The black and white of the skull and bones made the women shriek while the men stared in awe.

They finally entered the dead end, not knowing where to go on from here. They shined their lights back and forth, looking for anything that would give away the location of the missing teens. They began talking and Mr. Draben cursed aloud. The echo vibrated off the rocks above them, and then they realized what they had to do. They had to climb.

The women were shaking their heads, saying they would never be able to do it, but the men gave their support and shortly after a slight cheerleading session, all six had successfully scaled the wall. They paused to regain their composure and noticed that in front of them now, was an old oak table. On the horizontal surface was a piece of paper held down by a knife with a red ruby in the handle. It read, "Congratulations for making it this far, but do not let greed be the end of you."

The group turned around as one looking down at what they had just accomplished, they all felt a sense of satisfaction even though the darkness masked the adventure that lay behind them. After another short break, they pressed on. This passage led them past six cave-like rooms. After an inspection of each, they realized that all were full of treasure: pearls, gold, silver, and riches beyond everyone's imaginations. As John Manry left the room, he snatched a gold coin and held it firmly in his hand, before placing it safely into his pocket.

It was the last room that was odd. There was nothing in view except for a staff with a scroll exposed, left unrolled. Before John Manry bent over to pick it up, he saw a jacket that appeared to have been thrown carelessly into the corner of the room. His wife recognized it immediately.

"That's Ben's wind breaker! Honey what happened to our children?"

Tom shined his light down at the staff and a rolled note as John picked it up. "It's in Spanish?"

He handed Linda the scroll and she began to read.

"What's wrong?" asked Margie, knowing by the facial expression something was amiss.

Linda regained her train of thought, "Well, it starts off saying something about how this treasure belongs to the pirate, Captain Blood Bones…and then it says how he amassed this wealth…and then something about this chest being cursed. It's signed 1763."

Linda was interrupted by her husband, "What chest, there's no chest in this room, what's he talking about?"

"Will you let me finish?" She continued looking over the large font that appeared through the message, "It says they were cursed to 1763."

Her husband interrupted again, "Our children were sent back in time? This is nonsense, it couldn't have happened. Time-travel is proven, it just doesn't happen."

They stood there, unsure of how to interpret the news. A faraway voice in the radio crackled, breaking the silence, "There's a robbery being held at the bank on Broadway Avenue. We need all units available."

"We'll resume the search in the morning, it's getting late anyways."

"Ben always talked about wanting to live in the past. I guess he got what he wanted. I hope he's all right," John thought of his youngest son.

The parents had their heads low as the policemen took the lead out of the empty cavern. Linda held the staff close to her chest as she fell in line behind the others. John Manry waited for all to file out of the room and as he peered back, he noticed a blinding light fill the cavern. For just a moment, he saw a black and white negative engraved into the stone, of four figures hovering around a chest. There was a scribbled line that wound itself between each. Within seconds, the vision dissipated and he let out a stressful sigh.

Lingering behind the group, he reached down for the golden coin. Just as he passed the side caverns; now just empty expanses, his fingers touched nothing but pocket lint.

18

It was a brisk night in Freeport, Bahamas, with a strong wind blowing in the scents of the surrounding waters. If all were quiet inside the merry tavern, Ben would have heard the wind howling throughout the streets.

"May I have all of your attention?" the Nelson cleared his throat. "As you'll know, we don't have enough men to continue on, so we'll need to recruit men for the journey ahead. Ben, Sal, and Harris, will you be the first to join us in our adventures?"

Ben looked over to his friends; he could read what his brother was thinking. He glanced back and said, "Well, you have three more added to your crew."

"Glad to have you aboard. Now let's eat," Nelson said as he noticed a group of servers carrying everyone's meal.

"The food's great, but what're we going to do until we set sail?" asked Harris curiously, eyeing around to see if anyone was listening.

"Eat?" Sal interrupted with a mouthful of seasoned roast in his mouth.

Ben watched his friend inhale the food. "Hey, try not to die eating."

"Hey, I'm hungry, man. Leave a fat kid entrapped in a skinny body alone for Christ's sake!"

"I was looking out for the both of us."

"It's okay," replied Sal with a large smile. A piece of chicken slipped out and fell to the table causing the group of friends to laugh heartily.

Ben stared around the oak table, studying the crew. To the left of Captain Nelson was Nate Brodkin, and to the right was Charles Marconi. "Captain, I have a few questions about the next few weeks," stated Ben.

"Go ahead lad," replied the feasting captain.

"Well, what're we supposed to do?"

"We need to work on our beauty, fix her up a bit, but that'll take maybe a week or at the most two."

"Then what after?" Ben asked curiously.

"Find something to occupy yourselves with, close to the boat while I take care of some business."

"I see," Ben said.

"Sure thing lad, tonight we'll sleep in this here tavern, and tomorrow we'll start work. Our darling took a few shots, there's a hole on the back deck, splintering on the mast, and a few yards of sail needs to be replaced. Other than that, we only need to replace a dozen boards on the stern and repaint the hull. We'll sell our wares tomorrow."

✖✖✖

After a quick breakfast, Nelson marched his men back to the pier, assigning duties and began an initial damage report on the *Frendrich*.

"John Borton, you're my new purser. I need you to sell all the ship's wares, at the best prices. The *Fantasma Negra* will certainly bring in a few thousand pounds. Come back with the money and I'll tell you my plans for what's next," directed Nelson.

The man nodded. He walked down the gangway, heading for the plentiful taverns of the booming settlement. He was previously the steward, and with years of faithful service had been promoted.

Nelson and McCafferey went below and brought up a pile of wooden planks to begin work on the port side. They lowered a stage, leveling off around two feet above the waterline. Two new crewmen, Christopher Bandoon and Joseph Lawen, began the work on the stage. Nelson ordered Ben and Sal to climb the foremast to check for damage. As Ben began his trek up the ratlines, his eyes stared up into the heavens, noticing a mess of tangled sail and line, one of the three sails on the mast.

He cupped his hands, with his elbow locked around a spar for balance, "Looks serious, tell the captain there's a crack a few feet below the crow's nest, and that we'll probably need a carpenter."

"Sal, are there any problems in the shrouds?" asked the captain with concern.

He nodded at his friend, who was still climbing down the tarred ratlines, "Uh, yeah. Ben mentioned a crack below the crow's nest. He said something about getting a carpenter to fix the mast, it looked pretty bad."

"Aye, I'll send you ashore now to find me the most reputed wood worker," said the captain.

Sal jogged quickly to the port side, showing excitement as he took large steps, passing closely beside Marconi and McCafferey.

"Eh lad, where are ye going?"

"I need to find a carpenter in town to fix the damaged mast and also for the journey."

"We'll accompany you. Perhaps we can recruit a few more hands on the way," the three paced down the gangway and left the dockside for the town.

✖✖✖

After talking with a friendly local, the three were given directions to the workshop of Henry Hughson. They traveled along the waterfront, making their way through the bustling streets. As they stood before the carpenter's home, Charles paced up the stairs. To his surprise, there were no squeaks, as is commonplace with wooden staircases.

He knocked on the door twice, paused to listen, and then struck his fist on the door for a third rap. A few moments later, a tall, middle-aged brunette opened the door. Sal noticed a little girl tugging at the back of her mother's dress.

"Who's that mommy?" the young girl asked.

"Sara, I'm not sure," she switched her gaze from her daughter to the open door, "But may I ask your names?"

He touched the brim of his cap, "Uh, hello ma'am. I'm Charles Marconi, this is Jensen McCafferey, and this is Sal Draben. Is your husband present? I need to talk business with him."

"Yes, he's in the shop behind the house. Come on in lads, would you like something to drink, tea perhaps?" Laura Hughson curtsied, before leading the way.

"No need to inconvenience you ma'am," replied Marconi as he took off his sailing cap.

"Oh it's not a problem, I don't mind," she said with a cheerful smile.

"Well, I suppose."

Sal walked in last and stared into a mirror on the left side of the hallway. His hair was in a dangle, unclean face, with some hair growing on his chin. His eyes moved down the mirror, he noticed he was still in clothes from his time.

Laura led the three men through their house into the kitchen, "And you guys can throw your coats on the bench."

"Thanks ma'am," replied McCafferey and Marconi as they stripped out of their pea coats and then placed them in a pile.

"You can go back and see Henry," said Laura.

"Thank you ma'am," replied Sal.

Laura motioned to the little girl to show the way outside. Sara moved her hand towards the far wall of the kitchen; she walked over to the opposite side and placed her small hand on the doorknob. Her little fingers turned the large, brass doorknob, ninety degrees until she opened the door with a gentle shove. She walked through the entrance and led the three into another corridor that passed two rooms.

She smiled, "That's my room."

After passing through the hallway, they were led to a small door. The girl opened it and showed them to the workshop. She paced across the grass, "Papa, there are men here who need to talk to you."

There was a muffled sound and then Henry Hughson replied, "Let them in dear."

Sal held the door for the other two and walked into Henry's workshop.

"Ah, you must be the fabled carpenter?"

"Yes, I suppose I am. Do you need my services?"

"My name is Jensen McCafferey, of the *Frendrich*. We came here only yesterday to refit our ship. We're in need of a carpenter for repair, and also for the journey that follows."

"Well, how much does the job pay? I'd like to get away from this boring town life and back to the sea."

"Ah so you're a sailing man? Well, the captain, Arthur F. Nelson, said to hire you for fifteen pounds a month," answered McCafferey.

"Aye, for that's a hard deal to reckon with. I make ten pounds a month here doing little jobs. Yes, I used to be a sailing man. How long do you think we'll be out?"

"If all goes well, you'll be back in a half year. We're going to sail the Caribbean, then on to England after."

"It sounds like a grand offer. I'll come back with you to the ship to finalize the deal with the captain. What're your names?"

"This is the First Officer, Charles Marconi, and this is my new acquaintance, Sal Draben, nice to meet you."

"I have a question Mr. Hughson," stated Sal.

"Go on lad," Henry replied.

"Are there any clothing stores around here?"

"Yes, but the prices are too high for any of the people in town to afford, why?"

"Well, I need to get clothes for me and my two friends." He added in a whisper, "Um, clothes from this era."

"All right, I'll give you each a set of clothing, and I think I also have a few extra pea coats that I haven't been able to fit into lately. They're yours if you want them."

"Thanks a lot Mr. Hughson," replied Sal.

Leaving the tool shed, the group entered the house, nearly bumping into a silver tray containing four cups of steaming tea. "Gentlemen, take a seat, my wife'll be down in a moment with the clothing."

They sipped at the tea until each slurped the last of the flavored water down.

"Ah, time to go," Henry began to stand from the chair.

Before opening to the door to leave, he called back to his wife, "Darling, where's Jacob?"

She grabbed Henry's hand, "Honey, is everything alright?"

"Yes, these men offered me a job. They require a carpenter's skill for the next few weeks to fix their ship and perhaps to join them afterwards. They're from the *Frendrich*, the vessel we heard about the other day. The pay is good too."

She placed her hands on her hips. "That sounds great, I remember when we first met how much ships and the ocean meant to you. How long would you be gone?"

"I'm not sure dear, I'm about to meet Captain Nelson to talk the details over. I wanted to let Jacob know also. We'll discuss this when I come back."

✖·✖·✖

They exchanged a kiss and then Henry left the room, Sal in his wake carrying modern clothing. He led the group down the street and hooked a left. They stood before a small building with the door half-open to ventilate the steam-filled space. Henry pounded on the door and entered with the three behind. "Uh, hello Dave," said Henry, "Is my son done yet with the lesson?"

"No, but if you need him he can talk with you."

Sal stared at Dave Hendricks; he was middle-aged man of forty-six, with broad shoulders and a massive beard clinging to his neck from perspiration. He had his thinning blond hair tied back in a ponytail, his apprentice by his left hip. Jacob Hughson stood proudly, with a strong built and his hair tied back.

Henry motioned for his son to come talk with him, watching his son walk slowly towards the entrance. "Son, these men gave me a deal I can't refuse. They need me to work on their ship and they asked me to sail with them for England."

"Papa, do you think that's such a good idea. I thought we were making enough money here. How much a month is it?" asked Jacob wiping specs of ashes off his protective sleeve.

"Fifteen a month, it's more than I make now. I really think my destiny's out on the sea, not making benches here on land. We would've passed by the shop anyways, so I wanted to tell you the news."

"Well papa, do you think they'd allow me to come with you?"

"I'd have to ask the captain, but we could always use another sailor," said McCafferey as he interrupted the duo.

"Really sir, do you think the captain would let me?" asked Jacob.

Sal stared at the happy expression on the young man's face. McCafferey sighed and then put his hands on his hips, "Well, how old are you lad?"

"I'll be eighteen in a few months. Am I old enough to sail?"

"You're older than I was when I first sailed. Yes, you're old enough," replied Jensen.

❌❌❌

"Henry, you'll make fifteen a month, and Jacob, you'll make five. You'll start working after this meeting and we'll log you onboard in our records and you'll receive your wares. Then tomorrow, bring all the tools, and equipment that you need. We have some on board, but if you prefer to use your own, go ahead. Now go off and work," said the captain with a smile on his face, both new hires showing great potential.

The sun was setting when a delighted John Borton came aboard.

"Sir, I sold the boat for quite a large sum of money, seven thousand pounds to be precise. As for the goods, we can make up to nine hundred pounds, I think more," he paused, looking at a pocket watch. "He'll stop by with the paperwork and make the deal final within the hour. I convinced him into giving us a down payment, I have the money in my pocket," said John as he handed the captain the sack of coins.

As the captain lifted it gently out of the outstretched hand he smiled. "Tomorrow, we'll purchase some goods and wares, but now we must unload the cargo to the pier."

During twilight, the last of the cargo was moved and was then transported to the buyers via horse and carriages that littered the wharf. It was almost nine before all the goods were sold, and all were tired.

19

acob knocked on the shop's door until he stared into the beard of his teacher. "I just wanted to let you know that I won't be attending anymore lessons, at least not for a while. These are my friends, Ben and Harris Manry, you met Sal already."

"Nice to meet you lads, why can't you make the lessons? I hope you didn't convert to the dark side!"

Jacob let out a laugh, "No, no I haven't become a carpenter. My dad has yet to change my mind. I love our work. It's just that I was recruited to join the *Frendrich* in a journey that will let me see the world beyond our town."

"The *Frendrich*? Wasn't that the vessel attacked by El Perro Loco?"

Ben chipped in, "Yes, sir. We fought them off. It was the captain and the three of us. It was an exhilarating feeling when we cleared the deck of the enemy."

The blacksmith was impressed. "If this is true, I would be honored to shake your hands. That bastard has been preying on our ships. I've lost several shipments of raw materials and some of the fine weapons that I've made over the years."

The man wiped his dirty hands on his smock and extended his

hand. The gesture circulated throughout the circle of men. "Oh and by the way, I forgot a few of the items I was working on before I left. Do you mind if I go show my friends?"

"Not at all Jacob, I'll leave you to show them around, my back is cramping up on me again. I need to retire; I've been doing this for too long!"

"Well, isn't that why you're training me?" he said with a smile. Still laughing, Jacob turned to the guys and said, "All right, I'll show you around and tell you how this whole process works."

The man left the teenagers to venture through the workshop. "Okay, where to begin?"

Harris looked around eagerly, "Tell us about the tools."

Jacob nodded, "Well, the key things we focus on are the forge, anvil, hammer, tongs, a vise, and a file. Coal and charcoal are used to fuel the forge. To soften the iron and steel, the fires need to be heated to approximately two thousand degrees Fahrenheit. We use leather bellows to feed oxygen into the fire; this creates a fire hot enough to prepare the metal for forging into different shapes. As the metal gets hot, we gauge it by the color. Iron is worked in a range of color between red and yellow.

"Next, when the iron is soft enough to work, it's brought from the fire to an anvil. We then hammer the metal into the desired shape. The shape depends on the job we are doing. Usually the metal would cool before it would be perfect, so then you put it back in the fire and heat it up again. Then you have to pound it continually and repeat as necessary. It requires a lot of strength and skill. Lastly, we heat it up again and then submerge the product in water. This rapid cooling gives it strength.

"We usually fix household items, gates, utensils, and make custom gifts. Sometimes we create a few swords or knives. My mentor has made several beautiful weapons and he taught me how to make one. Here I'll show you."

He walked over to a cabinet in the far side of the room. Bending down, he opened the drawer. The cabinet was oak, beautifully carved and stained.

Sal inquired, "Wow, who built this? It's magnificent. Look at the grain and wood work."

A smile came to Jacob's face. "That's my dad's work."

Ben could not help but release a laugh, "Jeez, a family of skilled workers. You guys should take us under your wings and we can help you out when we get back from sea."

Jacob looked at Harris, "You seem really interested in the forging process. If you remember my mentor saying that he wants to retire soon, maybe by then, I'll be put in charge of the shop. Then I can appoint you as my apprentice! How's that sound?"

"That would be great. I can't wait to make a sword! I've always wanted to do that."

Jacob tugged on the handle of the top shelf. "Hmm, that's not it." He pushed it in and then proceeded to the next. "Okay, here it is."

Wrapped in a leather cloth, he held a bundle in his hand.

Harris was curious, "What is it?"

He smiled and revealed his work. "Well, my father came home one day with a sword he received from a friend in the Royal Navy. It's a beautiful sword in the gothic style, with a lion's head pommel and back strap. The solid bowl guard is pebbled and in the center is a crown and fouled anchor. The slot in the guard has been rounded to allow for the cord knot," he paused for a few seconds as his available hand grazed the specific aspects of the weapon.

He continued, "Also there's the folding rear part of the guard, which latches into a stud on the brass top piece of the scabbard. The white fish skin grip is wrapped with gilt wire. The length of the blade is thirty-one and a half inches. The leather scabbard has all of its brass hardware finely engraved to produce the appearance."

"Wait, so did you make this sword?" asked Harris with a confused look on his face.

Jacob laughed, "Not a chance! I wanted you to see that first, before I showed you mine. I basically looked at it the entire time, carving and etching everything from eye, here's mine."

He took out another bundle, revealing a beautiful sword. "The only difference is that instead of a crown and fouled anchor in the center, I put my initials in it. See the JH?"

Harris stared at the sword; he was utterly amazed. "It's remarkable. How long would it take for you to make us all swords, maybe all of them matching, kind of like a secret club?"

"You know what? That's an excellent idea. I won't have time to do that now though. We only have a few more days here, but definitely when we come back. Anyways, I just wanted to show you the workshop and pick up my sword. You ready to head back to my house?"

✖✖✖

"Hello Jacob," Laura Hughson said as she opened the door. "Who are your friends? Oh, hello Sal, I remember you."

Ben stepped forwards, "Hello, my name's Ben Manry."

Harris bowed his head, "And I'm his brother, Harris."

"Can I get you boys something to drink, tea perhaps?"

"Sure mother, thank you. We'll be with papa in the back."

They went out the back door to meet up with Henry. He was in the process of sweeping the floor of the workshop.

"How about you lads grab a broom and help?"

"Yes sir."

Jacob placed the two cloth bundles on top of a long flat table and joined the group in cleaning the shop.

His father looked at the table and said, "Son, what is that you hide?"

"In one is the blade you let me borrow and in the other is my replica."

"Let me see it! You haven't showed me the finished product."

Jacob smiled, "Do you want to see it now or after we sweep."

"Lads, put your brooms away over in that corner. What's a little sawdust going to do anyways? After all, this is a workshop!" he laughed, excited to see his son's handiwork.

After the brooms were stowed, the group circled around Jacob. "Well what are you waiting for son, show me," the father smiled.

Henry supported Jacob in all his work, which made his son feel more talented than he already was. He slowly opened the first bundle, exposing the original sword. "Father, I believe this is yours."

Next, he opened the second bundle exposing the leather scabbard. He placed his hand around the grip and tugged. His father stared in amazement as the light shined off the heavily polished blade. "It looks exactly like my blade, excellent job! Let me handle it."

He passed the blade to his father, who weighed it in the palm of his hand. "It has remarkable balance." Henry then flicked his wrist a few times; watching the blade follow in the direction his hand went. "Mind if I test the blade?"

Before he let his son respond, Henry moved swiftly towards the end of the table. He squared his stance and drew back the sword. With a quick slash to the wooden support, the leg split in two. He then went to the corner of the room to a pile of three pine rocking chairs.

"This is a collection of failed experiments. I was working on a new style, but the engineering behind them did not work. Only my daughter could be supported by it."

Sal watched as Jacob's father swung at the top of the pile. The blade hissed through the air, hitting the seat perpendicularly. The sound of the wood crunching beneath the blade sent a shiver down the spine of everyone, except that of Jacob. He was proud that his sword not only mimicked the beautiful Royal Navy blade, but also proved its worth.

The blade went completely through the one-inch seat and continued its descent through the backing of the one beneath it. "Son, this sword is spectacular."

"Thank you."

Sal walked over to the chairs, studying the woodwork from his standing position. "Mr. Hughson, do you mind if I look at one of your failed chairs. I used to study carpentry."

He looked over to Sal, "Of course, if you could figure out what I did wrong, we can start building them when we return from sea. How's that sound?"

"That sounds great; I'll check it out now."

He stooped over and examined the chair. "Well what I would do is make the back inclined to a further angle. By doing this you would change all the angles of the joints and strengthen the chair. Also, I would make the length of the rocker longer. How long is it now?"

After looking at a number six etched in pencil on the chair, Henry looked at a notepad on the table, "Um, for that trial, the curved piece measured thirty inches long. So you think we should make it, say, thirty-two inches?"

"We can try that, but I'd go for something longer though. I think if you alter those two specs, the chair would work."

Henry took out a pencil from his pocket and adjusted the drawing in the notepad. "Hmm, from a mechanical viewpoint, your idea would strengthen it. What if we also installed two vertical sections leading from the bottom of the curved legs to the backrest?"

Sal joined him at the table and looked at the diagram. His finger traced what was drawn, "Yeah, that should work also."

Henry let out a relieving sigh, "Ah, wonderful. Let's relax until dinner and then we'll return to the *Frendrich*."

20

FEBRUARY 18TH, 1763
THURSDAY: THREE DAYS UNTIL DEPARTURE

Nelson watched as a handful of his crew walked down the gangway to enjoy a sunny, but brisk winter day. Ben went off with the large group and walked through the crowded streets. Some trickled into the numerous taverns, but the four youngsters stayed together, exploring every nook and cranny of the town.

It was around five o'clock, the sun low in its descent to meet with the horizon, yet her hair lit up the street like a lantern. The light glimmered off her blonde hair; the flowing locks almost looked as if it were alive, dancing upon her head. Ben glanced up and down, looking from every perspective.

"She is the most beautiful girl I've ever seen," Ben whispered, caught in a dream as he was nudged by Jacob to enter the tavern.

"See that girl over there; I'm going to ask her out tonight. I'll meet up with you in Sally's. If I'm not there in ten minutes, I got a date."

He watched his friends duck below the wooden sign that swung with the breeze, entering the warm tavern from the chilly evening air. His focus shifted back to the street. She was just forty short feet away; sitting on a bench, reading a book in the last rays of sunlight.

But love at first sight makes forty short feet, into forty million long feet. A nauseating feeling developed inside of Ben.

"Come on Ben. Keep yourself together. Just walk up to her and ask her out. It's as easy as back at home. Come on now."

In his peripheral view, a woman emerged from the general store; arms full of red, silver, and bright yellow fabric. Out of earshot, he could only see his fair maiden stand up to greet her mother. The daughter helped carry half the load as the two left the bench. Ben's eyes drifted, watching as they made their way down the main street.

✖✖✖

A cool breeze blew through the streets, the smell of the ocean spray wafting with each gust. Even with the warm shawl draped around their shoulders, the two women had a chill race up their spines. The scent of alcohol and warm food filled their noses as they shuffled past the taverns that lined the street. Through each doorway, boisterous laughter and the clanging of cups echoed into the cobblestone-lined road.

They were noticeably edgy: the daughter clasped her mother's upper arm firmly as they made their way down the main street. They were preoccupied in their shopping for satin for a new dress, and had, most regrettably, lost track of time.

"Just stay close to me, Leah," Mrs. Williamson whispered to her daughter, in the most composed tone she could muster. Leah glanced up into her mother's worried eyes, her mother's hand tightening around her own.

"You bloody, yeller' bellied…"

Both women jumped back and gasped as two men vaulted out of the doorway of the Boar's Head, pummeling each other in the face at the feet of the startled women.

"What animals!" the mother said moving quickly away from the tavern.

A little flustered, she took hold of Leah's hand and sped her gait.

Leah's hands began to shake. Her mother took notice of this, and gathered up as much confidence as she could. "Now dear, I understand your father's warned us to never walk this street alone, but it's the best lit and is the shortest path home. And you have me here. There's nothing to worry about. We'll be home shortly."

Leah's grip on her mother's arm loosened as she stood straighter, shoulders back, attempting to give off the air of self-assurance she so wished she truly had.

✹✹✹

*B*en still gazed down the long stretch of road before him; two men stumbled out of one of the taverns, almost falling at the women's feet. He then saw the women alter course, watching as the two men bashed each other with closed fists. From a side alley a shadow emerged. The man kept several feet behind, staying along the buildings, his shoulder brushing against the stone. The moment his eyes focused on the object in the man's hands, he broke off into a sprint.

✹✹✹

*T*he women continued on their hurried mission to get home. Leah's acute hearing picked up the sounds of pursuing footsteps, just behind them, and closing in. Her pulse began to race. Her grip on her mother's arm, once again, tightened.

A silhouette of a figure barreled towards her and her mother; Leah instinctively broke free, dragging her bewildered mother behind. Leah glanced over her shoulder to see who their assailant was, just as the hulking man lunged at them and pushed them into the entryway of a side alley. The women were just about to let out a shriek, when a strong, broad hand was placed over each of their mouths and midsection. There in the alley, another foul smelling man, also reeking of liquor and body odor, had been awaiting their arrival.

She was able to note that the original attacker was dressed in a thin, tattered white shirt and had a green handkerchief draped around his neck. His partner in crime was wearing a disheveled leather coat and a moth-eaten beaver felt hat on his head. As for their faces, with all the tumult, one could only conclude that they were sea-weathered and dark.

Leah withered and squirmed, flailing her limbs in every direction, attempting to hit her attacker. She saw that her mother was doing the same, sobs of fear and anger breaking through the hand holding her mouth. Beaver Hat had managed to unfasten his belt while pushing Leah against the wall, having his back to the street that laid only a dozen paces behind.

She bit down at the man's fingers as he attempted to constrain her. "Help…."she cried out.

"What ye think that'll do?" he slapped the girl, causing a welt of tears to form in her eyes.Blood trickled down his fingers, but this only made him more content. His hands then probed the inner workings of her petticoat, receiving another slap for the deed. He put his massive frame against her, pinning Leah against the brick facing. He began unbuttoning the silk red gown, her outermost garment. She closed her eyes, only hearing the screaming of her mother and the heavy, raspy breathing of her attacker.

✖✖✖

*R*ounding the corner carefully, Ben entered the dark alley. In front of him, he witnessed the ravaging of the women by their grotesque attackers. The man with his back to him had both hands exploring the crevices of each fold of his young love's corset. His eyes flared up in disgust, his pulse increasing as adrenaline flowed through his veins, fueling his anger. He scanned the area for anything of use, but it was a difficult task without sufficient lighting. He watched, as the men continued to undress the unrelenting women, hearing the sounds of pain and suffering that should never have to be screamed.

Then his eyes fixated on his weapon of choice, a piece of scrap lumber: three feet long by four inches wide. It was propped against the wall, just within reach. He stooped down and grabbed the base, his fingers wrapped around the wood firmly. He tiptoed behind the man, as to not make his presence known, but it was excruciating to have witnessed the scene. He then stood directly in back of Beaver Hat, staring into the eyes of Leah. She noticed his handsome features, contrasting greatly to the man that was ravaging her. Ben sent the wooden club to meet the man's earlobe, sending the man reeling sideways. Still holding on to Leah, the man tripped over his own feet bringing the girl down with him. She fell to her knees, squealing as her half naked body jolted from the impact with the ground. In a smooth motion, Ben gave his hand to the fallen lass, strings of muscle stretched as he lifted the girl to her feet.

✹✹✹

Isabelle Williamson, pinned against the back wall of the enclosed alley, watched as her daughter fell to her knees, being dragged down by the weight of her attacker. Emerging into her view was a young man, not even twenty years old, wielding the wooden club. He then helped Leah stand with a comforting squeeze of her hand for reassurance. She sighed with content as her daughter was out of harm's way for the time being.

✹✹✹

Green Handkerchief adjusted his head as he heard the shuffling of footsteps behind him. His comrade lay motionless on the ground as he saw blood trickling down the side of his head. He then slammed the woman hard into the wall. With a tug, he ripped open her laced bodice and turned on a heel to face the Ben.

"Get out of here, that's no way to treat these women," he yelled.

"And may I ask what'll ye do to stop me," replied the drunkard, the smell of stale grog carried to Ben's nose.

The man reached into his shirt and pulled out a large knife from its scabbard. "I think after I carve ye up, I'll steal yer money and have my way with these pretties. Maybe after that buy me some more grog."

"Not if I have a say in this," said Ben angrily, his eyes turned red, his heart pounding loudly.

The man walked forward a few steps, leaving Isabelle white with fear. She then sidestepped towards the same wall that her daughter leaned against. As the two men continued exchanging threats, Isabelle remained one with the wall, until finally she found the comfort and warmth of her daughter. The two women sighed heavily in an embrace.

The situation raced through his head as he paced forward. They stood an arm's length from each other. Ben's wooden club held tightly in his hands, anticipating the worst.

"He's still drunk," thought Ben, noticing the villain's uncoordinated movement.

The blade danced around, swing after swing, leaving just tenths of seconds for Ben to slip away unhurt.

"Yer think you can avoid me, heh?"

His large build powered each stroke, missing Ben as he swiftly moved aside to avoid yet another blow. He knew he could not match Johan's strength, but was confident he could outsmart his opponent; all he needed was an opening in the man's defense to swing the club.

Ben looked for the pair of women; a smile came to his face when he realized they had moved out of danger's way. His eyes now focused solely on the man's green handkerchief. In his mind he began to think of his past or rather, the future and of the days he used to know. This man in front of him, would be arrested for abuse, locked up and thrown in jail. But, there were no police around. He was the police. He had to do something about it. It was just the way it had to be.

He ducked under another series of wide arced swings. He maneuvered his body sideways, luring the man to follow. He then backed himself against the brick wall, hoping that the wide arced swings would catch. On the very next swing, Ben ducked as the blade smashed into the bricks, revealing the man's entire right side. Ben took advantage and swung with all his might.

Ribs cracked from the initial impact, causing the man to stumble back a few feet. The blade fell to the ground as he held his stomach. As Ben wound up for another swing, the man lunged forward. The two bodies mingled in a mess of flailing arms as they crashed back against the wall. He felt the man take hold of his shirt; ripping his issued work clothes. The man's fists began pounding into Ben's chest like a downpour of rain. He managed to throw a solid left jab, followed by a quick right hook. The man countered with another body lunge, his massive two-hundred pound body crashed into Ben, bringing them both to the ground.

Leah watched as the large man straddled her rescuer. His sheer size completely pinned him against the muddy terrain below. With one hand, the attacker searched for his fallen blade. Finally, the man's fingers grazed the hilt. He stared into the piercing blues eyes of the man below.

"Are you ready to be run through?" He managed between heavy wheezes.

With all his might, Ben contorted his body, sending the man sideways. He quickly rolled away and stood erect. With a swift kick to the man's arm, the blade flew from his hand, clinking against several stones. The man remained on his hands and knees, panting at a shortage of breath from the efforts.

Flight or fight. He turned his head towards the street and his legs soon followed. Isabelle Williamson studied the cuts and bruises on the boy's face, looking at the open wounds and fast flowing blood.

"Oh, my! Are you all right? We must get you home immediately!"

On the way navigating the streets to the Williamson estate, Isabelle held her daughter's hands while continually thanking Ben.

"Nonsense ma'am. I'm fine, just a little scratched up is all."

✖✖✖

They rushed along the winding road that led to a large colonial house on the top of an inclined hill, finally arriving at the wooden stoop. After pacing up the stairs, the mother knocked on the door twice, jiggled the knob, but it was locked. She waited a few more minutes, and then knocked again. On the second round of knocks, the door opened slowly. A weathered face peered out.

"Hello dear. I expected you earlier, dinner is on the table."

Ben noticed that Leah's father was in his late fifties, judging from the gray hair and his aged face. His voice was low, but clear.

"Pray Heavens, what happened? I thought you were just going to the store," Nicholas Williamson studied the three bodies in front of him. His wife's bodice was ripped, his daughter had tears in her eyes, and the young man in front of him stood hunched over, sore and bleeding.

Once inside, Isabelle began retelling the story that was so fresh in her mind. His face sunk with the news.

"Tell Juanita to boil a pot of hot water for Ben to clean himself off and give him a suit of yours."

Although Mr. Williamson had great power in the city being the Governor, at home, his wife held all authority. He called aloud to their servant and the elderly Spanish woman hobbled down the central staircase. Ben nodded as Mr. Williamson motioned for him to follow.

✖✖✖

The woman led him across the large house into a small dressing room with a bench on one side, and a chandelier hanging from the high ceiling. He noticed the candles burning slowly, flickers of light bouncing off the mirror in front of him. She then left and closed the door for privacy as Ben pealed his shoes off. He undressed quickly, piling his light cotton shirt, brown cotton pants, and moccasins at his bare feet. With just his undergarments on, Ben opened the door once Juanita knocked, entering the room with a jug of warm water in her hand. She slowly covered her eyes with her free hand after placing the jug down.

After she left, he stared down at his feet, noticing the torn and bloodied clothing. He let out a sigh as he recalled the day's events in his mind. His hand reached into the jug of water, feeling for the sponge. On top of the bench was a soap dish. His eyes stared back at him in the mirror.

"Jeez, that guy landed a few good hits on me."

❌❌❌

*I*sabelle Williamson watched as the young man walked out of the room with their servant. Her husband turned their daughter. "Leah, excuse us. I must talk with your mother. Go clean yourself for dinner."

Leah kissed him on the cheek and then hurried towards the stairs.

He turned to his wife, "Darling, are you okay?"

The two embraced and she let out a disheveled cry. "Yes, yes I am. It was very scary though. To reward Ben, I'd like if we could have him for dinner tonight."

He looked at his wife. "Of course dear, but just for dinner, you are well aware that I have promised Leah's hand in marriage. It would bring great dishonor to my name if knowledge of his stay here were to spread around town."

"How does having dinner with the people he rescued have anything to do with Leah's marriage to a man she's never even met."

He shook his head, "Dear, that's not the point. My point is he cannot stay with us for a length of time. I will feed him, give him a suit of mine, and then we shall part ways."

She grew flustered. To avoid further argument she said, "Well, I'm going to doll up. I am a mess. My favorite corset was ripped!"

The two went their own ways to ready for dinner.

❌❌❌

*L*eah stared into the mirror; she had just cleaned her face and changed into a lovely white gown that ruffled at the bottom. She applied the scented fragrance, the smell of the tulip dispersed through the air. Pulling open several drawers of her cabinet, she found what she was looking for. She smeared on lovely rose-colored rouge that accented her face. Next, she found a darker colored powder for around her eyes. She let off a smile, as she was pleased with how she looked.

✖✖✖

*M*r. Williamson led Ben into his personal quarters. They moved to a walk-in closet and he noticed a row of suits. Out of all the colors and patterns of material, a plain blue suit with matching pants attracted his attention.

Nicholas coughed to clear his throat and said, "Ben, what do you like the most?"

Ben made a second glance and walked in carefully, stepping over a pair of wonderfully crafted leather shoes. "This one, the blue suit, my eyes seem to be unable to look at anything else."

"Ah, that's the very same suit that I was in when I met my wife."

Ben smiled at the thought in his mind. Mr. Williamson reached in and placed it in Ben's strong hands. "Sir, where can I change?"

"There's a wash room over there. Just open the door and you'll find a chair where you can sit down."

Ben offered his hand in thanks. After a moment of hesitation, Mr. Williamson finally reached out and shook the lad's hand.

✖✖✖

*H*e pulled up the pants, reached for the belt, pushed the leather through the belt loops and began to think of Leah. He pulled the shirt over his head and finally tied the laces to the black leather shoes. Before donning the jacket, he washed his hands once more from a jug of cool water. With wet hands, he swept through his hair until he was satisfied with how it fell. He opened the door and walked through the room to where Mr. Williamson and his wife were standing.

The familiar blue on blue rekindled happy memories for Isabelle. "You look delightful, Ben."

He smiled at the gesture, "Thank you ma'am. It's a cozy outfit, much better than what I was wearing."

It seemed that Mrs. Williamson the talking for both her and her husband. "Ben, how did your clothes get so sullied?"

Ben smiled. "Well, I'm currently working on the beautiful *Frendrich*, a schooner anchored in port. Pirates attacked us just a few short weeks ago. We sustained heavy damage to the ship and we had to come to Freeport to refit and for repairs."

Mr. Williamson was shocked. "Ben, as Governor of Freeport, I had learned of your ship the moment it entered my waters. How did you manage to ward off the pirates? Usually we hear of these attacks through sole survivors or ransom notes."

He paused, realizing he was talking to a high official. He had to impress him now, for not only was he the father of the beautiful Leah, but because of his rank in society. "Sir, well we started out with about forty or so men. They emerged from a mist, taking us by surprise. Most of us were below deck, sleeping in our hammocks, so we had to rush to our battle stations. When we were boarded, they killed almost half our men with their handguns. We were then paired evenly. My friend, brother, and our captain were fighting a gruesome looking horde of pirates. We killed their captain, El Perro Loco. At the conclusion of the battle, a few pirates jumped overboard when I screamed a threat in Spanish," Ben answered knowing that he stretched the truth a little, but the effect on the man was in his favor.

Isabelle's jaw dropped with the story. "That's remarkable! I cannot wait to hear all your stories. You must have many more," she turned to her husband, staring directly into his eyes, "Darling, don't you agree?"

With a hidden smirk of anger, he nodded, "Of course."

There was a period of silence that lingered in the air. Ben's mind was elsewhere, picturing the epitome of perfection. He wanted to talk with her, get to know her, understand life in the eighteenth century through someone his age. His daydream ended when he heard the creak of the staircase as Leah came into the room with a white gown on. She dazzled Ben's senses. His heart seemed to protrude from his chest. The very hairs on his neck straightened as he glanced over to the girl.

With a warm smile she said, "I am ready for dinner."

✖✖✖

The sound of the fiddler filled the merry tavern, packed with several sailors from the *Frendrich* along with a wide variety of locals. Jacob, Harris, and Sal sat at a corner table discussing the day's events.

"So you think Ben got that date?"

Sal looked at Jacob, "Yeah. He's pretty good with those sorts of things."

Jacob looked at Harris, "What do you think?"

He took a sip from the mug and then said, "Eh, I bet you my brother will walk through these very doors shortly. He'll take a seat next to us and say 'Man, she was just out of reach.'"

They let out a laugh and returned to drinking.

✖✖✖

Ben, Leah, and her family sat around the large round dinning room table. He studied the scene in front of him, looking at the hordes of silverware that coincided with each setting as the servant poured fresh water. Nick Williamson recently purchased several new tureens, sauceboats, and centerpieces, all imported from Germany. Each piece of culinary aid was made of porcelain, designed with wonderful gold leafed prints. In front of each table setting sat a burning candle, the flame melting the scented wax, giving the room a nice, cozy cedar smell.

His gaze brought him to the numerous breadbaskets, accompanied by jars of spiced oil and vinegar, bowls of freshly picked vegetables, soups and stews, vegetables and boiled fish and meats arranged around the grand centerpiece.

"Wow, I've never seen so much food on one table for only five people," he thought.

Ben studied the Williamson family, glancing at similarities between father and son, mother and daughter. Both the females in the family had locks of soft, long blonde hair that curled at the tips. As for their faces, both had high cheekbones with a sleek profile. Their eyes were bluish-green in color. If that were not enough, their complexions were equally enviable, with soft pale flesh imbued with a healthy blush.

His gaze slipped and studied the males. The elder Williamson had bright red cheeks the contrasted greatly with his pasty face. He had black eyes and curly gray hair, peppered with brown. His aged face was clean shaved. His son had features common to both his parents, giving him his mother's eyes and high cheekbones and his father's curly brown hair.

A moment of silence was broken when the man of the house began to say a prayer. Once complete, each individual began loading their plate with the food stationed around them. After Mrs. Williamson finished chewing the oil soaked bread, she cleared her throat.

"Ben, so tell us of your background."

He first glanced at Leah's mother, and then around the table. "Well, I'm seventeen and come from a family of four. My father and mother's names are John and Margie Manry. I have a brother who's a year older, named Harris. I'm named after Benjamin Manry, who was widely known..."

"I can't tell them that he was a famous hero in the Revolutionary

War it hasn't taken place yet," he stared off into space, thinking of his past, or rather, his future.

"…And we live on a nice piece of land that was passed down in the family, it used to be a farm. There's a lovely stream that leads to a large lake with an island in the middle. When I was younger, I would always go off and explore and have adventures. Now I'm in the midst of my own adventure. I joined the crew of the *Frendrich* and then discovered something about myself I never knew, that I was fairly good at swordplay. Well, after my comrades and I defeated the hordes of pirates that had attacked us, we entered the harbor shortly thereafter.

"We then began the process of fixing all the damage the vessel sustained while selling off our wares and captured goods. We hired a new crew, and were then granted liberty since we worked hard and finished the job ahead of schedule. We're actually departing this coming Sunday."

The family nodded as they watched the young man introduce himself. Ben was content that no one pressed any further questions as the servants took away the first course off the table. In the several moments that lingered, Leah's parents conversed between themselves, leaving Ben in the presence of the pair of siblings.

"Ben, what do you have planned tomorrow?"

He turned to face Leah, "Well, the typical day lately has been waking up for morning colors at 0700. After that, we have the day to ourselves. Captain wants us to relax and enjoy the last few days before we sail for Havana."

Mr. Williamson heard the last sentence and ended the conversation with his wife. "Ben, not to impose, but what exactly is your duty?"

He was not positive; the captain never really stated a clear purpose, "To trade sir, though it seems like Captain Nelson might have other plates on his table. Anyways, I enjoy the ocean very much. Have you seen a sunset at sea? It is the most beautiful thing you'll ever see, nothing to block your view."

Nicholas nodded content that he ended his daughter's questioning with Ben.

Ben remembered a trip his family took a few years back. They went on a five-day cruise around the Caribbean and at the furthest distance from land; they were able to have an unobstructed view of the sky, without disturbance from the city lights and atmospheric pollution.

The same servant brought out the second course, consisting of steamed vegetables, an exotic pheasant pie, and a plateful of gumballs and cheese wigs. The latter two dishes Ben had never seen before.

"Excuse me miss, what is that?"

The servant curtseyed and replied, "Gumballs are in this basket. They were made this afternoon. In the other are cheese wigs."

"May I ask what that is?" Ben asked curiously.

"Of course sir, gumballs are made from eggs, sugar, flour, butter, mace, aniseed and caraway seeds mixed together to form a paste, which is then baked. Cheese wigs are small bread buns coated with cheese sauce so they resemble the shape of a wig resting on a wig stand."

"Thank you," he held the silverware in his hands, eager to try the unique food.

Back at home, his family typically stuck to barbequed chicken, ribs, or steak. This was a treat for his stomach. The freshly churned butter melted over the steamed vegetables. The family and their guest began to pass food around, shortly thereafter; Ben's plate was full of food.

His mouth was in a state of amazement the moment the delicacy hit his tongue. It was soft and the tasteful meat dissolved on his tongue. They continued eating the main course, the contents on each plate continued to diminish in size. When Ben consumed all that was in front of him, he soaked up the flavored marinade with a piece of bread. It looked like a steak sauce, but tasted nothing like what he expected.

Mrs. Williamson looked at Ben again. "Do I know your mother?

What church does she belong to? The name does not sound familiar. I'm a member of several women clubs around town."

"Well, I'm not from around here, so most likely not; we're members of the Presbyterian Church. Um, what else can I tell you?"

The more questions she asked, he noticed that her husband grinned look of disapproval on his face. Before she could muster another question, Mr. Williamson looked down at his empty plate.

"Dessert would be delightful now," he said for all to hear. "The sooner dessert would be served, the sooner their guest would leave," he added silently.

Ben could not believe that throughout the conversation, he had managed to devour the pheasant pie. After Mr. Williamson called for the servant to bring out the next dish with a ring of a bell, the group waited in silence. In the minutes that followed, the group continued their conversations.

"Ben, what do you usually do after a meal? We usually drink tea and read, followed by a lovely music session. Does that sound to your liking?"

"Yes, Mrs. Williamson, that sounds great."

The man of the house clenched his fork tight, his fingers turning a beat-red as he made the attempt at oppressing any comments from being said.

Sweetmeats, sugared fruits and pudding were brought out on several trays and handed out. The sugared peaches were Ben's favorite. The plums and apricots were also tasty, but Ben decided to spend the rest of dessert eating the peaches and the chocolate pudding. Once the dessert dishes were cleared off the table, the Williamson's and their guest moved into the next room. Walking down the hallway, Ben passed several paintings on the wall. One particularly caught his attention.

On the large wooden frame, a placard hung. He turned towards the elder man as he read the metal engraving.

"Sir, this painting is extraordinary. The details of each brush stroke are amazing. Is Governor James Williamson II a relative?"

Nicholas smiled, temporarily relieved of being put on the spot by his wife. "Well, I am glad you noticed that. I love telling this story; it is one of my favorites. It began roughly twenty years ago when my wife and I lived in Bristol. Like my father before me, I attended and graduated from the University of Cambridge in 1738. There I studied under one of the most prominent professors. He taught me everything there is to know about politics and government.

"Between that and the discussions with my father, who held a position as Statesman of Bristol, I learned many things that I used later in life. When my father was sick with smallpox, I was appointed to fill in for him. In his absence, I improved Bristol and the surrounding areas significantly. Luckily, he fought the disease and was cured within a year. I was noticed in his stead and after several months, I was recommended for a governorship in one of the provinces outside of the Empire.

"I later received a letter and was granted a permanent position here in Freeport. I moved here with my wife, Isabelle, and our two children. They are actually now in England furthering their studies. A few years later, Leah was born and then two years after that, Nicholas Jr. was born. Since arriving here in Freeport, I believe I have made great changes and am quite content with how the town is run."

Ben was pleased that the father actually conversed without displaying an evil grin. He could tell that there was still something that the Mr. Williamson was not telling him.

The large reception room contained ten chairs that were beautifully carved and stained with exotic colors. The carpet that lay across the floor was purchased when the governor made a trek to the Orients on one of his several trips as a child when his father decided to travel the world.

Each sat in a chair with a table next to them. On the small sitting table, there was a plate and a cup of herbal tea that filled the room with a nice smelling aroma. Bookshelves lined the room, every possible inch on every shelf was crammed with books that both husband and wife inherited over the years or collected. The governor was proud of this collection, as he saw Ben's mouth drop he smiled.

"Ben, as you can tell, I enjoy a nice book to read once in awhile. Go look through them, if you see anything you like you can start reading it while we drink tea. In about an hour we can then part ways and get you off back to the ship before it gets too late. How does that sound?"

As Ben sat up, he replied, "Sir, it sounds great."

He replaced the cup of tea back on the ceramic saucer and then walked towards the first series of bookshelves. His eyes strained towards the top shelf, noticing that the first book was by a man named Aaron, and the one after that was by Adams.

"He really organized his entire collection alphabetically, that is remarkable." He skipped from A to B to C, and stopped at D. "Hmm, when was Defoe popular"

As Ben was trying to put a date to his thoughts, his fingers slipped upon *Robinson Crusoe* a book that he knew well. He took the book from its spot and then opened the cover. After scanning the title page, he found the print date, 1719.

As he sat down, Mr. Williamson looked at the cover to the book, "Ah, wise choice Ben. It's one of my favorites. My father actually gave that to me when I was just a boy of about eight. Now let us enjoy our tea and read in silence for an hour."

The leather chair engulfed Ben as he began to fall into Crusoe's world.

❈❈❈

Mr. Williamson placed a feather between the pages to mark his place, "Well, the hour is up."

She knew that her husband wanted their guest to leave, but she then stood up and moved quickly towards Ben. "Benjamin, come. You must hear this new song that I learned on the harpsichord. It's simply beautiful. I've been playing it for several months now."

Mr. Williamson turned red. He could feel the heat of his wife's eyes on him. "Sure, a music session sounds lovely."

The group migrated to yet another room; furnished with paintings, fancy chairs, and cabinets upon cabinets of musical instruments containing every variety of stringed instruments from a variety of countries. In the corner of the room, there was a large harpsichord. Isabelle paced gently over the large rug and took a seat. Her audience each took a seat with the exception of Leah. She moved towards her mother's side.

There was no single word to describe the sounds that filled the room. With precision, Mrs. Williamson plucked a sequence of strings, setting the pace of a grand story. The mother-daughter musical pair was simply outstanding. Leah's voice was relaxing yet tense at the same time; he sat on the edge of the chair to hear the conclusion to the song.

Ben was at a loss of words. "Um, that was, amazing," he struggled with finding the right words. "I've never heard anything like that before. The combination of each merged so well."

The two women curtseyed and then Leah turned to her parents. "May I be excused for a brief moment? I will return shortly."

Her father was equally amazed and did not further interrogate, only approving with a nod of the head.

✖✖✖

Once Leah had left the room, she walked quickly straight for Juanita's quarters, pacing through the grand hallways that stretched throughout the household. She knocked at the closed door. Once it opened Juanita smiled, "Hola, Leah."

She replied the gesture and spoke slowly so Juanita could understand. "...Just slip it in the pile. You don't have much time. He's about to leave."

Leah could only smile at the prospect of the following day. She then returned to music room, rejoining her family and Ben. "I apologize for my delay."

Her father stood once again, smiling as he said with outstretched arms, "Ah, just in time to say goodbye to Ben."

The group walked over a large oriental carpet, until they found themselves in a side hallway. Ben followed the pack until they arrived at the front door.

Juanita arrived with a stack of clothing. "Good evening, señor."

Once the servant left the group, Ben looked at Mr. Williamson. "Sir, I'm still wearing your clothes. Thanks again. May I change before I leave?"

"Nonsense, keep it. It is my gift to you."

Leah remained quiet, while her mother talked. "We cannot thank you enough. Good luck on your voyage, and if you're ever in Freeport, just drop by. You're more than welcome."

With this, they bade farewell.

❉❉❉

It was after ten o'clock when he walked down the stoop. The moment he left the protection of the overhang, a strong breeze ruffled the pile of clothing in his hand. The top layer fell off, revealing a small folded paper, sealed with a wax stamp: *LW*.

He wondered what it was as he put down the pile to read it. He opened the seal and then scanned the contents with eager eyes. It read:

Ben,

> *Thank you again for coming to our rescue. If you would like to see me before you leave, meet me tomorrow morning at eight. I will be in front of the General Store on the same road where fate crossed our paths.*

> *Yours truly,*
> *Leah Williamson*

He smiled and then turned his head back towards the house. In a window on the second story, he saw a pair of eyes stare back at him. It was the same blue-green colored eyes that he remembered gazing into earlier in the evening.

"Goodnight, Leah," he whispered, his words carried by the wind.

✖✖✖

Still new to the town, he tried to navigate his way back down the main streets. He traveled in the middle of the street, staying within the candlelight emitted from each post. Often times, he heard the neighing of a horse in the distance. Otherwise, the trip back to town was quiet. He walked down the same street where he had witnessed the brawl, passing by the same unlit side street. The thoughts of the event sent a shiver down his spine. Then above his head, the sign for the tavern came into view and he pushed open the door to enter.

Once inside, Jacob smiled and waved as he saw the familiar face enter the room, "Looks like Harris was right after all! Ben come sit."

He joined his friends and they stared at his outfit. His brother was in awe. "Dude, where'd you buy that?"

Ben smiled and then recapped the night.

Sal interrupted, "So wait. You fought off two guys, ate dinner with the beauty and her family, got that amazing suit, and got a date tomorrow morning?"

Ben answered with a smile and a nod.

Sal looked straight at Harris. "Ha! I knew I was right. Take that. Score one for the home team," he said, slapping Ben a high five.

21

Ben had hung his suit on a makeshift hanger on the forepart of his hammock, sleeping in just his underwear. Below decks often got hot and stuffy, the majority of the crew slept in just their undergarments. It was seven in the morning when the bells for morning colors echoed through the maze of ladders and passageways of the ship.

Each man dressed in their gear and paced the stairwell to meet at the sternpost. A bugle man played revelry and then Nelson spoke loud for all to hear. "Men, two days left. Today you can venture off, but on the morrow, we'll stay close to the pier. I'd like to leave Sunday morning with the rising sun. Go off and enjoy this fine day."

The crowd then went their own ways, some leaving the ship right after, while others went below decks to unite once more with their hammock. Ben went into a water closet and found a basin full of fresh water. He got his wrists wet and then gently massaged his face with the cool water. Walking back to his hammock, he began to change out of the work gear, and into Mr. Williamson's gift.

"That sure is quality fabric."

He turned to put a face to the voice. "Hey Jacob, I haven't worn such a nice suit since my confirmation. What are you and the guys doing today?"

Harris and Sal emerged into view and joined in the conversation. "Probably just walking around, maybe buy some things. We do have some loot now that Nelson gave us that chest to split. Let's not blow it all in the taverns like the others."

He watched his brother talk. "Yeah, I'll try and meet up with you later in the day maybe for dinner, if that's cool with you. She's real gorgeous."

Sal remembered every detail of the description last night. Everything from her eyes, hair, and skin, to personality was described with such precision his audience felt as if they had already met her.

"She sounds nice, you going to bring her?"

"I assume she'd like to meet you guys. Maybe she can bring a few friends of her own."

He winked at his friends at the prospect of playing cupid.

Harris replied, "Very funny. We are quite capable of getting our own girls."

✖✖✖✖

*H*e found himself venturing the streets alone. He was vaguely familiar with the area by now, but he was too caught up in the moment. Part of him wanted to remain with his friends, but figured he would see them all the time on the ship. In the meantime, he walked down the wharf, humming, as the rays of light felt warm on his back. It was a quarter to eight when he arrived in front of the General Store, and to his astonishment, Leah was already sitting there with a wicker basket on her lap. It looked as if she had camped the night there, hidden beneath an oversized red cloak.

"Wow, a girl who's on time, amazing," he thought.

He slowly approached the bench she sat at. Making a sweep through his hair, he then smoothed out the front of his suit. "Good morning, Leah."

She looked up from her book, from side to side, acting like she could not find the source of the greeting. A smile grew on her face as Ben began to laugh with his hands on his hips.

She replied, "And good morning to you, Benjamin."

She stood up and slowly approached. She put out a hand and in that brief second, Ben had absolutely no idea what to do.

"Should I kiss her, hold her hand, kiss her hand, or shake her hand?"

He then bowed, remembering several movies of the era and slipped his hand below hers. Bringing his head down, his lips met her soft velvet gloves.

She replied with a curtsey and the two began walking down the street.

"Did you enjoy dinner yesterday?"

As they walked, he turned his head to face her. "Yes, it was remarkable. I haven't had such delicacies. The rest of the evening was great. Thank you very much for your hospitality."

"Well you have nothing to thank us for. It was the least we could do. My mother is very fond of you."

Ben smiled. "Yes, that may be true, but I sense your father doesn't like me much."

Leah let out a sigh. "Yes. Well there's a story behind that."

Before she continued, he wondered what it was, "Hmm, a story behind it? I wonder if any of my relatives did something to him," he chuckled at his own thoughts.

He shook the idea out of his head and concentrated on Leah. "Well. I am seventeen. My birthday is in three months. In my family, we have a tradition that on your eighteenth birthday, the females are to be wedded."

Ben replied, "Isn't that kind of young to be wedded?"

She laughed, "Nonsense Ben, my mother married at that age as well. He was much older than she, but they sure do get along swell. Anyways, my father received a letter from an old friend back in England. It said something along the lines that the man's eldest son had just made rank of Captain in the Royal Army and that he is unmarried. Well, this man is nearly twice my age, and requested my hand in marriage. Our families would merge and we would then become quite the landowners, having many estates in England and in the Colonies. We are fairly wealthy already though, so I do not see why I should marry a man I've never met, nonetheless, a man who is thirty-two."

Ben's heart sunk. "Yeah, I understand. That isn't fair for you. So,

I'm guessing your father doesn't want me around because you've been promised away?"

She nodded. "Yes, around these parts, giving your word for something such as that is a great deal. If you break that word, then you are considered a coward and traitor."

Ben was puzzled. "So why did you want me to meet you here?"

She tried to hide a smile. "Well, it was my father, after all, who promised me away. I talked with my mother all night last night, and she agreed. She fell in love with my father *before* they married. However, that was a rare case. His father, and his father's father, all were appointed their wives. But because of that, my mother suggested we meet up before you sailed away. It is not that I am in love with you or anything like that, you just seem like a nice boy to take a walk with on the beach," she turned her head, averting his eyes.

Ben's cheek flushed at the compliment. "Well, I'd be honored to walk around town with you." He paused, "Do you think your father has spies? Like, do you think he's watching you? How'd you leave the house this morning without being interrogated?" he asked in what seemed one excited breath.

"Well, my father had to leave very early this morning to tend to business with government officials. Mother said he'd be gone until at least midnight. So she encouraged me to come."

Ben sighed with relieve. "Last thing I want is for you to get in trouble."

"There's nothing to worry. He is on the other side of town, plus I escaped under a cloak, so even if he did have anyone looking for me, they would not notice. We are going to the beach first."

"Are we going swimming?"

"No, just for a walk…"

The two made their way through the streets, walking along storefronts and through side alleys. She walked with a smile now, not like the previous day where she had short, quickened steps. Leah was not worried about getting mugged now; she was quite content with her company.

Finally, the two made their way through a wooded path, leading to a beach. He stared ahead, taking in the scene. The waves crashed into the shore with a loud yet relaxing clap. The grass ended roughly two hundred feet from water, and from there, was a mixture of sand and rocks.

On an outcropping, she sat down on a raised jetty of rocks. "Take a seat."

Ben joined her and then they sat in silence. "It's beautiful."

She looked at him, "Yes, it is. My brother and I come here often. We found a small cavern that the water carved out. Since its low tide, we probably can go in without getting too wet."

Ben thought of all the caverns and caves that he's explored in his time. He smiled, "I love exploring. Let's go!"

The two ran around the weathered outcroppings, fast, but careful not to slip on the sea growth. Finally, Ben saw what she was talking about and stared into the cave's entrance. There was almost like an inner harbor guarding it, the rocks formed a barricade that created a still pool of water at the base of the cave.

"Take off your shoes and pull up the pant legs. Sometimes I get my dresses wet and then my mother or father asks what happened."

The two placed their socks inside their shoes and rolled up their leggings. Ben led the way through the four-inch pool, his feet enjoying the cool water. Stepping over several coral formations, Ben approached an incline. Arriving at the entrance, he waited for Leah. The cave height was no greater than four feet high, so Ben ducked his head under.

He took a deep breath, smelling the air he was about to enter. It was well ventilated and smelled like the ocean.

"I suppose you don't have a light?"

He could see the white of her smile through the darkness. "I am one step ahead of you."

He heard the commotion of her hands lifting the top of a wooden box located in a groove of coral. She withdrew a small lantern and then closed the box. "You probably won't believe how this works. My brother is very smart. Instead of actually striking the flint on steel, he developed a different way to do it, and the spark is directed towards a charred cloth. The spark then ignites the cloth. The compartment inside the lantern is completely sealed off, so to feed the flames, you have to open the side latch for air."

He took a few steps back towards daylight. "Can I see it?"

She handed him the lantern, and he studied the flint wheel. Attached to the wheel was a dangling string. "Hmm, so I pull on the string?"

She nodded, "Yes, after you pull the string, the wheel rotates. There's an angled piece of steel that connects the wheel and inside compartment. This so-called 'path' is where the sparks fly. When the sparks land on the charred cloth, it sort of stays there, and with more oxygen, it lights up pretty quick. Then you have to blow into the lantern for it to spread completely. Once it catches, leave a little window open on the hinged door. Just close the door and we have light!"

Ben was amazed. "Your brother seems to have quite the ideas."

She nodded in agreement. This essentially "modern technology" caused a flashback in Ben's mind, remembering the lessons his science teacher taught about the first friction matches developed in the late 1820's.

He came to his senses when she nudged him to try it. "Come on, go ahead."

He set the lantern down on the wooden box and then tugged softly on the string, watching the flint wheel rotate one-fourth a turn. Several red sparks shot up the steel file, entering the compartment, landing atop the charred cloth. As the strip of cloth heats up, it gives off volatile gasses, which ignite. Within twenty seconds, the flame grew several inches tall. Remembering what she had told him, Ben had already opened the hinged door and blew several times into the lantern. Moments later, the entire cave had come out from hiding, revealing several chairs and a cabinet towards the back of the space.

"Wow, it's bright!"

"My brother also changed out the glass of the lantern. Don't ask me why it makes everything brighter, but there are patterns in the glass and I can only assume that that is the reason."

Ben then closed the hinged door, leaving the window open for ventilation. His eyes scanned the interior space of the cavern; he could only guess the dimensions to be six feet wide, about the same high towards the middle, and maybe twenty long. He felt like he was inside a submarine, hearing the crashing of the waves against the one side of the coral wall.

"This is our secret spot. Only my brother and I know of it. I figured I'd share it with you."

Ben replied, "It's beautiful, so what do you do down here?"

She reached over towards the cabinet and pulled out a pile of papers from the top drawer. "We do a lot of thinking in here. It's quiet besides the surf. I usually write poems, he tends to draw and design things. I think he's working on some sort of two-wheeled contraption. He looked through a book of Leonardo DaVinci's and is working on it now."

"What sort of poems do you write?"

She filed through the stack of papers, placing several on her lap. The rest she replaced in the cabinet drawer. "I wrote this one a few months ago, it's called Dreams."

Dreams
After all those years of wishing upon a star
Tracing the tail of the night's scar
Until it disappears into the sky
Those stars that hold your dreams
One by one, you'll put them to sleep
Wherein the heavens they lie
Once put to rest, these stars will stay
There for gazing to waste time away
Another wish burns so bright
Head back, glancing skyward once more
Your dreams knock upon heaven's door
In hours of darkness reigns the star's shine

Ben was speechless.

"So, what do you think?"

He looked at her. "It was amazing. I've written several poems in my day too, but nothing as good as that."

Even in the candlelit area, he could see her blush. "Thank you. It means a lot when someone appreciates your work."

"Yeah, I completely understand."

She handed him a handful of papers and she sat in silence while he read through several of her poems. It seemed that each one progressed in skill, the first few not as good as the ones towards the bottom. After half an hour, he handed the stack of parchment back to her with a smile.

"To be honest, I can't think of a phrase to capture its beauty."

She tried to hide her smile, but could not hold it back. There was a brief moment of silence, and then she muttered, "Let's continue our walk."

Leah grabbed the lantern from atop the cabinet, and then closed the window, suffocating the oxygen inside the lantern, dousing the flame. The room went from candlelit to dark within seconds and Ben bumped into the chair as his eyes slowly adjusted. He heard Leah's laugh as he toppled over. It was all right though; he was used to being mocked for his clumsiness.

His eyes had yet to completely adjust and he was probing the darkness with a wandering hand. His fingers then grazed the flesh of a soft and warm hand. Leah did not back away, nor did she take his hand in hers right away. The hands sort of hovered near each other; a magical force began to take its toll, bringing the hands slowly together. She then squeezed with reassurance, just like he had done for her in his rescue.

They continued walking along the beach, watching as the surf crashed at their feet. Ben held both pairs of shoes while Leah had a crooked arm holding the basket full of food. The pair left a trail of footsteps behind them; the incoming tide would erase the trail just moments after being created.

"So, where are we going?"

She smiled at him. "You'll just have to wait and see."

He could only assume they were going somewhere to eat. He had been on several family picnic trips in his youth.

"Ben, are you engaged?"

He wanted to laugh, but thought it inappropriate. Quickly, he responded, "No. As much as I would love to, I just don't have the time. With all this traveling that I've done, it's difficult to."

Ben saw the slightest hint of a smile form on her lips, suggesting some deep, inward thought arising. She replied. "That's too bad. A woman would be lucky to find a young lad like you."

She turned her head to hide yet another growing smile.

For the length of the beach, they continued in silence. Ben could finally see the tall masts of the ships in the harbor. He began kicking a rock along the sand, watching it cut grooves in the wet beach below.

"Ben, is there something wrong?"

He looked at his feet and then back to her, "Of course not. It's a habit that I have trouble breaking. So, what shall we talk about?"

Her gaze fixated on the water. "Tell me what you want to accomplish in life."

"Probably work with Captain Nelson for awhile," he began thinking of his old life and how he wanted to graduate high school, go to SUNY Maritime College and sail the seven seas. He continued, "Maybe settle down and buy a nice piece of property. Raise a family of my own. Change the world for the better. You know that sort of thing."

She nodded with a smile. "Yes, similar to what I want to do, besides the whole sailor thing."

Ben's smiled, "Why not? That's the best part of the deal. I may just have to take you sailing someday."

Her smile receded. "That would be lovely, but my father would not approve."

"You came out to meet me today though; do you think he'd approve of that?"

She remembered the conversations she had with her mother the night before. "Of course he wouldn't approve, but I don't know..." she trailed off into a mumble.

He sensed he touched a sore subject. "Hey, how about we just walk for a bit. Enjoy the nice sounds and take in the beautiful scenery. Words can't describe it."

The two continued their walk along the beach, finally reaching the dockyards. They continued walking across the wharves, following the water's edge until they reached another stretch of beach. As they walked, they continued to talk. The sun had reached its apex in the sky; Ben noticed the angle beginning its decent towards the horizon.

"So, are you going to tell me what's in the basket?"

"We are going to have a picnic."

✖✖✖

On a hill that overlooked the bay, she shook out the blanket that was packed in the wicker basket. Ben took one side and together they laid it flat on the ground. Once both were seated, she placed the open basket between them. Reaching in, she brought out a dish of sugared fruit, laying it by her side. Next, she removed a cloth, unfolding it revealed two freshly baked wheat rolls. Lastly, she took out an apple pie that Juanita had made for her before the day had begun.

Ben's stomach growled with hunger. The aroma that filled his nose created a fresh flow of saliva in his mouth. "I can't wait to eat. It all looks so good."

As Ben reached for the food, he caught Leah's glare on his arm. In mid-air, he paused as she began reciting a prayer. "…And bless us, God, for the food you have provided…"

He silently scolded himself for his blunder. They sat under the boughs of a large tree, out of the sun's rays on the beautiful day. As Ben chewed, he looked up and saw the slight ruffling of the leaves, feeling the breeze sliding gently through his hair.

✖✖✖

*I*t was now two hours before sunset, and Leah made the motion to pack up. Ben helped her fold the blanket and place everything back in the basket. She stood up with the basket under her crooked arm, but Ben placed a hand on her arm. "Don't worry about that. I'll carry it."

"It's not heavy."

"You carried it here, it's the least I can do."

She slowly relented, handing it over to Ben.

The two made their way through the streets. Ben saw several familiar street signs and storefronts, finally taking a bearing as to where he was. He smiled. "Hey, do you think we could go to Sally's, my brother and two best friends are there."

She smiled, "I would love to meet them."

He led the way to the tavern, towing his beautiful date behind. "Do you want me to tell you about them now, or would you prefer to hear it from them?"

She squeezed his hand tight, "Let's enjoy the evening's silence for now. Sally's is one more street down anyways."

✶✶✶

*T*hey paused at the tavern's door, "After you."

She pulled her cloak's hood over her head a few more inches than she had during the walk, and entered. Once inside she waited for Ben. The three waved at Ben, welcoming the two newcomers.

"Hey guys, this is Leah."

She curtseyed politely, "Gentlemen, it is my pleasure. May I have the honor of your names?"

The individuals shook her hand and introduced themselves. She left the cloak wrapped around her body as they all sat down and chatted.

"So tell me, what's it like onboard the ship?" she looked at the four males. "I've always wanted to see the world, but my father won't let me yet. He says I'm not old enough. I am seventeen though. My sister, three years my elder is studying abroad in England. She has another two years of schooling left. My brother lives and works in Liverpool as well. On this island it is just my mother, father, younger brother, and I."

Ben smiled as he listened to her speak. She had just asked a question, but continued talking. Her personality radiated throughout the group. Jacob responded, "Leah, to be honest, I haven't even sailed yet. So you can't really call me a sailor. I actually just joined the crew and have been lucky enough to befriend these lads. I am more of a blacksmith than a sailor, at least for now."

"That is very interesting Jacob," she turned to Sal, "Tell me about you, kind sir."

She shot Ben a quick glance and smiled.

"Well. I have known Ben and Harris for what seems forever. Our families are quite close. The three of us are inseparable. Usually we seek adventure and explore the outdoors. We just had a…"

Ben stared fully at Sal, causing his friend to stop for a moment.

"You just what?" she inquired.

"Sorry, I get distracted easy. Did you happen to see the juggler over in the corner?" he pointed to the side of the group.

She looked towards where he pointed, giving him a few seconds to think. "Yes, so continuing on. We just came into port not too long ago. I'm sure you have been told. Well, have you heard of our misfortunes upon the seas?"

She ignored that momentary pause before and decided to hear Sal's version of their adventure. "Of course, I would love to hear your tale though!"

"Okay, so it goes like this…my story begins as we were standing watch on the lovely vessel the *Frendrich*. There were four of us looking around; making sure the ship was in proper keeping, one cabin boy who will remain nameless, and the three of us. He was dosing off so we had to pick up his slack. Well, I took out my scope and scanned the horizon. There was nothing on the port side. Ben climbed up the ratlines to get a better view. Harris was twiddling his thumbs or something along those lines."

Harris went with the story and slapped Sal on the arm. "Hey, you sure you didn't get that backwards?"

The group laughed as a waitress was flagged over by Ben. "Hello, can your bring us something to drink?"

She said, "Certainly, what can I get you?"

Leah spoke for the couple, "Some warm cider would be great."

The moment the waitress left the group, she turned back to Sal, "I believe you left off with Harris twiddling his thumbs."

Sal let off a smile; he could not resist it either, "Okay, well I left off where I spotted a vessel emerging from the mists. It had a black hull and dark sails, almost perfectly blending into the darkness. Before I could alert someone, I saw several rounds fly towards us. The captain got his awakening as the balls crashed into our hull. Well, I've been talking for a while, why don't you pick up where I left off?"

Harris felt Sal's eyes, "Of course. So, Leah, we wrung the bell rapidly to wake the crew. Within several minutes, we had a quick formation to take accountability as we maneuvered with the wind. The cannons were primed and loaded, ready for action. Several of us manned each gun and carriage, while the others waited along the rails for battle. I was stationed as gun crew, Ben was stationed in the ratlines, and Sal stayed along the rails. My main job was to swab out the cannon's barrel before each volley. Ben was in the crow's nest, equipped with a long rifle to prevent borders. Sal brandished a boarding axe to chop the lines that they threw over to bring our ships together.

"The two vessels zigzagged with the wind, trying to get the advantage over the other. Finally the ships met and the pirates threw over more hooks than Sal could cut. Ben shot a few down while in the process of the boarding while he swung his axe fiercely. The gunners continued shooting into the enemy; we aimed for the waterline continually smashing it. Somehow their vessel stayed strong and did not sink. We fought a terrific battle, overcoming disadvantages to win. Then we sailed here with the vessel in tow after losing most of our crew."

She was amazed, "That story was excellent! Ah the cider is here,

I am quite thirsty from our walk," a waitress placed a tray with the drinks on the table.

She looked at the grandfather clock in the corner of the room to gauge the time they had left. The group drank while going in the circle telling stories. Each hour's tick of the clock combined as one. It was just after six when she stood up to say goodbye to her new friends.

"I hope to see you all soon, it was a pleasure."

The three gentlemen said their goodbyes and watched Ben escort his lady out of the tavern.

"See you on the ship?" Ben asked before he ducked under the sign.

"Yeah, catch you later," Harris responded.

✖✖✖

A few streets from her house, Leah stopped walking. She turned to Ben and placed a hand on his arm. "We should stop here; I don't want anyone to see us."

He then placed the basket by his feet. "Thank you for a nice day; I had a lot of fun."

She smiled, the last rays of daylight sparkled in her eyes. "As did I, so am I going to see you again tomorrow?"

Ben shook his head. "Captain wants us to stay close to the ship tomorrow. He probably is going to ask us to do some last minute things. I mean, I'll be around the dockyards if you want to say goodbye."

He noticed her smile start to fade. She was thinking of that too soon goodbye. "Of course, what time are you leaving?"

"After morning colors, so if you could be here by like quarter to seven, that would be great."

She quickly picked up the basket and began to walk away. She turned her head and stared right through Ben. "Then I'll see you quarter to seven."

With that, he watched as her figure got smaller with every step.

22

DEPARTURE

She looked into Ben's eyes, staring deep into his pupils. She noticed a tear rolling down his cheek. Although they had only known each other for a couple of days, they held hands as if they were saying goodbye forever. After several moments passed she hugged Ben and kissed him on his wet cheek.

She sniffed to clear her nose, and then said, "Ben, I hope you have fair winds on your journey. Most of all, I have a gift for you."

She reached into a fold of her blouse, searched for her gift, and pulled out a beautiful locket. She placed it in Ben's hand and smiled.

"Open it."

As he stared in, he noticed a small painting of Leah. He studied the picture; he was surprised that at how closely it resembled her. He closed the locket, and then allowed Leah to place it around his neck. She did not notice the leather strip hidden beneath his shirt.

Ben needed to give her something; he reached into his pockets of his breeches, searching for anything. A sack of coins, a handful of nails; he then realized the cursed medallion still around his neck.

"Well, I guess I don't need this anymore; without the staff, the medallion is of no use. I guess this is the life I am destined to live…"

"Close your eyes."

He held the medallion in his hand for a moment. The realization of what he was giving up, weighed him down heavily.

"Open your eyes, dear."

If there were any combination of words to describe the expression on her face, Ben could think of none.

"Ben, it is beautiful. Where did you get it? It is pure gold."

He scratched his head. "Darling, this is my most treasured possession. It is nearly 150 years old, passed on from generation to generation. It has special powers and cannot fall into the wrong hands. This is why I entrust this to you. For you not only have my trust, you have my heart."

Her face flushed as he snuck in a kiss goodbye.

❉❉❉

The longshoreman took the eye of the hawsers off the bollard, untying the ship from the pier. The wind began to fill the sails; the vessel began its passage through the harbor. Ben stood, leaning out over the handrail as he waved to Leah. He screamed something to the distant figure, but the sound of the wind disrupted the message. The bows lifted to the harbor swell and the great ship began its voyage of adventure. Sailing southwards, the *Frendrich* headed for the straights of Florida, in which they would transit through and continue on to their destination of Havana.

Captain Nelson had scheduled combat practice, everyday after lunch. He said if they were ever to be attacked again, they would be well prepared. During the day, the vessel calculated its speed to be less than seven knots. Around midnight, the wind died down to a light breeze. The progression was turtle-like, going less than a knot.

Once out of sight of land, Captain Nelson called the four youngest crewmen into his quarters. Ben, Harris, Sal, and Jacob reported, thinking the worst.

"Afternoon lads are you all ready for a good day?" asked the man in charge of the *Frendrich*. They nodded. "Well, until we arrive in

Havana, I'm going to teach you some nooks and crannies about the ship each day. Celestial navigation will be the topic today."

He gathered the teens around his desk. On it was a nautical chart, dividers, triangles, and a pencil. "I guess I'll start off by introducing each item," he began, taking hold of the dividers. "You spread the legs of this tool, to measure distances or make markings on the chart." Next, he held up the triangles. "This enables you to slide your angles to advance or retard a fix, or just for a straight edge." After that, he held up the pencil, and with a straight face said, "And, this is a pencil."

The four laughed at the joke, and then began their work. "First you have to lay down the track line." He took the straight edge of the triangles and marked a line across the chart. "Next, we use an estimated speed to predict where we will be in a certain period of time," he paused for a second and then proceeded with the lesson, "Let's use five knots for the speed. My father taught me this when I was a kid, ultimately he taught me one of the most important rules of seafaring calculations, and it's called, sixty D-Street."

Puzzled faces looked at the captain. Nelson smiled, "Well, sixty, relates to an hour, sixty minutes in an hour. D is the distance you travel, S is the speed, and T is the time. So basically I can give sample problems now, and all you have to do is substitute the values into this equation."

He scribbled a handful of numbers on a scrap piece of paper: D=1.5 nm, S= 5 knots, T=?

He turned and faced the students, "I want you to think of the answer in your head. To be a proficient mariner, you have to go with your gut instinct, you have to know what to do at all times," he took out a windup pocket watch and looked at the time, it read 1105-15. "You have thirty seconds."

Each closed their eyes, carrying numbers in their head, dividing and multiplying number.

Ben called out, "Eighteen?"

The captain replied, "Good, very good. What if the time was six minutes, and we were solving for speed."

The four students again began thinking the problem out in their head. Jacob beat the others to it, "Fifteen!"

Nelson smiled, "Good. There's a rule of six. Any period of time divisible by six, twelve, twenty-four, etcetera, are all related to a fraction of an hour. Six of sixty would be one tenth; twelve of sixty would be one fifth and so on. I'll give you some problems to do by evening watch. Next on the list will be to lay the track line out. So now that we know how to figure out the distance to advance the fix, using speed and time, you just go from the last known position, to the estimated position, using the equation I just told you about. You guys got any questions?"

Nelson peered around to astute stares. Using the original question five knots, and thirty minutes for every fix, Nelson began marking lines on the chart. "So, every two and a half nautical miles, we would place a mark on the track line…"

"So you understand the concept of this?" there was a puzzled look on Jacob's face. "Well, say its 0800. You want to know roughly were you are in an hour, so at 0900, you have a decent idea using what I just showed you. Can anyone think of what could make us not be at our predicted spot?"

His eyes stared at each young man. Ben replied, "Change in speed?" Sal pondered for a moment and then said, "Change of course?" Harris now felt the eyes on him, almost staring directly through his body. He answered, "Maybe the wind pushed us off course?" Finally it was Jacob's turn. "Hmm, I would say something similar to the last one, but instead of wind, maybe the ocean itself. We could've drifted."

The captain beamed with content. "You lads will surely make a good crew. All you need is some more experience," he paused for a moment, "Oh yes; we have twenty minutes before noon."

"What happens at noon?"

Nelson looked at Jacob, "We're going to take a sight with a sextant, and then do some calculations to figure out what our latitude was at the time of the sight."

There were four nods, as Captain Nelson stood erect from his leaning position over the desk. He walked to the bookshelf that was carved into hull of the ship. His eyes moved from shelf to shelf, finally spotting the box that contained the sextant. His hands reached upwards and reached around each corner of the wooden box firmly. He rejoined the lads at their seated positions, placing the sextant on the table in front of them.

"All right, I guess I'll show you the parts of the sextant first. First off, can anyone tell me why a sextant, is called a sextant?"

He waited for an answer, but got none. His smile began to fade. Ben noticed this and raised a hand. "Um, well from what I've heard, a sextant is one sixth of a circle, or sixty degrees. They used to have octants for the navigation also, those instruments represented one eighth of a circle and are forty-five degrees."

Captain nodded his head, "Correct. Okay, so let's begin."

The captain gripped the wooden handle, caressing the instrument. "Be careful when working with these instruments. I've seen the ship roll; causing my shipmates to stumble, and then they drop it. Then we have to fix all the mirrors and readjust everything. I trust you all though, so I know that won't even be a problem.

"Well, what I am holding now, as you can guess, is a handle. What you put your eye to and look through is simply a scope. I've heard it called a telescope, or glass, but it really doesn't matter, it's all preference anyways. When looking through the scope, you will glance into the horizon mirror," his fingers began pointing to each part of the sextant, "The second mirror on this helpful tool is the index mirror, which is right here. For both sets of mirrors, there are several shades. Can anyone guess why we have these there?"

Harris squinted as he answered, "To protect the person's eyes."

The captain's face brightened once again with the student's progress. "Ha! Very good, so next, we have this pincher. We squeeze it to adjust the angle of the sight, bringing it down in the mirrors to align with the horizon. We finely tune it with this cylinder here, that's called the micrometer head; it has dashes and marks tenths of a degree. Do you guys see the notch here," he pointed to the window on the swinging arm of the sextant.

With nods of confirmation, he continued, "All right, so this is the arc. It's got numbers etched into it. When the sun, moon, or star is looked through in the index mirror, and then brought down to the horizon on the half horizon mirror, this reading on the arc is your observed altitude of the body. As this is read, have someone record the time of the observation. I'll get into more details later about the conversion of this number to finally the line of position."

The captain rubbed his goatee before speaking, "Hmm, so shall we go up on deck and take a noon sighting?"

The young men stood up, nodding, eager to learn everything the captain would teach.

✖✖✖

Once on deck, Ben felt the wind blowing across the deck. Ben breathed in the fresh air, feeling the sun's rays beating down through a cloudless sky. The five men walked to the starboard railing, the captain leading the group with the sextant in his left hand. Nelson took in the scenery, ocean in every direction, nothing in sight. "Well, judging by the height of the sun, we have a few minutes before we take the sight."

They waited paitently, eyes on the captain as he glanced upwards at the sky. With his free hand, Nelson dug into his pocket, taking out his windup watch. "Ben, would you do the honors in noting the time of the observation?" the captain turned to the rest, "You guys can stand beside me and watch the procedure."

Ben reached out, grasping the captain's heirloom. As he brought it to his eyes for closer inspection, he noticed every detail of the timepiece. "It sure is a beautiful watch, cap."

"It was my fathers," the captain gripped the wooden handle, lifting the sextant. After using his left eye for a rough estimate of the sun's location in the sky, he began adjusting the index arm with nimble and skilled fingers. "Watch what I do lads."

With all the mirror shades up, the sun's halo could be seen slightly. The next step would be to move one or two shades so that the entire sun's image could be seen next to the horizon, once the index arm was moved to allow that. His eyes watched as the sun's reflection in the mirror continued to ascend in the sky. Once it seemed to stop, he knew he only had a few seconds to take the sight before the sun would descend.

"Time?"

"1204-18."

Nelson now held the sextant out before him in plain view so that his students could easily see the reading in the index arm window. He then looked at the four faces on either side of him.

"So, does anyone know what 74.3 degrees is?"

Ben was about to speak, but thought he'd let someone else answer. Harris looked straight out into the horizon, clearly seeing the line between the dark blue ocean and the light blue sky. "It's an angle, so probably the angle between the sun and the horizon we brought it down to."

The captain nodded. "Let's go back to my quarters to finish up the calculation of Lattitude at LAN."

Once in the comfort of the his cabin, Nelson sat in his chair, and showed Ben, Harris, Sal, and Jacob the proper technique for a site reduction by doing a step-by-step mathematical procedure. The final result yielded a latitude of 25° 46.8' on the 23rd day of February, 1763.

"Good work lads, after doing this, you have to write it down in the logbook," he opened the journal that sat in the left corner of the desk and spread it before him, looking at Ben while doing this, "This is a good habit to do once you become the master of a ship. Well now that our work is done, let's go up and finish some chores and maybe we'll get Charles or Nate to teach some knots after the work day is finished."

"Aye captain," they replied.

After an afternoon full of manning the sails for maneuvering practice, the crew of the ship began to settle down and relax for a cozy night of music and song. It was several hours after sunset when Ben joined the group by the forward mast, as Marconi blew into a hand carved harmonica. The tune drifted in the night air for a moment, finally arriving to the expecting ears of the crowd. Nate Brodkin approached Ben and his three friends as they all stood amongst the men.

"Hey lad, shall I show ye some knots?"

Ben looked at Second Officer, watching as the broad shouldered man tossed the bitter end of a two-inch diameter line into the air. The coil of rope landed on the deck, just at the feet of Ben. With a quick flick of the wrist, Brodkin let the rope skip off the wooden deck, back into his awaiting hands.

Ben was impressed with the speed of hand, "Ah, nice! You got to show me some of the ins and outs of it."

Nate smiled, "You should see us when we have line throwing contests. The captain often wages an extra cup of rum to the winner. Charles and I are the victors almost every time, but if and when cap joins, he wins by a landslide."

As the conversation continued, Ben scanned around the deck for the captain, looking for the familiar swirl of blue smoke that emanated from his pipe. His focus shifted back to the man before him, and the group of four circled around the ship's officer.

"The first knot that we will tie is the bowline. If you know this, you pretty much can use it for anything."

He paused until he knew he had all eight eyes on his hands. "Here's a little saying I was taught many years ago," holding the bitter end in his hand, he continued. "Well, see this here bitter end? Picture this as a bunny rabbit, but before I get to this carrot eating creature, I'll start you off."

Holding the length of line in his hands, he made a loop using his right hand. Pinching the loop with his left thumb, he picked up the bitter end with his right hand.

"All right, so we have a hole, and there's this curious bunny. He can smell a bunch of fresh carrots that the hunter has picked out to use as bait from his backyard garden. The rabbit stirs from the Earth, coming out of his little bunny hole. The hunter smiles, knowing his lure worked. It brings out the carrot, but luckily for the bunny, he smells the hunter hiding in a bush. In a mad dash, he runs around the tree to confuse the hunter. Just as the hunter began to chase, the bunny dove back into the safety of his home, evading the man."

"Sounds like an episode of Bugs Bunny," Sal glanced towards the Manry brothers.

He received a smile and the slightest chuckle, if any, from Ben. Sometimes Sal got carried away with his attempts at humor, but the brothers were so used to it that it didn't matter.

The captain continued, "So, now that you have all been taught the beautiful knot story, share the line and practice. I'm going to join the captain for a pipe and then we'll continue the lessons another time."

"Sounds good," said the group.

✖✖✖

A week passed as the winds were fair, increasing their progression to their destination. McCafferey stood before a crowd of sailors. He cleared his throat and began, "All of ye shall listen, because this is extremely important in a fight. The swivel gun, or patarero, as it is also known, is used like this," he placed a hand along the barrel. "This is one of the most priced weapons on board because it can be mounted any where on deck where there is a mount, thus increasing potential damage. You see, first you mount it like this," he lifted the entire contraption until the vertical mount slipped into the bracket. "After mounting, you can see how it has the capability to move in a three hundred and sixty degree circle. The best is grape shot, because of its wide spread and anti-personnel capability."

Ben was listening intently. Storing the information he had a feeling he might need later. The carpenter, Henry Hughson, had made a target using a barrel connected to a ten feet long board. He had painted a face and a Spanish captain's hat secured to the top of the barrel. He secured it to the grab rail and the practice began.

The mass of people wandered to the starboard side, watching McCafferey with determination and awe. He double-checked the powder and ran through the process mentally and then said aloud to the bystanders, "Are you ready mates? Stand back."

He aligned the sight with the target and then placed a match to the hole. After a slight delay, a loud explosion broke the silence as the deadly projectiles were fired out. The shards smashed through the barrel, breaking it into pieces. When Ben looked over to where it was, two things remained; the rope that it had been secured with and the board it was tied to.

McCafferey said aloud, "Now ye mates know the power of the weapon. Next is hand to hand combat training."

Harris shook his head and then said, "Sal, imagine shooting that into an enemy of boarding pirates. That would mow them down."

Even seeing this weapon in the fight against El Perro Loco, Sal was still perplexed by what he just saw, and could only nodded in agreement.

☠☠☠

McCafferey came back on deck and walked up to the group of men that were singing and talking. "We've an order to tack portside, until we reach Havana. So I want you to split into two groups, and adjust the sails."

Gray clouds moved in with great speed, blanketing the sun, causing day to turn to night. The dense fog limited visibility to less than a quarter mile. You would be lucky to stand on the stern, look towards the bow and see the foremast. The decks became slick with rain, making walking dangerous, and the risk of being washed overboard increased substantially. Ben's body was soaking wet just after a few minutes of the hard rain. The sky above swallowed them whole; the gray clouds the whale, the ship the minnow.

Rain crashed heavily upon the deck at his feet. He looked up, seeing several figures hanging dangerously in the shrouds while others were on deck beside him hauling in lines. Behind the two men, Ben put his full body weight into each tug on the block and tackle.

His fingers were slick and he felt the line slipping though his hands. He struggled to keep his grip but the lines continued to spill out. Muttering through the pain, he stressed his body until he heard a voice call to him from in front of him. He looked up to the faces of the captain and Marconi.

He liked these opportunities of challenge and disorder, a firm believer in the learning process of the sea.

"Before we begin a valuable lesson," he looked into the faces of Ben and Charles, "we'll help you secure this line."

Between the three, they hauled in the remaining fifty feet, wrapped it around a cleat, and tied it off securely. "Ah, all right. So it seems we have found a storm. What do you think it is?"

Charles brushed his hair with the back of his hand; bullets of water flew from his knuckles. "Well, it isn't good. From my observations, it could be a squall, with very strong winds, upwards of fifty knots."

Nelson nodded, "Well, what can we do to stop this thing from causing damage to my vessel?"

"We need to minimize the sail area or the canvas will be destroyed by the wind, which we're doing now. We need to ride it out. Hope that the rigging and masts don't break," Marconi answered, "That's all we can do."

Nelson nodded with the input, "Charles, you are dismissed to attend your duties, Benjamin, tag along with the mate. Just remember that the weather is like a woman, fierce and unrelenting if they are upset, but can also be lovely and most desirable. Mother Nature is feminine for that reason, for if weather we like us men, it'd be hell to pay all the time," he slapped Ben on the shoulder with a hearty laugh. "Ha! Now go off and help Marconi."

Rain pellets the size of marbles crashed down from the skies. Lightning and thunder made it difficult to perform their duties. Ben was now in the shrouds, shortening sail. Hand over hand, Ben pulled up the heavy cloth. Once hauled in, the crew tied rope around it, securing the sail from the devastating winds. Even without the canvas flying, the *Frendrich* was still making fifteen knots. All were seasick as the ship bobbed up and down. The storm was at its worst now, pitch-black skies, and blankets of rain pouring down. The schooner tilted to twenty degrees causing three men slip, one of which was Jacob. None of the three feel overboard, but Jacob was injured and brought below into sickbay.

❌❌❌

The after mast split in half by a tremendous gust of wind of sixty miles per hour and all they could do was head into the waves and ride the storm out. Another hour passed and Nelson took out his spyglass. He scanned the limited view, but saw something disastrous. Just a quarter mile ahead was a large island. In the back of his mind, he was certain of would happen.

The crew received an order, hoping to save the vessel from the devilish storm. Marconi's voice rang out for all ears, "Let out anchor, it's the only way."

Steering was impossible at this point; the storm controlled the ship's every move. His hopes were to create a drag and avoid the island, but no one could predict what may happen in a storm like this. Nelson walked carefully to Marconi and tapped the man on the shoulder.

He seemed white as a ghost, shivering from the cold wind, "Charles. I've some good news and a whole lot of bad news. Which do you want first?"

He looked at the Nelson, "The bad."

"The storm is taking us straight into the island. The good thing is that we could possibly find shelter, if we're *lucky*."

Marconi looked into the worried eyes of Nelson, reading his thoughts. "All right captain. Any other commands, sir?"

"No, but nature's a bitch at times, especially now. Go, muster the men and get the longboats ready."

23

elson watched Marconi herd the men to one side of the boat as a sudden jolt knocked his balance. The schooner crashed into a large rock off the coast of the island. The ripping of planks under them made Ben's face pale. He heard cracks as the deck beneath him began to break in half.

The bow and the stern both lifted, as the boat turned acute. Ten men flew off landing on the sharp, jagged rocks below, sending them to a painstaking death. Of the two longboats, one survived the initial impact. He then remembered that Jacob had slipped earlier, losing consciousness from a blow to the head. He was in sickbay strapped to a table, the knowledge of potentially losing someone he had grown so close to ate at his heart and head. He rushed down the flights of companionways, bumping off each side as the storm had its way with the vessel.

Moments later, Ben entered the room as the water was at ankle level and rising quickly. He was in a hurry and could not afford to delay their escape any longer. After releasing Jacob from the straps, he reached down and tossed the frail body onto his shoulder.

Jacob's head bobbed as Ben took each step at full gait. "What's going on, my head hurts," he moaned.

"Shhh, we're almost out."

Ben ran through the doorway and up the staircase with the heavy body on his right shoulder. He nearly slipped on the wet deck until he reached the starboard side. "Captain, wait."

Nelson looked over and pulled hard on the rope to stop the boat from proceeding downwards. "Get in now! There's not a second to delay!!"

Ben put Jacob down gently on his feet. The long boat was three feet below the railing, but he handed his injured friend to the awaiting hands of Henry, who took his son's head and secured his body into a seated position. Ben then leaped in immediately after and squashed into the crowded boat. They sat down and looked up.

Nelson released the rope and jumped into the boat as the longboat crashed into the undulating waters below. The captain held an oar and pushed as hard as he could to free the longboat from the suction created between the vessels. Each man had an oar in a hand and began the laborious row towards the island. Even though the storm was fading, it was still strong enough to make the progress excruciatingly difficult. In just a few short minutes, the crew's arms were fatigued from the strenuous rowing.

Once the boat finally touched bottom on the sandy beach, they jumped out and pulled the longboat to the forest's borderline. Nelson turned to Ben, there was a serious expression on his face as he looked to Ben and said, "Ben, I need you to make a list of the dead, and see what supplies we have with us. Report back as fast as you can."

"Aye, cap."

The high force winds and heavy rain continued to fall. Ben looked at the survivors, making a mental chart of who were present, then he thought about who had died. He talked to every man to see what the individual had managed to grab before the ship went down. Ben then searched the long boat from the bow to the stern and realized the seriousness of their situation.

Ben approached the captain, listing the men who died the moment he stood face to face with Nelson. After a few seconds of hesitation he continued, "On the longboat I counted two handguns, one musket, one machete, some gunpowder, and a cask of fresh water. Our crewmen have some valuables, and Henry has two swords. Clayton Burns has his medic kit with him too."

Nelson stared with approval, "Good work lad. As long as this storm is still churning like it is, we need to make camp and get out of this blasted rain."

The surviving eleven men dug a large trench, two feet deep and eighteen feet long. Then they flipped the heavy boat over and propped it against a tree. Now they could sit relatively comfortably under the protection of the boat and the enormous palm leaves. The men positioned themselves side by side, keeping warm under the protection of the boat above them. Most fell asleep right away, but the noise of the storm was enough to make Ben stay conscious. After about two hours he finally fell asleep between bouts of uncontrollable shivering.

✖✖✖

It was about six in the morning when Ben awoke to a bright and sunny morning. He sat up to find the rest still asleep. He crawled from under the boat and stood up. Cracking his back and he was ready to start the day. He reached for Leah's gift around his neck and opened the clasp, viewing the water-soaked painting. Ben walked down to the water's edge with a sense of hope after dreaming about her blonde hair and beautiful smile. The fine sand felt comfortable under Ben's shoeless feet. He walked in a figure eight along the beach and saw a crippled body wash up. He suddenly ran over to it and realized the familiar face. It was Corey Fester, and though dead, still had his menacing grin that was typical of his personality.

Ben knelt down and smacked the man's face to see if there was any life in the body. He felt for a pulse, but he was long dead. He dragged the limp body back to the longboat. He dropped the water-logged corpse onto the ground and walked back down to the beach. His eyes searched the surrounding area to see if anything else floated from the wreckage. He saw pieces of wood, empty crates, and a sail, but nothing else. On his last crusade back, he noticed Brodkin and

Marconi in the process of making a large bonfire. Ben placed an empty crate on the ground next to them and said, "Top of the morning guys, I searched the beach and found some things."

Brodkin nodded and replied, "Well, good morning Ben, we can use some of it."

After all were awake and talking, an announcement rang through Ben's ears. Nelson stood on a large sand dune, clearing his throat to get everyone's attention. "I just need to tell you this. If we're to survive on this island, we'll need to live here for a while. In an hour, we'll row out to the *Frendrich* and see what is salvageable."

Ben was curious to explore the island. He walked away entering the forest beside camp, following game trails. He walked for fifteen minutes and emerged roughly a half mile's walk from the bonfire. He was whistling to himself as he strolled back into the camp.

Harris looked up from the spear he was carving out of a sapling, "What you up to?"

"Just walked along a few animal trails, trying to get some alone time. I figured it'd be a good idea."

"Nice. Check this out, it's pretty sharp so far. I've been sharpening it since you left."

He nodded to his brother to give him the spear. Ben weighed it in his hand, tossing it softly up and down. Finally, after approving of the weapon's potential, he gripped the spear in the middle of the shaft. He eyed a bush that was just several paces away. As he stepped forward with his left foot, his body contorted and the spear spiraled through the air, wiggling sideways in mid-flight, slamming to a halt as the missile ripped through the bushes' leaves.

"It needs more balance, but overall it's not bad. Maybe shave off some weight along the shaft."

He looked at his brother. "Yeah, I agree. Do you want me to make you one?"

Ben nodded, "Yeah. I think I hear Nelson's voice. Save it for later."

❉❉❉

The captain called for another meeting, "Well, it is time to journey back to the *Frendrich*. We'll take six men; the five others will make a shelter. Brodkin, Sal, Harris, Ben, and Marconi will accompany me. Any questions men?"

They walked the longboat to the water's edge, placing it down gently. After sliding the boat out a few feet, the six men stepped in. With an oar in each man's hands, the boat proceeded slowly against the current that crashed slowly into the beach. The oarlocks rotated with each pull as the blades reached into the water. Stroke after stroke, the vessel made progress towards the wrecked ship. Only the stern remained wedged atop the jagged rocks, for the sailor's sake, the tide was not strong enough to completely pull the section under. Somewhere, in an area of about sixteen hundred square feet, the bow section sat on the bottom of the ocean.

Captain Nelson threw down the sea anchor to keep the longboat steady. For several moments, they discussed a plan of action while studying the ruins of the *Frendrich*, the vessel that had brought adventure, and recently misfortune. Ben was thinking of the dangers of boarding the boat.

Ben stroked his chin, finally coming up with something. "Captain, we have no chance of boarding the *Frendrich* again, the stability would be completely off. It's too dangerous. We might be able to drag the section back to our camp."

All were silent; picturing what had just been said. Nelson was thinking out loud, "That could actually work. You're right about not going onto the *Frendrich* due to the danger, but it seems like you might have an idea."

Marconi added in, "Well, I suppose we could make two rafts. Somehow attach them to the boat and float her back to the island. Then we could use the boat for wood. Who knows, it just might work."

Nelson was proud of his men. "Now that we have a plan, let's secure the *Frendrich* to the rock, so it doesn't float away. Though it's wedged, I'd rather have more than one safety precaution."

Ben thought of something else, "Captain, the *Frendrich* is caught up on its own rigging, it's not going anywhere. It'd take something drastic, like the storm that brought us here, to knock her off the rocks."

Brodkin gave it a thought, "Ben's right, the rigging's enough to hold the *Frendrich* here. It would be a waste of rope, rope that we don't have. We need to focus on surviving on the island first. The *Frendrich* should come later."

Nelson nodded in agreement, "Yes, yes, you're both right. Let's head to camp. We'll discuss this later when all are present."

☠☠☠

The sun reached its apex when work began again. The captain ordered Ben and Harris to go off and explore, the goal for the mission was to find edible plants and to hunt if possible. Sal and Henry Hughson went to look for a source of water. The remaining seven searched for material to finish the shelter.

Harris led the way through the dense forest, stepping over fallen trees and around small rocks. They were twenty minutes into the hunt when Harris paused. "Hey, let's take a break; my feet are beginning to hurt."

Ben was also feeling miserable and they sat down on a fallen log, talking silently when he heard a noise from a place high in a tree. Ben craned his head and looked straight up. Up the palm tree, leaves were shaking, causing two coconuts to fall. The large nuts fell at the feet of the relaxing young men.

Ben whispered to his brother, "Give me your spear. I think I can get it, whatever 'it' is."

Harris handed his brother the long spear, placing the weapon into Ben's eager hands. He then balanced the spear in the middle of the shaft and began the process of the throw. His arm went back as he located the rustling leaves and released. The spear flew from his hands with speed, spiraling through the air. Through the leaves the spear flew, and then there was a strange, almost eerie sound.

Thud.

The spear crashed through the palm leaves, getting stuck into a small coconut. Almost a split second later, a larger object fell to the ground, landing lightly on its feet. The small monkey ran off, but then turned around to face its attackers. It eyed the humans with curiosity just as the humans eyed the animal.

Only thinking of food, Ben reached into his pocket for a knife, but it was too late, the monkey screeched and then hobbled away, climbing high into a neighboring tree.

"Well, that failed," Harris said sarcastically.

"Not really, what about the coconuts?" Ben asked.

Without hesitation, he ran towards the large palm tree and climbed fifteen feet up. As Ben held onto the limb, he noticed the spear sticking out of a coconut. There was a milky substance oozing from the hole once Ben freed the spear. He lifted the coconut high and drank the sour milk until there was nothing left. Pulling off several coconuts from the tree, he hailed Harris and then began dropping the large nuts one by one.

"Collect the nuts I throw down. It's about time something's going right."

An hour later, the brothers walked into camp, a dozen coconuts in each shirt used as a stretcher. They dropped their loads next to a small hut that was half completed. The brothers dozed off for not even five minutes, when a large commotion broke the silence of the camp.

A swarm of bees followed Sal and Henry along the beach, bees that have never been seen by white man. They were extremely large, the size of thumbs; their stingers were four inches long, and their bodies black and orange.

The buzzing blocked out the sound of the screaming men. The rapidly moving cloud was several feet behind. They nearly stampeded Ben's outstretched legs; the commotion caused them to jump immediately.

Ben gazed at the scene and said the first thing that came to his mind, shouting over the disorder, "Jump into the water."

They jerked left, heading straight for the rolling surf. Henry, an old man compared to Sal was running stride for stride. In one giant leap, the two dove headfirst into the water, allowing the waves to crash over their heads. Upon being submerged, the bees circled around, hesitating, and then returned into the jungle.

Sal and Henry walked back to the hut after waiting a minute. They sat down across from their friends who had just witnessed the humorous event. The remaining seven returned to camp, finding many long, plank-like posts.

"Ben and Harris, did you find any food?"

Ben replied, "Yes, captain. We could only carry two dozen coconuts though; I figure I'll trek back in there with maybe a sail or something, so we can carry out more."

"Great," Nelson paused and turned to the soaking wet Sal and Henry, "And what happened to you two?"

Henry took responsibility, speaking for both of them, "Well cap, we were looking for fresh water, we found a stream about two miles that way," Henry pointed to the north of the camp, "Then we were chased by bees of enormous size, I've never seen anything like them."

"Of course you have never seen them, you've never been on this island before!" said the captain trying to lighten the situation.

"Cap, that's not what I mean. I'm talking about a species I've never seen before. They're orange and black and extremely large; the size of thumbs, with stingers four inches long."

Before the captain could say anything, Sal chimed in. "Captain, we need protection from these bees!"

Nelson was a little irritated after that comment, "Well then, just what do you think we should do?"

Sal's expression was blank, "Cap, I have no clue what we should…"

Ben had enough, "Guys, the only way to prevent contact with these bees of yours is to finish this shelter."

Nelson was surprised by Ben's quick comment, but liked his attitude resembling leadership. Leadership was greatly needed if they were to survive here.

"This boy Ben, just a young man, has so much leadership potential. He reminds me of myself when I was a lad. He will soon be my right hand man in my future dealings, but he's still unaware of our true intentions. Well, it shouldn't matter now, at least not yet."

Nelson nodded in agreement, "You're right. Let's finish it as soon as possible. The sun's strong now; we need shelter from this heat. It'll be getting warmer everyday now too."

❊❊❊

The next morning came by fast and with time, hunger. The fresh water and food supply were dwindling quickly. With the captain quite impressed by Ben's marksmanship, he appointed him the hunter and Harris the weapon maker. The remaining men continued construction on their quarters; thatching palm leaves for a roof to the sleeping and supply huts.

Ben decided he would find the stream that Sal had found after walking along the beach. He enjoyed the water as it brushed the bottom of his toes. He pressed on, searching for any marine life that was within a reasonable distance, but there was nothing but water. He then approached an opening into the dense forest and stepped through. Palm trees loomed overhead, along with many unknown flora species. He searched high in the branches and overturned logs and rocks for anything of value to eat.

He continued on, but found nothing that would provide sustenance. He approached a clearing and heard a sound. About fifty feet ahead of him was the stream, a beautiful stream that meant life. He ran for it and once there, stuck his head in. The rush of cold water on his sun baked body felt refreshing. After taking a long drink, he stood up and made a swift circular path back towards camp. About a hundred feet away, Ben noticed fallen coconuts. After scrounging the ground for ten minutes, he had a large pile in front of him.

Pulling off his cotton shirt, he tied off both sleeves and placed the coconuts inside the makeshift sack.

✖✖✖

Around the fireplace, the group was singing songs and telling stories of adventures and treasures. The first to speak was Henry Hughson, "Back when I was thirteen, I worked with my father in his shop. I was his apprentice, learning the skills of carpentry. Then one day he died and I took over. Business grew until I had a premier shop, money flowed in and I became rich. Then I married Jacob's mother. Well, a few years later Jacob was born.

"Those ten years or so were the most productive years for my business. So to celebrate I took a vacation, well not really, and I joined an eighty-foot boat, and I sailed around the Atlantic for two years while Jacob was in a private school. On that sloop, one of my greatest adventures happened. There was a storm, worse than the one that sunk our ship. I rode it out and finally it was over. The rain stopped completely, as did the wind and my crew was forced to let the current have its way with us.

"Before we reached home safely, the Spanish pirate named Captain Blood Bones attacked us. We were lucky to survive, because rumor is he usually eats the captured men, or sells them to slavery. He and his cousin, Blood Spot roam the Caribbean, if you ever meet them, you will be grateful to be sold into slavery because my friend, Sam, was eaten while still alive.

"Anyways, after our boat was captured, I escaped with three others in a small rowboat when the pirates were all drunk. We rowed home to safety, about ten miles."

He cleared his throat and continued on, "Well, it happened on a dark and dreary night, such as this night. My captain told me to stand the portside watch, along with my friend Sam, the one eaten alive. Anyway, I took out my scope and scanned the horizon. I focused on a blurry object about a mile off. I awoke the captain and told him of the news. I said 'Cap, they be pirates to the port, a mile and closing.' Well, our fifty men gathered our weapons and prepared for the deadly battle. Later we found out that the pirates had about five times our men, so we knew we had no chance for a straight up fight. That's how Blood Spot and Blood Bones are so successful; they either outnumber or completely deceive their enemies.

"Well, we tacked back and forth, shooting broadsides of grape. Then we loaded with chain to take down their masts. I saw the cannon ball wrap around the mast, breaking it into a million splinters. After a day of chase, they seemed to give up, but oh were we wrong. That night we took it easy; we drank and sang, celebrating our lives. I was asleep on my hammock on deck, swinging lightly to the roll of the ocean under our keel. Sometimes I hate sleeping below decks, that night was different however. Well, I heard a noise; it sounded like a fallen sword. My eyes adjusted from the sleep, and I saw five men climbing over the railing. I knew there was trouble so I unsheathed my sword. Before the first man made it over, I had slain the first raiding party. I called out to the watch, and soon our men were engaged. Attack after attack we drove them back, until they lost half their men. The pirates still had the edge, and the fight was in their favor, almost two to one.

"I had command of a swivel gun. I loaded and reloaded the small gun. After shooting into the hoards of pirates, I took down a dozen at a time. This is just one reason we killed so many. The other reason is that we weren't taken by surprise thanks to me. Well, they came in from behind us somehow and slaughtered my crew. I was taken prisoner, along with a few others who surrendered. And like I said before, we escaped when the pirates were intoxicated."

All were clapping at the terrific tale; it was well spoken and interesting. Jacob had a dumbstruck look on his face throughout his father's entire story. Ben said aloud, "That was the best story I've ever heard! I'll tell one now."

The men sat in silence, and then Ben spoke at last. "Back, into a time no one will ever see again, an adventure occurred. This is a tale of a treasure hunt, of the pirate named Blood Bones," the audience gasped again at the sound of the horrible pirate, "Harris, Sal, and I found his treasure. We walked impassible places, climbed high mountains, and accomplished the most difficult of obstacle courses.

"Then, as we were sitting in front of a treasure room, filled with diamonds, pearls, and coins, something dreadful occurred. That was the day we three were sent back into time, roughly two hundred and fifty years. What we knew as home was the twentieth century, where we had inventions that would make dreamers cry. This was a time of peace and prosperity, where our nation, the United States triumphed. It was a time were one could feel lost, but would always be with friends. I miss my home, my family, and the friends I once had, but I probably will never see them again. So I must focus on my new life, my new home, and my new friends," Ben raised his arms, pointing to all.

He continued on, "We must survive this island, so we can live out our destiny to a full and happy life, whether we know what it has in store for us, we must look forward to it. The night we were locked up for being thought stowaways was the changing point of our lives. Now I must succeed in my new life, defeat pirates and help save princesses. This is what must happen."

Ben bowed as he finished his last lines, then he sat down looking into the flames of the burning fire. Jacob had a funny smile on his face; he was getting better from his injury everyday, gaining more strength as he helped out more with the construction of the camp. He stood up slowly and said, "Well done my friend. For all you've said is true, because friendship is more important than materials, and I'm glad to have you as a friend, for you have saved my life, in a time that seemed so long ago."

They walked towards each other and clasped hands by the fire-light, the bond of brotherhood contagious amongst the men. More stories were told, more clapping, and of course, the unions of friend-ship growing stronger with each moment passed on the island.

24

Weeks passed as the men dwelled upon the island, searching for food and large trees for the construction of the rafts. John Borton walked along a game trail, eyeing a dense bush that obstructed his path. He paused when he heard a rustling of leaves on the hilltop. Through the leaves, he could see the whites of a boar's eyes. The colossal beast, a member of the largest-sized animals that inhibited the island, could kill a man in seconds. It weighed close to two hundred pounds, all muscle. Its razor sharp tusks could rip a man into shreds.

The boar targeted Borton and charged at him, lowering its head to take the victim at the knees. About fifty feet away, John noticed the heavy steps as the boar pressed on. Aware that something was wrong, he screamed out loud to warn Ben and Brodkin of the trouble about to occur. It had been a month since the wreckage at this time and they were well prepared: all three had a bow and a quiver of arrows with them and were also armed with the pointy spears that Harris made.

Ben stared at the scene, calculating the place where he should shoot to bring the boar down with his large fifty-pound pull bow. He took aim, muscles straining at the effort. He released the string. He later would consider this the ultimate test of skill, being the best hunter with the bow as well as the spear. He once took down a large bird, flying at a high altitude. Another time he had hit a fish with his spear.

But this time it was different; the arrow missed its mark, nailing the boars mid-section. Instead of an instant death, the boar stumbled. The men could not pass this opportunity with the animal on the ground momentarily. They took aim as the boar rose to full height again, about twenty feet away with its eyes full of rage. Ben placed another arrow into the boar, penetrating the right lung. But it was still not enough.

✖✖✖

Brodkin had also let loose two arrows that struck the shoulder and the hip, both doing absolutely no damage. John eyed the boar as it continued on its enraged stumble towards him. The boar was right at his feet when he jumped to the side just in time to avoid being trampled. The spear was thrust right into the neck, penetrating the vocal chord. The boar's knees gave out as flesh met ground. John pulled out his knife for the final kill, slitting the boar's neck from side to side, and then plunged the blade into its heart.

As he was doing this, Ben and Brodkin were at their friend's side, with spears ready for any new development.

"Wow, this meat will last for a few months," Brodkin said with a little smile as he wiped his blade on the boar's thick skin.

"Yeah, I'm happy we can eat something else besides fish and coconuts, but it wouldn't have been worth dying over."

Ben replied as he lowered his spear, "I know what you mean. Johnny, I'm so sorry my arrow missed the first time. You gave me a scare; most men would've been run through."

John had just turned twenty-three the other day, and with the months of continuous labor, strings of muscle grew on his arms. "I thank you both for your help, if you were anywhere but here, I might have not been eating with you by the campfire tonight."

Ben was a man now, gaining thirty pounds of solid muscle. He had great marksmanship with weapons and equally talented in hand-to-hand combat, due the captain's training program.

"All right, we need a long pole and some rope, this boar's going to be heavy..." Brodkin said to his fellow hunters.

Ben reached into a hip-sack that he made of piece of sailcloth, pulling out a length of line. "This long enough?" he asked.

"Yeah, that'll work; just cut it into equal halves. Johnny, look where I'm pointing," he angled his hand to the right. "Bring that over."

Borton reached down for the eight-foot long pole. The hunters worked together in the tedious process of tying the boar to the pole and then began the laborious work of carrying the beast back to camp.

✹✹✹

That night by the fire, John told of their adventure. All were attentive and enjoyed the good story, there was much added however to make the tale larger than life. After telling a short recital of his background, the men talked of the future plans.

Nelson called the attention of the group, "With us, the surviving eleven, it will be difficult to get back to civilization. We need those rafts completed as soon as possible, because there's something extremely valuable in my vault. Something that will be split amongst us equally, for you have all contributed so much to the survival of our party. We have just begun the first raft, and progress is slow, but it can be done, and it will. We are strong men, capable of anything."

The discussions lasted for hours until the stars filled the night sky, and all fell asleep where they were seated. Ben observed his friends and had a sudden flashback to his old life, of a lazy weekend morning after having friends sleep over. This was different though, he didn't just go down to the kitchen and pop some bread into a toaster or pull out some leftovers from the fridge, he had to build weapons, hunt, and survive only by the means he himself possessed.

✹✹✹

The next morning, all was well. Jacob was in good health and had recovered completely. The men had cut the boar into strips and smoked the meat, enjoying it during the months of vigorous work, making rope out of the bark of saplings. This process of fabricating rope took days on end to make just ten feet. For weeks, they split the group up. Ben and Harris the hunters, the rest either made rope, or looked for logs. All day they worked, eating the jerky and drinking fresh water from the stream.

One morning Ben ventured down along the beach, on a comfortable stroll to clear his mind. His bed was made of four logs tied together with small sticks tied across to make a frame. He covered the frame with palm leaves and then put moss on for additional support. It was a comfortable bed and most of the men had copied the design.

His eyes then saw something floating in the corner of his eye, about a dozen feet off shore. It was his backpack and ironically, his only possession from his previous live came back to him. The crew's quarters were in the stern of the *Frendrich* and the bag must have floated out of the wreckage.

Ben did not hesitate a second and ran for it, splashing through the warm water. He scooped up the waterlogged pack. Glad to see it, Ben sprinted back to camp excitedly. He dumped the contents out next to the palm leaves that made up his bed, scattering the items onto the sand. The hatchet was still there, a case of waterproof matches, a flashlight with dead batteries, and a length of rope. The rest must have fallen out of the hole that appeared along the backing, but he was still lucky to have some of his things.

"Thank god my mom got me this awesome bag, it floats, it's strong, and it's lasted since grade school!"

✖✖✖

Using the Hughson's swords and the newly retrieved hatchet, Harris made many weapons and new ammo. The arrows were now straighter and more efficient. The first raft was complete after a little less than a month and a half. It was large enough for seven men comfortably and if need be, it could fit all eleven, but would be crowded.

To test the raft's effectiveness the captain chose four men to row out to the *Frendrich* as a trial for sea-worthiness.

They paddled until they were near the rock. The crew cheered and raised their hats in a salute when the stern section revealed itself to still be salvageable. After paddling around the area, the general consensus was that their plan could actually work. They rowed back to report the news to the others.

The night went by fast, but as the new day arose, there was a problem...

✖✖✖

"Someone, or something, broke into our food supply during the night. And if it's someone that means we're not alone on this island. If it's something, we must keep a lookout for any wild boars," the captain stated as they sat around the fireplace, with empty stomachs.

Ben closed his eyes, thinking, "The door was closed, and tied. That means if it were a something, it'd need to have hands."

"Captain, I think I know what did it..."

"You're saying that that monkey did this?" his brother asked with a weird look on his face.

"Sure, why not? Maybe it followed us after we ran into it by the coconut tree."

The captain rubbed his beard, going unshaven since the ordeal began. "You know what, that is feasible. We must keep an eye out for it, but until then we must get more food. Ben, you know what to do."

✖✖✖

Ben, Harris, and Jacob were elected for an overnighter to hunt. Carrying the pack on his shoulders, Ben led the way through the dense jungle. They hiked towards the stream to get a drink; the humidity and the heat of the island was overpowering. Staring towards the mountains about five miles north, they traveled quickly.

He slashed through foliage, making a way for the others. They walked another mile uphill until they heard the familiar gurgling sound. Each man washed his face and hands, and then drank until their stomachs hurt. The day only grew hotter as their brows consistently had to be wiped from sweat. They continued on, walking uphill until the brook was out of sight. The terrain grew difficult now, making it arduous to hike the hills without having to zigzag around obstacles. Finally the ground became level and the group could see the mountain peaks ahead.

✖✖✖

*H*arris stared up at the peak, his mouth hung loose. "Wow that's high. It must be at least a mile high."

Jacob nodded with agreement. "Well, I think we should start the climbing now and camp in the middle."

"Yeah," Ben said, "that'd be the best thing to do. Let's take a few minutes to rest and then we'll start climbing."

The group sat chatting for ten minutes and then began the long trek up the steep hill making good time. The first mile of the winding trail was a piece of cake for them, only getting difficult once the mountainside turned nearly vertical. Ben looked around for another way up, but saw nothing.

"Guys," Ben said with a hint of bad news, "I think we have to climb this section, it looks about twenty or so feet. After that I'm sure there will be level ground."

Ben started up the cliff side, placing his hands into small crevices, lifting himself higher up the wall. He hesitated because there were no grips overhead. To solve this problem, he climbed sideways a few feet and continued his way up the peak. Placing a hand on a small outcropping, Ben pulled himself up. Swinging his leg over the ridge, Ben stood erect. Looking down, he gave acknowledgement for the others to climb up.

Harris craned his head back to see his brother waving down. "How was it?"

Ben replied, "Easy. Just begin to climb five feet to your right, there's not too many holds where I started."

Harris walked down two paces and then stared up. He was talking to himself for encouragement, psyching himself for the challenge. Remembering the American Gladiators he used to watch on television, he spit in his hands, and rubbed the moisture in. He began the ascent slowly, but he finished with the help of Ben's tug on his shoulder. Jacob started climbing once he saw Harris's foot vanish over the ledge.

About a half-minute later, the three men were drinking from their boar skin canteens. They started off again, following an animal trail that led around a large boulder. The group hacked its way through the dense vegetation. As Ben moved a branch to clear his view, something very unusual appeared before their eyes.

25

IRAJAN VILLAGE

A village containing roughly twenty huts emerged into view. Ben could only assume that the largest shelter was the chief's. He studied the intricate statues that surrounded the doorway from afar, taking in the scene he remembered in several of the history lessons back at school.

"Hey, what ya'll think we should do?" Jacob tapped Ben on the shoulder.

Ben hesitated, pondering for an answer. "Well, I suppose we can avoid it. If there's one village, there'll probably be more."

The group stood there for a minute, planning a route. "Yeah, you're right," Harris replied in a whisper, "Let's find away around it."

A loud crunching of twigs in the form of a footstep was heard, then another, and yet another.

"Ahiko sum taka et bega!"

A warrior standing six feet tall stood with a spear, his muscles shining in the light that shone through the leaves above.

"Ahiko sum taka et bega! Ya Hinda, su trepas a ur vilge!"

Five others jumped from around, hidden amongst the vines. One warrior, standing to Ben's chin, repeated the lines that Hinda said. There was brown and black paint covering his olive colored skin.

The only clothing worn by these tribal people was loin clothes tied around the waist.

"I am Ben, the leader of my people. This here is my brother Harris and my friend Jacob," he gestured with his hands, spreading them as wide as possible.

"Taka ahiko taka!"

"What are they saying?" Haris asked, "I've never heard this language."

Ben replied, "Well, I don't want to find out. On the count of three, let's run."

Silence hung in the air, no one moving in the stand off, "One…two…three."

The three men ran in different directions, knocking down anyone who stood in their way. Ben wrestled with a man about his age. He was huge, muscles stretching as Ben struggled in the man's grip.

Harris struggled with the man who introduced himself, his sharpened spear ready to take a life.

"Taka ya Hinda!"

Harris threw a solid right, catching the warrior in the cheek, "Well, I'm Harris!"

Meanwhile, Jacob broke through the line of men and managed to break through a patch of bushes. Stumbling over a fallen log, Jacob continued on, darting between bushes and small trees that lined the game trail. For five minutes he ran, not looking back for fear of being captured.

Harris and Ben were cornered. Nowhere to retreat to, they had to fight or surrender.

"Taka ahiko. Com prisner. Ya Lepo!"

The brothers looked at the old man, around sixty years of age. After several moments of studying the figure, Ben thought he was the leader by the way he carried himself and gave orders to his men. The brothers were then herded, walking in a tight-knit group until they emerged in the village.

Ben noticed the young playing in the street, the women making baskets, and the men smoking through some sort of reed pipe.

They were foreigners in this strange place, just like these people were strangers to the white men. The villagers looked at them eccentrically. Ben noticed a few curious looks in their eyes, glancing at the clothing on his body.

✖✖✖

"What should we do with these strangers?" Hinda spoke with his chief, Lepo.

"I am not sure young warrior; I think they are sent from the Gods. The man named Ben resembles Glepos or even the Sun God, Hitylo. We must wait until the Gods tell us what to do."

"I understand, Lepo, but these men are strange. Did you see them? They look like Yalodo. We should find the one who got away, before something happens to him. He might fall into the enemy's hands. We can get information from him."

"Hinda, you are my greatest warrior, I respect you. These strangers could be dangerous, but we have no way to talk to them."

"What about the old man, he is of their color, and looks like them too. Maybe he can speak for us."

"You are wise. I hope the counsel approves of your union to my daughter. You will then be leader of the Iraja."

"Yes. That day will be here soon, until the next moon."

"Hinda, I want you to take them to the supply shack, give them food and water. We can move the supplies into my hut until the decision is made."

"Yes, chief."

✖✖✖

Hinda led the two prisoners into a small shack. Once inside, the warrior motioned the prisoners to help move the supplies. Looking around, Ben noticed some clothing that looked familiar, coats with buttons and stripes of the British Navy. He looked more closely and noticed a few chests, rifles, and a keg of powder.

Hinda lifted a small chest, motioning the two men to do the same. Each man carried a few items and walked into the chief's hut about fifty feet away. Once inside the largest hut, they stacked the items on the ground. Ben was the last in the line of carriers, and before he left, he snatched a leather pouch and filled it with gunpowder, slipping it slyly into his pocket.

When they were walking outside again, four men joined in helping with the moving. After a half hour, the small supply hut was empty and the two prisoners were locked inside. The warriors did not check their pockets, only confiscated the visible weapons.

Ben pulled the objects from his pocket, emptying them onto the damp earth. Out fell his pocketknife and the pouch of gunpowder.

Harris looked over curiously, "What are you doing?"

"I am evaluating our situation. I have a feeling Jacob's going to come back for us."

❊❊❊

They slept for an hour when a Hetran slave brought them meat and water. When she left, the brothers ate in silence. They closed their eyes to lay back down with full stomachs, not sure of what was going to happen to them the next time their guarded door would open. Before they could fall asleep, a warrior with skin hardened by the years came into the hut. Harris noticed the paint on his face and the patterns of stars on his cheeks. The warrior nodded his head towards the door. Ben and Harris followed.

They were led to the chief's hut. Lepo, Sepa, Hinda, and a white man were sitting around a small fire talking when Lepo stood. "Ahiko, ya Lepo."

The other members nodded, supporting their leader. The white man had a gray beard hanging from his sagging face. He then spoke, representing their captors. "I am Yalodo. I was born forty or so years ago in a small town in England. I do not remember much of my past life."

Ben interrupted the man's speech. "Can you help us escape?"

"Only if I can come with you, these people are nice, but once a war comes, as it does frequently, they became ruthless animals. Yes, I will help you escape."

"Thank you, Yalodo."

"What is your name, friend? And your acquaintances?"

"My name is Ben, this is my brother Harris. Jacob is the one who escaped. We were shipwrecked on this island during that storm, in transit to Havana."

"Ah, I once sailed these seas, but I was a child then. We are in the middle of a common shipping lane. Like many before us, the ship hit a rock in a violent storm. We were deserted onto this very island. We hiked these mountains and the Hetran killed our group. I managed to escape and was found by an Irajan woman and was adopted as one of them. That was in the year of my seventh birthday. It feels so long ago."

"What do they want with us?"

"Well Ben, the Iraja want nothing to do with you. They'll most likely make you slaves or adopt you into society. Lepo is the chief of the Iraja, this tribe. Dating back towards a time unknown, the Iraja fought with the Hetra, the other tribe on the isle. They fought fierce battles on every new moon, losing many warriors monthly. The two tribes had once been united, but there had been a conflict that separated the Asturas, the ancient name of the tribe."

He paused, catching his breath. "Lepo wanted the Hetran chief named Derkata to unite once again, to end the constant struggles, but his counterpart wanted war instead of peace. The witch doctor had read Lepo's future and predicted his death on the next moon, which is coming quickly. This would mean Sepa would take over the reign of the village and marry a warrior appointed by the counsel. But I have one question for you."

"Yes, what is it?"

"Ben, are there others of our kind?"

"Yes. We're a hunting party for an eleven-man group. That storm awhile back shipwrecked us and now we live upon the beach."

The islanders conversed for several moments, while the brothers sat in silence.

"Lepo wants to know if you are messengers from the Gods."

"Tell him that we are the Gods of War, we are here to help the Iraja."

Yalodo turned to Lepo, "Et wartos a diso, et dira a Iraja!"

"If you are really Gods, show us your powers."

Ben reached into the pouch without an eye's notice and pulled out a pinch of powder. Ben closed his eyes, bowed his head in a dramatic exaggeration, and snapped both hands like a composer, throwing the gunpowder into the fire without a glance from the viewers. The small fire erupted, touching the ceiling, but not setting fire to the hut.

Yalodo translated once again. "You are Gods, I am sorry if I have offended you."

Ben hid a smile; his plan was working well. "Tell him we forgive you and that we must be released at once."

"We cannot let you leave just yet. You must help us defeat our enemy, the Hetra."

"Tell Lepo that we agree to those terms. That we can help them only if they help us in return."

"What is it you need?"

"We need to get off this island. We need to build a ship worthy of traveling the seas."

The chief nodded and stood erect, walking towards Ben with his hand extended. Ben stood, gripping the man's weathered hands, shaking to signify their new alliance.

❈❈❈

"I wonder what they did to my friends," he thought. He had ran until he couldn't run anymore, his lungs stretched and burned with every breath. "What should I do? Go back for them, or warn the others?"

While he was pondering this decision, he heard an owl's call from behind him. It was still day though. He figured it was not an owl and that it was the warriors communicating with each other. Jumping from the log he sped off down a winding path, improvising his escape; at forks in the path, he went with his gut instinct. After breaking through the foliage lining the forest, he emerged into a field of grass.

There were posts sticking from the ground, tied to these posts were skeletons. Jacob continued running through the field and stopped at a rope bridge that spanned the valley below. The bridge connected two mountains, on one mountain lived the Irajas and on the other lived the Hetra.

The two warriors never emerged into the open field that their tribe called the Forbidden Area. Since the beginning, the Hetra did the attacking, and by leaving dead Iraja at the entrance to the bridge, they had protection from attack due to their opponents' fear. Jacob was unsure of why his pursuers stopped the chase but did not complain. He just stood their, debating to surrender, wait the warriors out, or to cross the bridge. He weighed the options and figured his best chance was to wait.

He kept a careful eye on the tree line, to his content, the two Iraja warriors turned around on a heel and ran back along the paths cursing in their language. He waited nearly half an hour, regaining his breath and then walked along the border of the forest and the grass, looking for another trail.

There was a slight opening in the brush in front of him, about a foot and a half wide. He decided to follow the animal trail, crouching low and staying amongst the earth. Following this windy trail, he peered out through foliage and saw that it paralleled the main trail.

His progress was slow, but he eventually ended up a dozen yards in back of the village. He saw the hut where his two friends were being led. As the sunlight diminished, the sky became dark. Thick, dark clouds hid the moon, which made the village pitch black. Jacob crawled towards the hut through the vegetation and underbrush. He squatted next to the vertical sticks, which made up the wall of the building.

"It's Jacob, are you there?"

"Hey buddy, good to hear your voice, I thought you got captured," replied Ben.

"I'm going to sneak around and open the door."

"Don't, be careful. There's a guard. Don't worry about us, we made a deal with them. They promised us to help get off this island. Go back to camp and bring the rest here. You remember the way we came right?"

"Uh huh, I remember every left and right we took. I'll go return to camp and then we'll come back tomorrow morning."

"All right, see you soon."

✖✖✖

Jacob made his way back to camp, slowly and carefully to avoid detection from the Iraja. After he descended the rock wall, he sprinted along the trails, trying to get to camp as soon as possible. At around midnight, he burst into the camp sweating and panting. The crew was sitting by the campfire, singing gaily and roasting crabs that were caught that evening. The captain looked up from the fire and said, "Jacob, where are Ben and Harris?"

"Captain, something went wrong…"

The captain threw his roasting stick down quickly, "Are they okay?"

Jacob continued, "Well, at first it did not look good. We were climbing the mountains looking for game, when we stumbled into a village. Warriors surrounded us. I ran for it while the other two got caught. A few warriors pursued me until I somehow escaped. It was at some bridge, which connected to another mountain peak. There were dead bodies in a circle around the perimeter of the field, right in front of a bridge…"

There was silence for a moment and then Jacob resumed his speech, "Yeah, I guess I stumbled into some forbidden zone because the warriors stopped where the forest ended, and then turned around and ran. So then I waited awhile, and discovered a game trail, which paralleled the route I was on, and it eventually led to the village. It became dark and I snuck up behind this hut that they were held in. I whispered to them and they said they made some kind of deal with the chief. If we help them they will help us."

The group cheered at the thought of seeing civilization once more. The captain stood on the log. "Men, on the morrow, we shall follow Jacob to where the village is. We'll help the tribe with whatever they need us for, and then we'll get off this bloody island and finish our business."

There was a brief period of silence and then the gathered crew began a chant, "Three cheers for the good news, hip hip, horray, hip hip, horray, hip hip, horray."

26

Ben had been awake for a few minutes before he heard the fall of footsteps outside the hut. Lepo knocked upon the frame of the door to the quarters of his guest. With him were Yalodo and a few warriors who bowed their heads in greeting.

"I hope you had a goodnight's sleep. We have much to do today. I suspect your friends will arrive soon?"

Ben nodded his head, "Yes, last night Jacob returned to the hut and he will bring the remaining men to help in the efforts."

"Ah, yes. They should arrive before the sun has reached the heavens. Let us prepare a welcoming for them."

***

*T*hey sat by the fire and had a light breakfast of crab and coconut meat. They divided the weapons, both newly made and ones from the ship between the nine men. Jacob took lead of the party, while the captain trailed behind a few steps. Traveling at a quick pace, he escorted the party along the paths until they were finally at the wall.

Marconi touched Jacob on the shoulder, "You climbed this?"

***

*B*en and Harris stood up to greet Jacob and the remaining sailors, "I'm glad to see you all!"

The nine men reunited with the brothers and then all took their respective seats amongst the villagers. Yalodo and Lepo stood by the fire while the rest sat talking. From a pouch at Lepo's side, he brought out a medicinal bough from their sacred bushes. He threw the branch into the fire and blue smoke spread throughout the village, carried by a gentle breeze that circulated over the mountain. The smoke spiraled in shrouds around the chief. He began talking in his native tongue, the villagers nodded in approval. The foreigners stared at the old man in confusion.

Yalodo translated for the new guests, "Welcome to my village. I am Chief Lepo. I have been the leader of my people, the Iraja, for nearly five hundred moons. We have been at war with the Hetra since the Great Battle, when the main tribe split in two. Ever since then, the Hetra have been attacking us with the coming of each new moon. They hang our dead by the edge of the bridge. We are afraid to pass through the dead. We are a very superstitious people. Your unexpected visit has given me an idea, and if you help us, we will help you. To get off this island, you will need our help. We have things your people would love to possess and they will be yours if you help us fight our enemy. Let us eat before you make your decision."

There was a brief moment of silence in the village. Slaves were busy handing out wooden trays to eat upon. A jug of water was passed around the circle. The food was sliced off the pit, cut up, and distributed to the children first, then the women, and finally the men. They ate and drank in silence until there was no more left to consume. Finally, Captain Nelson stood up to say something. He looked at Yalodo and said, "Kind sir, I like these terms you speak of, let me discuss this first with my men."

Nelson then turned to his crew, removed his cover and swiped his hand through his bushy hair. "Men, we've gone a long way these past few months; battling pirates, storms, and these island hardships. To come all this way and give up, it'd be nonsense. If we help these people out, they promised us help in return. We could soon be on our way to Cuba and then on to England and resume our duty. So men, raise a paw if you agree with me in my decision to accept their alliance."

Nelson stared at the raised hands, and then looked into the chief's eyes and said, "You have a new friend and an ally. We will help you and later you will help us."

Ben sat with closed eyes, the message was relayed and the rest of the night was spent eating, drinking, and smoking a peace pipe. "What exactly is our duty? I have a feeling something onboard will answer this question, but now we have other things to do, other things to conquer."

✹✹✹

The crew of the *Frendrich* sat beside the fireside, watching the sun streak the eastern sky. Captain Nelson came out of the chief's hut with a smile on his face. As he approached his men, he began to speak. "I have agreed to will help Lepo and the Iraja in their victory over their enemy. In return, they'll give us a boat capable of cross the ocean, so we can finish our voyage. This ship will be laden with things they have collected over the years such as gold, weapons, and other ship's particulars.

"I think this would be a most profitable course of action for us, since we are in dire need of a ship. They will only have bows and arrows, axes, and primitive tools. We have our guns, powder, and experience. So men, let's do it. We'll teach them how to handle these modern weapons. He told me they have a decent amount of them from wrecks. With our knowledge and training with this technology, we have a huge advantage. This evening we will have the first training session."

✹✹✹

Later that evening, the warriors gathered around their guests. Yalodo translated the captain's orders as every would-be soldier had a rifle in hand. "Place the musket at your feet with the barrel pointed away from the face. Take the charge and ball out of cartridge box and bite off the top of the paper wrapping. Pour the powder down the barrel and then push the ball down the barrel with your thumb. Remove ramrod from beneath the barrel, pulling it straight out, then turning, and placing ram head on the ball. Ram the ball to the breach; remove the ramrod straight out, and return to the slot under the barrel. Bring musket up to your abdomen, bring to half cock, hold with one hand, and with the other, and get a percussion cap from your cap box. Place cap on the nipple, wait for command, on the command "ready" bring to full cock and raise the rifle to your shoulder, aiming at the target, and on the command "fire" pull the trigger."

"Men, this will be our first test. Form up in a single file line, side by side and face the bushes. Let's give it a try."

The men formed up as ordered. The captain stood in back of the men, relatively in the middle so everyone could hear his voice. The loading took some but, but within several minutes every rifle was raised, ready to be shot. Every man tightly shouldered the deadly weapon, looking down the barrel, sighting the targets ahead.

"Fire!"

❈❈❈

"Chief, those sounds heard moments ago, it is an omen. Thunder without clouds? I have only heard this once, many, many years ago. It is not a good sign my friend. I wish you would think twice," the village elder proclaimed to Derkata.

"Nonsense, we will attack our enemies. The new moon arrives shortly. Soon we will control both mountains. I will name you chief of the captured territory after we behead Lepo."

"But father, I thought you said I would lead the conquered people?"

The old chief let out a hearty laugh and reached for a pipe. He smoked from this prized procession, passed down through the years by past chieftains. Ignoring his son, he turned to the village elder, "How many warriors do we have?"

The wise man closed his eyes; picturing every warrior he has been training with, "We have thirty strong men, a handful of older men, and a few children old enough to carry bows. They could be of use if we arm them as scouts. They are quick and agile in the woods."

"Yes, we will start planning our attack tomorrow. I have a feeling this will be the last battle we fight."

The wise man shook his head in disbelief, "And it will be so if you lead these men in this battle."

✖✖✖✖

Ten of the Irajan warriors struck the bushes, the remaining men sprayed dirt everywhere. The warriors practiced the loading and re-loading process, repeating every step except the execution phase. For hours the warriors trained with this new technology while the crew of the *Frendrich* was taught archery. For the next several days, the men worked together, planning their strategy for the battle, which crept closer with every sunrise and sunset. They practiced formations and went over the smallest details of the plan.

Captain Nelson stood beside Lepo as they oversaw their re-spected training programs. Each group of rifles and bows rehearsed the plan a dozen times until the day before the battle. On this day, they relaxed, sharpening and cleaning their weapons, knowing that this would be the last battle on the island of constant toil.

27

The moon was not visible that night; only an outline of the celestial body was seen through the clouds. A new month began, which meant another battle between the island natives. The Iraja dressed their guests in their tribal war attire. Around his shins, she wrapped deerskin, tying a little knot by his calf to secure it. Ben's fist was placed into a glove, which slid down his forearm. He noticed two thick bones running the length of his arm. She motioned him to put his arms in the air. As he did this, she placed a leather chest protector over his head. She tightened the straps under the armpits until it stayed sturdy. Once she was finished, he joined Nelson and the translator.

"Are you ready for battle, my friend?"

He looked at Nelson with a grin, "Yes, but this chest protector thing is doing more damage to me than good. It's crushing my ribs."

The captain let out a hearty laugh, "It makes you tough. Don't worry, it should be over within the hour, then you can take it off and relax and bask in the glories of a new beginning."

***

From their positions the Iraja watched as Hetran warriors crossed the bridge, marching to the cadence of a loud horn. Derkata had a staff in his right hand that went to his chest when placed on the ground. The long piece of wood had intricate carvings designed in patterns, which grew in size as it went from the pointed tip to the handle. In his left hand he carried a throwing spear, roughly a foot longer than his staff.

Lepo and his warriors waited by the tree line for the advancing Hetra. All were crouched, knees bent in a power stance so they could easily spring into a full sprint. As soon as his enemies were across the bridge, Lepo led the charge forward. He knocked an arrow into his bow, brought the string beside his eye and released it. The arrow spiraled through the air, plunging into a man's shoulder.

The man still charged his spear ready to be thrown. Hinda saw that the enemy had raised the spear, his arm bent to ninety degrees, ready to deliver a deathblow to his leader. He quickly knocked an arrow, aimed with precision as he focused in on the man's throwing hand. The arrow penetrated the wrist, steel and wood ripping through flesh, tearing muscle. The spear dropped with a loud thud against a rock.

Soon the battle spread out across the open field; men were wrestling in close combat, fists and spears thrown. Losing a handful of men early in the fight, the Iraja fell back towards the tree line. Derkata and his son led their warriors forward, forcing his enemy backwards, into the woods.

Lepo decided it was time to fall back further into the safety of his territory. His men never exposed their backs in their planned retreat, but rather ran from tree to tree, loosing arrows before retreating further. Two archers, high in the trees, let arrows rain down upon the horde of enemy warriors just as they were inside the trap. The plan could not have been executed any better than it was.

✖✖✖

Ben closed his eyes, listening to the cries as men were slain in the open field. He was not sure if they were dead or injured, but he decided he could not do anything for them anyways. Looking for the enemy, he strained his eyes and scanned the woods through the thick vegetation. He reached around his neck, holding Leah's gift for what could be his last time. He said a silent prayer, watching as the first wave of the enemy emerged into view.

The charging men stopped in mid-stride, facing a U-shaped formation of long barreled rifles. Each warrior or crewman in the squad lay flat on their stomachs behind strategically placed logs, eying their enemies down the sights of their rifles.

"Fire!"

The command was given, yielding devastating results. As the dust and smoke settled, the clearing was full of mangled bodies. The three men that had survived the onslaught stood facing the U-formation, in plain view of Lepo's piercing stare. The arrows ceased as Lepo gave the signal to the treetops. The Iraja circled the three men, moving slowly, cautiously.

"Spare my father, the chief, and this brave warrior," called out Wilkamay.

His father turned to him, "How dare you converse with the enemy!"

As the Iraja surrounded the three Hetran warriors with spears, Wilkamay only stood taller. His chest stuck out with pride. He turned his head to the right and noticed that his father and the other warrior began to kneel. Derkata lowered his body to the ground.

"The village elder was right about it all along. Why did I refuse his advice and attack the Iraja full strength? It was a bad omen to hear thunder when there were no clouds or rain. For my entire reign as chieftain, we have known victory, but now I will be known for defeat, I cannot let this happen."

Lepo stopped an arm's length away. "You have been defeated. All that belongs to you now belongs to me. We will now live in a united tribe. Why can't we just live in peace like we once did, when our tribes were one? I will let you live, but you must recognize the fact that your tribe will no longer be *yours*. And that, the Hetra will no longer exist, except in the discussion of memories or in dreams..."

Before he could finish the last sentence of his speech, Derkata reached into a satchel around his waist. He pulled out a dagger and made a move towards Lepo. Wilkamay noticed the movement and then shifted his weight to prevent his father from a certain death, but he was too late.

✖✖✖

The archers in the treetops noticed the change in footing of their targets. They knocked an arrow in their bow and studied the scene. Listening to the speech, they noticed another slight movement. As the dagger was pulled out of the satchel, each archer let off a shot. Two sharp arrows struck Derkata, causing him to trip over himself and stumble at the feet of their chief.

"You could have just surrendered and lived a long and happy life amongst the Iraja."

"I would rather die. You may be content with your peace, but my tribe has developed into a warring people. To win is to have conquered your enemies and grow stronger. To lose is to have been conquered and grow weaker. I cannot let myself grow weaker," he struggled with his breath. "Out of the many battles we have fought, I have never lost. The village elder advised me about today and I let my way of life take precedence. Therefore I cannot live amongst you and your followers. They will look at me. They will say, 'Look at him. His head is hung low because he lost.' Do you know what that makes me? I cannot even say the word…"

Before he could continue, he plunged the dagger deep into his chest. Lepo watched as his enemy took his own life; forever escaping the ridicule that may have ensued as a result of surrender and having the two tribes unite as one.

✖✖✖

Hours later, the rising of the sun marked the beginning of another day; the Irajan villagers celebrated their victory. It was the battle that ended battles and they were eternally gracious to the ill-fated crew. Lepo, the translator, and Captain Nelson sat in the chief's hut to discuss the future of the two and their people.

"My friend, would you like to hear a story of the stars and constellations?"

He turned to the weathered man, "Any story told by such a wonderful host, warrior, and leader would be a shame to be not be heard. Tell me of this story about the stars and constellations."

"Well, it began a short time ago, before our paths crossed. I had my fortune read. I was destined to die on the next moon. This battle was supposed to be my last and because of you and your followers, I will lead the two tribes. We will unite once again. We must honor those who were lost in the battle with a ceremony tonight. The men who were slain will be remembered as heroes who ended the constant battles between our people."

Captain Nelson rubbed his beard. Without shaving for so long, his well-groomed goatee became a tangled mess. "You are great speaker. It was a well-told story. I wish to share many stories in the upcoming months while we prepare to leave the island."

He passed Nelson a tobacco pipe and said, "Yes my friend, after we deal with bringing the tribes together, we will work on getting your crew home safely."

✖✖✖

*T*he Hetran village was quiet that night. After several hours revealing no returning warriors, the village elder feared his prediction had come true. He called a meeting for all those of age; everyone else remained in the huts. The fire was crackling and he began speaking, "What I have seen in a dream has come true. We have been defeated. Our lives will change drastically, from a warring nation, to a peaceful society like it once was. I do not know exactly what will happen. In a dream last night, all I saw were white ghosts amongst our village. They were not the ghosts of the dead though, but rather living ghosts similar to the sacred Gods. Sleep well tonight. For tomorrow, everything will change."

✖✖✖

Lepo and his daughter met with Hinda to discuss the wedding arrangements. She had a pretty smile, the corners of the lips flared as she talked.

"...And father, I would like the wedding to be like yours to my mother. I remember the stories she used to tell me before the Hetra took her away from us. She would say how the entire village came out into the streets, while music and festivities filled the air. I want to walk through the village and have everyone stare at the attire I will wear. I was looking through Lerta's belongings and found her old marriage robes. If you don't mind, I would take great pride in wearing it."

"Yes, you can wear your mother's robes for the wedding."

Before the camp settled down for the night, Lepo called Captain Nelson to his hut for another meeting. "With the sunrise, we must enter their camp with the body of Derkata. I will go, along with you and three of your most loyal warriors. Many moons ago, there were ghosts like you who walked our beaches after a storm similar to the one that brought you to us. It was here where we had our first encounter with your kind. They raided and pillaged us, but left shortly after because we did not have any of this precious yellow metal they were looking for. Well, the moment they left us, we thought it was a present from the sky and adopted them to become our Gods. When we saw Ben, Harris, and Jacob, we knew we were blessed because my people believe that the second time something happens, that it will be the opposite of that coming before.

"Since both of our tribes believe in these same Gods, they will be under the impression that their way of life will change for the better, which it will. It is a shame that we've been constantly fighting, I have sent over many treaties of roasts and brew, but to no avail. I cannot thank you enough for bringing the island together."

"It is my pleasure to help you and your tribe. Let us sleep and rest up for the new day. We've much to do in order to adopt them into your society. It will take awhile to adjust, but I believe you are quite capable of this. I am impressed and pleased to have the honor of your presence."

The captain knew how to speak to people, knew what to say, how to say it, and when. It was a skill that promoted him up the chain in such little time.

28

After breakfast, Captain Nelson held a meeting with his crew. "Men congratulations, Lepo asked me for one more favor. I need three men to go into the Hetran village to accompany us. We are thought upon as Gods by these peoples. We will bring the envelope to a seal, the tribes will unite, and then peace will occur."

Throughout the speech, the captain eyed Ben. He continued talking, "As usual, Charles and Nate will accompany me," he paused, building the tension for the third member. "Ben, I'd like you to come to. The rest of you can relax until we return. Again, good work."

The crew let out a cheer. "All are dismissed except for the three I mentioned. Good day to you all."

❌❌❌

As they advanced through the woods towards the bridge, Lepo could still see the blood smears on the ground of his men and his enemy. Shortly after the battle, they took all their dead and injured back to the village to be buried or treated. Lepo and his fellow Irajan warriors decided that the dead enemy warriors would be buried just like any of theirs, a normal ceremonial burial for each; so that they could live a happy life after their soul had left their body.

Lepo led the party of six along the game trail, passing through the battlefield of the previous day, until they reached the clearing. Once at the bridge, they continued on. Lepo paused at the tree line and kneeled. His eyes strained for the entrance of the trail that would lead to the Hetra village. He saw a few broken branches, probably where the warriors emerged from the day before.

He pointed the way and pressed on through the foliage. Breaking a path with Derkata's staff, they found the trail. It was a quick walk and they soon emerged into the village. Several children were running around, stopping the moment they saw the ghosts escorted by an elderly chieftain. The children of each village were taught how to read the feathers or beads of a man's clothing to determine his approximate age and rank in society.

The children ran into a hut to warn the village elder. "The ghosts are here. The ones that you have told us about in the stories passed on. Why are they here?" said the eldest child.

Garcha turned to the young one, "I will talk to them now. Children stay here."

In the center of the village, the seven men stood. All other life seemed to disappear, leaving Lepo and his five ghosts with the Hetran elder to converse on the matters. "My name is Garcha, I am the village elder, high counsel of my people. I had a dream that this battle would end the tensions between our people. I am glad it has happened too. I have seen too many of my grandchildren go off to fight a battle that was started many moons ago."

"Yes, I agree. I have two ideas for what follows. You and your people can move over to my village. You will remain village elder and spread your wisdom to the young. My son will replace me for I have seen much in my life and would like to rest until my death. Or the other option is you and your people continue to live on this side of the mountain, while my son rules this village and we learn of peace and the Irajan way. I will let you and the men of your village discuss the two options. We will remain here. Also, we have two of your warriors. They were the last, the bravest of the bunch. They are safe."

"May I ask whom?"

"Yes, the chief's son, and also a warrior named Listroken. Derkata took his own life."

The village elder shook his head; a slight smile grew knowing that the two nations would now never have to fight again.

❊❊❊

"But why do you want to continue these battles? We are fresh out of warriors. Look around; there is scarcely a male between the ages of sixteen and forty. Most here are young or too old to yield weapons. I, as village elder, think it wise to join the Iraja like we once were."

He was interrupted by Teshnay, two years his younger. "Brother, we are a fighting people. We cannot just give up. I know at least I am not a coward. If you give in to them, you will disgrace all those who have gone before us."

He shot back, "What do you propose we do? There are ghosts walking with the chieftain of the Iraja. This is the second coming of the ghosts, which means it is good luck. We must cease the opportunity. Men and women of the tribe let us vote on it. Raise a hand if you want to continue the fighting."

His brother and several of the elders raised their hands high, leaving the majority with their hands by their sides. As he cocked his head to make a mental note of each vote, Teshnay's hand slipped back down to his hip without any notice from Garcha or anyone surrounding.

He smiled, "I will go tell our new friends that we accept their terms and will unite."

Teshnay stood up, "I will go with you."

❊❊❊

The two left the large thatched hut to join up with the men waiting in the center of the village. The Hetran elder continued to question his brother's true intentions, he knew him well, but was still unsure.

Lepo greeted them with open arms, "My friends, have you made your decision?"

The elder spoke for the two, "Yes, my tribe has voted and we agree to your proposition."

Lepo smiled, "It is with great pleasure to reunite once again. I have been looking forward to this moment for many moons."

As he said this, Teshnay bowed his head in submission. He watched as Lepo's eyes moved towards his brother. He unsheathed a short throwing knife from a leg strap and in one smooth motion, launched it towards the distracted chief. Ben dove at Lepo to knock him away, but the blade sunk deep into the man's chest. Garcha ran to the aid of the fallen leader, kneeling over him to examine the wound.

As the turmoil began to spread, Teshnay sprinted off. Without thinking, Ben pursued him, hot on his trail. Teshnay had a four second lead on the white ghost.

The village center was in a clearing of the woods roughly a hundred meters in each direction. Ben looked ahead and saw several trails that led deep into the woods. The Hetran man now had a two-stride length advantage over his pursuer. Even though he was in his later years, he moved swiftly and gracefully. He looked back and saw the ghost closing the distance.

Ben rushed forward, at the stage in the pursuit where his steps were a stride length behind. The foliage was within arms reach now as the warrior broke through the dense foliage, forging his own path. This slowed him down enough for Ben to make his move.

✸✸✸

Lepo's body contorted with each violent shudder, coughing up dark red blood. His eyes were closed tight, the pressure in his head immense. He let out a scream as blood dribbled out from his nose. The captain stayed behind with Garcha and Yalodo. The two tribesmen discussed a plan to save the struck man.

Nelson ripped off a three inch by foot long strip of his white cotton shirt and then poured the contents of his canteen out, soaking the cloth. Garcha ran off to a hut calling to his wife, "Sritchaka, bring out my herbs and medicinal items."

Yalodo removed the blade and squatted beside his fellow white man, "Captain, this does not look good."

A moment later, Garcha returned with a deerskin pouch that had several leaves and branches protruding from the inside. "My friends, we need to get him into a hut without disturbing his wound. I need time to brew a mixture that will make him better. We just need time. By the look of the wound, we might not have time."

✸✸✸

Marconi and Brodkin were about two hundred feet behind when they saw the two figures break through the foliage.

Ben was within arms reach just after entering the wooded area bordering the village. He leapt forward and reached around the man's neck. The body below maintained the grueling speed regardless of carrying the load. Ben then hooked his left foot around the man's knee, tripping him instantly. They crashed through several saplings until Ben straddled the warrior, locking his legs around the man below. He wriggled free and struck Ben in the chin with his elbow. He stepped off to sprint away but Ben threw in two quick kidney punches that knocked the wind out of the man.

Teshnay doubled over, exaggerating the aftermath of the left-right combo. Ben sidestepped and let off a kick aimed for the man's throat. He dropped to his knees, but before Ben could solidly plant his feet, Teshnay released a solid uppercut to the inside of Ben's thigh.

Ben's leg went numb instantly, causing him to back off slightly. Adrenaline flowed throughout his body. The thought of him losing to a man at least three times his age sent a message from his brain to his fist. Blood seeped through both nostrils as Teshnay hit the floor, crashing through a tangle of bushes. His back hit hard on a jagged rock, slicing his left shoulder. Ben covered him immediately, using pressure points to control the man below. On either side of the man's neck, Ben stuck his thumbs with great force.

✸✸✸

The two sailors crashed through the path at full speed causing a shower of debris to fly about. They stepped on the back of Ben's leg in their entrance to the woods. Ben's grip on the man was hindered just enough to allow the man to twist his body and deliver a blow with a rock in hand. The hit sent Ben reeling back.

✖✖✖✖

*I*nside the village elder's hut was a pot, cooking over an open fire. Inside were several roots and leaves that Garcha handpicked several days before, in preparation for healing wounded Hetran warriors. He stood over the boiling water, gauging the brew's completion by the smell.

As he was preparing the medicine, Captain Nelson and Yalodo cleaned the wound as best they could with a wet rag. After it was cleaned out, they alternated putting pressure on the injury. It helped a little, but the cut deep. It sliced an artery and blood soaked through each rag.

Captain Nelson turned to face Yalodo, "Friend, can you ask Garcha what he is making?"

He was familiar with medicine. Since his early days of the monthly battles, he was asked to create various brews for different injuries ranging from cuts and bruises, to removing arrowheads and blade wounds. Thinking of the familiar smell, "Captain, he is making a brew using several roots and the leaves of a plant that's sacred to our people. The mixture thickens the blood so that the bleeding will clot. Once the mixture is boiled enough to almost a sappy consistency, the victim must drink the substance immediately while still warm. If it cools before ingested, the brew regains its poisonous characteristics."

The captain looked Yalodo in the eyes, "So the heat breaks down the poison?"

He smiled, "I wouldn't say that. The roots and leaves, while heated are a beneficial poison. The body recognizes it and allows the liquid to seep into the bloodstream and spread throughout the body. On the other hand though, once the mixture cools to room temperature and is ingested, the properties of the poison are recognized by the body as harmful and the body shuts down."

✻✻✻

$\mathcal{M}$arconi and Brodkin grabbed the runaway with strong hands, preventing another possible escape. Ben still remained on the ground, holding his cheek in his hands. The blow left a long gash across his cheekbone to his ear. Standing up slowly, he stood before the man, striking him once in the gut. After Teshnay regained a normal breathing pattern, Ben led the group out of the woods as Charles and Nate maintained their grip on the man. The Hetran villager occasionally tried to wriggle free, only to meet a closed fist. As they reentered the village, Ben noticed smoke from only one hut. "They're in there," he pointed.

✻✻✻

$\mathcal{A}$s the brew finished heating and Garcha was satisfied with the consistency, he took the pot off the coals. His fingers moved quickly into the pouch. He took out a strip of Moringa bark and then stirred the mixture with it to soak the pores with the liquid. He said to Yalodo, "Let me apply this strip to the wound. Tell your friend to take that water gourd hanging on the post and fill it with the liquid in the pot."

The message was relayed and Captain Nelson and Garcha swapped positions. The strip of soaked bark was placed softly on Lepo's chest. Yalodo reached into a pile to find a four-foot long ribbon of fabric. He wrapped this across Lepo's chest and continued under his back and around again. The chief flinched as he was touched by the wet bark and then the fabric was tied off snuggly in a knot.

Nelson's strong fingers reached towards the gourd, lifting it off the post. He walked briskly towards the hot pot located on the earth. He forced the liquid into the hole using a long wooden spoon. "How much should I fill the gourd?" His question was directed to Yalodo.

His fellow ghost replied, "Fill it half way, then replace the pot on the fire. We might need it later."

✕✕✕

*B*en pushed through the hut's entrance to see Lepo horizontal on a wooden table. "How's he doing?"

Yalodo turned to the young man, "What happened to you? We'll find out how Lepo fares once the herbs kick in. Captain Nelson just finished administering the medicine."

"We captured the runaway. He's outside being held by Charles and Nate. I got into a scuffle with him; he hit me in the face with a rock. I'm not sure if anything is broken, but it hurts like hell."

Garcha said to Yalodo, "Tell Ben that we will deal with my brother once Lepo is treated. I need a few more minutes and then he just needs rest. I've examined the wound multiple times. In all my years, I have not seen a cut so deep. If we treated him quick enough, he might live. It is all in the God's hands now."

The message was relayed as Garcha continued doctoring the Irajan chief.

✕✕✕

*S*everal women and children cleared out a hut as they listened to the orders given to them by Garcha. After several minutes, the three sailors forced Teshnay into the empty space. Following quickly behind was Yalodo and Garcha. Captain Nelson stayed behind to watch over the fallen chief.

Garcha stared into his brother's eyes. He shook his head, "Breaking your word is also a disgrace, more of a disgrace then accepting change. By lying to me you disgraced our family. You struck a near fatal blow to Lepo. He will most likely die tonight. He promised us peace for our tribes, a united people without war. I cannot believe you. You are my brother by blood, but a brother no more."

As he said this, his open hand left his side. The slap was delivered, causing Teshnay to flinch. He did not flinch at the pain, but rather at the message his brother demonstrated. Family loyalty was one of the major beliefs between both the Hetran and Irajan villages and when this honor was deliberately disobeyed, there was only one thing to do about it.

✖.✖.✖

The wind blew strong in the clearing, ruffling the makeshift ceremonial tent. Inside of the hide pavilion, Lepo lay stretched on a hammock. The hides were drawn back to allow Lepo to view the ceremony.

Teshnay's wrists were lashed together behind his back with strips of a thorn bush. Each time the man attempted to rid himself of nature's handcuffs, the thorns would rip the skin raw until the green shrubbery turned red.

Garcha spoke to Lepo before continuing with the ritual, "My friend, I brought you here so you can watch the man who felled you perish. Although he is my brother, he has betrayed the virtues that are famous among our people. I have thought many hours on the subject. In any other situation, we would just embarrass the traitor in front of the entire village and then let him or her walk amongst our people once more. We cannot let Teshnay do this though. His beliefs are set in stone. He is stubborn and will not accept change. Most likely he would lead a movement, which would be detrimental to our reunited tribe."

Lepo was feeling weak; the infection spreading throughout his body. The medicine was ingested several hours prior, just long enough to maintain a slight equilibrium in his health. All that was needed for him to return back to health was time. The sun knocked twice on the western door, bringing a close to yet another day on the island. A fire was blazing as Garcha herded the ghosts around. Yalodo translated, "Once the Gods have lowered the sun, we will begin the ceremony."

Garcha took out a branch with colorful leaves from a pouch slung on his hip. He placed it on the fire, watching the flames consume the greenery. Instantaneously, the wind carried the cloud of colorful smoke in swirls around the group.

Nate and Charles positioned Teshnay so that he could view the fire while having his back to the cliff's edge. The air was full of smoke and suspense. All that went through his mind was for this mockery to end soon, but his brother deliberately took his time. Garcha sung out in a sweet and gentle voice an ancient prayer passed down from father to son. At the conclusion of the tune, he bowed his head, looked at the sunset and then stared straight into his brother's eyes.

"Next time we meet, I hope you have changed for the better. Goodbye, brother."

Instead of the ceremonial burial, which consisted of burying their dead with possessions to carry into the next life, a body somersaulted off the cliff's edge, falling into the depths of the rock that spanned between the two tribes. With one act of violence, the seed of peace was planted and with time, prosperity would soon develop.

29

The camp quieted as a group entered the Irajan village. On a stretcher laid their leader carried by the officers of the *Frendrich*. Hinda and Sepa ran to inquire, "Yalodo, what happened?"

Lepo was in a state of semi-consciousness, mumbling something incomprehensible. The white man cleared his throat, "There was an accident. Teshnay, one of the elderly Hetran villagers, was stubborn and refused the theory of our village's union. Lepo received a knife wound to his chest. Captain Nelson decided that his own witchdoctor would look at the wound and cure it with his medicine. He needs rest. We will place him in his own hut to sleep for the remainder of the evening."

The limp body on the stretcher suddenly jerked back to life, "What happened? Why am I being carried?"

As quickly as his body sat up, it went limp again. Yalodo directed Nate and Charles, watching as the train of men walked towards the chief's hut. "Sepa, he should be a little better in the morning. Hopefully you can have your wedding then or we can wait until your father is fully healed. We will discuss this more tomorrow morning."

As the village retired to their sleeping mats, the crew of the *Frendrich* met by the fire pit. All were seated except for the captain and his two officers, remaining silent and off to the corner.

He began, "Men, I believe on the morrow there will be a huge celebration, the marriage between Lepo's daughter and one of the tribe's bravest warriors. I've been informed from Yalodo that not only is the entire Irajan tribe participating in the feasts, but that the new members of their society are also joining in. Tomorrow is a huge day for Lepo's people. It is the beginning of a united tribe.

"The way I figure it, after the celebration, we will head down to the beach and finish up construction on the second raft. With the help of our allies, it should take less than a week. We will use Ben's idea and float the rafts out to the rock, tying it off on either side to the *Frendrich*. Next we will stabilize and ready the ship for the tow back to the island. Sliding long poles underneath the hull and tying off to the rafts will accomplish this. After that, we'll start cutting the rigging that secured the ship to the rocks. Ideally, the stern section will slide out and be supported by the rafts and we can use our long-boat in the effort also."

Ben was thinking further into the future, "Sir, after we salvage the stern section and rescue the items in your quarters, how will we construct a ship that will bring us to Havana? I know we lack the tools to build one, unless our friends surprise us with the required items. Between all of us, I know for a fact we each are somewhat skilled with carpentry. We lack plans and sketches too, so we wouldn't be positive if the ship's design is seaworthy."

He paused for a moment and continued, "I have been told that there are indigenous island tribes all throughout the Caribbean that use huge dugout canoes made usually from the Ceiba tree. These were capable of holding over one hundred men over long voyages. I think this would be the easiest type of vessel to build. I mean, we can ask the tribe for a guide to take us to Havana. I'd be surprised if these peoples did not have a pier loaded with some canoes."

The crew took in the useful knowledge. The captain smiled, "That would make our lives a whole lot easier. Building a European style ship with little tools and no real ship builders would be a difficult task, but building a dugout, I could see us on our way to Havana within a few months. Unless they have one like Ben mentioned. Well, for now let's rest. Tomorrow will be a fun filled day."

Ben remained seated as he watched his friends heading towards their hammocks in several extra huts set aside for the visitors. He stared deeply into the flames, watching as the fire spread to the fresh logs. The sap that was trapped inside the wood began to pop; the familiar sound sent him on a flashback. He was back home, anticipating the treat laden with butter and salt. A movie he rented earlier in the day was sitting in the DVD player as his family was seated the controller held lightly in his fathers hands, his finger eager to hit "play."

He would open the hot bag with nimble fingers, pouring the contents into a large blue salad bowl. Once seated with his family, his father pressed the green "play" button, beginning the movie.

"Why sit around, letting this movie present itself to me? This new lifestyle is completely different than what I used to know, but it's almost as if I'm in a movie. I'm an actor, foreign to this era, acting out a life as I please. I have no restraints to hold me back, only a drive to push me forward."

He smiled with the thought and then went to bed.

✖✖✖

Throughout the night, Clayton Burns tended the injured man. With what little he had in his medic kit, he managed to clean out the wound completely. The gash required several stitches, but Lepo did not flinch throughout the entire procedure. Once he applied gauze and then wrapped a strip of cloth around his chest, he wiped sweat out of his brow.

"Yalodo, he is a very lucky man. The knife entered here," pointing to the gash, "and missed the vital organs in the chest. The blade did strike bone though, so he will be in some pain for the next few weeks, maybe even months. He should be fine for tomorrow morning's wedding if they decide to have it."

Even in his deep sleep, Lepo heard the phrase 'tomorrow morning's wedding', causing his brain to internalize the statement. In a dreamlike thought, he envisioned the Hetran people uprising and destroying all that he had created. His village burned to the ground, as his fellow villagers ran around screaming. The cause he believed was his daughter's marriage to an Irajan man, instead of a Hetran, which would have united the two tribes forever.

✖✖✖

Garcha checked on Lepo periodically throughout the night, and after making a slight commotion, he awoken the injured man.

"Mmhm, uhh," the man moaned in pain.

The Hetran elder moved beside the man. "How are you feeling?"

"Mmhm, uhh," he moaned again.

Suddenly Lepo's eyes opened and his mouth to move. The pain limiting him to short phrases, "In pain…stop wedding to Hinda…get counsel…must talk when sun comes up…"

Before Garcha could reply, Lepo's eyes and mouth closed, his body accepting another wave of deep sleep.

✖✖✖

The melodic beats that emanated from the Irajan percussion instruments slowly woke Ben and the rest of the crew. He rolled out of the hammock and slipped into his leather moccasins, pulling his shirt on. His hand reached for the corners of his eyes, rubbing the sleep out.

He yawned and then cracked his back.

"Guys, wake up. Something's going on outside." This was purely directed at his brother. Still, Harris remained silent. "I know you heard me, get up."

Jacob and Sal dressed quickly as Ben shook his brother's feet, "Top of the morning."

All Ben heard was a muffled, "Eh."

As Ben and the rest emerged from the huts, they saw the eldest members of both tribes surrounding the fire pit. Yalodo was there, sitting to the side, internalizing everything. Ben ran over to his new acquaintance. Even after treating his wounds from the scuffle with Teshnay, Ben's face was sore and in pain as he talked.

"What's happening?"

"Hold on," he paused, listening to the conclusion of a statement from one of the counsel, "Sorry my friend."

Ben interrupted, "It's all right."

He continued, "Well, it seems the wedding is off," this caused Ben's jaw to drop, "It appears that Lepo had a dream about another war if Hinda was to marry Sepa, so they wish to marry Derkata's son, Wilkamay, to Sepa. This would unite the tribes and will result in a competition. It is a ceremonial sport that is played in the courtyard. I've seen many games over the years, usually it decides who marries whom, or who takes what hut when someone passes away, or who replaces whom in the counsel. It's actually quite exciting. Oh wait, hold on, the counsel speaks again."

…"Yes, I propose that we play a match of batey, Hinda and a companion against Wilkamay and Listroken. The ghosts can be distributed five to each, their leader can join us."

A Hetran man sighed, "Do you think that is wise? They do not know anything about this game."

The Irajan man chuckled, "Yes, which is why I think it wise. It will be humorous. Why not enjoy it? In reality, it will be a fair match, our two greatest warriors versus yours."

The counsel continued their discussion, coming to a conclusion.

Yalodo returned his gaze towards Ben, "I regret to inform you, but you are to play in a game that decides who will be wedded tomorrow."

Ben's eyes looked at the man, then down to the ground, then back to the man, "Wha…what?"

He let off a laugh. "They have agreed that the game will be seven on seven. We will begin when the sun has reached its highest point, and if the team led by Hinda wins, it shall be an Irajan wedding, but if Wilkamay's team wins, then it shall be the first Irajan-Hetran wedding since the days of the Great Tribe."

Ben internalized the information. "Okay, so when are we getting briefed on the game? What's it even called?"

Yalodo smiled as he said the word, "Batey."

30

The crew of the *Frendrich* met with Yalodo by the fire pit several hours after the counsel had came to a decision. Burns arrived late after rewrapping several gauzes around Lepo's chest. The white Irajan asked his friends to take a seat around him so he could speak to them all.

"All right, I've already told Ben of the news, but here it is. Lepo decided that the counsel should decide on whom Sepa will marry. To decide this, two Irajan warriors and two Hetran, will pick five of you for each of their teams on the batey field. Captain Nelson was chosen to join Lepo, Sepa, and the counsel to view the ceremony."

The captain stretched his back before speaking. "Yalodo, tell me of this game."

With a smile, he replied, "Ahh, I was just getting to that my friend."

The crowd hushed to allow the man to speak. "So let's talk about the field. We are in it right now. I've been around neighboring islands where they used stone pillars to lay out the field. We have built our huts to replace those stone pillars. If you noticed, there is a decent sized space in the center. The field is just over fifty paces long, and twenty wide in the middle, twenty-five at each end. It is similar to a capital cased 'I'. Well, you have to move a large rubber ball or sometimes a vegetable leaf ball, from your end, to the opponents…"

Sal turned to Ben and Harris, laughing, "Ahh, like my pastime, soccer."

The brothers chuckled slightly, trying to not get in the way of Yalodo's description of the game.

"…You cannot move the ball with your hands or feet however. Any other body part is allowed, usually heads, elbows, shoulders and knees. Typically the game is played with more participants; the last match was twelve on twelve, so there will be a lot of running involved. The rules have been decided, we shall play until the winning team has ten scores. The team would lose a point, if for any reason the ball stopped moving. The score is kept with a mark on the ground and the game will end after the losing team receives a certain amount of points, ten for this event. In higher status celebrations, the winners are treated like heros and the losers are sacrificed, but no one will be sacrificed today."

The entire crew seemed to sigh at the same time.

Yalodo nodded, "Yes, for now. The women and children will remove the logs around the fire pit and clear the playing field."

"Wait, what about the fire?" asked a voice.

Ben began to picture what the game would be like if there was a burning flame in the center of the field, people being knocked into it with a bump of the shoulder.

"That marks the center. Be careful and avoid it," Yalodo began to turn his shoulder to face Henry, "See that scar? That's from a game I played in years ago, when I was bumped into the hot embers of the flames."

The crowd went silent. Now, each pictured an innocent man burning as they accidentally slipped into a fire in the middle of a game of batey.

Yalodo could not hold his composure anymore; a rather serious look disappeared, revealing a humorous laugh. "I played a joke! They break down the fire and the black embers mark the center of the field."

Robert Linton looked around, noticing each man's reaction to the news. "I still don't understand why we have to do this. Why's it so important to play games. Can't they just like fight over it, whoever wins gets the girl."

Yalodo snapped back, defending the culture of the people who sheltered him for the majority of his life. "First off, we've been fighting for years. This 'game' is part of each and every one of us. It decides everything from agriculture, to boat building, to everyday activities."

Now all eyes were on Linton, the least liked of all the sailors under Captain Arthur F. Nelson. He didn't pull his weight at sea, or ashore. Nelson stood up, "Well, if you do not feel like enjoying a nice Irajan celebration, I suppose you can sit and watch in company of the young and old. I'd gladly take your spot on a team. I suppose it's up to you though, in the meantime, you don't have to attend the meeting if you aren't playing. See you around camp."

Linton picked up the hidden meaning as he lowered his head to the others. "Bloody Hell, I'll play."

✖✖✖

As the participants of the game geared up in several huts, women and children of both tribes swept the area of stones, branches, and leaves. They left the fire pit burning low, to be put out on the second call of the game. The first call was a rapid beating of the mayohaucan for ten seconds; this signified that the field was clean and ready. The next call was that of a seashell. A man would blow into the shell to call the men to the field. The third and final call, a mixture of both the tambour and shell, was to begin the game.

A female villager, roughly fifteen in age, moved towards Ben and Jacob with a handful of deer hides. She nodded for the men to bow their heads so that she could place the hides on their bodies. As Jacob bent down, his medium length hair fell over his eyes. As he parted the hair, he caught the glance of the Irajan girl. She smiled as she placed a hide over the young man's head. As the dark hair plopped out of the neck hole, his handsome features emerged before the cute Irajan girl.

Ben watched the facial exchanges, smiles and smirks, and quickly turned his head, avoiding an invasion of privacy. His eyes turned to Yalodo, supervisor of the gearing of the men. Robert Linton, John Borton and Clayton Burns were being tended to as a young Hetran girl was strapping Ben's shin guards on.

Yalodo sighed at the sight of the joint efforts from the tribes, "Ah, it sure is nice to have peace."

✖✖✖

The acoustic sound emanated throughout the village, causing Ben to jump from the chair he was seated on. Both shin guards and arm guards were tightly fastened with a leather strap. His deerskin hide covered his entire upper body, reaching down towards his hips. Each man was given leather helmets, padded circular hides that had two straps on either side, which would be tied around the neck. The young women went from player to player, putting on the red and white face paint on each man.

The shell whistle rung out now, and Yalodo stood. "Men, are you ready?"

Nodding heads convinced the elder to take lead of the group and escort them to the field. As Yalodo prepared the five sailors, Garcha overlooked Harris, Charles Marconi, Nate Brodkin, Henry Hughson, and Sal. Their face paint was blue and black. All participants of the game had deerskin hides, shin guards, and arm guards.

After the ten sailors emerged onto the field, Yalodo and Garcha showed each team their respective sides. The villagers began to clap as Hinda and Jesetpunta, and Listroken and Wilkamay emerged from different huts and walked to the playing field.

A group of united elders entered center field, standing around the blackened hearth.

"I believe the teams are ready?" said one.

"Indeed, we shall begin shortly," replied the next.

✖✖✖

The tambour played in tandem with the seashell whistle as one of the elders held the vegetable leafed ball, cradling it in his arms. After the third call signaled the beginning of the game, the man threw the ball skyward towards the Blue-faced team, led by Wilkamay and

Listroken. They were the visiting team since the ceremony was held in the Irajan village.

The ball of green, flexible leaves secured together by several wrapped leather straps, rotated through the air. Reaching its maximum height, the ball began to fall to the ground. The men stood in a wall-shaped formation, awaiting the ball. Listroken adjusted his torso to let the ball bounce off his chest. Before it hit the ground, he sent his knee arcing sideways to pass the ball to the right. Henry stood flatfooted, awaiting the pass. As the ball spiraled towards him, he felt the hot breath of a man behind him, waiting as well.

The moment the ball bounced off Henry's shoulder, Jesetpunta bumped him, causing the carpenter to tumble. The contact changed the direction of the pass and the ball rolled towards the red team. Clayton Burns slid to the ground, nudging the ball to his left with his thigh. The ball bounced upwards, and Hinda kneed the ball into the air. On the run, he headed the ball to himself twice before the broad shoulders of Nate Brodkin bumped him.

Several of the sailors stood back a few paces to watch how the game was played, noticing the four natives gracefully using their bodies to move the ball back and forth. This ball was always in motion, never stopping. Slowly each man picked up on the rules.

The focus of play was ten paces, from center field, towards the Blue's end. Hinda and John Borton sent the ball back and forth using their elbows and shoulders. Sal lowered his body for a shoulder tackle, sending John and the ball backwards. Only shoulder tackles or body bumps were allowed, unlike the methods used in American football, these rules were more like Gaelic football.

The ball bounced into the shin of Robert Linton who was playing way behind the tangled men. With a swift movement of his leg, the ball spiraled high into the middle of the men. Each waited nimbly on their toes to jump and bump the ball to another teammate.

Harris was one of the tallest on the field and his full body stretched upwards. With a forearm smash, he send the ball hurling over Linton's head. Before landing, Harris could see the remaining thirteen men scramble for control of the ball. Once his feet touched the smooth dirt, he ran forward to meet the clashing of bodies.

Somehow, Ben ended up with the ball. He bounced it to himself off the ground, making progress towards the other end. He made a successful five running paces before being hit from the side, causing the ball to roll forward. Marconi made a dash for the ball, running stride for stride with Jacob. The two of them dove on the moving ball, shooting it out between the two.

The ball bounced several times into the awaiting elbow of Hinda. His pass went to his fellow warrior who then passed it to Ben. After entering what would have been the twenty pace line, the ball was well into Blue's side. His brother bumped him and the ball arced high into the air.

Sal held his hands together and then bumped the ball with the bone armguard, propelling it into Red territory. Harris was already sprinting that way before his teammate made the hit. He beat out Clayton Burns in a footrace and then slid on the ground to keep the ball in motion.

Both teams ran towards the ball. Harris was almost trampled as he quickly jumped to his feet. The ball passed deep into Red territory, ten paces from the scoring zone. Three men jumped onto it, two Red and one Blue. All were expecting the ball to plop out, but it didn't.

Dead ball.

One of the united elders ran onto the field, blowing into the seashell. The sound meant to break off the play and for the players to return towards their respective side. Since Henry had covered the ball, Blue had to throw off to Hinda's team.

Fifteen minutes into the game, the ball had entered the zone of sand, called the zonetchka by the islanders. Earlier in the day, the women and children who prepared the field spread out a layer of sand five paces from each scoring zone. Once the ball passed this line, a flag was raised. As Red was pushing the ball into Blue's sand zone, then a blue flag was raised. If this flag lasted upright for longer then a flip of a sand dial, approximately one minute, and the defending team would be awarded a point. To reach ten, meant a loss.

Hinda flicked the ball off his hip towards Ben. With an awaiting forehead, he propelled the ball forward. The ball went through two Blue defenders. Just a few feet before the ball would have passed the scoring zone, Wilkamay made a diving effort, deflecting the ball towards the sidelines. A sideline judge raised a Red flag, showing that the Red team had possession of the throw-in.

The sand dial continued to pour its contents from the upper compartment down to the bottom. Time was running out for the Blue team.

As Jacob reached the sideline, he picked up the ball. His eyes looked for an opening, and then he nudged the ball into play with his knee. Jesetpunta waited for the ball as Listroken saw the trajectory of the ball. The two men collided, sending the ball vertical. Wilkamay went to bump it with his hip, but lost his footing at the last second, slipping to the ground.

Now the sand dial was three fourths gone, only fifteen seconds left for Blue to rid the ball out of their zonetchka. As both teams scrambled for possession, Jacob nudged the ball towards Ben. He bounced it into the air once with his forearm before he went to pass the ball. Harris knocked his brother to the ground, but before he got hit, Ben passed it towards Hinda.

The sand dial was empty. An elder blew into the seashell whistle, signifying that the Blue team was scored on. Another whistle blew shortly afterwards and the seven-man teams returned towards each end.

✖✖✖✖

After the next point, the score was scratched into the ground, 6-3 in favor of the Red team. The Blue team could only afford three more points before a Red victory.

After the sixth Red score, Blue kicked the ball deep into Red territory. Both teams collided for the ball, causing it to bounce in every direction possible. After a scramble, the ball popped out into Wilkamay's reach. With a quick wrist bump, he sent the ball hurling towards the zonetchka. It rolled through the area and into the scoring zone. As quickly as the play began, it ended.

6-4 was etched into the ground.

Jesetpunta kicked off for the Red team, sending the ball hurling into the air. Sal positioned his body, craning his neck backwards, so that he could use his head on the return hit. With a snap of the head, the ball arced well past the center field mark, and ten paces into Red. The Hughson father-son rivalry battled over the ball, moving their bodies back and forth to prevent the other to advance. Hinda ran in between the two and cleared it with a solid thigh kick, sending the ball back to midfield, only to be sent back with another great header by Sal.

Just short of the zonetchka, the ball was tipped fifteen paces into the Red territory. The fourteen men bumped into each other, tripping over their teammates or the opponents in the scramble for the leaf ball. Blue pressed on strong, taking inch by inch as the Red began growing weak, allowing Wilkamay's team to capitalize.

Listroken and the two officers of the *Frendrich* charged the ball in a powerful effort, driving the ball into the zonetchka. Several passes later, the score was then changed to 6-5.

Another kickoff, and yet another strong effort led by Wilkamay. Shortly thereafter, the score was tied at six. After clumsy handling by the Blue team, Hinda and his red-faced companions worked together in a graceful display of Batey, sending the ball person to person, scoring within a minute.

The scorekeeper held the stick tightly in his hands, moving the tip through the ground, sketching 7-6 in favor of the Red team. After a solid kick off by Sal, Ben and Jacob passed the ball between each other. Ducking over a high shoulder tackle by his brother, Ben watched as Harris cartwheeled over his torso. The ball was knocked loose in the hit, but the surgeon of the *Frendrich* dove, sliding into the ball, propelling it into Blue territory. Hinda kneed the ball about shoulder high to his fellow Irajan warrior, who with a solid shoulder hit sent the ball into the scoring zone. 8-6.

✖✖✖

Sweat glistened off of every body; all were fatigued and out of breathe from the quick paced game. The score was now 9-8; Blue only had one more point before they lost to Hinda's team. Wilkamay had passed to Sal for their eighth score on a headshot. Red kicked off to Blue, sending the ball spiraling through the air to the far side-line. Before the ball could bounce out of bounds, Henry Hughson knocked it back in play, sending the pass towards the middle of the field.

There was a scramble for the ball, Ben and John knocking into Harris, popping the ball sideways to the left. Wilkamay had studied the progression of the play and stood off to the left of the play, once seeing the ball pop out in his general direction, he let out a whoop and sprinted for the ball. As his wrists touched the ball for a solid hammer hit, Ben lowered his body, sending the Blue team's top player cart wheeling over the young sailor's shoulder. He lay there for a moment with the wind knocked out of his chest. Ben reached his hand down to help the man up, and Wilkamay generously took it. The two darted off into Red territory where the ball was now being forced forward by the combination of Marconi and Listroken.

Both teams pushed hard against each other, but the Blue team continued to force its way through every opening that occurred. Harris took control of a lost ball and kneed it to Henry for the team's ninth score of the game. Wilkamay led his team back to the Blue team's territory as an elder took the ball and handed it to Jesetpunta, the Red team's main kick off man.

With solid contact between his foot and the lower right side of the ball, Jesetpunta sent the ball deep into Blue territory. The ball took a weird bounce off Listroken's head, sending the vegetable leafed mass rolling to the zonetchka. The moment the ball entered the area; an elder raised a blue flag and flipped over a sand dial.

Listroken back peddled and then made contact with the ball with a swift thigh kick.

Ben closed in for the kill, gaining speed as he watched the ball sail towards him. His head craned back for the game winning score, but before contact was made, Wilkamay intervened, crossing the path and passed the ball to the broad shouldered Second Officer of the ship. Ben stumbled as his body clipped the native's hip. Both men fell, but only one stood up.

"Shit!" Ben punched the dirt, disappointed in his failure to end the game.

Now the ball crossed center field, and continued into Red territory. Sal let off a beautiful headshot that sailed over two defenders, heading towards the chest of Listroken. The surgeon noticed that the ball was still in his reach as he crashed into Listroken, hitting it with his elbow, sending it to Hinda. The Red team's captain dribbled the ball with his elbow, sending the ball off the ground, keeping it within his reach. He saw an opening between Wilkamay and the elder Hughson, and darted between, continuing the dribble.

Wilkamay knew that if his opponent passed him, Hinda would be married to the beautiful Sepa. As the figure moved quickly before him, Wilkamay lowered his shoulder, sending his bone square into the man's deerskin padded chest. In the hit, the ball ricocheted off a fist, sending the ball diagonally through the air. The ball bounced once before being swollen up by a horde of diving men. As the men piled on, the ball squeezed out, rolling into Red's zonetchka.

The elders on the sideline raised a red flag and flipped over a fresh sand dial, marking the beginning of a one-minute allowance period.

Sal sent the ball up to his chest with a quick flick of his knee. With a chest thrust, he sent a pass that split the defense, right into the path of Wilkamay, who was running full speed on the attack. He dove forward, striking the ball with all his might, his forehead angling the ball towards the scoring zone. Hinda changed his footing so that he moved his body into the ball's path.

All eyes were on Wilkamay's shot, and Hinda's deflection. The sand dial had dwindled down halfway, the game thirty seconds from being over unless the Red team could knock the ball out of their zonetchka.

Hinda stretched his body as best he could, using every muscle in the effort. The ball ricocheted off his outstretched forearm, bouncing up over his head. It then landed an inch before the scoring zone, causing spectators to stand on the edge of their toes. The momentum from Wilkamay's shot caused the ball to roll in for a Blue victory.

The crowd clapped as an orchestra of chimes, seashell whistles, and tambours all rang out the excitement that filled the village. The two teams huddled at their respective sides, and congratulated each other with a pat on the back. Words were not needed, and even if they were, each player was too sore and winded to speak. Hinda and his opposing player, Wilkamay, embraced on the sidelines, happy with the way the game had unfurled.

***

Lepo watched the entire game from a horizontal position, resting on a wooden platform. He smiled with the results of the game, content that what he had dreamed would happen. It would be an Irajan/Hetran wedding, a ceremony uniting the two tribes forever.

After a warm meal and a speech given by Lepo, the participants of the Batey game retired early, leaving the rest of the united tribe readying the grounds for the ceremony that would follow the next day.

31

The united village sat on logs around the fire as the sun rose the next day. A group of elders played the mayohuacan, a sacred tambour in which they believed the emanating sound was the voice of the Gods. Yalodo stood to greet the sailors and the four natives as the group approached the fire pit.

"Captain, take your men and join the tribe on the logs. After another melody from the village counsel, the ceremony shall begin."

Nelson led his men towards an empty log and each man took their seat. The acoustic sounds reverberated throughout the camp; the sound instinctively caused each listener to sway with the melody. After several minutes of this, the music stopped.

Ben looked around, noticing several men dressed in what seemed to him, women's robes. He later learned that this was a practice for the single males of the village to ask the moon for a wife. His eyes then gazed around the flame, noticing a male and a female with a knot tied around their wedding clothes, which symbolized the myth of the marriage between the two moons of Venus.

Lepo remained horizontal on an elevated stretcher, constructed of wooden strips, beside his daughter. Sepa was standing beside Wilkamay, both with smiles on their faces. Yalodo spoke in a hushed whisper to the two young ones waiting to be married. He turned towards Lepo and with a nod, began the ceremony.

✖✖✖

The village counsel began their constant beat on the tambours as the smoke from the fire pit began to swirl with a gust of wind. As this was going on, Ben gazed around the center of town, remembering the large area of open space that they had played on the day before. The echo of the last tune disappeared into the morning air as the couple faced each other.

Wilkamay bowed his head then untied the knot around his waist. Sepa did the same. With another series of beats from the drum, the crowd began to clap their hands. The white men clapped along, mimicking their hosts. After the music died once more, the couple exchanged the ceremonial cord, made of a red dyed cotton fiber. Wilkamay made a knot around his waist with his wife's gift, just as Sepa did the same. The ceremony did not last long like the weddings Ben were familiar with, but were rather short and meaningful.

Several hours of dance and music played throughout the courtyard, the majestic ceremonial dances kept the foreigners quick on their toes, all were sore from the previous day's activities. None of the crew could keep up with the fast and melodic beat of the percussion instruments. Wiping a flowing river of sweat from his brow, Ben was relieved when the music ended and then the courtyard cleared out.

❉❉❉

After two weeks with help from the villagers, Captain Nelson was content with the constructed rafts, pleased that each were sturdy and seaworthy. After a day's rest, the crew of the *Frendrich* searched the surrounding woods for long, thin poles that would secure the stern section between the two rafts. The work was tough, as each man had to climb through the dense woods and find a tree the right size. Each pole had to be thin enough to bend, but strong enough to not break. This lasted several days and soon enough, he stood in front of his men, two constructed rafts, and a mound of poles. Lepo had agreed to send down several coils of rope that his tribe had amassed over the years, and with the manila line, all were confident of the rescue mission's success.

Studying the waves over the past several weeks on the beach, they decided that in order to easily transport the two rafts via the longboat, it would have to be done just after sunrise. Of the eleven men, all were included in the rescue mission. On raft "A", Charles Marconi led Ben, Harris, Sal, and Robert Linton. The Second Officer was in charge of raft "B", overseeing John Borton, Jacob, and the doctor. Nelson and the elder Hughson remained in the longboat; each would be responsible for the raft's proper securing to the *Frendrich*.

✖✖✖

*A*ll eleven men sat in the longboat, with their oars in the U-shaped oarlocks. The pile of thirty feet long poles were split up, and secured to each wooden raft. The longboat set out, the men rowing as the vessel began to tow the rafts behind, the site of the beach where they had first settled, disappeared in the distance. They found themselves at the familiar jutting rocks. The jumble of sails, stern mast, and stern section were still jammed tightly into the rocks. The rigging could often be seen wrapped around or caught on pieces of rock.

"All right men. Haul in the rafts, and then I want all designated persons to join their respective raft. I'd like Marconi's men to take on the starboard side, and Brodkin on the port. Once in position, the group leader will raise their hands high in the air. Remember men; this is a critical rescue mission. There are several valuables in my cabin that we must recover. Men, are we ready?"

The men nodded with the plan, letting out a "hoorah" and then began executing the first phase carefully, as to not capsize either the longboat or the rafts. Now that all men were in their places, Nelson began letting out the line that secured the longboat to raft "A." As the captain was doing this, Henry Hughson did the same. Both rafts maneuvered slowly as an oarsman propelled the vessels into position.

Each raft leader raised a hand high in the air, signaling that all was well. Ben could see the insides of the stern section from where the raft lay against the ship's starboard side. Meanwhile, he could see his fellow crewmen on the other raft, against the last remaining side planking of the *Frendrich*.

The plan was rather simple; to place the thirty foot long poles between the two rafts and free the rigging and anything else on the ship to allow the remaining vessel to slide backwards off the rocks. If all went to plan, the stern section would plop down on the fifty long poles, evenly spread out every foot of the raft. Once all the poles were strung out between the two rafts, the men began securing the pole down to the raft's edge, using Lepo's much-needed gift.

It was go-time. Both rafts were ready to take on the load of the aft section of the Frendrich. While constructing the rafts, the captain made sure that each was large enough to hold the thirty-five feet of stern that was stranded on the rocks. They figured that the rafts would be pushed somewhat below the water level, but between the buoyancy of the fifty by fifty foot long rafts, it should allow for the towing back to the beach. To calculate the exact data would have been possible if they had the weight of the section and several other factors, but logically, they could only use rough estimates.

Marconi instructed Ben to be the first to climb aboard the starboard side, since he was one of the lightest and most agile of the group. Several of the other men held the raft close to ship so that Ben could easily step over the gap of the moving water beneath him. Studying the scene before him, he noticed that it might be easier to just enter the hull breach and then pace the companionway to get on deck so that he could begin work on chopping caught lines and sails. Once his hands were around a jutting plank, he tested the strength of the wood with a quick jerk. Confident that it would hold his weight, he shifted his body and swung around into the opening. His feet landed with a light thud and he paused in his footsteps, fearing the worst. If any amount of weight shifted the balance of the ship on the rocks, all would be lost.

After waiting for a moment, he turned his head and looked back to his raft leader, "All seems sturdy. Let me get on deck and then send up Linton once Brodkin sends one of his. We got to keep the vessel steady, it's like a seesaw."

Marconi nodded, "Aye, thanks for the heads up."

Ben analyzed the damage of the storm on the interior of the deck he was in. He began picturing in his mind what had happened that night. The ship crashed hard into the rocks, almost completing going over the tip. It ripped the entire bow and a good portion of the middle off, leaving what remained. The stern section was partially in water. The storage deck below where he stood was completely flooded with water. The cool water came in little surges at his feet. He looked down, only seeing less than a centimeter of water covering the second deck.

His gaze then changed upwards, looking at splinters of wood where the deck above had ripped apart. The companionway seemed in decent shape, capable of allowing Ben and the other three to pass from the second deck unto main deck. He called over his shoulder as he began pacing towards the foot of the ladder. "In a minute, call Brodkin and inform him to send one of his men. Wait another few minutes and then send Linton."

"Sounds good, Ben. Be careful, it looks like the seas are picking up."

Ben paced up the stairs, his hands gently grazing the handrails just in case something went wrong. He heard the creaking of each wooden stair below him, but he paced slowly and cautiously. Once he opened the hatch that allowed him onto the main deck, he moved sideways towards the starboard side. He was just four short feet from the splintered edge, he could see in detail each grain of wood as it jutted upwards. Cracks zigzagged all about on the deck. His gaze focused on one man, Captain Nelson. "Cap, all is well so far. Starboard side is ready to receive guiding lines."

After a very tense and long ten minutes, Linton and Ben stood on the starboard side, and Jacob and John Borton on the port. The captain called up to the four men from the longboat, "Good work lads, Brodkin and Marconi will throw up the guiding lines. Once secure to the railings, Henry will heave a line to you. I want that tied to the after mast."

Simultaneously, the two raft leaders tossed up a coil of line, which landed in the awaiting hands of the men on board the *Frendrich*. After the manila ropes were securely tied to the railing, Ben raised a hand. Several seconds after, John Borton also had his hand in the air. The captain saw this and nodded to Henry Hughson to make the long heave.

Henry had coiled the line in his hands, weighing the bundle in his right hand. With his left, he used it to hold the draped line, so that in mid flight, there would be no tangle. Back in his old shipping days, he could make a forty-foot throw accurately. But this was different; he had to clear the fifty feet of poles, and also the distance between longboat and rafts, and rafts and the *Frendrich*. With fingers, he guessed that the throw was slightly over sixty feet. "Captain, this is quite the throw. I'm not sure if I can make it."

Nelson rubbed his beard, pondering an alternate idea. "Well, give it a shot. If it doesn't make it, we can always do a two-step throw, first to a raft and then up to the deck. Then we'd have to straighten out the line. I'll leave the decision up to you."

"All right, cap. I'm going to heave it, see if it makes it."

Ben and the three others stood facing the longboat, seeing Henry Hughson step around the captain so he could be closer to the target. With his left foot on the rear bench, and his right foot solidly planted on the bottom, he breathed in deeply. "Here it goes," he whispered to himself.

His right shoulder dipped slightly backwards, his body turned, left shoulder leaning forward as he prepared for the throw. His entire weight lay on his back leg. With one last set of breaths, his body contorted quickly. Muscles moved through the air at an amazing speed, his body weight shifting to the front leg as his body twisted. The coiled end left his hand, departing his fingers. The release was at a picture perfect 45° angle. The line continued to lengthen in midair, the captain and Henry both allowing for the line to move forward.

All eyes watched as the rope soared high through the air, floating above their heads.

It had just passed over half the cluster of poles, when the coil began its descent to the water. Eleven pairs of eyes watched it continue its fall, hoping the rope would land on the main deck. Even if it landed where Ben had entered the breached ship, all would be impressed with the master carpenter's throw. The seconds strung together, though it seemed more like minutes.

The coil crashed into the water just feet before the breach. It floated there for a moment before anyone acted. Ben shook out of the temporary fixation on the throw's distance, and then quickly hurried towards the hatch and descended the companionway. He stood in the very same spot he had entered the compartment, kneeled down, and then reached his hand into the lukewarm waters of the Florida Straights.

In his bent position, his face stared inches from the blue water below. His fist opened and then his fingers latched around the rope. As he began to stand up, he paused for a moment. He noticed that there was about another inch of water in that compartment. "The ship must have shifted on the rocks or something, hopefully it's not too bad," he mumbled to himself.

He heard a voice from above; it was that of John Borton. "Ben, toss the line up so we can tie it to the mast."

He craned his neck to look at the target, and then shifted his body to allow for the toss. Lowering the coil to about knee level, he began to bend at the knees. With a powerful arced swing, he sent the line upward. The rope fought gravity, but eventually found the hands of the master purser. By the time Ben joined the three others on main deck, John had tied the manila line around the after mast.

Several minutes later, the captain called out to the four men the order of what he wanted cut first. "If you can manage to salvage the sails, try and cut free the rigging. I see some spars that are also caught. Good work so far lads."

The four men got to work, using blades and hands to free the sails and rigging. The idea was for the men to continue this process of freeing the ship until there was only little left holding the ship to the rock. Once complete, then they'd time the swell right and chop the remaining constraints. The remaining crewmen would pull on the lines connecting the longboat and rafts to the stern of the *Frendrich*. The four daring sailors would then hold tightly to the railings, as the ship would slide onto the poles. That is, if all went according to plan.

✖✖✖

Ben held a boarding axe in his hand. He called over to John Borton, who also had a similar cutting weapon. "On the count of three, let's cut this last section of caught rigging." His gaze shifted to Jacob and Robert Linton, both of who were latching their grips onto the wooden railing.

"One…two…three," Ben called out and with a slash, sending the boarding axe ripping through the tarred ratlines and rigging.

The vessel began to shift slightly, the four men held on for the ride. Both Ben and John had hacked the axe into the deck, burying an inch of the blade into the wood. Captain Nelson gave the orders and the sailors at water level began pulling hard on the connecting ropes. The seesaw-like ship began to sway. Creaking of the wood below reverberated through the decks, shaking the very clothes on the men.

As the ship began to slide onto the poles, something beneath the water line got caught on the jagged rocks in the depths of the sea. The ship stopped its descent and listed to port, sending the men stumbling. Ben fell to his knees still with a handhold on the railing. Robert Linton had lost his grip and began to stumble sideways, losing his footing. With a violent shudder, the ship hurled upwards, and then slammed into the water. As this was going on, the tension on the lines that connected the rafts and longboat to the stern section began reeling to and fro. The men on the rafts got low, holding on to the individual logs that made up the large rafts. Captain Nelson and Henry Hughson both took seats on the benches, watching as their vessel began to shift once more, both in question of what would happen.

✖✖✖

*T*here was a slight splash and a shooting of pain, as Robert Linton crashed through the railing and over the side of the ship. His body landed between the jagged rocks below. He scrambled for a hold to pull him away from the ship that was just several feet in front of him. The vessel swayed again, whether it came from the wind, or from the current, it did not matter. He pressed his body close to the rocks to avoid the oncoming hull, but it was not enough. The ship's side banged against the sharp rocks, crushing him. Screams of unearthly pain emanated from his body.

✖✖✖

*B*en could hear the screams as the boat continued to shift; slamming, and sliding off the rocks. Water began to fill the second deck of the ship, causing the weight to shift once more. The very end of the section rose as the breached section filled with water. Once they reached the hatch, they climbed down the companionway in single file. The ship surged once more, sending them stumbling down. As they hurried to the breach, they could see that the ship had landed on the first few poles that lay between the rafts. The raft leaders called to the men to hurry, the stern section looked as if it were to reunite with the bow on the seabed below.

"Marconi, relay a message to Ben. Tell him to rush into my quarters, and go to the second drawer on the right side of the desk. Take out the lock box. Once the *Frendrich* slides off the rocks, we must rescue Linton."

"Aye, captain," Marconi passed word to Ben, just as the two others began boarding the rafts by stepping from pole to pole. Both men made it to safety as Ben ran towards the passageway that led to the captain's quarters. He passed by the companionway, around several shipboard items that had fallen, and then placed a hand on latch. His shoulder pressed against the door, as four inches of water flowed in, spreading throughout the captain's quarters. This was the very same room that he had learned all about charts and navigation, but now it looked like a tornado had ran through it. The books had fallen off the shelves, maps lay strewn about, cabinet latches had broken, revealing items upside down and fractured, the desk had flipped over and sat upside down against the far wall.

Ben made his advance, stepping over fallen items and then reached the desk. Looking for the drawers, he realized he would have to adjust the desk. He reached around and tugged on the corner, pulling it away from the side planking. Ben then heaved upwards, setting the desk back on its four wooden legs. He situated his position beside the desk and then pulled open the second drawer like he had been requested to do. Reaching in, he pulled out the lock box.

"I've always thought that there was something that Captain Nelson hid from me, and now it's time to find out the truth!"

He looked at the portholes and the window-like veranda at the very end of the stern. That was where Nelson and his Officers would stand and smoke their pipes, relaxing after a day's work. The sun shined in, allowing enough light for Ben to weigh his decision once more. He shook the thoughts out of his head, and opened the unlocked lid. He stared into the lock box, fingers sorting through papers. The first paper was a list of ten names; El Perro Loco was the last one with a line through it. There were three more names that remained; Blood Spot, Blood Bones, and a name that had been smudged.

The next item he pulled out was the captain's Letter of Marque. He replaced the two items into the box and then shuffled his hands around. He then pulled out two sacks, full to the top. He decided there was not enough time to look through each one, so instead he rattled the contents. He distinctively heard the clinking of the gold pieces. Glancing down, he noticed the water was now knee-high.

He closed the lid, locking the box as he made his way towards the entryway carrying the box under his armpit.

✖✖✖

*A*s Ben emerged into view the Captain sighed with relief, fearing the worst. The wooden poles that had joined the two rafts, no longer supported the weight of the stern section as it slid off. Ben jumped the six-foot distance and landed beside Marconi, Sal, and Harris. There was a moment of silence as the ship lay there, continuing to fill with water.

✖✖✖

*S*till holding onto the rocks, Robert Linton screamed out in pain as the vessel moved off of him. A jagged rock outcropping pierced straight through his right leg, spewing blood in every direction. His left leg felt that every bone was broken. He lost his grip and then slowly slid down into the water.

Captain Nelson shouted to Marconi's raft, the closest raft to the jagged rocks. "Cut all lines made fast to the *Frendrich*!"

If they had not acted as quickly, the sinking ship would have flipped the rafts and longboat. Once all lines were cut, Marconi sent out Harris to jump in and swim to the injured man. Linton's head popped out of the water every so often, but he could not tread water with his lower body. He arced his shoulders back to allow his head to keep his head out of the water.

Harris dove in and swam quickly with strong strokes to the rescue of his shipmate. Positioning his body in back of Linton's he reached under Linton's left arm and grabbed the right shoulder. With his right arm and legs, he began to stroke sideways, pushing through the water back towards the rafts. Once he was close enough to the raft, Marconi and Sal reached out and lent a hand in the effort. They pulled the injured man into the safety of their arms, and then helped Harris climb up.

32

Beside the fire pit, the roaring flames touched the evening sky. Clayton Burns doctored the wounds as the captain stood at his side.

"He will most likely die within a week, unless I can successfully amputate his right leg and close the wound. He has lost too much blood. His wounds are large and deep. His left leg will heal if infection does not set in."

The captain's face grimaced at the news. "I shall go with whatever you think is best. If you think amputating his leg will save his life, then do it."

"I only have several tools in my kit, hopefully I can manage."

"When would you prefer to do the amputation?"

The doctor looked at the setting sun. He shook his head, "Well, it should be done as soon as possible, but it will be dark soon. We could either wait until morning when I have good visibility, or we can attempt it by the fire."

"That is what I thought. It's a life or death situation now. We must act quickly."

❈❈❈

By the fireside, Clayton Burns sifted through his medical kit. With the help of his shipmates, he laid out a spread of sail on the smooth sand. "Get Linton and place him here. I need water, some strips of cloth to clean the wound and wrap the leg, and a strip of leather. Lastly, I'll need a wooden stick for Robert to bite down on."

The joint mission scrambled around camp to get the requested items. Minutes later, the doctor stared at the tools he had assembled and placed beside the injured man. Usually he would pour a bottle of alcohol onto the wound and even give the patient several sips to calm the man down, but they did not have any available.

"Put a towel under his head to make him comfortable, tilt his head like this," he motioned for Nate Brodkin for the proper angle. "Good. Charles, if you could hold down his body near the shoulders. Henry, retrieve your sword, we'll need that to heat the blade and close the wound. Jacob, hold down his right leg."

Moments later, all were in their positions. Linton was in and out of consciousness; the pain he was suffering from was unbearable. The flames flickered off the scalpel that his hand stretched out to reach. Brodkin placed the stick in the man's mouth; his limp body reacted slowly. "It'll be all right, Robert," he called down to the man.

With the scalpel in hand, the doctor walked over to the collection of water, dipped in the blade, and then progressed to the fire. Holding the blade in the flames, the heat cleansed the blade of germs. Closing his eyes, he said a silent prayer for God to guide his hands, skillfully and carefully.

Jacob had one hand on the man's right hip, and the other pressing down on the kneecap. The doctor straddled Linton, and began measuring the distance from the hip that he wanted to make the cut. After pealing off the man's breaches, he realized the wound tore away most of his thigh, calf and shin. The hairs on his neck rose.

He tied the strip of leather just above where he would make the incision, and pulled it tight. Touching the blade to Linton's thigh, an inch above the wounds, he cut through the first few layers of skin with the sharp scalpel. He continued around the thigh, just cutting deep enough all around. Next, he poured in warm water into the cut, to cleanse the area for the next procedure. As he dipped his hand into the warm water a cloud of blood spread through the water. He continued making incisions so that he could peel the skin back, allowing for a passage to the thighbone. Once the V shape incisions were made, he poured more water into the wounds.

There were periods where Linton would wake from the pain. His face would grimace, wrinkles of skin would form around the eyes and his mouth would contort. The last incision caused the man to jump, but the men forced him back down. Clayton Burns placed the scalpel down beside a handsaw at his side.

✖✖✖

*B*en, Sal, and Harris stood to the side, trying to get their minds off everything that had happened earlier in the day. The plan had failed miserably, besides saving the lock box. Now all that was on the *Frendrich* was lost to the depths of the sea. The wind had carried the screams and moans to the furthest reaches of the camp. All could hear the bone crack as the saw cut clean through.

In a panicked rush, the doctor retrieved Henry's long blade from the flames. "Men, hold him down!"

He pressed the blade to the stump of his thighbone, closing the wound. The heat from the blade seared through the skin, burning the flesh. The air carried the repugnant smell to all the sailors on the beach.

The doctor then wiped the area with a wet cloth and dressed the wound with dry strips of cotton. As twilight had turned to darkness, the procedure was complete. Captain Nelson called the remaining men to meet to discuss the following plans.

"We will continue to doctor Robert until he shows signs. If he looks to be getting better, we shall bring him on the journey to Havana. Tomorrow morning, I want a party of about six to come with me to talk to Lepo and his village. We will then arrange for our departure from the island. Do you have any questions of what is to follow?" His gaze looked around at his on looking crew.

All shook their heads. He began to speak again, but decided to save it for a later time. Ben picked up on the lip movements and thought to himself, "I wonder what he was going to say."

✖✖✖

*T*he men retired to their leaf frond beds. Ben, like usual, sat by the fire and stared into the flames. He heard footsteps behind him and saw that it was Captain Nelson.

"Hello, cap."

"You got something on your mind, lad? Every one's fast asleep."

"Eh, just thinking about things. I like to get everything out of my head before I sleep, it's something I've done since I was a kid."

"Ah, I understand. By the way, I know that you know."

Ben looked into the captain's eyes. "What do you mean, sir?"

Nelson smiled, "Lad, I'm not dumb. I can see you are quite intelligent. You always seem to be pondering things, all the time. I've seen your face react when you pick up on key words when you hear conversations that I have with Nate and Charles."

"Oh?"

The master of the *Frendrich* continued, "Yes. Do not fret though; I will make the announcement public before we make the trek to the Irajan village."

"Sir, but why have you not told us this before?"

"Well, it is simple. It is easier to recruit men for a leg of a journey. They think that they are delivering cargo to a port, as merchants. Well, not only do we do that, we also carry out missions. I am entrusting you with this knowledge because I see something in you. Anyway, the engagement with El Perro Loco, it seemed that we were the prey in that case, but it's the other way around. I know you saw the documents. I remembered that I forgot to lock the lid before the ship went down. When you brought it to me, it was locked. I didn't want to say anything to you until we were alone."

Ben nodded throughout the conversation. "So, it's true that the *Frendrich* was used as a privateer? I saw names that were crossed off, and then there were three after that. Uh, Blood Spot, Blood Bones, and one I couldn't make out."

"Yes, it is true. Captain Blood Bones and his crew had infiltrated an English ship in the harbor of Boston. There was a little skirmish between *La Monzón* and the two remaining English vessels. Blood

Spot was found in a rowboat once his ship went down. The captured pirates were sent to the dungeons of Castillo de los Tres Reyes del Morro in Havana, Cuba. Our mission is to interrogate Blood Spot. We have to find the whereabouts of their hideout. I've heard rumors that it is somewhere near Port Royal, but if we can get an exact location, we can surprise him and his men. I believe that his hideout, houses a town. It's, how you say, a pirate domain, something along those lines. Not only will we have to fight Blood Bones, but we will have to contend with many others."

Ben realized that everything added up. "I see. We'll need to get a lot of men then for this raid. So how many of the crew knows besides me?"

Captain Nelson replied, "Only my officers. You may think this strange, but we get a new crew for each leg of a journey. Until now, that is. You, your brother, and Sal, have shown dedication that my officers and I have noticed. The eleven of us, if Robert survives and is in the mood to, will remain part of the crew, unless they wish to part company. We will have to obtain a new ship, bigger than the *Frendrich* with a larger complement. Usually we would carry about ten more crewmen than a normal merchant. Our typical missions are to deliver notes and messages between governors, but until recently, Blood Bones and his horde of men have wrecked havoc upon the Crown. Three months worth of colonial taxes were stolen in his deception. I was recruited for the daring mission; I have never failed, and I do not plan on it."

He paused for a moment, letting the words sink into Ben's head. "Yes, you may be thinking that we are stranded on an island, in the middle of the shipping lane between the Bahamas and Cuba. Ships may pass by, but we do not have time to wait and twiddle our thumbs. Tomorrow we will get our gear together, and obtain a canoe that you had previously mentioned."

Ben nodded, "Yes, I told you all how the Caribbean islanders would travel island to island with huge dugout canoes. So, you plan on rowing to Havana from here?"

"Well, with the help of Lepo's warriors. I had a dream the other night. Lepo directed several of his best warriors to escort us there safely. If this does occur, we will be there quicker than if we tried to navigate there. I have no charts, or navigational equipment."

"I understand. So we'll get a new ship, interrogate Blood Spot, and then hunt for his cousin? What will we do after that?"

As Ben asked the question, a familiar face popped into mind, it was that of the beautiful Leah Williamson. Nelson replied, but Ben was still fantasizing about the young woman he had met on their port call in Freeport.

At the conclusion of their conversation, the two retired for a night's sleep. Clayton Burns would wake up every few hours to check up on Robert Linton, changing the dressing to the wound and cleaning it with warm water. He checked Robert's forehead, and he could tell by the complexion on the man's face, that he was burning with fever.

✖✖✖

When all were awake and sitting on logs by the fire, Captain Nelson had cooked up some warm water, and made coconut tea. They poured the scalding water into a coconut shell, and each man drank. The shell gave off a unique flavor, and no one complained.

"Men, I have something to tell you all."

They opened their ears, and listened to the captain as he told the news about their true intentions, and the plans that were to follow. After cleaning the boiling pot, loaned to them by Lepo, Nelson had picked the men to accompany him to the village. Henry, Sal, Harris, and Jacob remained to look after Robert and ready the camp for departure.

Retracing the familiar paths that linked the beach to the Irajan village, the five men walked. On arrival to the clearing, Lepo's men greeted them and brought them to the chief's hut. Lepo was resting on a bed of hides. His complexion was normal now, but he could still feel the pain of the wound he suffered from Teshnay. Through Yalodo, he said to the sailors, "Good to see you once again. We have much to do on getting you off the island."

The two leaders communicated for several minutes as they had reached an agreement.

Lepo stood up slowly and told them to follow. He led them to a pair of surplus huts, a storage facility for all white men's possessions that had accumulated in the frequent shipwrecks around the island.

Yalodo spoke with Ben, telling him of the rocks and reefs that surrounded the island. In the sand, he drew the diagram. "Here, you see," his fingers traced an X. "This is where you had your encampment. We are here, in the Irajan village. There is the bridge that links the two villages. There are two piers, located here and there. Both tribes use canoes to communicate and trade with other islands. I'm assuming we will carry these goods and wares down to your encampment. I heard about Robert, it is quite a tragedy. There is no use to carry him all the way to the pier. So we'll have to row the dugout canoe to where you're beached."

Ben replied, "Yeah, that's what I was thinking. So, Lepo is giving us everything in these huts?"

Ben had remembered the huts that he entered when he was a captured prisoner; the many uniforms, weapons, crates of goods, and gunpowder. It was almost enough to supply a small army and a small army they would soon plan to be.

33

The following day, all the supplies from the Irajan and Hetran collections had been carried to their beach encampment. The sailors helped out with the effort, as they made several trips back and forth carrying armfuls of goods. Lepo had appointed eighteen of his strongest warriors, led by Hinda and Yalodo, to escort them to Havana. This pleased Nelson a great deal, and Lepo would always reply, "It's the least I can do, you helped bring these constant battles to an end."

The forty foot long canoe was placed in the water from its storage and circled the island, navigating between rocks and reefs that plagued the islands coasts. After the sailors helped Hinda and his men pull the vessel onto the beach, they returned to the village for one last feast. On the morning after, they would depart.

✖✖✖

Lepo was now strong enough to walk without much assisance, though occasionally requiring support. On one of the previous trips, he brought along his stretcher and let Captain Nelson use it to carry the Robert Linton to join in the festivities.

All waited around the fire as the villagers slowly cooked the pig roast and the smaller game on sticks. Ceremic pots boiled the vegetables to make a delicious soup of the various harvested crops. Yalodo translated between the sailors and the natives, discussing plans of what was to come.

"…Lepo, once we get to Havana, we will continue our journey, interrogating Blood Spot until we learn the exact location of Captain Blood Bones."

"But friend, will you ever come to visit my people? After all, you did bring peace amongst us."

Nelson smiled, content with the allegiance he had made. Soon, they would head out for Cuba, talk to a representative of the Crown, and then get a new ship. He needed one capable of attacking an island full of the most dangerous pirates that looted the Caribbean and the colonies' coasts.

He snapped back into focus as the first servings of vegetables came out on small wooden platters. After a long and hard day's work, they swallowed the food without even chewing. The next dish consisted of the small game that the children had caught. The barbequed rodents and birds were the appetizers for the huge pig roast. Women poured the island's brew into drinking bowls, all were eager for the prospects of the future. The two leaders continued speaking, discussing possibly developing settlements after all of Captain Nelson's business was attended to.

With a tip of a blade, the woman in charge of the roast decided it was time for the meat to be distributed. Once the main course was in front of each villager or sailor, the familiar tune on the mayohuacan rang out. Lepo stood up to speak to his people. After a short speech with the village elders, he turned to their visitors. "It is with great honor for us to have you here that you have joined us for this feast that we have before us. In the morning you will depart our island, and I am looking forward for you all to visit once again."

After Yalodo finished translating, Nelson replied, "And yes, I will not need Yalodo as a middle man then. I plan on having him teach us your tongue."

The two representatives laughed as the sailors cheered and the villagers slapped their thighs. They ate until the sun had set, and continued as the mayohuacan continued its constant beating throughout the meal. Finally it stopped, as did the food and drink. With one last grand speech, the entire village retired to their sleeping mats.

The sailors would enjoy their last night on the island, for once the sun marked the beginning of a new day, and all the last minute food provisions were loaded for the weeklong journey, their next sequence of adventures would soon begin.

✖✖✖

Linton was positioned on a bed of deerskin, as supplies and men filled the interior space of the canoe. With the thirty-one people, half of those who would row at a single time, there was not much room to move freely. Just before loading, Hinda and Lepo met with the captain of the crew, informing them that they could island hop until they reached the end of the Florida Keys, which would take about half a week. Once past, it would be a straight four days due south to reach Havana.

Villagers who stood at the water's edge waved to their departing warriors and their new friends. The canoe shoved off, Hinda at the stern steering with an oar, as seven on each side rowed. Yalodo taught the warriors basic phrases in English, so that the helmsmen could call cadence for each stroke. As the canoe moved swiftly through the water, the beach faded slowly into a memory.

Ben gazed at the beach, the place he called home for the past few months. He waved goodbye to the several huts, the longboat that had been tied off to a tree, the two rafts, and the fire pit where he had learned so much about himself and to his shipmates. He turned his attention to the task at hand, and enjoyed the breeze on his face as the sun beat down on a warm Caribbean afternoon. The canoe was wide enough to fit four across; one would sit closest to the edge and paddle, while his replacement would rest beside his shoulder.

They navigated around the jagged rocks, which had brought such trouble to their ill-fated crew. Nelson sensed a huge sigh of relief once they were well pass, touching the brim of his hat in salute to the graveyard.

"Men, it is time for us to forget the past and move on to the future. We are looking at a nine to ten day journey ahead of us. I plan to make camp every other night to stretch our legs and get off the canoe now and again, but for the most part, we will rotate out, continually keeping the vessel in motion."

The men continued rowing until the sun was halfway in its descent to the horizon. As the men shifted positions, the canoe drifted with its momentum, so that fresh pairs of arms could propel the vessel. The men who had just been replaced each were handed a handful of berries and strips of dried meat. A pouch of water was passed around to quench their thirst.

Ben's eyes moved around as his body leaned forward to get the maximum pull on the stroke, catching glimpses of airborne birds slicing through the clouds. He pulled the paddle through the water, his hands moving towards his body. They sighted the neighboring island, traveling just under twenty miles since they began their journey.

They continued rowing, switching two more times before the sun met the horizon. In the last rays of twilight, Nelson asked for a torch to be lit at the ends of the vessel. Yalodo spoke to a resting Irajan and watched as the man took out a large bowl from among the pile of goods. He opened a satchel full of twigs, leaves, and dry grass. From another leather pouch, he took out a torch, placing it by his side. On his hip, he had a small tool bag, and took out flint and steel. Within a minute, he was blowing into the bowl, providing sufficient oxygen to strengthen the fire. He then grabbed the torch, and dipped the flammable cloth on the end of the handle into the flames. Once the fire spread, he passed it to the after end. Spreading another handful of kindling onto the fire, he let it catch before placing the second torch in. Soon, both ends of the dugout canoe were lit, providing enough visibility to continue their rowing.

Hinda stood at the bow with a hand over his eyes, straining to see a landmark on a distant island. There was a patch of trees in the middle of the beach, and when viewing this dead-on, the canoe would have to adjust course a few degrees to the left. After the canoe edged closer to the coast, Hinda sighted the marker and called over his shoulder to Yalodo. He then passed word to the port side;

the rowers took the wooden blades of the paddles out of the water for half a minute as the starboard side continued to row. The men could feel the change in angle as they continued in their plight to Havana.

Ben could only guess it was a little after ten when the rowers switched out once more. He ate another handful of berries that were passed around and then slumped over, his head leaning against a pile of British uniforms. His muscles ached with the two hours of straight rowing. Within moments, his eyelids lost the battle with gravity, and he was sound asleep as the helmsmen called out the melodic cadence, "One, two, pull."

While Ben was asleep, the dugout canoe passed by a handful of islands comprising the middle section of the Florida Keys. Once awaken for the next shift, he dunked his hand over the side into the water and let the refreshing liquid trickle by his fingertips. He brought his hand back and then wiped out the crusts of sleep that had formed around his eyes. His hands then combed back his hair. "Man I need a haircut," he mumbled to himself.

✖✖✖

Upon daybreak, Nelson caught sight of the next spit of islands that they were to pass. They've been nearing twenty hours of straight rowing, and he could see that his men were aching with pain. After one more switch of rowers, Yalodo ordered Hinda to make an approach to the white sand beach. The canoe maneuvered around a reef that the Irajan were familiar with, and then circled around another outcropping of rocks. Shortly after, the canoe touched bottom.

Hinda and three other warriors hopped out from the bow into the knee high water, taking grips on the canoe's shell. Waiting for the right wave to come along, the men dragged the canoe five feet up the beach. The remaining men filed out one by one, the last two carrying the stretcher holding Robert Linton. Once all were out, they continued beaching the canoe.

Yalodo and Captain Nelson spoke off to the side, and then returned to the mix of men. "Make a fire, and relax. We'll stay until sunset, that way we aren't rowing in the hottest part of the day."

He watched as several men began searching the wooded area beside the beach for dry leaves, twigs, branches, and logs. One of the warriors had brought a crudely fashioned axe with them for just this reason, and retrieved it from the canoe's stores. Within a half hour, a roaring fire warmed the areas of the camp. Clayton Burns doctored Linton by the flames, peeling off some bloodied cloth and applying another pad to cover his amputation. Once satisfied, he placed a deerskin hide over the man for additional warmth. The doctor then stood up, his neck craning each way to find the captain.

After seeing the bushy beard clinging to the man's chin, the doctor approached the master of the lost *Frendrich* and began speaking before he came to a stop.

Nelson looked back, nodding. "How long do you think he has?"

"The fever's getting worse. This voyage is killing him. I think we should've left him."

"Yes, I understand. He wanted to continue the voyage with us, but I should've thought with my head, not my heart."

The doctor replied, "I think he'll be all right as long as we stop each day like we did today. He'll rest by the fireside."

"Yes, but there are only so many islands we can stop at. Lepo said that once we reach the westward island, it's a straight shot south. You think he'll make that four day stretch?"

There was no need for an answer, the horizontal motion the doctor's neck proved his point.

"I see. Well, should we inform the men?"

He scratched his ear, shrugging his shoulders. "It's up to you cap. They are strong men, I think they can take it."

"Aye, that they are."

✖✖✖

The thirty men moved away out of earshot of the injured man, entering the first few feet of wooded area bordering the beach. Yalodo and Nelson informed the mixed group of the update on Linton's condition.

"I do not see him surviving the last leg of the journey. He has gotten progressively worse."

The men eyed the doctor, nodding at the unfortunate news. Nelson sensed the uncomfortable looks on his men's face and then called out, "Let's return to the fire and sing songs and tell stories. What Robert would want last, is for us to be dull and be unlike ourselves. I want Ben to tell us some of his classic stories, like the good ole days."

The sailors let off a cheer and then returned to camp with raised spirits. Ben took charge of the first song, as Yalodo relayed Hinda and his warriors each phrase. He went through the verses of "Drunken Sailor," as his friends slapped their sides, sitting crossed legged on the white sand. Morale boosted as stories were passed between individuals, being translated by Yalodo.

✖✖✖

They made camp several days later as the sun's rays scorched down upon them. Robert Linton continually degraded in health and spirits, quickly losing the will to live. The Irajan warriors had made a fire, collecting twigs, leaves, and branches when the canoe was first beached. Clayton Burns leaned over the feverish man, placing the back of his wrist on the man's forehead. It nearly burned the doctor's flesh on contact.

"Captain, I need a wet rag with warm water, he is entering the last phase before death. Look at his mouth, feel his chest. There's an irregular breathe, it's as if he was missing every other."

Several sailors ran to the side of their comrade. Tension kept the men on their toes as the doctor ripped open Robert's cotton shirt. Taking the wet rag that Nelson had handed him, he let the water drip over the man's chest. Rubbing the cloth side to side, he tried to circulate the man's blood flow. His head craned back and he let out an unearthly moan. Death was knocking on his door.

"Shit, don't leave us!" The doctor yelled, rubbing harder and faster, trying to stimulate the flow in the man's veins.

It was no use, Linton's complexion changed to a pasty white, life continued to flow out with each exhale. He passed away as the sun kissed the horizon, leaving the ten sailors mourning the loss of their friend as the last rays brightened the day.

"Find a length of canvas in the canoe," he called to the Ben and Harris.

The brothers jumped from their kneeling position and ran to the beached vessel. They went from pile to pile, rummaging with quick hands. Finally, Harris found the length of sail that was stowed beneath a pile of hides.

"Hey, help me out with it, it's stuck."

Their hands worked together, freeing the canvas sail. They returned back to the fire pit where the other men were seated.

"Here it is cap," Ben said.

"Good, place it on the ground. We are going to place Linton's body in it, sew the fabric around him, and have him a true seamen's burial."

They went to work, and began poking holes every half-foot with a blade. Once the holes were punched, Linton's lifeless body was carried and placed down gently in the fold of the sail. Before any stitching began, the captain had ordered a search around the beach for rocks to help the bag sink. Once the men returned with a pile of stones, they placed it in the bag by the man's toes. The stitching began by his feet, and then slowly moved up inches at a time. After crossing Robert's arms across his chest, Nelson continued the stitching until he stopped at the collarbone, leaving the man's ghastly face visible.

"I don't have a Bible with me, but I am familiar with these occasions. I've lost some great men in my days. Robert Linton was a good man, though he often did not pull his weight. It is still very unfortunate however," he cleared his throat, and then put his head down, closing his eyes. The sailors did the same, and Yalodo motioned for the Irajan warriors to do the same.

"In the beginning God created the Heavens and the Earth. Now the Earth was formless and empty, darkness was over the surface of the deep, and the Spirit of God was hovering over the waters. And God said, 'Let there be light,' and there was light. God saw that the light was good, and He separated the light from the darkness. God called the light 'day,' and the darkness he called 'night.' And there was evening, and there was morning, the first day. And God said, 'Let there be an expanse between the waters to separate water from water.' So God made the expanse and separated the water under the expanse from the water above it. And it was so. God called the expanse 'sky.' And there was evening, and there was morning, the second day. And God said, 'Let the water under the sky be gathered to one place, and let dry ground appear.' And it was so. God called the dry ground 'land,' and the gathered waters he called 'seas.' And God saw that it was good."

He paused for a moment's silence. "This trade that we partake on, venturing the seas that God, Himself has blessed as good, is dangerous. We battle pirates, fight the enemies of the Crown, and rough the seas that are thrown at us. Together we have fared well, with some bumps along the road of life. I am happy that this has happened though. I could not ask God for a better and more loyal crew than I have now. You have all shown your quirks and benefits in the past several months, and I am pleased to see that you have all improved. Before the voyage began, I had three dedicated officers. Jensen McCafferey was a good man. I could not ask for better service from Nate and Charles. Their leadership has been proven multiple times.

"The addition of you all now, will solidify our next mission. I plan on hiring at least a hundred for the next journey, from Havana to the pirate lair. This will be a test of intelligence, strength, and wit. I believe we have what it takes. Again, the loss of Robert will be felt in our hearts. He has come so far, just to be taken away from us half a week before we will walk the streets of Cuba. But, we must not let it get to us, we have lots to do, and we will need straight heads and clear minds to accomplish this.

"I will conclude this service with the 'Lord's Prayer'. Our Father, Who art in Heaven, hallowed be Thy Name. Thy Kingdom come. Thy Will be done, on earth as it is in Heaven. Give us this day our daily bread. And forgive us our trespasses, as we forgive those who trespass against us. And lead us not into temptation, but deliver us from evil. Amen."

The sailors opened their eyes and looked at the captain. Nelson had kneeled down once more to finish up the last bit of stitching; making sure that the entire body was wrapped in the canvas.

Ben stood off to the side of camp, twiddling around with a pair of sticks. He cracked them both in half, only breaking the inside, and leaving the sapling's bark still in touch. He wriggled each back and forth, and then was content as he slipped in the shorter branch over the other, creating a crude cross. Holding the remembrance in his left hand, he dug a few inches into the ground with nimble fingers. He placed the cross into the hole and then pushed surrounding dirt from around and four rocks on each side of base for extra support.

✖✖✖

There was still half an hour before the last rays of sunlight disappeared, allowing for the night to take over. The men hurried back to the canoe, lighting the torches at the bow and stern. Several Irajan warriors lagged behind, and once all were inside, they began pushing the dugout canoe over the smooth sand. The stern hit water first, Nelson who took over at helmsmen for the shift, began paddling sideways to turn the ship around. With one last push, the warriors jumped in and then the assigned men grabbed their paddles.

"All right men, once we are out a bit from land, we will finish the last of the ceremony."

The men paddled in unison, causing the vessel to glide through the water. A burden was lifted from the men's minds, and all were now focused. Robert Linton was in a far better place. Captain Nelson cleared his throat and began speaking, "Men, that's enough. Take the paddles in; we can glide for the time being."

The orders were obeyed and once each paddle was inside the boat, Nelson stood up. "I would like the body to be moved from the stern to the bow and from the bow back amidships. Each person must touch the canvas in remembrance of a lost comrade."

Nelson reached down by his feet and grabbed the canvas with strong hands. He waited for Marconi and Sal to also do the same. After the man's limp body was lifted chest high, they began passing the canvas burial bag forward. Each man had his turn, even the Irajan warriors joined in. This brought a sense of unity amongst the men of the drifting canoe.

The bag now returned aft, towards the center of the vessel, where it stopped by Ben and Yalodo. With the help of Hinda, the three each held the bag chest high. Captain Nelson called out, "Place the weighted side closest to the gunwale, and have his head pointed in."

The men did as told, and then angled the body at a forty-five degree angle. "Release the body."

"Aye, cap." They said as the men guided the body bag. Robert's feet hit water with a slight splash, and the rocks quickly took over. The weight began pulling the rest of the body down, and finally the entire canvas bag was underwater. Ben looked into the water one last time, seeing the bag get smaller and smaller until it met Davy Jones' locker.

The captain began reciting the Lord's Prayer once again, and the remaining sailors piped in. At the conclusion of the prayer, he paused for a moment, and then spoke once again. "The last rays of light are dissipating; let's get back to the task at hand."

The men picked up their paddles and began on Nelson's cadence. Hinda guided the canoe due south, heading towards the island of Cuba. They continued with their two-hour shifts, never stopping for longer than a minute to exchange the paddles to their partners. The vessel made little progress that first night after their friend's death, but the next day they continued at a quickened pace. By now, the men were already too sore to care, and their bodies accepted the grueling speed of their southward passage.

34

May 2ND, 1763
Havana, Cuba

everal days later Hinda and Yalodo guided the canoe around the shipping lanes that passed by Cuba. They knew that they were close, but from their low vantage point, they could not see land yet. They continued rowing, and after another shift had ended, Captain Nelson was the first to spot the two fortresses on either side of the entrance to Havana. Castillo de la Punta was southwest of Castillo del Morro, the fortress that housed the huge dungeon in the foundation of the battery.

As the two objects gradually increased in size, they soon found themselves only several hundred yards away. This rejuvenated their muscles and they increased their pace. They were nearer to Castillo del Morro, coming in at the southward approach. Once they were fifty yards off, they altered slightly to port, to stay towards the east-ward banks of the channel.

Once past Castillo de la Fuerza, the canoe maneuvered to the right, hugging to that bank as close as possible, straying away from the middle of the channel. A four-mast tall ship passed by just several cable lengths away; the pressure of the water below billowed out, sending waves on either side of the comparably larger sea-going vessel.

Captain Nelson noticed this and told all to take the paddles out of the water, just keeping the blades touching the white foam. The disturbance in the water caused the canoe to rock violently back and forth. When the waters settled, he gave an order and the rowing commenced. The paddles propelled the vessel forward and they headed southwest along a stretch of land that housed several docks.

Nelson looked dead ahead, spotting Castillo de Atarés. As the canoe neared the wharf, several dockworkers ran to the water's edge, awaiting their vessel. Nelson ordered a man at both ends to toss the lines to the men on the wharf. The manila rope soared through the air and landed in the awaiting hands of the longshoremen. They tugged on the line, pulling the canoe in towards the pylon bumpers. Ben glanced around at his surroundings, noticing that the bumpers were constructed of a series of connecting knots. He'd seen it before on the old tugboats but was used to the rubber bumpers at the pier in town.

When the canoe was properly tied up and secured, Nelson handed the group of dockworkers several coins each and they nodded with thanks. The men began unloading the wares off the vessel, placing the items on the wharf. Nelson and his officers rushed to the nearest house at a quick gallop.

✷✷✷

After thirty minutes, Nelson and his two officers returned to the pier. "Men, the harbormaster arranged several horse drawn carriages for the transportation of the goods," he turned to Yalodo, "Tell our Irajan friends that they will be thanked time and time again for taking us here."

Yalodo spoke to Hinda for several moments, and then turned his head back to the captain. "He says that they are with you until death. They swore an oath, offered to them by the Gods of Peace and War, saying that they are now your warriors."

He beamed a large smile, "Ask them what they want to do with the canoe."

Yalodo asked Hinda the question, and then spoke so that his fellow white men could hear. "He said that it is yours now, to do as you wish."

Nelson looked at Hinda and the eighteen warriors before him. They were all wearing their loincloths, their skin darkened after the weeklong journey, exposed to the sun. His gaze then shifted to the remaining men, all were sunburned to a crisp. They walked around with limps, obviously in dire need of a bed to rest in.

"Let's load the carriages, and return to our assigned berth. I just need a few volunteers to come with me to take care of some business, the others can accompany the carriage and you guys can rest once at the Main Street Tavern. Expect me no later than dinner time."

As he finished speaking, two horse-drawn carriages rolled around the corner, emerging into view. The drivers tugged on the reigns, causing the horses to stop their march. "Good'ay mate!" the man from the closest buggy called down.

Nelson waved towards him, "Thanks for the short notice, my men will walk beside the carriages and help in the loading and un-loading of the carriages. Here's your pay in advance."

Nelson moved to the first carriage and then flicked a few coins into the man's eager hand. As he passed by the horses, his hand grazed the mane of the lead. He always loved his adventures upon horseback, he wished his schedule would permit more, but he was a very busy man.

He paid the second man as his horde of sailors and warriors began placing the canoe's wares into the storage compartments of the carriages. He looked at Yalodo and called him over with a wave of the hand.

"Aye, sir, what can I do for you?"

"From now on Yalodo, we will call you Nathan. It seems to be more appropriate."

The smile on the translator's face was indescribable. The moment that he had stepped onto civilized land, he had a flashback of the last time he was in England. He remembered what it was like, when he was seven years old.

"Yes, I'd like that. Is there something you need before we finish loading?"

Nelson looked back towards his warriors, "Yes, fit them with modern clothes. See if our British uniforms fit, and if not, get measurements for each one. Compile a list, I'll ask for funds when I go meet with the governor in a bit. Other than that, I'll leave you in charge of the group."

Nathan nodded, "Sure thing. Who's going with you?"

Nelson replied, "Nate, Charles…and Ben. The rest can relax," he paused, and then reached into a sack that was tied around his waist. "Here, give each a share to get some food and drinks. Make sure the Irajan are not in their loincloths if they do go out. It would be an interesting night if that happens."

The surrounding men overheard the last part of the captain's speech and all laughed jovially. The captain led his three followers to the harbormaster's house as they watched their remaining men stacked the goods with the help of the carriage drivers.

❈❈❈

Once inside, Nelson asked the man behind the counter a series of questions. "Is Victor Jenison still Head of the Castillo de los Tres Reyes del Morro?"

The man's white beard clung to his chin as the harbormaster nodded his head, "Yes, I just spoke with him the other day actually, bumped into him while at the market. He's doing quite well, lives on the bluffs just off the fortifications."

Captain Nelson let off a sigh of relief. "That is grand; Victor and I are old friends. Well anyway, where's the nearest stable? I have to get to los Tres Reyes del Morro as soon as possible, unless you have four horses available?"

The man looked down at a half opened logbook. He reached down and adjusted the spectacles that hung loosely on his nose. "Yes, I still have half a dozen available out back. We have a few young lads who run messages now and again, so we thought we'd have a stable. To be honest, I like a good day out on horseback."

"Ah, very convenient," he laughed.

"Yes, well I'll need your names…"

Nelson took out a handful of coins and then placed it on the table, "We're really in a rush, my name's Nelson."

The harbormaster smiled, his customer's impatience yielded enough funds for a week's worth of work. "Aye let me call my apprentice."

With the rapid ringing of the bell on the countertop, two lads, barely in their teenage years, ran down the stairs, coming from their room on the second floor. The four sailors followed the kids through a doorway that led to the backyard. Walking to the stable, one of the kids began speaking. Ben figured he was the eldest due to his height advantage over the other. They had similar figures, probably brothers.

"Um, this is our fastest horse; I ride him all the time. His name's Bucko," the kid paused and then continued, "The gray one is Cindy, the brown one is Hero, and, I guess you can also get Old Thunder, we've owned him for over ten years."

"All right, thanks kid," Nelson said as the brothers readied the horses.

The captain replaced the coin bag in his satchel that lay flat against his hip and the four men hopped onto the backs of each horse, sitting squarely on the saddle. The only time Ben had ever been on a horse was when he was a toddler, and it was at a fair in one of those petting farms.

Ben watched what the others were doing, and then finally settled into the mode of horseback riding. He led the way at a gallop, the three followed behind. They took the main road of the town, always within a stone's throw of the water. Ben's gaze swung back and forth, looking at the ships docked or anchored in the harbor, and also as people passed by carrying their wares to be sold at the market in the center of town.

✖✖✖

*I*nside of the battery, a junior officer led the four men to the quarters of Victor Jenison. The man rapped on the huge oak door until it opened with a creak. His fire red hair burned on the top of his head. Sharp and clean facial features suggested a modest upbringing. When he focused on the man that stood before him, he couldn't believe the state that his visitors were in.

"Arthur, it is great to see you, but you look like you have died and gone to Heaven, or better put, Hell!"

The captain smiled as the two friends embraced, "Aye, it's good to see you too. Nothing better than hearing that I look dead."

"So, what happened to you? How've you been since I last saw you walk these streets?"

Captain Nelson retold the story as his audience gasped as the story unfolded.

"…And then you rowed here for the past week?" inquired Victor.

"Yes, it's been a tough several months. We should have been here, visiting you many a moon ago, but we ran into that unforeseeable tragedy. I came to you to inform that we have accomplished the task of eliminating El Perro Loco. In addition, I require a new ship. I have some wares with me that we managed to salvage when we were shipwrecked on that island. I have a handful of Irajan warriors with me who I shall take with me in the next quest."

"Yes, don't worry about a thing. Rest for as long as you need, Blood Spot isn't going anywhere anytime soon. He's chained to a wall about a hundred feet below where we are standing," Victor laughed.

"Good to hear that the bastard pirate is locked up. So, shall we interrogate him, let's say, in a few days?"

The man nodded, "Yes. I will write you an allowance letter to give to the shipyard. I believe they just are more or less finished with a vessel, and there are our several others that are in repair. So, maybe tomorrow if you want, swing by Alfred Jacobs, the master of the shipyard."

Nelson smiled, "Sounds great, Victor."

There was silence as the man scribbled down a note on a piece of parchment. He held a candle in his hands melting a bar of wax over the seal and then pressed his ring into, branding his initials into the letter.

Victor called to the junior officer at the doorway to bring drinks for the visitors, and he motioned for the four men to take seats and relax for a bit. The two friends conversed throughout the afternoon as Ben chatted with Nate and Charles.

It was just after three o'clock when Nelson stood up from the chair. Victor circled the desk to stand before his friend, in his right hand was the letter and in the left was a bag.

"Inside you'll find some funding to help supply and ready yourself for the journey after the interrogation."

"Thanks my friend, I don't think I would've been able to do this without you."

Victor smiled, "It's the least I could do after you saved my life time and time again."

"I suppose, but thank you anyways."

The comrades embraced one last time before leaving.

✖✖✖

Once outside, they saddled the horses and the animals beneath them galloped slowly. Throughout the ride to the shipyard, Ben tried to piece together a solution concerning that last statement of Victor Jenison: "It's the least I could do after you saved my life time and time again."

He rode up beside the captain with a confident stride. The horse below him matched the pace of Nelson's animal and the two began chatting.

"Sir, I have a question."

Nelson looked over his right shoulder, "Yes, Ben?"

"I noticed Victor mention that you saved him time and time again. For the entire ride since we left, I've wondered what you saved him from, or where, that sort of thing."

He nodded, "I'd love to tell you the whole story, but I believe we are almost at the shipyard. I guess I can summarize it and save the rest of the story for a later time."

Ben smiled, "That'd be great cap."

"Well, we fought on the same ship, multiple times throughout the wars with France. We attacked Guadeloupe and Martinique. I was then moved to a different squadron, focusing more on the colonies, while Victor accompanied troops in the seizure of Havana from the Spanish. He was appointed head of the eastern battery, los Tres Reyes del Morro, since English occupation of the city."

Ben nodded, "That's incredible. I'm looking forward to the other stories."

"In due time my friend."

They galloped in silence until they entered the shipyard and walked their horses to a tying post. Heading for the stairway that led to the main office, Nelson and his men made their way to the door.

35

He slid the letter across the desk to Alfred Jacobs, as he introduced himself as Captain Arthur F. Nelson, master of the ill-fated *Frendrich*, and close comrade to the honorable, Victor Jenison.

"I have heard much about you. If only I could have seen the details of such heroism with my own eyes would I not hesitate to give you any ship you desired! So, my friend, what brings you here?"

Nelson smiled, "Thank you, sir. My business here is simple. My ship was shipwrecked in a storm many months ago; we were stranded on an island for several months. On the island we befriended a native tribe, called the Iraja. After we helped them defeat their sworn enemy, they escorted us here via a huge dugout canoe. Here is a message from Victor," he said as he handed over the letter.

After breaking the seal, the man read with curious eyes. "Aye, I see what you need. I'll take his and your word on this. We have a ship that had just arrived here from Devonport, the *HMS Defence*, a third-rate beauty, with seventy-four guns. We are painting the hull now, if you'd like to see it."

Nelson let off a quick smile, "Ah, in the morrow. We just arrived today after a week straight of rowing. I'd very much like to come back and walk around her, see the lines and how she is laid out."

"Aye, sounds great, go get some rest, you look like you've been dead for years."

The captain nodded, "Should we take care of the paperwork tomorrow as well?"

"Yes, we'll do everything in the morning. I believe the ship will be ready to sail within the week, so you can have some time to rest."

✖✖✖

*T*hey rode out on their horses into the center of town. He remembered the place that the harbormaster would host his men for their stay in Havana. His eyes looked at each sign that he passed, that hung above doorways. Finally, he saw Main Street Tavern.

"Okay, now that we know where it is, let's return the horses to the harbormaster, and turn in."

His men nodded with excitement, ready to have a fresh meal, a bath, and a nice bed to sleep in. The last week, the concept of sleep was either leaning up next to a comrade or against the hull of the dugout canoe. Not anyone's idea of a good night's rest.

✖✖✖

*N*athan and the remaining men arrived at the tavern half an hour after they left the pier. After a warm meal and several rounds of drinks, the men washed themselves in the washing closets. There were two tubs inside and they all rotated through. The Irajan warriors watched as their white friends dipped their heads below the water and popped out, causing the water to drip from their long, entangled hair. Nathan ran downstairs to the tavern owner and inquired of the whereabouts of the nearest tailor to take the measurements.

Nathan and the tailor entered the rooms that the men were staying in and began taking measurements. He took down the dimensions for each man as the tailor worked his magic with the length of tape. There were twenty-five names scribbled on the page and then the tailor began measuring Nathan.

He spoke to the tailor, "All right, I still have four men to be measured, would it be possible if you could swing by again tomorrow after sunup?"

The prospect of making thirty customized uniforms and clothing caused the tailor to smile. "I am at your disposal, anything you need I shall get."

"Excellent. We need undergarments, let's say about two pairs for each man, breeches, waistcoats, and justaucorps. We have a collection of old uniforms as well, but we will save those for any new recruits to our outfit."

"I see. Is there anything else?"

Nathan thought for a moment, "I cannot think of anything off hand, but if I do, or if Captain Nelson does, we shall let you know tomorrow."

"Have a great evening my friend," said the tailor.

✖✖✖✖

*W*hen Nelson and his officers entered the room, Nathan joined up with them and informed the captain of the day's progress.

"Excellent. Yes, after sunup the four of us can be measured, I'm sure I've slimmed down a bit," he let out a hearty laugh that made his men smile. He looked around to get everyone's attention. "Tomorrow we will take a look at the *HMS Defence*, a lovely third rate ship of the line with seventy-four guns. I was informed it would be ready to sail in a week. I'm going to ask for a company of men to man the gun crews and hire some merchant sailors to man the sails. The horde of us shall be appointed the officers of the vessel. We started this together and we'll finish together. Blood Spot and several of his men are imprisoned beneath los Tres Reyes del Morro. Any questions?"

Nathan relayed the message to Hinda, who then passed word to his men. Nelson looked at his elder, "My friend, we must teach them English. I also want our men somewhat knowledgeable in the Irajan tongue. That is your job."

"Aye, cap."

After another hot meal, the men walked clumsily up the stairs from the tavern's first floor. There were two rooms that were connected by a door, which housed the thirty men. They lay sprawled out on blankets and slept on the wooden floorboards.

✖✖✖

After a quick breakfast the tailor showed up, taking the measurements of Captain Nelson, Ben, Nate, and Charles. He said that in a few days all the articles of clothing would be ready for a low price. John Borton, joined by Henry Hughson, took charge once again as master purser, going from store to store to chat with the store owners.

Nelson led the remaining men to the shipyard, stopping in to talk with Alfred Jacobs as the rest stood outside. The man stood up from behind his desk and shook Nelson's extended hand.

"If you'll follow me to the ship, we can do the paperwork once you are satisfied with the inspection."

Nelson nodded, following the man as they walked through the doorway. The remainder of men tagged along, trailing the two as they navigated through piles of wood, workers, and the shipyard. Tied up to the pier, was the light blue-hulled vessel, with two solid golden stripes along the gun ports on both sides of the vessel, reaching around the stern. They stood on the pier by the stern of the ship, the man began speaking, giving the tour of their new ship.

"Well, she's one hundred and sixty eight feet long, has a breadth of forty-six feet eight inches, and draws nineteen feet eight inches. Any questions before we board the vessel?"

A voice called out, "I see two gun decks, what's the crew complement?"

Jacobs replied, "Five hundred and thirty, it can be operated with less of course, but that is a good number to operate her for one hundred percent efficiency."

Nelson nodded, taking in the information beginning to think of a plan for the attack on Captain Blood Bone's lair. The voice of the guide continued, "We'll go on deck so you can look at the lines and then go below decks."

They paced up the gangway and greeted several workers who were doing some touchup painting. The group went forward towards the bowsprit. "The figurehead is a lion, it's hard to see from here, I should've showed you all when we were on the pier."

After the tour of the ship, Captain Nelson was thoroughly content with the new vessel's prospects for success. He turned to the man, "Thanks for showing us the ins and outs of her, she's a real beauty."

"Aye, yes she is. Let's go fill out that paper work and get you on your way."

The company of men walked back to the office, where Nelson and the shipyard officer entered while the rest chatted excitedly about the *HMS Defence.*

After taking out a brand new logbook from a stack sitting on a shelf, he began filling out several lines in the inside cover which constituted the registration process.

"The master of the ship will be in the name of Arthur F. Nelson. May I ask for the names of your Officers?"

Nelson hesitated; he did see remarkable progress with Ben over the past several months. "My first officer will be Charles Marconi, second is Nate Brodkin, and lastly, the third is Benjamin Manry."

"Excellent, just sign here and here," he said as he pointed to several blank spaces between various terms and agreements.

36

From the main road, they could see the battery hidden within the cliffs. On the opposing bluff, they could see its sister fort, La Punta. The combination of these two fortifications had made it the safest port in the Americas against pirates and invasion. Continuing on the path that led to the castle's entrance, Nelson spoke of the history of the fortification, telling them that the battery was christened as the "Twelve Apostles" and how an English fleet of forty-four ships, containing three thousand cannons and fourteen thousand men, successfully took control of the harbor. He always informed and briefed his men on topics that concerned them.

The entrance to the castle was opened in preparation for the men as they then walked over a drawbridge to the insides of the stronghold. Ben looked down at the deep moat below. They passed by several stables, wells, barracks, and a chapel. Finally, Nelson led the men to where Victor Jenison was located, pacing his room with anticipation.

"Good to see you once again."

Nelson returned the gesture, giving his friend the names of all those who stood before the head of the garrison. Victor smiled, "It is my pleasure to be surrounded by such men of honor and valor."

Charles and Nate let off a cheer, causing the remaining men to join in. Victor positioned his body behind the desk and then pulled open the top drawer of the mahogany. His hand sifted through the contents, eagerly searching for the set of keys that would later open the cell of Blood Spot and his gruesome lot. Finally, his fingers settled upon the metallic circle that hosted a variety of different sized and shaped keys that would open anything from the chapel doors, cells, or his office.

He jingled the keys in front of Nelson's men, "Can't forget these," he said with a laugh.

Letting the man pass, the group followed Victor Jenison out of his office, through corridors of highly decorated halls. Imported tapestries along with paintings lined the walls, as each set of eyes took in the wonderful sight. Once through the insides of one of the keeps, the group emerged into the sunlight, passing over stepped ramparts. Ben noticed several crumbled walls that had yet to be reconstructed after the English seizure just a year earlier. He looked around, noticing other piles of rubble that still lingered about. Several walls and ramparts were breached due to the explosions and impacts of over forty thousand bombs and projectiles.

In front of them was a watchtower, which, several hundred years later would be the main lighthouse of Havana, a symbol and a beacon of the city. Victor paced forward as the mingled group followed. He placed a hand inside his coat pocket and extracted the iron keys. Placing the key inside the door to the watchtower, he opened the gate with a turn of his wrist. Inside were four men, two sitting at a desk and two standing. With the arrival of the head of the battery, they all snapped to attention and greeted their senior officer.

"How are we doing today lads?" he inquired.

The men relaxed their postures and reported all was well. "Good to hear, we are going to interrogate the prisoners now. Hopefully we can learn the whereabouts of Blood Bones and restore peace to the Crown and hopefully rescue our captured marines."

They nodded with approval and let the large group pass. A voice from behind inquired, "Are we going up the watchtower?"

He smiled with a shake of the head, "Of course not. What good would a dungeon be if it was at the heights of a tower?"

The men let out a laugh at his humor and stayed at an even pace on his heel. Instead of pacing up the counterclockwise stairway, which allowed for an easier defensive counterattack to a raid, Victor rounded the corner, into a shadowed area. Little light filtered in through the small slotted windows, causing the inside to have a dark and eerie aura. Candlelight flickered by where the four watch standers stood, but the light did not carry the twenty feet distance towards where he stood. Inserting a different key into a slot in the wall, seemingly hidden and perfectly carved into the stones, he pushed through another door.

After pacing down the stairway, he placed his hand around a torch that flickered, lighting the space around his head. "If several of you can take a torch, just follow me."

The men behind followed his request, heading down the spirals into the depths of the rock. It seemed that the stairs were carved into the earth, as there were no differences or gap between. The light that flickered off the stones led the path for them as their shoes grazed the rocks at their feet, creating a melodic beat as they continued spiraling down. Ben thought the darkness would soon overcome the small light that was emitted from the torches, but finally they arrived at a level bed of rock. Victor led the men through a tunnel; the similar cavern-like quality of air reminded him of his previous adventures back on that island that brought him to the eighteenth century. Placing a different key into a solid oak door, he opened yet another door that would eventually led to the captured pirates.

✖✖✖✖

*N*elson split his men up, telling Nathan to stay with the Irajan warriors out of sight.

Victor spoke first, "Blood Spot come with me."

The man remained seated with his back against the smooth rocks behind him. These walls had imprisoned countless traitors, heretics, and prisoners of war since it was first constructed in 1563.

"I said come with me!"

His legs were shackled together, connected by a short length of chain and a cannonball. Blood Spot smiled and refused to reply.

With an open hand, Victor slapped him, causing blood to squirt out as the lip split, dripping slowly until it met the scraggly, dust-ridden beard that grew on his face. His expression had little reaction to the event, his mind obviously elsewhere.

With the help of Captain Nelson, the two men lifted Blood Spot's hefty frame and pushed him back to the wall. He spit at the Englishmen; only to receive a solid blow to the ribcage. The remaining pirates all sat in the shadows of the dungeon, looking on as the two men continued their onslaught on their leader. Blow after blow, fists crashed against the man's soft flesh. Within minutes, he was bleeding from the wounds that covered his body.

"Now where is your cousin?" screamed Victor.

To no surprise, he bit his lip, holding in the reply. It would take a lot more than physical abuse to extract the information from him.

"Someone go to the watch desk and get a cat-o-nine and a blade."

Blood Spot only stared directly into Victor's eyes, smiling.

"So you think you're funny, eh?" he said with another blow to the pirate's jaw, sending his head crashing hard into the rock wall behind.

The two continued bashing the man, continually doubling him over with hits to the chest and stomach. A series of footsteps halted the onslaught temporarily as Charles and one of the junior officers of the dungeon entered with the items.

"Here, sir," the young man said as he handed the objects to Victor.

With only one man holding Blood Spot against the wall, it left open a slight chance and he sent forth a head butt to the bridge of Nelson's nose, sending the captain reeling back.

Shaking off the pain, he let off a smirk, "You messed with the wrong man."

Taking the coiled cat-o-nine from his friend, he gripped it tightly. In one smooth motion, the coiled whip arced through the air, hitting the man in the eye and cheekbone. Still, the cousin of Captain Blood Bones would not relent, would not give in to the torture and physical abuse. After turning his body, they pressed his face against the wall. Everyone took several steps back as Victor grabbed the whip from Nelson.

With a snap of his wrist, he sent the leather whip flying through the air. Flesh separated as the nine knots met skin. The tattered rags that covered the man's body cut with a shredding sound. Another crack of the whip, and Blood Spot's body remained motionless, completely accepting everything that was thrown at him. Victor continued sending the whip at half-minute intervals. His entire back was now raw, and as each stroke of the whip landed, flesh and blood stripped off his backside.

Nelson placed a hand on his friends shoulder, whispering so that Blood Spot could not hear.

"You're wasting time, he will not give in."

"What do you suppose we should do then?" he turned to face Nelson.

"I have an idea…" he whispered the remaining of the plan.

✖✖✖

The seven pirates were now standing beside their leader, all facing the wall. Each man flinched after the violent strike, all except Blood Spot. The two men continued switching off between the blade and the whip, ensuring that each villain had their fair share in the punishments.

After ten minutes of the intense beatings a man screamed out, "All right, stop it!"

He nodded to Victor to stop the torture.

"Speak!" screamed Nelson.

The victim paused, knowing that if his fellow comrades and he ever saw the light of day again, they would kill him without hesitation. He finally muttered through clenched teeth, "Near…Port Royal…in Hunt Bay…a few miles northwest…of the settlement of Kingston, Jamaica."

"You have just earned extra rations," Victor began to coil up the cat-o-nine. "We shall return in an hour with fresh shirts and some grog. How does that sound?"

The seven prisoners grunted as Blood Spot angled his head towards the man who gave in to physical pain.

"Drink up, for I shall kill you in your sleep."

Nelson nodded to his men to begin the trek back up the winding staircase that led out of the bowels of earth. On the way out, Nelson and Victor stopped to chat with the junior officers stationed on the post.

"I want you to bring a cask of grog to the dungeon, leave it there for them to fight over it," Victor said with an evil smirk. This was his way to get back at the scum who had killed many of his friends in battle, his own sweet revenge.

✖✖✖

Captain Nelson sent Nathan and the rest of the men back to the tavern to celebrate while he and his officers talked business with Victor Jenison.

"So how many men do you need, my friend?"

Nelson rubbed his clean shaven chin. "I'd say between two hundred and three hundred marines, and another fifty to a hundred seamen. This next mission will be very critical."

Victor paused for a moment, thinking of the sister fort just across the entrance to Havana, "I know of a non-active company of men across the bay. I can also spare around a hundred or so."

Nelson smiled. "Excellent, on our way back we'll do some recruiting for the ordinaries. I shall return in the morning to check in."

"Aye, sounds like a plan, my friend."

Victor then led the four men out of his quarters and through the mazes of corridors that comprised the inner workings of los Tres Reyes del Morro. With a wave, the group departed and found themselves on the road that led back to the center of Havana.

Captain Nelson placed a hand on Ben's shoulder, getting the lad's attention. "When we get back, I'd like you to come with me to the general store. I have something to get for you."

As they approached the general store, Nate and Charles continued down the street as they entered the doorway, masked in a shadow of the setting sun. Nelson maneuvered around several customers that were gazing at the storefront. Searching through a bin, he found two-leather bound notebooks.

"Every officer should have their own log book. You are quite the storyteller and I figured you should record the past events. After all, we have had quite an adventure," he let off a smile

Ben nodded, picturing everything that had occurred in the last several months since they first found the treasure map in their wine cellar. "I agree. My story should be heard. I'll start writing it tonight."

Nelson let off a smile. "Yes, let's purchase these and then catch up with Nate and Charles. They should be in one of the taverns."

They approached the storeowner, who looked up from his cash box. "How are you this evening?"

Captain Nelson replied, "Aye, all right lad and you?"

The lanky man ran a quick hand through his hair and then readjusted the glasses that sat on the bridge of his nose. He studied the object as he rung up the price in his head. After stating the price, Nelson dug into his pocket for the coins and then handed them to the man.

"We'll most likely be back in a few days for wares and supplies. We have to load our ship, the *HMS Defence*."

"Oh? She's a beauty that she is. I saw her come into port just last month. I have yet to be aboard her though; I've always wanted to board a naval ship."

Nelson sensed an opportunity, "Yes, I'll be her master. If you'd like to come aboard we can show you around."

Ben could feel the atmosphere changing before his eyes.

"Oh, did I say the journals were four, I meant two," he said as he gave back two coins, placing them into Nelson's hand.

"No, my friend, those are yours. Just give us good deals on our wares."

"Well, all right. I have off tomorrow, if that is a good time to take you up on your offer."

Nelson studied the enthusiastic face on the man before him. "Yes, actually we are to return to los Tres Reyes del Morro, and we were going to stop at the shipyard on the way."

"Aye, should we meet somewhere or shall you come here first, I live above my store."

Nelson thought for a moment, "It doesn't matter, my friend, whichever is easier for you."

"Hmm, I can meet you at the shipyard. What say you for a time?"

Nelson replied, "Say around ten."

"Excellent. Again, thank you."

The captain of the *Defence* nodded, "Not a problem."

They left the store and went from tavern to tavern in hopes of recruiting men for the journey to Port Royal. After passing through the first set of taverns, they met up with Nate and Charles. The four continued through the streets, drafting about five in each place they entered. They told each man to go to the shipyard the next day at ten in the morning.

Several hours passed as the men turned in, calling it quits for the night. They joined up with their friends, spending the rest of the evening by the open fire in the center of the tavern. Ben sat by himself as he began retelling his stories, dipping the quill in a jar of ink every time he needed. He could feel his brother looking over his shoulder.

"Just writing, figured all of our adventures would be a good read."

The sound of his brother's laughter echoed throughout the busy tavern.

✖✖✖

After a quick breakfast, Nelson and his three officers made their way towards the shipyard while the remaining men lounged around town. The tailor brought back the customized uniforms for the men as their meals were being cleaned off the table.

Ben carried a logbook in his hand to record the names of the men who had just joined the ship. Once at the pier, the four waited as men filtered through the shipyard towards their ship. He counted roughly fifty men after only a night's notice.

The newcomers circled around Ben, as they began giving them their names. They waited for a half hour before walking up the gangway onto the main deck. Nelson led the men towards the ratlines and masts, talking as he did so. He placed a foot on the first horizontal tarred line, and then leaned against the triangular shaped rope supports.

"Afternoon to all, I'm glad you could come out for the interview."

The men littered the port side, circling around the captain and his officers.

"What we'll do is show you the ship. If you don't like what you see, we'll cross your name off the list. If you wish to stay, move aboard tomorrow, for we have much work to do."

He led them through each deck, showing them the spaces where they'd eat, sleep, and work in the many crucial compartments aboard the vessel.

"Does anyone have any questions?"

Several eyes peered at the captain, one hand raised vertically. "Yes, would it be all right if I get my old crew aboard? I was a captain of a merchant vessel; our run ended this past month. Since then I've kept landside looking for work."

Nelson glanced at the figure speaking. "What was the complement?"

The graying hair on the man's head moved as he jerked his head to get a crick out. "Well, including me, we had thirty. If you'd like I can round them up for you."

"Yes, once we part paths, get them. We'll need all the men we can get."

"Yes sir."

The tour continued. Once back on main deck, Ben was told to climb each set of ratlines as the others viewed the scene. With agility, he maneuvered quickly up the tarred rope, finding himself at the top of the forward mast.

With a wave of the hand, he sensed that he raised the spirits of the men that seemed to be heavens below him.

The officers of the vessel watched their future subordinates walk down the gangway onto the grounds below. The crowd of men filed down the pier and along the well-used path leading out of the shipyard.

✖✖✖

"Let's move quickly. Victor is awaiting us," the captain said.

His men fell in behind his quick gait, leading them on the walk through various terrains, finally ending at the familiar spectacle of los Tres Reyes del Morro.

The guards at the drawbridge knew their faces and let them pass without any serious interrogations. Knocking on the wooden door, the men waited beside, listening to a set of footsteps clatter towards the doorframe. After the pins were pulled out, the door opened and he welcomed the visitors inside.

"Good news Arthur, I was able to find a pair of one hundred and fifty men companies. I think three hundred marines should suffice, don't you?"

He smiled with the good news. "Are they ready for battle?"

Victor nodded, "Yes, they've been in training for the last four months. I'd say that the majority of men have seen battle at least once. There are several veterans, near our age, strewn throughout the mix."

"Good, what I'm thinking is I'll set in charge several of my men, for each of those veterans, who in turn will lead a handful of marines."

"That seems like it would and will work. How was your luck with recruiting the ordinaries?"

"About fifty showed up with a night's notice. One man said that he could get near thirty more. Overall, I'm quite content with our efforts. The ship is nearly ready to sail, my men have rejuvenated their health and are eager to press on."

The two friends embraced one more.

"I couldn't have done it without you."

"Stay safe Arthur."

"I will. I shall send word of our success, until we meet again."

entlemen, we now have plenty of men and high spirits, but we will be fighting against a pirate colony housing God knows amount of men."

Charles placed a hand on the captain's shoulder, "Remember the upsets that we have conquered prior?"

He knew that his men would never falter with pride, never be scared or burdened with fear. By stating that they were facing large odds, he balanced things in his favor. The four officers began drafting the plan for what would commence within the week. By the end of the first full day of sailing, they had rounded the most westward spit of mainland Cuba.

The helmsmen altered course heading southeast, just north of the Cayman Islands. Once through, the winds and currents pushed the ship forward, sailing along the northern coasts of Jamaica.

※·※·※

Five days into journey, Ben thought it time for him to ask for the remainder of the captain's story. He made sure his uniform was squared away, the undergarments tightly tucked into his pants along with flattening out the jacket. In a mirror, he stared at the hair atop his head, noticing the brown, tangled mess level with his brow. Clawing his hair back with wet hands, he finally was content with how the hair fell.

Ben stared at the propped door, about to knock but was interrupted by the captain's voice, "Come in."

He approached the desk, seeming to slide over the smooth wooden strips that lined the floor. His chest stuck out with pride as he stood before the captain.

"Sir, I was wondering if you could finish up the story of Guadeloupe and Martinique."

A smile developed on his face, "Ah yes. The year was 1759, January to May. This was one of the first times that Victor and I fought together. We departed Bristol, heading across the Atlantic to on a several week trek to Guadeloupe. As per orders from Commodore Moore, I fought with a squadron who bombarded Basse-Terre, Guadeloupe on January 23, 1759.

"The day after, our fellow English forces captured the city of Basse Terre under an invasion led by General Hopson. A month later, on February 23 1759, General Hopson dies and was succeeded by General Barrington. Slowly, after a three month long campaign, we conquered city by city. The French surrendered Guadeloupe to us on the first of May, 1759."

The captain continued, "Well, after our victory in Guadeloupe, we were assigned to join up with troops on the French island of Marie Galante. That soon fell on May 26, after a solid attack by our troops."

"Another victory, so what's next?"

"Well, after this last conflict, Victor and I were split up. He stayed around in the Caribbean and I was moved to a squadron that attacked Montreal. After several smaller and less significant encounters in the Americas, I was shipped back down to the Caribbean in the first few weeks of 1762. Under Admiral George Rodney, my squadron conquered Martinique. During the summer months, I found myself fighting beside Victor once again, laying siege to Havana, which was a battle unto itself, if you noticed the layout of the defense in the cliffs."

Ben was taken in by the knowledge. "Unbelievable. You've got a lot of experience."

"Yes, you're right. And since the capture of Havana, Victor stayed, while I ran back and forth between the colonies and England. Then I found myself appointed to capture several pirates and traitors to the Crown. There is just one more mission that I have after we succeed in our efforts soon to come."

They continued their conversation until the middle of the night. After they decided that there was nothing else to talk about, they shook hands and departed. Ben paced through the decks of the ship towards Officer's Way, the passageway leading towards the three small quarters of the ship's officers.

✖.✖.✖

By candlelight, he wrote in his journal, dipping the quill into the inkwell between thoughts. He noticed that this ship's layout was quite similar to that of the *Frendrich*, in the aspects of sleeping quarters, besides the fact that the officers each had a small room for themselves. The remaining men stayed in two holds sleeping in rows and columns of hammocks. In these common areas, at the innermost extremes of the ship along the side planking, there were a sea chest and cubby for each man aboard.

After writing for a half hour, he stretched his back, drawing sketches of the obstacles that he and his friends conquered in the depths of the caverns on Roosevelt Island. Wiping sleep out of his eyes, he remembered that he had the morning watch, eight to twelve. He blew out the candle and found comfort under the cotton sheets of his bed for the rest of the night.

✖.✖.✖

The vessel tacked around the easternmost part of Jamaica, now on a due west course. They sailed several miles away from land, still in sight, but far enough to stay without scope view from any possible onlookers. Captain Nelson stood on deck, pacing back and forth before the helmsmen. "Come to port one point. I think we are still within sight from the beaches."

The *HMS Defence* continued its westward passage, noticing several ships exiting the port of Kingston. From Captain Nelson's telescope, he could make out several flags that just peeped over the horizon. These vessels flew the British flag and they knew they were friendly, but you could never be too cautious in the Caribbean.

After several hours on this course angle, the helmsman was instructed to come to starboard. Now the ship came closer to land. The men on deck noticed the hills and tall trees slowly grow in size.

Nelson called his officers and the previous sailors of the *Frendrich* to come on deck. "Men, here's what we are going to do…"

✖✖✖

It was just after sundown when the ship weighed anchor several miles southwest of Hunt Bay. The ordinaries readied two long boats and Nelson began hand picking a crew for each. When he and his officers stepped into one, he watched as the block and tackle shook above his head, as the men on the deck began lowering it towards the water. The hull of the longboat kissed the smooth crystalline waters with a slight rock. The oars were run out and each longboat captain called a cadence, propelling the small vessel towards land.

Nelson and his three officers scanned the area, looking for anything unusual, as the two longboats remained beached. After walking through a wooded region for about a hundred paces, the four men found the incline of the terrain increasing. There was then, a clearing, where they moved to the base of a steep hill.

Ben lowered his center of gravity, shortening his tall frame, to a hunched position. Left foot, right foot, he paced to the top of the hill. In a smooth motion, his stomach met the ground below and then edged to the crest, getting the full view that emerged before him.

"Do you see anything?" the captain asked of Ben.

"Eight ships at anchor and a campfire just over there," he pointed. "I'll do a quick count."

He scanned the area with the captain's spyglass, moving in a pattern that covered the surrounding waters, beach, and wooded area that lay behind the settlement. "There's a large canopy that seems to house the prisoners. I can't distinguish the numbers, but they seem to be clad in our red uniforms. There's also a half constructed pier, I think it's a pier, at least. Looks like there's a field over there," he pointed to the sugar field.

Nelson smiled, knowing that a rescue mission was still possible, "Excellent, what else?"

He regained his focus, placing his eye once again next to the lens, "Look towards the entrance, cap. I know why this is their hideout. From sea, you can't distinguish the opening," the bay was enveloped in a ring-like manner, of elevated hills, which concealed everything from view that lay inside the protected bay.

"Aye, you're right."

"Do you think they have lookouts?" asked Marconi.

"Yes, most likely at, or near the entrance. We are anchored far enough to the southwest of here to be out of sight. That wooded region that we just traveled through is quite sufficient in masking our intentions," replied the captain.

Brodkin scratched his head. "Sir, they're pretty much trapped inside the bay, if you think about it."

The four studied what lay before them, passing back and forth the gold plated spyglass, each noting a certain aspect of the layout of the camp.

"Yes, you're right," the captain agreed. "Enough for tonight though, we have a long few days ahead of us. The coming battle will be a test of pure strategic planning. There are eight vessels there, anchored silently. Each, I'd say, has about a hundred or so, depending on the size and type. To be on the safe side, let's say they have around seven hundred and fifty."

The number seemed to weigh down each man, pushing them further into the earth, a mixture of sand and grass.

The captain continued, "Though we are severely outnumbered, we have the element of surprise. They do not except us. If they did, they would have expected something many months ago. I guess our little misfortune with the shipwreck was to our favor."

All agreed with a nod.

"So, let's return to the ship for the night," he said as he led the three officers down the hill and through the woods.

The group emerged before the two boat crews, who had emptied out of the vessel to stretch their legs. "Aye, cap," said a man snapping to attention, giving respect to the oncoming group.

"Ready the longboats, we're sleeping aboard the ship tonight. In the morrow, we shall begin unloading the men onto the beach here, and begin the planning segment of our scheme."

They all filed back into the longboats, except for a pair of men who stepped through the knee-deep water, pushing the vessel into the water. Once the water level reached their hips, the four individuals climbed back in with the help of those around. They rowed the slight distance towards their ship, and to the awaiting men on deck.

The lines were secured and the longboats were raised. Hands were extended to help the men board the ship, as word was passed of the findings and discoveries, and the plans that would follow in the morning.

Ben retired to his cabin and reached a hand into the sea chest beside his bed. Placing his journal on the desktop, he opened to where he had left a feather in to mark the place. Dipping the quill, he continued with the story, summarizing the events and drawing sketches of how he perceived things to be.

The wick of the candle beside him burnt out, casting a darkness that filled the space around him. Without hesitating, he extracted a new candle from the desk drawer, lit it with a few aimed strikes of flint and steel, and then continued in the journal for another hour until his seated posture evolved into a horizontal sleep.

🕱🕱🕱

*D*reams and nightmares plagued Nelson's mind, the entire night. A plan slowly formed; at first in small detail and then were refined as the hours progressed. The moment the sun had breached the horizon, something inside him jumped to life. It was time to start the day; he knew they had much to do. After going from hold to hold, he woke the ship. Those already awake followed his shadow as he paced the deck until all were up changing.

After the men flowed through the mess hall, they mustered on main deck, standing in ranks and columns as the captain and his officers made their way through the ranks, discussing the plans for the day. The two companies of marines were split into groups of seventy-five. The original crew of the *Frendrich* was then distributed between each of these four squads.

Nelson stood before the formation, running a hand through his hair. He replaced the cover atop his head and then began speaking. "First squad, eyes," the men in the first squad stared at the captain. "I need thirty men to join Ben and eliminate the outpost near the entrance. I believe I saw a structure through the boughs of trees that line that far coast," he paused, and then continued staring at first squad. "The remainder of you, forty-five, shall join me on this lovely vessel. Our job is quite simple. Once we get the message from Ben, a white flag that is waved, we'll sail into the harbor, bombarding the coasts and the ships that lay at anchor. We mustn't hit the *HMS Courtesy* though, that will be our prize ship for us to take back to Boston."

He then shifted his gaze to the second squad. "You will follow Nate Brodkin, Jacob, and Harris. You shall attack from the north side of the beach," he then looked at the third squad. "Third squad will be led by Charles Marconi, Clayton Burns, and Sal. You will push on a northward attack, starting from the south."

He paused for a moment, and then glanced around, getting a crick out of his neck. "You most likely see where I am going with this. If there is water on the east side of the camp, attacks from the north and south sides, there's only one side left for them to go.

Which is where the fourth squad will be, led by Henry Hughson and John Borton. Accompanying you will be Hinda, Nathan, and the Irajan warriors."

Nathan passed word in the Irajan dialect; Hinda nodded and then spoke to his men.

"When shall we act on this plan?" Nathan returned his gaze from Hinda, focusing on the captain.

A wrinkle in the corner of the mouth showed slight hesitation, "We must do it on the darkest night possible. The new moon will be in four days."

"So in four days?" he questioned further.

The captain nodded. He then looked at Ben and then to the squad of men that would follow the young officer. "You have the most crucial job of all. The ability to get her into the harbor is of grand importance," he let it sink in for a moment. "Once you and your men are finished at their outpost, join in with Brodkin's forces. My one thought was that you could maybe sneak on ship to ship, but that might be too dangerous."

Ben thought for a moment. "Well, that might be the best idea. If we can take control, or just set fire to their vessels, it'll cause more pandemonium. Between ships blowing up and shots from the *Defence*, they'll be running for cover. We'll sandwich them, pushing them into our trap in the west."

"Yes, good insight. So, instead of joining up with Brodkin, make your way to the ships. If I remember correctly, they are all anchored. Their pier is half constructed as well, so the only way to get on is to swim or get a small dinghy to row out to each."

Ben nodded, "Do you think there will be any men aboard?"

A smirk of doubt appeared on his face. "That, is something I do not know. I've always kept a few hands on deck when we were at anchor. They may do things differently. For all we know, they might all be drunk and passed out, but assume the worst."

"Aye, that is true," stated Brodkin and Marconi with a nod as well.

"For the next several days, we shall ready ourselves, while studying and taking notes on the enemy."

✖✖✖

"Split the men up into your groups, we will further discuss and plan for the day that is soon to come," Nelson said for all to hear.

Ben led his group of thirty to the water's edge. The waves occasionally reached up to tickle the backs of his legs, but it was a lovely spot to rest and talk, gaining insight from his men, while proving himself as a leader.

"What I'll need, are at least two men to be relay messengers," he took out a dagger from its sheath that sat loosely on his hip. Pressing the blade into the sand, he began sketching out a diagram. "Here's where we are now and this is the ship. Here's the blanket of trees that separate the hideout and us. I need one flag messenger to stand here," he pointed to the very edge of the trees, where the terrain began to slope upwards to form the ridge. "I need another man on the ridge here," he pointed, marking an X at his feet. "So what'll happen, is that once we overthrow the lookout over here," he pointed to the northern spit of land that cradled the entrance. "We'll wave the flag three times back and forth. The first relay man, will wave once to confirm the message. He'll then relay to the man by the foothills, who will do the same confirmation, and then run through the trees to here," he marked where they gathered.

"So the ship will see it and then raise anchor and sail into the harbor?" asked a man.

He looked up from his diagram in the sand. "Yes, that's the plan."

"What about the two relay men, once they have passed the message?"

He thought for a moment and then answered. "Meet on the ridge and follow it until you join Marconi and his men."

"Okay, so we have the plan for the relay messages. What we first must do is travel west, past the bay several miles, staying out of detection of the hideout. This is what everyone will be doing," he began slicing into the sand, in paths all departing where the X marked their current location. "We'll go north and then head east, back towards the water's edge and the lookout. We'll eliminate the pirates located in the watchtower; Captain Nelson mentioned it is critical. We'll find out soon enough, though."

He heard a cough and paused for a moment. "Well, there are eight ships that lay at anchor in the bay. The likelihood that we can set fire to all is unlikely. The way I figure it is we'll set fire to the first ship. It will explode and everyone in the bay will run out of their huts, probably asleep and drunk. They'll stare at what's going on, and as this happens," he began marking the spots of where Brodkin and Marconi would be coming from. "Our friends will begin their onslaught from here and here. They will spread out, most likely taking up the majority of the beach and raking through the enemy. They will notice a fight coming from both sides, and then will head inland to seek shelter," he paused, and then stuck the end of the blade deep into the sand. "This is where our Irajan friends will close the deal."

His men nodded throughout the speech, approving the plan.

"Any questions?" he looked into each man's eyes.

"And what do we do when we set fire to that first ship?"

"Jump off?" he said as laughter filled the air. "Well, two choices; we can either swim to the beach and create a third force to push against the enemy, or we can swim out and join in with Brodkin's men, since he'd be the closest force to us."

"I think we should to the first idea," a voice called out from several ranks back.

He weighed the idea in his head for a moment. "That may be wise. From their perceptive, it'd be like us emerging out of a flaming fury. So, are we in agreement to all that was discussed thus far?"

Ben's eyes gazed at each individual of who he was in charge of. Fully content, he replied, "All right, let's assign the two relay men."

Two hands flew up.

"Great, you both know what your assignment is, right?"

"Aye, sir."

38

everal days passed as the men continued to go over every small detail of the plan. The officers met in the captain's quarters one last time as the sun began to set over a glass of red wine, aged twenty-one years. Ben's gaze looked at the bottle as Nelson poured a second glass for each man.

DWV

At first, Ben did not pick up on the initials engraved into the bottle, but with the delayed realization his jaw dropped. Nelson noticed the change in his expression and asked what was wrong.

"Um, I'm fine sir," he shook his head. "By the way, I thought of several changes to my original plan."

"After we attack the outpost, we'll swim out to the closest ship and set it on fire. That's when you'll be in the bay already, shooting into the huts and encampment. We'll jump off and swim to the beach, at a headfirst charge into the enemy, just as Nate and Charles swing in. I figure, why set fire to all these boats? We'll have these guys by surprise. Some might not even be armed when they jump out of their huts when they hear the explosion. Imagine when we set sail from here, and we have two lovely British ships flying England's colors, followed by six other ships," he let his idea settle. "Just a quick question, sir."

Nelson responded, "Aye?"

"There were a hundred and fifty marines aboard the *Courtesy*, right?"

"Yes."

"Okay. So what I'm thinking is that we're fighting with three hundred marines. We've got Irajan warriors, and us. The shear fact that we have this all planned out to pinpoint perfection, seals the deal. I don't see us losing that many. If the cards we're dealt are played right, there's no reason why we can't be sailing out of here the following day, with captured pirates in the holds of our convoy and our saved friends on deck enjoying a couple of sunsets and fresh air. We'll sail back to Boston and be deemed famous for capturing Captain Blood Bones."

The thought of such recognition brought smiles to the men's faces. The captain smiled, he knew why he had chosen Ben as his Third Officer; motivating his comrades was just one thing that he could do so well.

"Well, the sun has set. It's time to move the men into positions. Good luck and God speed."

The captain stood up and shook each man's hand before leading the group out of his cabin.

✖✖✖

The men assigned to the ship stayed on deck, watching as the squads mustered one last time before they would move out. Ben told the two designated men to fall out of rank and come forward.

"Move to your posts," he offered his hand. "Stay as low as possible until you see us wave our flag."

The first messenger grabbed his hand firmly, "Aye, sir."

He shook the second man's hand, and then watched as they shuffled into the dense woods before them. Ben focused on the squad that would follow him into battle.

"Men, are we ready?"

In unison, he heard a cheer that shook his insides. He felt something spread through his entire body, pride. They began their march westward. Following behind Ben and his squad of men, the rest of the team leaders marched in their wake. They stuck to the most easterly passage, only going south if there was a break in foliage. Occasionally, when the trees could not sufficiently block out the bay, they saw the rolling hills that separated them from the hideout.

It took half an hour to move the men to where they changed their path to a northward angle, skirting the back end of the sugar fields through a strip of dense vegetation. Marconi's men stopped at their assigned position, as the four other groups continued making their way.

Henry Hughson gauged the distance traveled since they had wished Charles luck, and then his group, along with Hinda, paused. Henry shook Ben and Nate's hands, before the two last groups departed.

After a hundred paces, Brodkin took his men out of the march to wait at the foot of the hill. He made his men kneel, as he watched Ben and his twenty-eight men turn to the left on a path that would lead them through a dense patch of foliage.

✖✖✖

*H*e led them into the thicket and then paused when he heard a loud crash in the air. He inched his head through a brush into a small clearing, just big enough to allow the construction of the lookout tower. Ben eyed the legs of the crude building; high in the trees and large enough for the four-man complement with plenty of storage of weapons and food. He paused, judging how he wanted to carry out the attack. Studying the men for several more minutes, he heard another crash above his head. Laughter followed, followed by a loud burp.

The smell of rum wafted down from the platform, making the call fairly simple. "They're drunk. I'm thinking if we throw a rock into that thicket over there, one of them will go investigate. Then we'll knock him out, and rush the outpost. Make sure they don't fire a shot," he whispered to the men behind him.

Ben reached down by his ankle, palming the fist-sized rock. He tossed it high into the air, losing sight of it as the pitch-black night engulfed the stone. With a loud thud, the night's silence was broken.

❈❈❈

Captain Nelson paced the deck, waiting anxiously for the relay man to break through the dense vegetation and signal their ship. He had a handful of sailors standing by the anchor, ready to raise it at a second's notice. His entire squad of marines and half the ordinaries were below decks, manning the gun carriages.

He glanced upwards into the rigging, seeing the bodies of the sailors ready to drop each sail, smiling with the thought of what was to come.

❈❈❈

"What was that?" said a man with a sullied bandana fastened around his head. His long, soiled blonde hair fell out from the opening on the side.

After his comrade stumbled to the edge of the railing, he looked out and returned to the middle of the platform.

"Ah," he hiccupped, "it's a nothing. Pass me the bottle!"

"Here you go. I'm going to investigate."

The only sober man of the group, stood up, cracking his back. "I'll go with you," he said to the blonde.

❈❈❈

The camp lay restlessly, some sitting by the fire, others drinking from bottles in the comfort of their huts or beside the many campfires. Captain Blood Bones smiled as he thought of the progress made on the pier that day, along with how well the sugarcane fields produced.

He kicked off his leather boots. The feeling of bare skin on the sand below relaxed him. Adorning his quarters were several stacks of plunder from the *HMS Courtesy*. Popping the cork out of a bottle, he began sipping from the white wine. He had a sudden flashback to his earlier days of being a messenger in the Spanish navy.

He stood before his Commanding Officer, awaiting duties for his next assignment. A gentle breeze carried the distant sound to his ears. He ignored the noise, pressing his lips into the glass, letting the fluid infiltrate his mouth. The taste was pleasant and he smiled. He was living the life that he loved, the life that he knew.

***

"You think it's those blasted squirrels again?" the man over his shoulder, sifting through the undergrowth of the foliage.

"Eh…I ca…can't tell. Pro-probably," he slurred.

He stuck his entire hand into a bush, feeling around for anything that moved. Nothing. He moved to the next bush, repeating the same technique yielding the same result.

He was about to give up when he heard something, a sound that made him pause with fright.

***

With a quick snap of the wrist, Ben sent the butt of his rifle arcing through the air. The oiled wood met the man's forehead, bringing him to his knees. Several marines swarmed the other, covering the victim's mouth as they launched several strikes into the man's gut. It wasn't much of a fight as the sailors waited anxiously once both were subdued, hoping that the sound of their efforts did not carry to the outpost. Ben and his men had tied the two prisoners and gagged them with a strip of cloth. Convinced that no one had heard anything, he crept through the underbrush towards the ladder.

Stretching his arm upward, he placed a hand on the outer edge of the vertical wood. He felt its smooth texture, wondering how many hands have slid down it over the past few years. He paused, breathing in the night air into his lungs, calming his senses. He placed his foot on the first rung, feeling all the weight of his body leave the ground once he continued up the ladder.

He watched as each rung dwindled in count, until finally his head bordered the opening. Ben listened in, straining his ears for something to gauge where the pirates were located on the platform.

He then shifted his grip, trying to edge ever closer to the opening. The rifle that hung on his side clinked loudly against the ladder as he the wooden rung gave way under his weight. He paused, holding on tightly hoping that no one had heard the noise.

✹✹✹

"*I* wonder where they went," he said aloud, knowing that the only person around was long passed out.

He answered for himself, "They probably discovered another bottle to drink. That's all we do," he hiccupped, "on this island."

The man continued rambling, pacing back and forth, occasionally staring off into the darkness. From his vantage point, he could see for miles, a stretch of visibility that housed the entrance to the hideout.

Then he heard a loud thud below, the sound emanating from the opening, just several feet behind him.

✹✹✹

*B*en saw the man's face hover above him, he knew that if he did not act quickly, their mission would fail. In a stunt that could only be described as acrobatic extravagance, Ben launched himself up through the opening. His body stretched to its full length, wrapping both rms around the man's thighs. Their entangled bodies tumbled over a table, knocking off stacks of papers and a small lantern. The lantern's flame sputtered, almost becoming extinguished from the fall, but the floor caught instantly.

Sheets of documents rained down on the two figures as they struggled for positioning. This continued for several moments when Ben began to hear a crackle of fire beside his head. While he turned to investigate, his opponent had struck him with an elbow to the chest, knocking him off and to the side. Before both could stand tall, a marine had entered the platform and drew his sword, pointing it at the man who had a hand on his pistol holster.

"Don't even think about it!" the Brit said with stone cold eyes.

Ben saw the man's gaze focus on the marine, and with a solid sweep of his leg, he brought the full effect to the man's kneecap. The flames behind him roared with life, the heat tickling his back. The marines entered quickly, standing at their leader's side. A redcoat pointed his blade into the fallen man's neck. After a quick slit of the throat, the marine wiped the blood that soiled the blade on the dead man's chest.

"All enemy are eliminated, sir."

As the report was given, the men began swatting frantically at the flames. To their advantage, there were several basins of water on a shelf. Their combined efforts extinguished the fire before it could spread any further.

Ben sighed with relief, closing his eyes as the realization overcame him. He snapped out of his hypnotic-like state of mind and then led the small group to join the rest of the men below.

"Run to the clearing and send the signal!" Ben called to the relay man.

With a nod, the man broke off at a sprint, the remaining British led by Ben, quick on his heel. The messenger broke through underbrush with swinging arms, doing all that he could possibly do to speed up the process. Now on a downhill trek, he ran to the beach. He reached the water's edge, feeling the cool water soak through his leggings. The flag swung back and forth wildly over his head, signaling to the man who lay atop on the hilltop opposite the bay.

✖✖✖

Captain Nelson paced the deck, humming to himself as he ran a hand through his hair. "What's taking so long? I hope they didn't run into trouble," he whispered to the night's sky.

He stared at the constellations, following each pinpoint of distant light. His gaze was still in the heavens when a sailor announced, "There he is, the messenger!"

Giving the orders, the ship weighed anchor and the sails let out, slowly filling with wind as the vessel lunged forward. He looked skyward, praying for a stronger wind and a more favorable current.

✖✖✖

*B*en and his men stayed low to the ground as they maneuvered in a single file along the water's edge. They spotted the bare masts of the eight ships that were anchored in the waters of the bay. He figured that the depth was just enough for the vessel currently there, and hoped that his captain would be able to sail safely once inside the harbor. He scanned the beach, seeing an empty camp.

"We're almost there. Just another fifty or so paces and then we'll have to swim out to it," he whispered over his shoulder. "Pass the word back."

He forged the path into the water. Every few feet he would put a foot down to test the depth. The terrain below sunk at a steep angle halfway out. After several minutes, they all floated alongside the ship.

"Let's swim towards the bow."

The twenty-nine men swam along the ship's hull, feeling its curves through the water. It was a beautiful two-mast sloop. Ben could count six gun ports overhead, figuring a total armament of thirteen including the stern chaser.

His fingers then touched the metal links of chain. He called to his men, "Here we are."

Hand over hand; he climbed the length, pulling his waterlogged body up each link. His men followed, feeling the water drip from his body on their foreheads.

✖✖✖

Once all were on deck, they snooped around to see if there was a watch stationed on the ship. Content with seeing no one, Ben led his men below deck towards the powder stores. Once at the lowest level of the ship, they discovered fourteen barrels of black powder.

"Shall we just set off a fire in this room?" asked a voice from behind.

He closed his eyes, trying to come up with a method that would bring the most attention to the vessel, luring all to come out from the comfort of their tents in the encampment to witness hell on earth.

"No. Remember, we are below water now. An explosion would sink the vessel, but we need something, well, more elaborate..."

The men carried the tall barrels, placing them on second and third deck, at the furthest breadths and in the fore and aft. They went from room to room, carrying back anything that would catch fire quickly. After the network was set up, Ben sent twenty of the men up to main deck, the remaining were to start the fire.

"One...two...three!" Ben yelled loud enough so that his voice would carry up the companionway.

His pistol was cocked and primed, ready to shoot. The pointer finger pulled on the trigger, feeling a click, propelling the round forward. His aim was at a strip metal covered with powder. The sparks showered the explosive dust, spreading the flame down the line. He eyed the scene one last time before he turned on a heel and hurried towards the companionway.

He joined his men at the bow. "It's time to depart the vessel. Swim directly to the shore and wait at the water's edge. Stay as low as possible."

His men began jumping off, two at a time. He heard the periodic splashing as he fiddled with his leather satchel on his hip. He extracted a short telescope and aimed it towards the bay's entrance. He scanned the area for the white sails of their vessel, but could not see anything. "I wonder what's taking so long," he whispered.

***

*B*lood Bones jumped from his sleeping mat as the loud explosion shook the contents of his hut. Without hesitating, he pulled on his breeches and threw on a stained shirt. Over his shoulder, he placed a scabbard and then reached into a drawer for a pair of pistols.

Flames danced upon the deck of the two-mast sloop, spreading into the rigging. Spars and sails began falling to the deck, spreading the fire ever upward. He heard footsteps in the other tents as hi men stumbled from their drunken sleep.

"Get to your stations!" he yelled, his voice carried across the camp.

***

*H*e reached into his pouch, retrieving the coiled line of knots. He moved to the railing as his fingers unrolled the line. Tossing the corked end into the water below, he closed his eyes, concentrating on the knots passing through his hands. Captain Nelson sighed with the low speed estimate. He knew that if he was to succeed in the mission, every aspect of the plan would have to mesh together perfectly. A late arrival on his part could mean the loss of many good men.

***

*B*en and his men crouched down as low as they could, feeling the cool water splash on their legs. From the water's edge, they could see all around the relatively flat beach. About forty pirates were now walking around, investigating the night's disturbance.

He stared at the sloop, wondering how the ship would have sailed with a steady wind. By the time his eyes adjusted to the darkness from the bright blaze, the enemy numbers doubled. They poured out from every nook and cranny that was deemed a hut; roughly one hundred pirates beginning to rake the beach in hopes of finding what had caused the fiery display of pyrotechnics.

Looking over his shoulder once more, he vaguely picked out the white sails penetrate the darkness. It seemed to be motionless, just sitting there on the near windless night. He snapped back into focus when he heard the sounds of guns shooting wildly into the air.

They couldn't wait any longer. With every minute that passed, another twenty or so pirates appeared. He looked back once again towards the entrance of the bay, seeing the bowsprit and the first set of sails slowly emerging into view.

"Men, it's time," he called to his troops.

As one, the men raised from their crouched position. Ben took the first step, as he had his sword drawn, whooping to his troops.

"Charge!"

The twenty-nine men ran in a V formation, with Ben at the focal point.

✹✹✹

"Change of plans," he watched as Ben's men moved forward from the water's edge. "Charge!"

Marconi's troops poured out of the woods heading on a full out sprint to join in with the others. Moments later, Brodkin joined the efforts from the north side of the beach.

Complementing the clinking swords, the eruption of pistols ripped through the mass of tangled men. The group of pirates split up to focus on the two English squads of seventy-five men. Ben worked this to his advantage and attacked on a flank, ripping through the enemy's lines.

The pirates outnumbered the English two to one, but fighting on these three fronts balanced the equation for the time being. Like the leaves of autumn, men fell left and right. The sands were stained red, littered with fallen soldiers. Blood Bones called for a triangle formation, only exposing two sides as they pushed the English towards the water's edge.

Sidestepping from a high-arced swing, Ben avoided a blade and then slashed quickly at a man's thigh. Driving his body weight into the man, he knocked his opponent over and made a quick kill. Taking several steps back, he counted the marines who were fighting with him.

✖✖✖

"Hard to port!" the captain yelled to the helmsman. "Skirt perpendicular to the beach, when we're nearing the end of the stretch, come around and make another pass," he said as he began to head below deck to consult with the gun crews.

"Where's the senior officer?" he called out to the listening marines.

A man came to attention. "Aye, sir. Lieutenant Thompson, what your orders, sir?"

"At ease, nature held us back. We're at least a half hour behind because of the wind and current. Our plan of bombarding the beach will not work; all our men are there too. Aim high; shoot into their huts and storage."

"Aye, cap."

He hurried to main deck and stood beside the starboard rail, watching as the muzzle flashes scarred the night sky.

✖✖✖

Inside the thatched hut, the captured Brits woke to the sounds of explosions and gunfire. Shackled together, men towed their accomplices to get a view of the battle ensuing on the beach. The sight of fellow redcoats rekindled their spirits. The word of the good news spread throughout the tight quarters of their lodgings.

✖✖✖

Ben pushed forward, though the majority of his men had succumbed to the pressures exerted from Blood Bones. He wiped off splattered blood and sweat from his face with his sleeve. His eyes had a burning sensation in them. In an enraged fury, he charged into a tangle of men, hoping to find Captain Blood Bones and kill him himself. Through a mingled scene of faces, he saw Sal and Marconi fending off an attack. Off a dozen skirmishes away on his right side, he noticed his brother and Jacob touching swords with the enemy.

The pirates were well trained from years of pillaging the seas, while the English were young, some only in the fleet on their first mission. The pirates were a collection of rough-edged, seafarers, while the English were an anthology of young paper pushers strewn in with an occasional veteran. But, the English did have one advantage; nearly a hundred fresh troops off to the west, eager to join in the fight.

※※※

They were tired of waiting to execute the plan. They were sick of watching their friends fall. They had to do something about it. The olive skinned men launched arrows on the run, sending volleys into the enemy's flanks. A group of pirates turned around to face the oncoming rush of men, only to find English blades and pointed bows.

As the men rushed in, the seesaw tipped towards the English side. Modern and ancient weapons clashed together; guns versus bows, swords versus clubs. The Irajan warriors could let loose a dozen arrows before anyone could successfully locate a figure in the mass of quickly shifting conflict. They've seen more battle than anyone on their moonless nights combined.

※※※

Captain Nelson looked through the telescope once more as he watched the red coats engulf the enemy, suffocating the pirates until there were virtually none left. From over three hundred, the numbers of Captain Blood Bones and his men dwindled down to just a mere thirty-six. With pointed blades, the English herded the remaining pirates until they were tied up and a guard was set.

The *HMS Defence* shortened sail, slowing to a stop as they pointed the bow into the wind. Dropping anchor, Captain Nelson and a crew of six lowered a longboat and rowed ashore. He walked through the battlefield, receiving greetings and congratulations for the victory.

"Let's free our captured friends, they've been treated poorly and deserve it," he called out to his officers. "Nathan, make a head count, sift through the bodies for anyone still alive," he paused to find the doctor. "Clayton, I need you to set up an area to doctor wounds. Jacob, Sal, and Harris, go get a fire going," he pointed towards a part of the encampment.

✖✖✖

"Hundred and twelve dead and maybe a dozen on there way there, a handful injured," he entered the inner circle of officers, reporting the news to Captain Nelson.

"Thanks Nathan. Continue to guard Blood Bones and his men. For now, let's retire for the night, when the sun comes up we'll bury the dead and explore the camp."

Nelson looked around at each man's face after he heard the receding footsteps of Nathan. "So, someone tell me what went wrong and what went well?"

There was a moment of silence, the flames that consumed the wood popped sporadically.

Brodkin was the first to answer. "Well, we never drove them westward like planned. I think Ben made the right decision to push forward when he did."

Marconi chimed in. "Yes, I agree. If he didn't act then, it could've been worse."

The captain added, "Well, we did not take into effect the current and wind. The past few days there was a moderate breeze, but tonight there was none, if at all."

"I watched the pirates multiply and had to do something about it. Their total complement would have been geared and ready if I didn't act when I did."

"Well it's all right. We probably should've set fire to the gunpowder just as the *Defence* entered the bay. So, what went well?" he said as he saw the flames flicker in each man's pupils.

"Henry and Hinda pretty much came to our rescue. Other than that, I think we executed the plans well," Marconi answered.

"Yeah, we took out the outpost with relative ease. The message was relayed quickly."

Nelson eyed Ben and then moved his gaze as Brodkin added in, "Our attacks went well too, but Blood Bones had his ranks shift to avoid fighting on three sides."

"Well, it's been a long day for all of us. On the morrow we'll ready camp and set sail for Boston. It's time to turn in, we've earned every moment of rest."

Ben waited anxiously for the others to leave before he gathered the courage to ask the captain for a favor.

✖✖✖

As the sun rose the following morning, a man approached Nelson, "I cannot thank you enough. We've been slaves to these men for the last several months. Several have died from heat exhaustion since we've landed."

"It's all right, my friend. I'm Captain Nelson, call me Arthur."

They shook hands and the man introduced himself as Alistair James, the second in charge. "Blood Bones killed our captain in front of the entire crew. We were placed in ankle shackles and put below decks until we arrived here."

"I apologize for not coming sooner; we were delayed with many unfortunate events. But there is still much to do, we need to bury the dead and sail to Boston as soon as we have given respect to our fallen friends."

"I believe the men would find console in having the burial in the sugarcane fields," Alistair said with closed eyes.

39

The realization of having walked along the same street, the same path on a course of destiny made Ben think for just a moment before rapping upon the door of the Williamson estate. His knuckles met the wooden frame and moments later, the familiar face of Juanita smiled at him.

"Ben!"

Along with his brilliant smile and a large hug, she welcomed him in. "The señora is in study, reading. Both boys are out of the household," she paused, debating if she had the right to inform him, "Mrs. Williamson, we have a visitor!"

She put down the book on the table beside a cup of steaming tea. She walked towards the front door and stopped in mid-stride.

"Benjamin! It is so good to see you!"

She rushed to his side and squeezed the life out of him.

"Come inside."

As he followed her into the study, "Take a seat, tell me how you are."

"Well, we just got in today ma'am. We have had quite the misfortunes on our voyage…"

"Oh dear, and where are you off to now?" she moved to the edge of the seat, eager to hear the rest of the story.

"Well, sitting in the pier right now are the six ships that we captured; among them, the *HMS Courtesy*, which was commandeered by Blood Bones."

The two continued talking between sips of the tea.

"You're probably going to ask where Leah is," she began, watching as Ben's head bobbed up and down. "Well, she left with her father and her husband about two weeks ago. They were married on her birthday. He's the largest landowner in South Downs."

Ben let out a sigh of disbelief. He traveled so many miles, for so long, battling and braving the elements. To come this far and have a door slammed in his face.

"Well, thanks for the tea Mrs. Williamson, it was good to see you, but I better be going."

He stood up, placing the three-quarters full cup on the table.

"I'm sorry if the news upsets you. I personally would rather see you two together, but it was Mr. Williamson's doing."

The two walked to the door. "Good luck in your ventures and swing by if you're ever in Freeport again," she said.

"Of course, I don't know where I'll end up in the years to come though. I was appointed Third Officer under Captain Arthur F. Nelson, so I'll follow him wherever he goes."

"That's great, Ben. I have a feeling you'll move up the ranks quickly."

With the compliment, a smile formed and he went on his way through the lanes and streets. As he passed by the bench, the same bench where he had first laid eyes on Leah, he let out a chuckle that carried down the street.

✖✖✖

As the ships weighed anchor, Ben stood by the bowsprit with Captain Nelson. The two figures leaned out, staring at the waves crashing against the hull as the helmsman maneuvered the vessel.

"Well, was she there?" he asked.

Ben shook his head. "No, she's off in South Downs. I missed her by just a month!"

"Ben, if it's one thing I know, it's that time is never in our hands. Don't let it get to you."

"Yeah, I guess you're right," Ben agreed.

"So," Nelson tried to change the topic. "While you were gone, we loaded fresh supplies for the leg to Boston. We should be there in about a week or so."

"Good to hear."

They talked well into night, discussing the plans to come.

40

BOSTON, MASSACHUSETTS
JUNE 1ST, 1763

Four figures left the fleet of ships moored in the bay as they walked hurriedly through the streets of Boston, heading for the family home of the Elliot's. Knocking upon their door, Nicholas Elliot received the visitors.

Nicholas studied their uniforms, instantly knowing who they were. "Captain Nelson. It is a pleasure to meet you in flesh and not in a name scribbled or a name mentioned," he offered his hand. "Please, tell me of the outcome."

"We engaged the pirates at their hideout, killed the majority of them, a handful are below decks in shackles, to do as you wish with."

A smile formed on the man's lip. "Johnny, come down, I have good news."

He briefed his son quickly, "Run a message to the fort. Tell the new Dominion Governor the news. Ask for the earliest time we can have the hangings."

The young lad nodded. "Yes papa. Have a good day, gentleman," he waved towards the four men.

"I'll have a messenger bring you the news," Nicholas told the captain.

"Good, I'll be on the *Defence*," he replied.

"See you soon, my friend."

❌❌❌❌

*A*s the sun reached its apex in the sky, commoners and English officials alike crammed into the courtyard housing the gallows. Executioners dressed in black robes with black masks covering their faces led a long line of scurvy looking men from the corner of the courtyard. The shuffling of the chains created a melodic chant that echoed off the brick facings of buildings. Nelson and his famed crew stood in the center, in the company of the highest-ranking British Ambassadors in the colonies. Word had passed of their arrival and days later, on the anticipated execution, all that could come to witness the event, came.

The mob cheered as each man's head was pushed through a swaying noose. Children threw rotten vegetables at the pirates, while merchants who had lost many ships and friends cheered and cussed. With a nod, the lever was pulled and the man closest to the geared station fell. The rope jarred as the weight tugged, sending a jitter of gruesome interest throughout the crowd. Thirty seconds later, the next man fell, facing the same time consuming struggle for death. Cheers rang out as the series developed, a domino effect extracting the life out of each man who was next in line.

Captain Blood Bones eyed the last few who stood before him, awaiting their deaths to reunite once more in the afterlife. His gaze shifted to the faces of those who had captured him. No, he was not upset nor did he fear death; they were brave and they had fought well. He smiled as he heard the click of a gear. The door beneath him dropped, sending the most feared pirate of the era to his death; the spark of light fading quickly from his eyes, but the scarlet stone around his finger continued to shine brilliantly.

❌❌❌❌

*O*n a due east course, two vessels sailed out of Boston harbor. One captained by Nelson, with Brodkin under him, and the *HMS Cour-*

tesy, mastered by Charles Marconi with Ben as the First Officer. Men scurried along the ratlines, exposing canvas for the wind to catch.

His brother, Sal, and Jacob approached him from the side, congratulating him for his promotion.

"I couldn't have done this without you all," Ben said as he stared each in the eye. "I talked to Nelson before we departed; we're heading to England for one last mission."

Sal chimed in, "It's a shame that we weren't allowed to keep all that gold of Blood Bones' spoils. Three months worth of taxes! You realize what we could do with that?"

Ben tried to hide a smile, "I wouldn't be worried about that…"

They followed him to the deepest part of the ship, navigating the wooden framing by candlelight. Covered by a blanket sat a stack of chests; four deep, four wide, and two high.

"What are we going do with thirty-two chests?"

A smile formed on Ben's mouth, "Whatever we want."

41

MODERN DAY
ST. AUGUSTINE, FLORIDA

Margie Manry yelled through the corridors of their large home. Her voice traveled down to the cellar where her husband was cleaning to start the project on the extension. After shifting the large wooden cabinet, he paused and then ran up the stairs for lunch.

It had been a month since they had searched the island for their lost. After that day, they returned regularly, only to find nothing. Every possible location inside the maze of caverns was empty, free of life.

For the past several days, John would slave away in the cellar cleaning the space out, or digging in the grounds surrounding the house. The work kept his mind off of everything, which was good because his children were his life. Their pictures hung on every wall of every room. It was a timeline; pictures of Ben and Harris as kids playing on the beach, frames of their track meets, and pictures of the holidays.

Margie had hung two last picture frames on the wall, apart from the other collections. Inside of the red oak frame there was just the black background of the cardboard inside. Through the glass, she could see herself as she gazed in. There were no pictures in these last two frames, just a blank space yielding the possibilities of what their children were doing, of how they aged, and how their life has fared.

✖✖✖

After the meal, John Manry walked to the gray shed in the back-yard. Turning the handle he stepped in, grabbing a pickaxe and a shovel. He began digging out another corner of the foundation that would connect to the cellar. A space twenty by twenty feet that would serve as a game room, connected to a stone inlaid walkway from their driveway.

They talked about selling the place once the work was finished, since they had nothing to look forward since their children were gone, off in another time. Swinging the pickaxe, John parted the earth, digging the blade inches below the surface. Putting his weight against the shaft, the ground split. Continuing this process of open-ing the top layer, he began to shovel out the remains. Sweat began to form on his brow, on the warm spring day.

An hour later, he was knee deep in the brownish soil. He bent down and pulled out several rocks that lay at his feet. He heard the clink of rock against metal as he tossed the chunks into a wheelbar-row. He slowly inched his way down as the hours passed him by.

"Margie, can you bring me some lemonade!" he called loud enough for the sound of his deep voice to carry to his wife inside.

Though her gaze drifted away from the two blank pictures, her mind was still thinking of her children as she emerged with a tray, two glasses, and a pitcher of lemonade.

"It's ready when you are, dear."

"One moment, I want to clear off this last layer before I take a break, I've head enough for the day. I'm beat."

Scrape, scrape, scrape. Clink.

He paused. The sound got his wife's attention also.

"What was that?" she asked.

"I'm not sure, let me clear it out."

After kneeling down, he saw a wooden object, with strips of steel bracing the chest. His hands sifted through dirt. He knew something drastic was to occur; it's not an everyday occurrence to find a chest while digging in your backyard. No, not just one, two, and then three. He unveiled the outline of a fourth one.

"Oh my God," she dropped the tray.

Her gaze shifted between the pit where her husband kneeled and the spilt lemonade on the ground. She moved towards the edge and hopped in.

He took the edge of the shovel, inching it into the gap. Applying pressure, the metal hinges gave way. Before his eyes emerged a scene that could only bring tears of joy to a parent's face, a face that was down with strife and sorrow.

There was a note. He bent down immediately and brought it to his face:

"*Mom and dad,*

> *Don't be worried we're fine. Harris, Sal, and I have joined up with a lovely crew sailing under a man who can't be described with a single word. We've had many adventures so far in this new age, this new time that we were thrown into, but it's all right. I've been promoted to First Officer of the* HMS Courtesy. *I've sailed around the Caribbean, along the coasts, and transited the Atlantic several times. I've even met a girl named Leah. She's gorgeous mom. You'd love her, dad, you too.*

> *I hope everything's well back at home. I'm actually standing where you're standing, building the very home that I grew up in, that you grew up in, that grandpa and his father as well. There's a few letters in the other chests, along with some of our spoils of war. If you could give a chest to Sal's parents, that would be great. The three of us are even closer now and we've met a great lad named Jacob. The four of us our deciding what we want to pursue, how we want to spend the rest of our lives. We've*

got more money than we know what to do with. We've saved countless people on rescue missions, protected ships and ports, and have gotten to see the world. I couldn't have asked for more. I wish I could see you both again, but I know it isn't possible.

I'll leave some more notes and letters throughout the house. Check the attic when you can, there will be something in there.

Love,

Ben"

The tears welled up in the parent's eyes. The fact that their sons were all right, in good health, and happy, brought a smile to their lips. Now they could move on with their lives, free from the burden of worry.

The End

About the
Author

My name is Owen Palmiotti. I call home Monroe, New York, but am most likely elsewhere in the world. I am a sailor, serving Third Officer with Military Sealift Command. I graduated from SUNY Maritime College with a Bachelor of Science Degree in Marine Transportation and International Business, and with a United States Coast Guard License. In my free time I love to write and read. *Benjamin Manry and the Curse of Blood Bones* is my first novel in *The Adventures of Benjamin Manry* series.

Printed in the United States
113813LV00005B/28-42/P